TAKEN

The Deception Series - Book One

By

Barbara Freethy

D1114305

TAKEN
@ Copyright 2011 Barbara Freethy
ALL RIGHTS RESERVED

For information contact: barbara@barbarafreethy.com

PRAISE FOR THE NOVELS
OF BARBARA FREETHY

"Freethy has a gift for creating complex, appealing characters and emotionally involving, often suspenseful, sometimes magical stories." -- Library Journal

"Barbara Freethy delivers strong and compelling prose." – Publishers Weekly

"Fans of Nora Roberts will find a similar tone here, framed in Freethy's own spare, elegant style." – Contra Costa Times

"A fresh and exciting voice in women's romantic fiction." – Susan Elizabeth Phillips

"Freethy skillfully keeps readers on the hook." – Booklist

"Superlative." – Debbie Macomber

"If there is one author who knows how to deliver vivid stories that tug on your emotions, it's Barbara Freethy." – Romantic Times

TAKEN

By
Barbara Freethy

Prologue

"To my wife." Nick Granville gave Kayla Sheridan a dazzling smile as he raised his champagne glass to hers.

Kayla tapped her glass against his. As she looked into the gorgeous blue eyes of the man she had married, she felt a rush of pure joy. She could hardly believe she was married, but an hour ago she'd vowed to love this man above all others. He'd put a ring on her finger and a diamond necklace around her neck and he'd promised to stay forever, which was really all she'd ever wanted. A child of divorce, she'd split her time between two houses, two sets of parents, two cities, and she'd said more than her share of good-byes. That was over now. She was Mrs. Nicholas Granville, and she would make her marriage stick.

The champagne tickled her throat. She felt almost dizzy with delight. "I can't believe how happy I am," she murmured. "My head is spinning."

"I like it when you're off balance," he said.

"I've been that way since the first second we met," she confessed. "Marrying you tonight is the most impulsive, reckless thing I have ever done in my life." She glanced down at the two-carat diamond ring on her finger. It was huge, dramatic, and wildly expensive. It wasn't the kind of ring she'd imagined wearing. She'd thought she'd have something set in an old-fashioned silver band, and in her wildest dreams the stone had never been this big; she was an incredibly lucky woman. And Nick was a very generous man. He'd been spoiling her rotten since their first date.

"You do impulsive well," Nick commented. "Better than I would have thought when we first met."

"Because you're a bad influence," she teased.

His grin broadened. "I've been told that before. Life is supposed to be fun. You are having fun, aren't you?"

"Absolutely. This day has been perfect. The chapel was lovely. The minister made a nice speech about love and marriage. I was afraid it would feel like a quickie wedding, but it didn't. And this hotel room -- it's incredible." She waved her hand in the air as she glanced around their honeymoon suite. Nick had ordered in scented candles that bathed the room in a soft light, riotous colorful wildflowers on every table, rose petals lining a romantic path to the bedroom, and silver trays with chocolate-covered strawberries, her favorite dessert. She couldn't have asked for a more romantic setting in which to begin her new life. "You've made me so happy, Nick. You've given me exactly what I wanted."

He nodded. "I feel the same way." He leaned forward and kissed her softly on the mouth, a promise of what was to come. "I'm going to get some ice." He sent her a meaningful look. "I think we'll want some cold champagne...later."

A tingle of anticipation ran down her spine. "Don't be long."

He picked up the ice bucket and headed for the door. Once there, he paused and pulled out the antique pocket watch she'd given him as a wedding present a few minutes earlier. "Thanks again for this," he said. "It means a lot to me."

"My grandmother told me I should give it to the man I love. And that's you."

Kayla wanted him to say he loved her, too, but he simply smiled and gave her a little wave as he left the room. It didn't matter that he hadn't said the words. He'd married her. That was what was important. She'd spent most of her twenties with a commitment-phobic boyfriend who couldn't bring himself to pop the question. Nick had told her almost immediately that he intended to be her husband. She'd been swept away by his love and his confidence that they were perfect for each other. Now, only three weeks since that first date, she was his wife. She could hardly believe it. Three weeks! This was definitely the craziest thing she'd ever done.

Well, so what? She'd been responsible and cautious her entire life. She was almost thirty years old. It was about time she took a chance.

Too restless to sit, Kayla got up to look out the window. Their luxurious honeymoon suite was on the hotel's twenty-fifth floor and offered a spectacular view of Lake Tahoe and the surrounding Sierra Nevada mountains. She was only four hours from her home in the San Francisco Bay Area, but it felt like a million miles. Her entire life had changed during a simple wedding ceremony that had been witnessed by only two strangers. It was her one regret that neither her family nor Nick's had attended the wedding. But the past was behind her. Tonight was a new beginning.

Turning away from the window, she entered the bedroom. She took off her dress and slipped on a scarlet see-through silk teddy that left nothing to the imagination. Then she drew a brush through her long, thick, curly brown hair that fell past her shoulders and never seemed to do exactly what she wanted. Her best friend, Samantha, had told her that the messy, curly look was coming back in, so maybe for the first time in her life, Kayla's hair was actually in style.

A flash of insecurity made her wonder if the hot-red teddy was too much or if she should have gone with elegant white silk. But the sophisticated white lingerie she'd considered purchasing had reminded her of something her mother would wear, and she was definitely not her mother.

Smiling at that thought, Kayla couldn't help but be pleased by her reflection in the mirror. There was a sparkle in her brown eyes, a rosy glow in her cheeks. She looked like a woman in love. And that was exactly what she was. She'd made the right decision, she told herself again, trying to ignore the niggling little doubt that wouldn't seem to go away.

The quiet in the room made the voices in her head grow louder. She could hear her mother's shocked and disgusted words: *"Kayla, have you lost your mind? You can't marry a man you've known for three weeks. It's foolish. You'll regret this."* And her friend Samantha had pleaded with her. *"Just wait until I get back from London. You need to think, Kayla. How much do you really know about this man?"*

She knew enough, Kayla told herself firmly. And this marriage was between her and Nick, no one else. Turning away from the mirror, she sprayed some perfume in the air and walked through it. Debating whether or not she should wait for Nick in bed, she tried out several sexy poses on the satiny duvet. She felt completely ridiculous and chided herself for being nervous. It wasn't as if they hadn't had sex. And it had been good. It would be even better tonight because they were married, they were in love, and they were committed.

As she stood up, the suite seemed too quiet. She wondered what was taking Nick so long. The ice machine was only a short distance from the room, and he had left at least fifteen minutes ago. He must have decided to run downstairs and pick up another special dessert or more champagne. She smiled at the thought. Nick was so romantic. He always knew just how to make her feel loved and cherished.

She walked into the living room and sat down on the couch to wait. She flipped on the television and ran through the channels. The minutes continued to tick by. Glancing at her watch, she realized an hour had passed. An uneasy feeling swept through her body. She got up and paced. Within seconds the room grew too small for her growing agitation. She had a terrible feeling something was wrong.

Returning to the bedroom, she slipped out of her lingerie and dug through her suitcase for a pair of jeans and a T-shirt. All the while she kept hoping to hear Nick's footsteps or his voice.

Nothing. Silence.

She grabbed the key and left the suite, heading to the nearest ice machine. Nick wasn't there. She tried the other end of the hall, the next floor up, the next floor down. Her heart began to race. She checked the room again, then took the elevator down to the lobby, searching the casino, the shops, the restaurants and bars, and even the parking lot, where Nick's Porsche was parked right where they'd left it. She stopped by the phone bank in the lobby and called the room again. There was still no answer.

Kayla didn't know she was crying until an older woman stopped her by the elevator and asked her if everything was all right.

"My husband. I can't find my husband," she muttered.

The woman gave her a pitying smile. "Story of my life. He'll come back when he runs out of money, honey. They all do."

"He's not gambling. It's our wedding night. He went to get ice." Kayla entered the next elevator, leaving the woman and her disbelieving expression behind. She didn't care what that woman thought. Kayla knew Nick wouldn't gamble away their wedding night. He wouldn't do that to her. But when she returned to her room, it was as empty as when she'd left it.

She didn't know what to do. She sat back down to wait.

When the clock struck midnight, and Nick had been gone for almost five hours, Kayla called the front desk and told them her husband was missing. The hotel sent up George Benedict, an older man who worked for hotel security. After discussing her situation, he assured her they would look for Nick, but there was something in his expression that told her they wouldn't look too hard. It was obvious to Kayla that Mr. Benedict thought Nick was either downstairs gambling and had lost track of time or he had skipped out on her, plain and simple. Neither explanation made sense to her.

Kayla didn't sleep all night. In her mind she ran through a dozen possible scenarios of what could have happened to Nick. Maybe he'd been robbed, hit over the head, knocked unconscious. Maybe he was sitting in a hospital right now with amnesia, not knowing who he was. She hoped to God it wasn't worse than that. No news had to be good news, right?

Finally, she curled up in a chair by the window, watching the moon go down and the sun come up over the lake.

It was the longest night of her life.

A knock came at the door just before nine o'clock in the morning. She ran to open it, hoping she'd see Nick in the hallway, wearing a sheepish smile, offering some crazy explanation.

It wasn't Nick. It was the security guy from the night before, George Benedict. His expression was serious, his eyes somber.

Putting a hand to her suddenly racing heart, she said, "What's happened?"

He held up a black tuxedo jacket. A now limp and wilted red rose boutonniere hung from the lapel. "We found this in a men's room off the lobby. Is it your husband's jacket?"

"I...I think so. I don't understand. Where's Nick?"

"We don't know yet, but this was in the pocket." He held out his hand, a solid gold wedding band in his palm.

She took the ring from him, terrified when she read the simple inscription on the inside of the band, FOREVER LOVE, the same words that were engraved on her wedding ring. She couldn't breathe, couldn't speak.

This was Nick's ring, the one she'd slipped on his finger when she'd vowed to spend the rest of her life with him. "No," she breathed.

"I've seen it happen before," the older man said gently. "A hasty marriage in a casino chapel, second thoughts..."

She saw the pity in his eyes, and she couldn't accept it. "You're wrong. You have to be wrong. Nick loved me. He wanted to get married. It was his idea. *His* idea," she repeated desperately.

She closed her hand around the ring, her fingers tightening into a fist. Her husband had not run out on her... had he?

Chapter One

Two weeks later

Nick Granville was happy to be home. He hadn't left his heart in San Francisco, as the song went, but he had missed the city of narrow, steep streets and sweeping bay vistas. As he set down his suitcases on the gleaming hardwood floor in the living room of his two-story house, he drew in a deep breath and slowly let it out. While the past three months spent in the jungles of Africa had been spectacular, engineering bridges in remote parts of the world had taught him to appreciate the simple pleasures in life, like a hot shower, a good cup of coffee, and a soft bed. He intended to enjoy all three as soon as possible.

He walked across the room to throw open the windows. He was surprised to find the blinds open. The cleaning service must have forgotten to close them. He'd hired a service to come in once a month while he was gone to keep the dust under control. They'd obviously done a good job. The air didn't smell nearly as musty as he'd anticipated, but he opened a window just the same, allowing the cool March breezes to blow through the room.

He'd chosen this small house because it overlooked the Marina Green, the bay, the Marin Headlands, and most important, the Golden Gate Bridge. Bridges were his passion. He was an admitted junkie. His living room walls were covered with photographs of his favorite bridges, a few he'd had a hand in building. There was something about the massive structures that made his blood stir. He'd decided to become an engineer before he graduated from high school, and he'd gone after that career with single-minded determination. It hadn't been easy. He'd had a lot of other distractions and responsibilities, which he'd acquired when his father had run out on the family, but that was water under the proverbial bridge, he thought with a small smile. He had the life he wanted now. That was all that mattered.

Turning away from the view, he caught sight of his telephone answering machine. The red light was blinking. He pushed the button on the machine and listened as the first message played back. A woman's voice came out of the speaker.

"Nick, it's Kayla. Where are you? Please call me as soon as you can."

Kayla? Who the hell was Kayla? The machine beeped.

"Nick, it's Kayla again. I don't know what to do. The security guard found your coat and wedding ring in a men's room at the hotel. I'm really worried. If you wanted out, you should have told me. Please call me."

His coat and his wedding ring? He sure as hell didn't have a wedding ring. She obviously had the wrong number and the wrong Nick.

"Me again," she said, her voice filled with panic. "I don't know why I keep calling, except I don't know what else to do. The police say they can't help me because there's no evidence anything happened to you. They think you ran out on me. I guess that's what you did. Don't you think you owe me at least an explanation? I love you, Nick." Her voice caught on a sob. "I thought you loved me, too. It was your idea to get married so fast."

Nick shut off the machine, reluctant to hear more of her desperate pleas. He felt as if he had stepped into the middle of someone else's life, and his relief at being home was tempered by the sense that something was very wrong.

As he looked around the room, his uneasiness grew. Small things began to stand out: the celebrity magazines on the coffee table, the wilted roses in a vase by the window, the empty coffee mug on a side table, the throw blanket that he usually kept on his bed now resting on the arm of his brown leather couch.

Unsettled, Nick walked into the kitchen and found a box of Lucky Charms on the counter, the kind of sugared cereal he'd never eaten in his life. In the refrigerator there was a half-open bottle of chardonnay and a carton of milk that had expired a month ago. His stomach began to churn as he considered the possibilities. Obviously someone had been in his home. The only people who had keys were his mother and the cleaning service. His mother would never leave sour milk in the refrigerator.

His nerves began to tingle. The air was filled with vague scents he couldn't quite place -- a man's cologne or a woman's perfume? The silence felt thick and tense. He turned around, feeling as if someone were standing behind him, but there was no one there.

He picked up the phone and called the cleaning service. "This is Nick Granville," he told the woman who answered. "I'd like to speak to the person who has been cleaning my house for the last three months."

He heard the flip of papers, and then she said, "That would be Joanne. She's not in right now. Can I have her call you?"

"Yes, I need to speak to her as soon as possible. It's urgent." He ended the call and punched in his mother's number. She didn't answer. Not wanting to leave a long message on her machine, he simply told her he was home and asked her to call him back as soon as possible.

He moved across the living room and up the stairs. The master bedroom was the first door on the right. He paused just inside the room. The cream-colored down comforter on his bed was pulled back, the sheets and blankets tangled, as if someone had recently gotten up. A couple of towels from his bathroom lay in a heap on the floor. An empty wineglass sat on the bedside table.

Every detail made his blood pressure rise. What kind of thief slept in his bed, took a shower in his bathroom, and kept food in his kitchen?

The phone rang and he grabbed the extension by the bed, hoping for some answers. It was Joanne from the cleaning service.

"Is something wrong, Mr. Granville?" she asked. "Laurie told me I needed to call you right away."

"Yes, there's something wrong," he snapped. "This place is a mess. There's crap everywhere, towels on the floor, and the bed is unmade. What the hell has been going on in my home?"

"Excuse me? I don't understand," she said, obvious confusion in her voice.

"What don't you understand? I've been out of the country. The only person to have access to my house is your cleaning service."

"But you were home a few weeks ago," she said. "I ran into you right before Valentine's Day. Don't you remember? We spoke about how funny it was that we were finally meeting face-to-face."

"What are you talking about? I haven't been home in three months, so you couldn't possibly have spoken to me." Nick's mind raced. Joanne had spoken to someone -- who? Obviously it had been a man, and that man had told her that he was Nick Granville. Who would do that? Nick didn't have any brothers, no friends who would play that kind of a joke on him.

The silence on the phone lengthened. Finally, Joanne said, "I don't know what to say, Mr. Granville. Perhaps you've forgotten. You should ask the woman you were with."

The woman? He was reminded of the pleading, desperate voice from the answering machine.

"You said you were getting married that weekend," Joanne continued. "You both looked incredibly happy. I thought it was so romantic that you were going to have a Valentine's Day wedding."

He couldn't believe what he was hearing. "That wasn't me. You didn't talk to me."

"The man I spoke to said he was Nick Granville," Joanne stated. "I didn't imagine it."

"I'm sure you spoke to someone, but it wasn't me. I'll need to talk to you further about what these people look like. First I'm going to call the police."

"I'll do whatever I can to help," Joanne replied, a nervous note in her voice. "But I swear I thought the man was you."

"I'm sure you did." Nick hung up the phone, feeling completely rocked by the conversation. He'd always prided himself on being able to roll with the punches, adapt to any situation, no matter how dangerous or bizarre. But this invasion of his home, his privacy, his life, disturbed him more than he wanted to admit. As he gazed around the room, he saw his computer on the desk. The monitor was dark, but the light on the hard drive was on. Someone had been on his computer. He cursed himself for never setting a password, but he'd put it off. No one used the computer but him. Now he realized whoever had been in his home could have accessed his bank accounts, his credit cards, and God knew what else. It occurred to him that he hadn't looked at a bank statement in a very long time. He hadn't felt the need. His income far outstripped his living expenses, especially when he was working in the field. He could have been ripped off in a big way.

He rushed across the room to check the computer. The machine whirred and whirred. It must have frozen. *Damn.* He turned it off, then back on. While he was waiting for it to boot up, he returned downstairs to the living room and replayed the messages on the answering machine.

"Nick, it's Kayla...."

Kayla. She had to be involved. How the hell was he going to find her?

* * *

As Kayla stared down at the shattered pieces of colored glass on her studio worktable, she couldn't help comparing the broken window to her life. In the case of the glass, a baseball had come out of nowhere, blowing the window apart without warning. In her life that baseball had been Nick Granville. She'd spent the past two weeks living in a whirlwind of emotions, one minute furious at Nick for running out on her, the next minute worrying that something had happened to him. She'd bitten her nails down to the quick. She couldn't eat, couldn't sleep, and couldn't go ten minutes without thinking about him. Not that anyone else seemed to care.

She'd filed missing-persons reports with the Nevada and the California police, but both, upon hearing that she'd known the man only a few weeks, seemed less than enthusiastic about pursuing the case. There was no evidence of foul play, and further questioning had produced few concrete details. It had become embarrassingly clear that she knew very little about her husband.

When the police threw her missing-persons report into a stack of thousands, she'd turned to a private investigator. He'd listened to her story, barely keeping a straight face, and told her he would need a thousand-dollar retainer to get started. Although she'd been tempted to empty her bank account, some part of her brain had finally woken up and said no. If Nick had suckered her into marriage, for what reason she couldn't fathom, was she really going to let herself get taken again? She'd walked out the door and prayed that Nick would come back to her, that there would be some crazy but logical explanation for his absence.

She was still waiting for that to happen and feeling more stupid by the minute. Her friends and her family had reminded her that they'd told her so, that no good could come of such a hasty marriage. They had encouraged her to simply get on with her life. How on earth was she supposed to do that with so many unanswered questions?

Stretching her arms over her head, Kayla gave a weary sigh. Work was the only thing that got her through the days and sometimes the nights. It was almost four o'clock in the afternoon, and she'd been working for six straight hours, trying to reconstruct the pattern of the window, so that she could see how best to attack the job. She would be able to use most of the old glass, but she would have to create several smaller pieces to fit where the shards of glass had splintered too finely to be replaced.

It had once been a beautiful window in a small chapel in the Presidio, intact for almost a hundred years -- until a group of neighborhood kids decided to play a pickup game of baseball in the field next to the church. Kayla wanted to restore the window to perfection for many reasons, but most of all to prove that nothing was irretrievably broken. Everything could be fixed. That was what her grandfather had always told her. And with her life in tatters, she wanted to believe that now more than ever.

She wished her grandfather were here today. Edward Hirsch, who had taught Kayla the art of stained glass, would know just what to do with this window. The Hirsch family had been creating and restoring stained glass in Germany for almost a century. Edward had passed the family talent down to her. He'd also passed down his house and the converted garage studio. Well, actually, her grandmother had passed it on. Charlotte Hirsch had decided to move out and start over somewhere new after her husband of forty-something years had died.

While Potrero Hill wasn't as fashionable or sophisticated as downtown San Francisco, the abundance of sunny days on the hill bathed Kayla's studio in beautiful light more often than not, and the studio was perfect for her needs. Her grandfather had worked with glass only as a hobby, a way to let off creative energy after his day job as a banker. Kayla, however, was turning her passion into a lucrative business.

The aging Victorian house also felt like home to her, and one day it would be perfect for raising a family, with its three bedrooms and basement playroom. Nick had loved it the minute he'd seen it. He'd wanted to explore every nook and cranny of the two-story house. They'd picked out the bedroom they would turn into a nursery. They'd talked about remodeling the old kitchen and tearing up the carpets and restoring the hardwood floors. She'd believed in him, trusted him, confident that his actions would follow his words. When he'd told her on their wedding night that he was going to get ice and that he'd be right back, she'd never thought for a second that would be the last conversation they would have.

Getting to her feet, she walked over to the counter and poured herself a cup of coffee. Taking a sip, she realized it was barely lukewarm. She made a face and tossed it down the sink. As she rinsed her mug, she glanced out the window at the wild cottage garden that was still very much one of her many works in progress. She'd planted a ring of wildflowers around the sprawling old apple tree and added a wooden bench and a birdfeeder to attract the hummingbirds. An arbor entwined with climbing roses stood in one corner of the yard; a thick row of shrubs ran along the perimeter, hiding the neighboring houses from view. She'd mixed rosemary and sage with currant and blueberry bushes. She'd added foxglove and sunflowers to attract the butterflies, and filled in the rest of the garden with whatever color she could find, cosmos, zinnia, and marigold. She especially loved the splash of lavender that spilled over the path leading back to the house.

She'd thought about trying to capture the essence of her garden in glass, but she was afraid that she wouldn't be able to do justice to the wild beauty, that she wouldn't be able to fully capture the nuances of the changing colors of each new season. She smiled to herself as she remembered Nick's face when he'd first seen her garden. She'd tried to explain the method behind the madness, but he'd simply shaken his head and looked at her as if he thought she was completely crazy. He'd said the only thing he'd ever wanted in a backyard was a pool or a hot tub. Funny how the bits and pieces she remembered about him now made her wonder just how compatible they'd really been. Had it all been a mistake? Had Nick changed his mind? Or had something terrible happened to him?

Turning away from the window, she forced her mind away from the frustrating questions that had no answers and started to clean up her work area. A few minutes later, the door to her studio opened unexpectedly. She couldn't prevent the involuntary skip of her heart. Two and a half weeks had passed, and she still couldn't stop jumping at every ring of the phone, every knock at the door. But it wasn't her husband entering the studio; it was her longtime friend and business associate, Samantha Jennings. A tall, thin ash blonde with an energetic personality and a sarcastic wit, Samantha was a marketing whiz who had built a thriving business representing various artists, including Kayla. However, their relationship went far beyond business, their friendship dating back to childhood.

Unfortunately, their bond had been strained since Kayla's wedding. Samantha had been in London for most of the month that Kayla and Nick were together. She'd begged Kayla not to get married until she returned, but at the time Kayla just hadn't wanted to wait one more second to have everything she'd ever dreamed about. Now she was left not only to repair her broken heart but also to mend her friendship with Sam.

Samantha perched on the edge of the worktable and glanced down at the glass. "How's the window coming along?"

"Slowly," Kayla replied, sitting down in her chair. There was a sparkle in Samantha's eyes. It was obvious that she was practically bursting at the seams to tell her something. "What's up?" Kayla asked.

"I just took a call from the Carleton Court Hotel in Sausalito. They're doing massive renovations, and listen to this -- they want you to bid on doing two stained-glass windows in the lobby. Isn't that cool? Not only will it be great money, but it will also be tremendous exposure for you as an artist."

"That sounds like a big job." Kayla felt both excited and terrified at the prospect. Living in limbo the past month had cut into her confidence, her trust in herself and other people.

"It is big, but you can do it," Samantha said. "You're so

talented."

"Still..."

"Look, I know you've been going through a rough time, but this will be good for you -- for both of us."

Her no-nonsense words reminded Kayla that she wasn't in this business alone and that she owed it to Samantha to keep putting one foot in front of the next, something she hadn't been doing particularly well since her aborted wedding night. "When do I meet with them?"

"Not for three weeks. You have plenty of time to get ready. They gave me some ideas of what they want." She handed Kayla a folder. "It's all there."

"I'll take a look later tonight," she said.

"Good. I have to run," Samantha said, sliding to her feet. "Tonight is my second date with Jeff."

"You brought him back for a repeat performance -- I'm impressed," Kayla said with a smile. Samantha was notoriously picky when it came to men, and unlike Kayla, she wasn't in any hurry to get to the marriage, kids, white-picket-fence kind of life.

"He made a good first impression," Samantha said. She paused, an uncomfortable note entering her voice as she asked, "Did you talk to your stepsister about filing for divorce?"

"No," Kayla said with annoyance. "It's only been two weeks. The police are still investigating."

Samantha shot her a skeptical look. "Sure they are. I'm sorry if I'm pressuring you, but you should be filing for divorce. Get the ball rolling, so you can put this whole disaster behind you."

"He could still come back."

"What if he does?" Samantha asked in amazement. "What could he possibly say, aside from that he'd been kidnapped or was suffering from extended amnesia, that would explain why he ran out on you without a word?"

"It's possible he was kidnapped. And amnesia is a real clinical diagnosis."

Samantha let out a long, disgusted sigh. "That's your imagination talking, Kay. You know it is."

She did know it. But the alternative left her feeling like even more of an idiot. "You're right, but it's easier to think something happened to him than to believe he ran out on me."

"Well, better he did it now than in a year or two, or after you had a kid. He probably just realized you'd both made an impulsive mistake and took off. You know how men are. They like to take the easy way out."

"I don't think I know men at all," Kayla said wearily.

"Well, I do. So next time you listen to me," Samantha said, shaking a finger at Kayla. "Call me next week, and we'll go to lunch. But don't call too early," she added, as she headed to the door. "I'm planning on some very late nights," she said with a wicked smile.

After Samantha left, Kayla got up, switched off the light, and headed down the well-worn path between her studio and the house. She checked her bare cupboards and refrigerator and decided it was time to find some food. Throwing a short jean jacket over her skimpy bright orange T-shirt, she pulled the rubber band out of her ponytail and shook her hair out, running her fingers through the tangled strands. She should probably run a brush through it, but what the heck -- it wasn't as if she needed to dress up to pick up a pizza.

When she got into her car, she told herself to drive straight to her destination, no stops, but the urge to take a little side trip past Nick's house grew stronger with each block. To be honest, it wasn't a side trip; it was a hike across town, and she really needed to stop torturing herself this way. Maybe this would be her final trip, one last good-bye, she told herself. Closure. That was what she needed to put an end to this chapter of her life.

Driven by rationalizations that didn't sound true even in her own head, Kayla kept going until she reached the Marina Green, a large expanse of grass that edged San Francisco Bay and provided a spectacular view of ships sailing under the Golden Gate Bridge. She couldn't imagine getting much work done if she lived down here. She'd be too tempted to take long, windy walks or simply stare out the window at the setting sun that even now was lighting up the clear, dusky sky with a wild splash of purples, oranges, and pinks.

As she paused at a stoplight, she drew in a breath at the awesome color palette provided by Mother Nature and immediately envisioned a new stained-glass window with exactly those colors. She doubted she would ever be able to match the perfection that was before her now. Even as she tried to commit the colors to memory, they began to fade into the night. Nothing ever stayed the same.

When the light changed to green, she turned left, her heart beating more rapidly as Nick's home came into view. She'd driven down this street a hundred times since her wedding day, hoping against hope to see some sign of life. Every time she'd been disappointed.

Until now...

The light in the window shocked her so much she blinked twice to make sure it was real. With shaky hands, she steered into a nearby parking spot and shut off the engine, her heart beating double-time. Nick was back. He was home. She was going to see him tonight, get the answers to her questions. So why couldn't she move? Why was she frozen with fear?

She shouldn't be scared. She should be angry, furious. She should go up there and give him a piece of her mind.

That was exactly what she would do.

Throwing her shoulders back, she stepped out of the car and walked across the street and up the stairs to the front door. Her knock brought the sound of heavy footsteps. She was afraid to breathe.

The door opened abruptly and a man stood before her.

"Who are you?" she asked in shock. This wasn't Nick. It was a stranger -- a man who towered over her five-foot-four-inch frame by at least ten inches. He had dark hair and the most piercing green eyes she'd ever seen. She took a step back, feeling an instinctive need to defend herself -- against what, she didn't know. "Who are you?" she repeated.

"I'm Nick Granville."

Chapter Two

The name slammed into her like a punch to the gut. Kayla's jaw dropped. Her breath came short and fast. She must have heard him wrong. He couldn't possibly have said Nick Granville. "No, that's not true," she said immediately, with a definitive shake of her head. "I know Nick Granville, and you're not him." She searched his face for some sign of familiarity, which was crazy, because this man was not Nick. Nick had blond hair, a wide smile, and a lean, wiry frame. This man was big, with broad shoulders, a deep tan, fierce eyes, and an angry scowl.

"Oh, it's true, all right," he said, his gaze fixed sharply on her face. "Now, you. A name, please."

"Kayla. Kayla Sheridan," she muttered. His sharp intake of breath surprised her. "What did I say?"

"You're Kayla? The woman who left a dozen messages on my answering machine?"

"On Nick's machine," she corrected, "and you are not him. I think I would know my own husband. What are you doing in his home?"

"This is my house."

"I don't know what kind of game you're playing, but I'm calling the police," she said with as much bravado as she could muster.

"I've already called them," he said, surprising her once again.

She stared at him in confusion. He wasn't making sense. Why would he have called the police when he was the intruder? And why was she standing here talking to a complete stranger, who might even be dangerous? As she began to back away, he reached out and grabbed her arm.

"Not so fast," he said, a hard glint in his eyes. "You're not going anywhere."

"Let me go." She tried to wiggle free, but he had an iron grip on her arm.

"After you've answered a few questions."

"Me? You're the one who needs to answer some questions. Like what you're doing in my husband's home."

"I told you I live here, and I have for the past six years."

"That's not true."

"Why would I lie?"

"Because... well, I don't know yet, but I still don't have any reason to believe you." She pushed back the niggling doubt beginning to take shape in her head. She told herself that she knew Nick and she trusted him. The only lies being spoken were by this man, this stranger. But weeks of uncertainty had blurred Nick's image in her mind, and her confidence in her own beliefs was not as strong as it had once been.

"If you want proof, fine. I can give you that." Without releasing her arm, he reached into his pocket and pulled out his wallet. He flipped it open to his driver's license and held it in front of her face. She stared at the photograph, which matched the face of the man standing in front of her. The name was Nick Granville. The address was this address. It was a perfect match.

"That can't be right," she said emphatically, but her mind was spinning. How could two men have the same name and address? "There must be some mistake."

"There's no mistake. I am Nick Granville. This is my home."

God! She had the terrible feeling he was telling the truth. But how could that be?

"Now it's your turn," he continued. "Tell me about this man you married and why you were living in my house."

"I wasn't living here. Nick was." She licked her lips. There was a knot of emotion in her throat that made it difficult to swallow or speak. She knew she needed to defend Nick, but she was having a hard time finding the right words.

"Since when?" the man asked. "When did he break in here?"

"He didn't break in. He had a key. I saw him use it more than once."

That bit of news seemed to take him by surprise. She pressed her advantage. "He told me he'd lived here for over a year. He even said hello to one of your neighbors. And the cleaning woman was here one day. He talked to her, too. She acted like he was the owner."

"Because she never met me in person," he muttered. "I hired her over the phone."

"So you say."

"It's the truth. I've been out of the country for the past three months on a job. I'm an engineer. I work for Coopers and James," he added, naming a large and prestigious engineering firm in San Francisco. "I just got back from building a bridge in Africa."

Which would explain all the beautiful black-and-white photographs of bridges that adorned the walls of the house. Nick had told her that he just liked bridges. But this man said he built them. He could probably prove that, too, or she could. A call to his company would confirm his employment, which meant he had to be telling the truth about his job, at the very least. Still, that didn't make him innocent.

"You're pretending to be Nick," she said defiantly. It was the only explanation she could think of that made sense. The fact that he had a driver's license in Nick's name was probably part of his plan to be Nick. "What have you done with him? Where is he?"

"You're fucking crazy, lady. You're in on it with him, aren't you?"

"In on what?"

"Whatever game the two of you are playing to rob me of everything I own. I know my credit cards were used, my bank accounts pilfered. I haven't discovered the extent of the thefts, but I will, and you will both pay dearly for what you did to me."

He was accusing her of robbing him? Her heart began to race. "I didn't take anything from you."

"But you have been here before," he continued. "There's perfume in the bathroom and I found lipstick on my dresser." His gaze fixed on her mouth as he said, "Cherry red."

She couldn't help licking that same color off her lips. It was her favorite.

"I assume those belong to you," he said.

"They might. I can't remember if I left anything behind. I haven't been here since before our wedding. Nick hasn't been here either, not for at least the past two weeks. I've left messages and I've come by almost every day. There was never a sign of anyone home until tonight. Now, let go of me."

His grip tightened on her arm, his fingers strong, unyielding. "I don't think so. Not until the police get here."

Why was he so eager to have the police arrive if he was the guilty party? She wished she had a good answer to that question. The way he was talking, she had a feeling she would be the one arrested.

The phone rang. He didn't move.

"Aren't you going to answer that?" she asked, wondering who was calling. In the weeks that Nick had been gone, she had racked her brain trying to remember the name of one of his friends or a coworker, but she'd finally come to realize that whatever friends Nick had, he hadn't shared them with her.

"You'd better come in," the man in front of her ground out, pulling her into the room. She tried to resist, but her strength was no match for his. He reached for the phone and said, "Hello? Mom. Look, I have to call you back. I've got a big problem on my hands."

Mom? What kind of a thief takes calls from his mother? Kayla felt suddenly overwhelmed by the whole situation. She didn't know what was true and what was false.

"I know I called you," he continued. He held the phone receiver away from his ear as an irritated female voice grew louder. "Yes, yes, I understand. I got it. I can't write down the address right now." He sighed. "Fine, hang on."

As he tried to juggle the phone and reach for a pen, he let go of her arm. Kayla backed away as he repeated an address while writing something on a notepad. She was out the door when she heard him swear. The clatter of the phone dropping to the ground made her sprint down the stairs and across the street. She jumped into her car as he reached the sidewalk. Jamming her key into the ignition, she prayed for a quick start. The engine roared and she peeled away, almost running him down in the process.

Her heart pounded against her chest. She swerved around one

corner, then the next. A quick glance in her rearview mirror showed nothing but an empty street behind her. Thank God, he wasn't following her. She needed time to think, to make sense of it all, if that was even possible.

His words spun around in her head: *"I'm Nick Granville."*

If that was true, who on earth was the man she had married?

* * *

"Dammit," Nick muttered as Kayla's car disappeared from sight.

The only lead he had was gone. And he'd let her go. Who the hell was she? A thief? An accomplice? Her big brown eyes had been shocked when he'd opened the door. When he'd told her who he was, she'd looked at him as if he were crazy or dangerous. But she was the nutcase, calling him a liar. What the hell was that about? He didn't know what to make of her.

Was she a victim? Duped by someone else? She certainly didn't look like a sophisticated thief, with her wild brown hair, tight-ass jeans, and clingy bright orange T-shirt clinging to a very nice pair of breasts. He frowned at that distracting thought and told himself to stay focused on the facts at hand. He'd just been robbed. And that woman had admitted to being in his house with another man.

He went over their conversation in his head, her contention that he was, in fact, the liar and that the other guy was the real Nick Granville. He'd never had anyone challenge his identity before. It was strange having to defend his name, to prove he was who he said he was.

Returning to his house, he jotted down the numbers from her license plate on a pad by the phone. He had a very good memory. With any luck this Kayla would be able to lead him to the man who had broken into his house.

Glancing down at his watch, he wondered where the police were. He'd called them over an hour ago. He hated to wait for anyone or anything. Patience had never been part of his makeup. He didn't like being out of control, letting someone else call the shots. He remembered all the times he'd waited for his father to show up for a visit. Nine times out of ten his father hadn't come at all. Nick could still feel the frustration and anger of those days. But that was behind him now. He was living the life he'd always wanted. He loved his career, especially the travel, and he was damned sure not going to let anyone steal that life right out from under him without a fight.

He was beginning to realize that his distraction with his work had made him vulnerable. He should have taken more precautions. He knew about identity theft, but he hadn't paid attention to his personal business, and now he was going to pay a big price. He still didn't know how much the thief or thieves had stolen from him. There were thousands of dollars charged on his credit cards, and his bank balances were far lower than they should have been. He had no idea if he could get all or any of it back, but he'd worked too hard to earn his money to let it vanish just like that.

Pacing back and forth across his living room, he went over his conversation with Kayla word for word. Had she left him any clues? Had she said anything that would help him figure out who had been in his home?

She'd given him her full name. Kayla Sheridan. She shouldn't be too difficult to find. For the first time since this nightmare had begun, he felt a surge of excitement.

* * *

Kayla was still shaking when her doorbell rang an hour later. Looking out the window, she saw the silver Porsche in front of her house and her stomach turned over. Was it Nick -- her Nick? Or was it the other guy? She moved slowly to the front door and looked through the peephole. Her heart sank. How had he found her?

Taking a deep breath, she opened the door to the same tall, dark-haired man with the furious green eyes who'd been at Nick's house. He'd traded the slacks and button-down shirt he'd been wearing earlier for a pair of worn blue jeans that clung to his long, lean legs, and a charcoal-gray sweater that was pushed up to his elbows. His brown hair was damp from a recent shower, his cheeks clean-shaven. His skin showed off a dark tan, as if he'd spent a great deal of time in the sun. There was nothing soft about his features. His face was hard and angled, his jaw set in an unyielding, determined line. With his hands clenched in fists on his hips, he looked ready to hit someone. She hoped it wouldn't be her.

"What are you doing here?" she asked warily.

"I have a better question -- what do you think of my new car?" he asked, his sarcasm clear. "I found it in my garage, right where I usually park my black Grand Cherokee. I also saw a payment made to the car dealer out of my bank account."

"My husband purchased the car. I was with him when he bought it. He said it was about time he picked a car just for fun."

"Oh, I'll bet he had some fun. What happened to my car?"

"He traded it in. He said it was too practical."

The man glared down at her. "Where is he? Where is the man who robbed me?"

She didn't want to admit that Nick had stolen anything. But he certainly had a lot of explaining to do. "I don't know. If I did, I'd be talking to him right now."

His ruthless gaze searched her face for the truth. She wanted to look away, but she couldn't. She didn't want to appear as if she were hiding anything.

"I spoke to the police," he said a moment later. "I gave them your name."

"That's fine." She straightened, throwing back her shoulders. "I filed a missing-persons report when Nick disappeared, you know, as soon as I got back from Lake Tahoe."

"You went to the police?" he asked in surprise.

"Of course I went to the police," she snapped. "My husband disappeared without a trace. I thought something terrible had happened to him."

"You got married in Lake Tahoe? Let me guess, one of those drive-through wedding chapels?"

He made it sound so tawdry. "It wasn't like that. We just wanted a simple, quick ceremony."

"Why? Are you pregnant?"

"No!" The word burst out of her. "Of course not."

"Just asking. It's a reasonable question."

"Not from a complete stranger," she snapped back.

"Oh, we're hardly strangers, Kayla," he drawled, bitterness edging each note. "You apparently took my name when you got married. You've been in my house, probably slept in my bed, used my shower--"

"Please don't go on." She put a hand to her stomach, feeling like she wanted to throw up. What kind of mess had she gotten herself into?

Nick shoved his hands in his pockets and looked down the street, then back at her. "So when did this guy take off -- when you got back from Tahoe?"

She licked her lips, knowing that her reply would make it all sound worse, but there was no point in denying what he could learn from the missing-persons report. "He vanished on our wedding night. He went out to get ice and he never came back."

"He left on your wedding night?"

"Don't make me say it again."

"How long ago was that?"

"A little over two weeks."

"What did the police do when you told them?"

"Nothing. They told me that with no evidence of a crime, it was more than likely he just decided he didn't want to be married. They said they didn't have time to pursue it. They have hundreds of more important cases."

"They told me the same thing. Apparently identity theft is a booming business. I don't think they're going to pound the pavement looking for my thief."

"I know you won't believe this, but I wish they would," she said. "Because I want to know what is going on, too. I want to find out what happened to my husband."

"If you wanted to know the truth, why did you run away from me before?"

"You scared me," she admitted. "And I was confused. You want me to believe that you're Nick Granville, that everything I thought belonged to my husband was yours -- is yours." She folded her arms in front of her chest. "It's not easy to stop believing in someone you love. But if the man I married was in some way impersonating you or stealing from you, I need to know that."

"Then you and I have to work together," he said. "I want you to tell me everything you know. I need every detail, no matter how unimportant you might think it is."

"That will take some time."

"So we'll get started now. I don't want to waste another second. The trail is already cold, and I can't let it get any colder. I intend to get my life back as soon as possible."

She nodded. "You'd better come inside then, but I have to warn you I don't know much. That's become apparent to me in recent weeks."

"You know what he looked like. We can begin there. I want to get an image of this guy in my mind."

She started, realizing she could do better than describe him. "I have a picture." She moved away from the door, grabbing her purse off a nearby table.

He followed her into the entry, shutting the front door behind him.

"We had a wedding photo taken," she added as she dug into her purse. As she flipped through her pictures, she came to Nick's smiling, laughing blue eyes, and felt an odd sense of relief that she could prove he actually existed, that he'd married her. It wasn't a dream. He had been real. She slid the picture out of its plastic case and handed it to him.

He gave it a hard look. "Damn."

"What's wrong?" she asked.

"I know this man."

Nick stared down at the photograph. Were his eyes playing tricks on him? Even though the face was older, there was no mistaking the sun-bleached blond hair, the shrewd eyes, and the knowing smile. He'd never thought he'd ever see him again.

"What do you mean?" Kayla asked. "How do you know him?"

He lifted his gaze to hers. "His name is Evan Chadwick. We went to college together." A burning anger swept through his body, making his hands shake and his gut twist into a hard knot. He wanted to rip the photograph in two. He wanted to tear up the image of Evan's face, but he couldn't do that. This picture was proof, evidence he would need later when he found Evan.

"You went to school together?" she repeated in surprise. "You're friends with -- with the man I married?"

"Not friends -- enemies." His jaw was so tight he could barely get the words out.

"Why? What happened?"

"A lot," he said shortly. "I shared an apartment with Evan in my junior year at Cal. It took me six months to figure out who he really was."

"I don't understand. What do you mean -- who he really was?" she asked in confusion.

"Evan was a thief, a con artist. He scammed his way into college with fraudulent transcripts. Once there, he ran small games, big games, whatever would make him a buck, give him a thrill. I'm not sure what he liked more, the game or the payoff. Actually, that's not true; I do know. Evan liked to make fools of people. He enjoyed playing them for suckers. It made him feel powerful, strong, bigger and better than he was." Nick tasted bile on his tongue. Anger rolled through his body in forceful waves. He'd thought he'd closed the door on Evan Chadwick. He'd believed that he'd won the last round, but apparently the game wasn't over. Evan had just been waiting for the right moment to strike back -- twelve long years later.

"That doesn't sound like the man I married," Kayla said, doubt in her voice.

She wasn't the first woman to defend Evan. His younger sister, Jenny, had once spoken very much the same words. She'd had the same confused look in her eyes then as Kayla did now.

"Evan was very good at being whoever someone wanted him to be." He deliberately kept his voice calm, even though inside he was seething. He had to make Kayla understand. He had to pull her over to his side, or they'd never get anywhere. "Evan was a chameleon. He could fit in anywhere, look like he belonged. Once he pretended to be a visiting professor at the university. He went to a faculty tea and mixed in as if he truly were a forty-year-old teacher of astrophysics. Evan knew how to get people to trust him, and then he betrayed them. That was the way he worked then, and it sounds like the way he's working now."

Kayla stared at him for a long time. He could see the indecision in her eyes, but at least she was still thinking and not jumping into rationalizations or defenses.

"What else do you know about him?" she asked.

"What do *you* know?" he shot back. "You married him a few weeks ago. You're probably more up to date than I am."

She hesitated. He suspected she very much wanted to blow him off. She wanted to believe in her dream marriage. It didn't surprise him. Evan had always known how to pick a trusting soul. He'd always chosen beautiful women, too. Dressed down in jeans and a T-shirt, not a speck of makeup on her face except a slash of red on her lips, Kayla had a beauty that was all natural: gorgeous hair, fine bones, clear skin, big, wide eyes, and curves in all the right places. He cleared his throat, reining in his wandering thoughts. He'd always been attracted to brunettes, not that he intended to be attracted to Kayla. He didn't need that complication.

"All right," she said finally. "We'll talk it out. I'm not saying I believe everything -- yet. But I'll listen. And I'll tell you what I know."

"Good idea."

"I hope so. I've been a little short on those lately." Kayla waved her hand toward the archway leading into the living room. "Why don't you take a seat? Make yourself at home. I'll get us something to drink."

As she walked down the hall, he blew out a breath of relief that she hadn't kicked him out. She was his only link to Evan. He needed to know everything she knew.

Entering the living room, he was struck immediately by the warmth of her home. There were colorful throw rugs on the hardwood floor, soft, pillowed couches along the windows, and flowers everywhere -- on the mantel, the coffee table, the old piano that stood in front of a beautiful stained-glass window that seemed to catch the light from the rising moon. Knitting needles sat atop a pile of colored yarn spilling out of a wicker basket on the floor.

The room looked lived-in and comfortable. It was a family home in a family neighborhood. He wondered if Kayla lived here alone. It didn't seem like a house for one person. It also didn't seem like a house Evan would choose to live in. It was too old-fashioned, too homey. What the hell had Evan been doing with Kayla, besides the obvious?

He sat down on the couch, feeling suddenly tired. It had been a long trip home. With everything that had gone on the past few hours he'd barely had a chance to catch his breath. Stretching out his legs, he sank back into the cushions and let out a long, tense breath. It didn't make him felt better. Fury raged inside him, eating him alive. If he found Evan tonight, he'd probably kill him. He could imagine himself putting his hands on Evan's neck and squeezing the life out of him. The depth of his anger shocked him. He'd never felt so much hate for another person. But Evan had conned him before, and it infuriated him that it had happened again. This time Evan would pay. This time he would not get away.

Nick looked up as Kayla reentered the room. She handed him a glass of red wine and sat down in the armchair across from him. Clasping her hands together, she asked, "Why do you think Nick -- Evan was pretending to be you?"

"That's what I need to find out. Obviously, Evan knew I was out of the country. He probably figured I had some money." Nick took a sip of wine and then deliberately set the glass down on the coffee table. As appealing as it was to numb his brain with alcohol, he needed a clear mind.

"If Nick -- I mean Evan was robbing you, why was he with me? Why did he marry me?"

"He must have wanted something from you."

She frowned at that. "I don't have much. And he didn't take anything from me."

"He didn't get you to put him on your bank account or ask you for a loan or anything like that?"

"No, nothing. There really wasn't time, because he vanished right after we got married."

Nick was surprised that Evan had married Kayla. Why had he taken that step? "Tell me again what happened the last time you saw him." He leaned forward, resting his arms on his thighs.

Kayla drew in a deep breath. "He went to get ice, and he never came back. I looked all over the hotel for him. I called security. The next morning they found his coat in a bathroom off the casino. It had his wedding ring in the pocket. That was it. I didn't know if someone had robbed him, kidnapped him, or hurt him in some way. I actually still don't know what happened to him. I just know he's gone."

"I wonder why he needed to leave that night. Did something happen between the two of you? Did you have a fight?"

"No, everything was perfect."

Nick watched Kayla play with the silver chain around her neck. The glittering diamond heart drew his attention. "Is that new?" he asked. "Your necklace?"

Her hand paused, her eyes widening. "Yes, Nick -- I mean Evan -- bought it for me. It was a wedding present."

"That explains the charges at Clarington Jewelers."

"I didn't know it wasn't his money." Her hand dropped to her side and a wash of guilty red colored her cheeks. A moment later she unclasped the hook and tossed the necklace on the coffee table between them as if she couldn't bear to wear it a second longer.

"Maybe you can take it back and get a refund," she said.

He didn't bother to pick it up. "Tell me more about your relationship. How long did you know each other?"

Her cheeks flushed again. "About a month," she muttered.

"A month?" he asked, sure he hadn't heard her correctly. "Are you serious? You married a man you'd only known for a few weeks?"

She fidgeted in her chair, crossing, then uncrossing her legs. "Yes. I know it was fast, but it felt right. For once in my life I wanted to take a risk, dive into the deep end. I wanted to feel alive, on the edge. There's nothing you can say that I haven't heard before. I was stupid, impetuous, crazy, foolish, reckless, generally an idiot... Have I left anything out?"

Her eyes sparked with anger, and he saw a touch of steel beneath her soft exterior. "I don't think so," he said prudently. "Where did you meet Evan?"

"At my grandmother's house. Evan was a real estate agent. He was selling the condo next to my grandmother's. They started talking about the market one day, and he offered her a free appraisal. She introduced us. That was it. It was fate."

"I don't think so," he said grimly. "Evan always had an agenda. And the way he left so abruptly... Evan was either done doing what he wanted to do, or someone was catching up to him. As for your part in it all -- there has to be a reason. Evan never did love for love's sake."

"You don't know that for sure," Kayla argued. "You're speculating about a relationship you know nothing about. You weren't there. You didn't see him with me."

"I saw him with plenty of other women, including my sister. Jenny thought he was in love with her, too. No," he said with a definite shake of his head. He knew their marriage hadn't been about love, not the way it had started, and certainly not the way it had ended. "You had something Evan wanted. What did he take with him when he left?"

"I told you -- nothing," she said, and then stopped abruptly, a light coming on in her eyes.

"What? What did you remember?"

"I'm sure it's not important."

"Let me be the judge of that."

"It was just an old pocket watch that belonged to my grandfather. It wasn't worth anything. It had sentimental value. That's all."

Nick's muscles tensed. They were finally getting somewhere; he just didn't know where. "When did you give it to him?"

She hesitated. "On our wedding night. It was my wedding present to him. He'd admired it earlier, and my grandmother had told me to give it to the man I loved."

"Bingo," he said, jumping to his feet. "The watch. He wanted the watch."

"Why? Why would he want a fifty-year-old watch?"

"It had to be worth something." He ran a hand through his hair, trying to think of how valuable an old pocket watch could be.

"I'm sure it wasn't," Kayla replied. "It's not as if it had jewels on it or anything."

"It had something." He was convinced of that. "Who can tell us more about the watch?"

She thought for a moment. "I guess my grandmother could. The watch belonged to my grandfather. He passed away two years ago. That's when she gave it to me."

"When can we talk to her? How about now?"

"Now?" She didn't sound enthusiastic when she said, "I don't know. It's not too late, I guess."

"Why don't you give her a call?"

"You're very pushy," she complained.

"I'm very motivated," he said shortly. "Aren't you? Don't you want to know why Evan married you? Why he took your grandfather's watch?"

"Of course I do. I want to get to the bottom of this as much as you do."

"Then help me. The sooner we find Evan, the sooner you get us both out of your life."

"Good point." Kayla stood up. "I'll call my grandmother." She picked up the phone on a side table. Before she could punch in a number it rang. "Hello?" she said.

Nick saw the blood drain from her face, and he suddenly knew who was calling. He moved quickly across the room, taking the phone out of her trembling hand. "Evan?" he said sharply. He heard someone exhale and then there was nothing but a dial tone. "Dammit." He turned to Kayla. "Was it Evan? What did he say?"

She stared at him, her eyes glittering with emotion. "He said, 'Tell Nick, welcome home.'"

* * *

Evan slipped his cell phone into the pocket of his slacks and smiled with satisfaction. Nick was back. Things were falling into place exactly as he'd planned. Nick and Kayla were puppets on his string, and now they would dance for him. He pulled out a cigarette and lit it, the flame brightening the dark shadows that surrounded him. He took a long drag as he leaned back against a pillar and waited.

Dusk had fallen over the city. The fog coming in from the ocean had obliterated the stars and the moon. He liked the cool, wet darkness around him. He'd always been a creature of the night. Shadows were his friends. Not that he was afraid of the light. No one was better than him at becoming part of the landscape. He knew how to blend in. He could be anyone he wanted to be, play any role, answer to any name, and wear any clothes. He was so good he could convince a mother he was her son or a sister that he was her brother. He knew how to sell dreams, and everyone had a dream.

He was the best. And soon everyone would know just how good he really was.

A flock of night birds squawked as they skipped off the water in the nearby lagoon. It was quiet near the rotunda of the Palace of Fine Arts. The building was closed. The tourists had gone home. But still he waited. A moment later a sleek, black limo pulled up. He gave it a long look, then tossed his cigarette on the ground and rubbed it out with the heel of his boot.

The driver got out of the car and held the back door open for him. He sauntered over, taking his time. He had not called this meeting, nor did he want it, but for the moment he would go along...

"You're late," Evan said, as he slipped onto the plush leather seat.

"Do you have it?"

His fingers curled around the watch in his pocket. "No," he said. "Your information was wrong. You wasted my time."

"As you wasted mine. You took too long with that woman."

"I had my reasons."

"I don't care about your reasons. I want results. We have only a few weeks to put the rest of our plan in motion, and failure is not an option."

"I never fail," Evan replied. He got out of the car and shut the door quietly behind him. The limo disappeared into the night -- as did he.

Chapter Three

Evan Chadwick. The name ran around in his head like a maddening refrain from an old song. Nick couldn't shake it loose; nor could he rid himself of the image of Evan on his wedding day dressed in a black tuxedo, a red rose boutonniere in his lapel, a knowing smile on his face, as if he couldn't wait for Nick to know exactly what he had done. *Damn him!*

Nick wanted to shout the words. He wanted to punch someone, preferably Evan, but he couldn't do anything but drive, his hands curled around the steering wheel of the Porsche Evan had bought with his money. *Damn him!*

"Are you all right?" Kayla asked, worry in her voice. "You're going awfully fast." She braced her hand against the door as he maneuvered around a bus, weaving in and out of lanes to avoid the slower traffic.

"We're in a sports car. We're supposed to go fast," he snapped back.

"Look, I know you're angry--"

"You don't know the half of it." The tires squealed as he spun around a corner.

"If we die in a car crash, Evan wins," Kayla said. "Do you want that?"

Her words cut through his rage, and he eased his foot off the gas, realizing she was right. He wouldn't give Evan the satisfaction of dying before he got even. Instead of blasting his way through the yellow light, he brought the car to a crashing halt, almost throwing them both through the windshield. "Sorry," he muttered.

Kayla shot him a wary look and straightened in her seat. "Why don't you take a breath? Get a grip."

"I'm trying."

"Try harder. Or should I get out of the car right now?" she challenged, her hand hovering over the door handle.

"I'm fine. Stay. Please," he added. He couldn't afford to alienate Kayla. She was the only lead he had.

After a momentary hesitation, she let go of the handle and straightened in her seat. "All right. But slow down."

"I will. I'm just so pissed off," he confessed. "I can't believe Evan came back into my life and ripped me off. I should have paid attention, seen it coming. I shouldn't have let my guard down, but it's been so long. I never thought I'd see him again."

"How long exactly?" Kayla asked.

"Twelve years. We met when we were juniors in college. We only knew each other a few months before everything blew up." At her questioning look, he shrugged. "It's a long, complicated story."

"Give me the short version."

He hit the gas as the light turned green, careful to keep his speed down as he maneuvered through the busy streets. "I thought Evan was just an ordinary college kid. But it quickly became apparent that he was far more interested in making money off his fellow students than getting an education. He ran cons, Kayla. Card games with marked cards, housekeeping services that were a front for prostitution. He sold drugs to kids who needed to stay up all night studying, and if someone needed copies of tests, he hacked into the college computer system and found them. Of course, it took me a while to realize what he was doing. By that time he was involved with my sister Jenny. I tried to convince her he was no good. She wouldn't listen. I decided to take him down right in front of her. Unfortunately, things went bad, and ..." He stumbled, wishing he didn't have to go back down that road, but it was too late now. He was already there, and maybe it was a good thing. He needed to remember just how dangerous Evan could be.

"And what?" Kayla prodded.

"Jenny got stabbed. She took a knife for Evan, and he left her bleeding on the floor."

"Oh, my God!" she breathed.

"It was my fault Jenny got hurt. I blew it. I didn't protect her." He could still see his sister's white face, her lifeless body, the slash of blood across her chest. He'd been terrified that he'd lost her.

"Was she all right?" Kayla asked.

"Eventually."

"And Evan?"

"He went to jail and swore he'd get even." Nick paused, remembering that day in the courthouse when Evan had been convicted, primarily due to Nick's testimony. Evan had turned to give him one last hateful smile, and he'd said, *"Someday, Nick, when you least expect it, I'll pay you back."* Apparently that day was now.

"I guess we know why he went after you," Kayla said heavily. "But it happened so long ago. Why now?"

"I don't know."

"And why me? How do you and I go together?"

He couldn't answer that question either. "That's what we have to find out," he said. "Hopefully your grandmother will be able to tell us more about the watch." He paused as a two-story development of town houses near the Embarcadero came into view. "Is this it?"

"Yes, her unit is down at the end."

He pulled into a nearby space and shut off the engine. He was out of the car before he realized that Kayla hadn't moved. He leaned back inside. "What's wrong? Why aren't you getting out?"

"I'm trying to figure out how to tell my grandmother that I married a thief without giving her a heart attack. She's an elderly woman. She lives a quiet life. This news will upset her. Yesterday I thought I was married to one guy. Now it turns out I'm married to another. None of this will be easy to explain."

He started at her words. Evan had married her using his name. He'd probably enjoyed that the most.

"I didn't mean I was married to you," Kayla said quickly. "In fact, the marriage can't be legal, because Evan used your name. Right?"

"Right. I'm sure it's not legal, but it's another piece of red tape to untangle. Let's talk to your grandmother. We have to find Evan before he can do any more damage."

"Is that even possible? What else is left for him to do?"

"We won't know that until we figure out what he's after."

Kayla took her time getting out of the car. Nick was in a rush to learn the truth. He would roll right over her if she got in his way. But she wasn't worried about herself as much as her grandmother. She wanted to make sure they did this as painlessly as possible. She put a hand on Nick's arm. "Wait. Before we go inside, I want you to promise to let me handle this. I don't want to upset my grandmother any more than I have to."

Nick looked like he wanted to argue, but thought better of it. "Fine. Just get the answers we need, and I won't say a word."

They walked up the path to the front door. As Kayla put her finger on the buzzer, she could hear laughter and loud voices coming from inside the apartment.

"Sounds like a party," Nick commented. "I thought you said your grandmother lived a quiet life."

"She does," she replied with a frown. As far as she knew her grandmother spent most evenings reading or watching television. "Maybe it's her bridge night," she said. Kayla rang the bell again. No one answered. She tried the door. It swung open. "I guess we might as well go in."

As she entered with Nick on her heels, she saw her grandmother sitting at her dining room table with three other women. They were playing cards, but judging by the array of colorful chips piled in the center of the table, they were not playing bridge. Cigarette smoke hung thick in the air. A half-empty bottle of bourbon was surrounded by used shot glasses. Old Broadway tunes played in the background of their rather loud conversation. To say Kayla was surprised was to put it mildly. She barely recognized the woman shuffling the cards like an experienced dealer.

The conversation at the table ended abruptly when one of the women spotted them. "Charlotte," she said. "You have company."

Her grandmother turned her head, her blue eyes surprised but sparkling. Her cheeks were flushed, and her hair looked blonder, shorter; she must have gotten it cut recently. She was different, Kayla thought, younger, prettier, and definitely livelier than she'd been in the past two years. Why hadn't she noticed the changes before? Had she been so caught up in her own problems?

"Kayla," Charlotte said. "I didn't know you were coming

over. This is my granddaughter, girls." She set her cards down and stood up. She was taller than Kayla, about five-foot-eight, and she moved across the room with energy and grace. She gave Kayla a hug and a kiss on the cheek before turning an inquisitive gaze on Nick. "Have we met?"

"No. I'm--"

"Grandma, what is all this?" Kayla asked, cutting him off. She didn't want him to say his name until she was ready.

"It's Friday-night poker," Charlotte replied. "The girls and I have a weekly game now. We're very good at Texas Hold 'Em. When we get better, we're going to take a bus trip to Tahoe and win some money."

"What happened to bridge?" Kayla wasn't sure she liked this new rendition of her grandmother.

"Bridge is an old lady's game," Charlotte replied with a dismissive wave of her hand. "Meet my friends. That's Bernice in the yellow. She lives next door."

"I remember. Hi, Bernice."

"And next to her is Donna from church, and Kathleen, who has a condo a couple doors down."

"Hello," Kayla said as the women waved to her.

"Since Kayla hasn't introduced us, I'm Charlotte Hirsch," she said to Nick. "And you are?"

"Nick Granville," he said, shooting Kayla a pointed look that told her that if she wasn't going to get on with it, he would.

"I was going to tell her," Kayla said defensively.

"She asked; I answered," he replied.

"I don't understand. What's going on?" Charlotte asked in confusion. "This isn't Nick."

"Actually, it is." Kayla searched for the right way to begin, but what could she say that would make a confusing situation understandable? "I wish there were an easy way to tell you this, Grandma, but there isn't, so I'm just going to say it. The man I married is not who he said he was. He took on Nick's identity as a cover. His real name is Evan Chadwick." She let the words sink in, then continued. "He lied to me about everything, and it appears that he's not just a liar but also a thief. While Evan was living at Nick's house, he stole his money, got into his bank accounts, and basically took over his life."

Her grandmother's jaw dropped in amazement. "Are you serious?"

"Yes."

"Oh, dear. You must be so upset, Kayla."

"I've had better days."

Charlotte nodded. "We need to talk." She turned back to her friends, who were listening with avid curiosity. "Ladies, if you'll excuse me for a few minutes ..."

"Take your time," Bernice replied. "We'll have a drink while you're gone."

Her grandmother led them into a small room off the living room where she did her sewing and reading. She sat down with Kayla on the love seat while Nick hovered in the doorway. Kayla had a feeling none of them would be going anywhere until he had the answers he wanted.

"Now tell me again what's happened," Charlotte encouraged. "I'm not sure I heard it right."

"You did. It's just as unbelievable as it sounds," Kayla replied. "I went by Nick's house tonight, thinking I'd check to see if he was home, the way I've done every night for the last few weeks." She waved her hand toward the man standing in the doorway. "This Nick answered the door. I was shocked to see him, and I didn't want to believe that he was Nick Granville, but he proved to me that that is, in fact, the case."

"Oh, my," Charlotte said, her expression growing more disturbed by the moment. "You're sure?" She sent Nick a wary look.

"I'm sure," Kayla said. "I checked it out, Grandma. Everything matches."

"What happened to your husband then?"

"I don't know. That's what I need to figure out."

"What a shocking story," Charlotte said. "I can't believe it."

"Me either, but the facts are too real to ignore. Nick says that the man I married is someone he used to know, someone he went to school with. His real name is Evan Chadwick, and he's a con artist."

Charlotte turned her attention to Nick. "How do you know that?"

"I recognized Evan from Kayla's wedding photo," he replied.

"I have no idea why he appeared now, or why he chose to impersonate me to your granddaughter."

"He seemed like such a nice man," Charlotte muttered, a troubled look in her eyes. "He had beautiful manners, and he was so charming."

"That's what I thought, too," Kayla said, "but I was wrong. I screwed up, Grandma. I made a huge mistake. I married a man I didn't really know, and look what happened."

"Oh, honey, you didn't do anything wrong; you just fell in love," Charlotte said with a sympathetic smile.

"With the wrong guy."

"Sometimes that happens."

"Now I need to figure out why this Evan Chadwick married me and where he is," Kayla said.

Her grandmother nodded in agreement. "Is there anything I can do to help?"

"Actually there is," Nick cut in. "Kayla told me that she gave Evan a watch right before he disappeared, an old pocket watch that belonged to your husband."

"You gave him your grandfather's watch?" Charlotte asked in surprise. "Why? Why would you do that?"

Kayla was taken aback by her grandmother's vehement response. She seemed far more upset by this piece of information than by any other. "You said to give it to the man I loved. Don't you remember?"

"But..." Charlotte swallowed back the rest of her sentence. "Of course I told you that. I just didn't realize you gave it to him before he disappeared. Why didn't you tell me that before?"

"I didn't think it was important. I forgot about it until now. I was worried about my husband's safety. I wasn't thinking about the watch. I'm sorry." Kayla paused. "Was it valuable?"

Charlotte hesitated, her lips pressed together in a tight line. "It wasn't valuable. It was just important to me. I guess it doesn't matter now. I gave it to you. It was yours to do with as you wanted. I just didn't realize that you'd given it away so quickly."

"I never thought he would take it and disappear the way he did."

"I know you didn't. Well, it's done. I guess that's that." Charlotte stood up. "I should get back to my guests."

She was startled by the abrupt change in conversation. "All right."

"It's not done," Nick interjected, barring the doorway. "If Evan wanted that watch, he had a reason. According to Kayla, it's the only thing he took from her. It has to be worth something. Can you describe it to me? Was it gold, silver? Is there any kind of history attached to it?"

"It was just an ordinary silver pocket watch. I have no idea of its history or where my husband got it. It was just something he treasured." Charlotte turned back to Kayla. "I think the best thing to do now is just go on with your life. The watch is gone. So is the man you married. Your relationship is over. It's time to move on."

She had never suspected her grandmother could sound so callous, so dismissive, so cold. Charlotte was clearly angry that the watch was gone, but Kayla still wasn't sure why. "I can't move on until I find Evan," she said. "I have to know why he did what he did. And I want to get that watch back for you. It obviously means more than I realized."

Charlotte gave a quick, decisive shake of her head. "No, the watch isn't important anymore. Forget about it."

"But it *is* important," Kayla said. "You're upset; I can see that."

"I'm worried about you," Charlotte replied. "Evan's explanations won't change anything. You made a mistake, Kayla. Just move forward. Trust me. Looking back is never a good idea."

"Kayla might be able to move forward, but I can't," Nick said, interrupting them once again. "Evan took a great deal more from me than a watch. He stole thousands of dollars, and God knows what else he did using my name."

"I'm sorry for your losses, but they don't have anything to do with Kayla."

"She was with him the entire time Evan was impersonating me," Nick replied.

"You can't believe she was stealing from you."

"At the moment, I'm willing to believe she was an unwitting victim, but I think that watch is the key to Evan's game. So if there's anything you can tell me about it, I hope you will."

Charlotte looked Nick straight in the eye. "There's really nothing else I can say. Now if you'll excuse me..."

Nick reluctantly moved away from the door. "If you think of anything, you'll let Kayla know?"

"Of course," she replied. "I'll see you out."

Charlotte ushered them directly to the front door. Kayla had never been kicked out of her grandmother's house before. It felt very odd. As soon as the watch had been mentioned, her grandmother's entire demeanor had changed. "I'm sorry we barged in on you," she said quietly.

"It's fine. Please just think about letting this go, Kayla." Charlotte sent her a pleading look. "I really believe it's for the best."

"I can't do that," Kayla replied as disappointment filled her grandmother's eyes.

"I see. Well, good night." As soon as they'd stepped onto the porch, Charlotte shut the door behind them, sliding the dead bolt into place.

"What the hell was that about?" Nick asked, an annoyed gleam in his eyes.

"What do you mean?"

"Your grandmother went a little nuts when we told her the watch was missing. She did not want to help us."

"She did act a little odd," Kayla admitted, still not sure exactly why. "I never thought the watch was a big deal. She never made it sound that important. It was just sentimental."

"She's hiding something," Nick said. "The question is what?"

"Don't be ridiculous. My grandmother is the most honest person I know," Kayla defended, but deep down inside she knew her grandmother's behavior had been off. Something bothered her about the watch being gone, something she hadn't wanted to tell them.

"We'll just have to get the information we need somewhere else," Nick said as they walked back to the car. "You obviously saw the watch. What did it look like? Can you describe it?"

She paused by the car door, picturing the watch in her mind. "There was an engraving on the front, the outline of a building, spires, columns, that kind of thing," she said slowly. "On the back was the phrase 'of Heaven await.'"

"What does that mean?" Nick asked.

"I don't know. I guess my grandfather just liked the words. He was a religious man."

"What else?" Nick asked.

"The watch flipped open like your basic pocket watch. It hung on a silver chain." She bit down on her bottom lip as she thought for a moment. "There were two initials on the inside cover. They were very small. I think maybe the letters were *D* and *R*.".

"Not your grandfather's initials?"

"No, his name was Edward Hirsch. I assume they belonged to the person who made the watch."

A light of excitement flashed in his eyes. "Could be. What else? What about a photograph of the watch? Does one exist?"

"I don't know. I suppose there could be a picture of my grandfather wearing the watch."

"Where would the photos be? Please don't tell me with your grandmother."

"Actually, no. My grandmother moved out of her house, which is now my house, two years ago, and she left a lot behind. She said she wanted to start fresh someplace new."

"So if there are photos, those albums would be ...?"

"In the attic at my house."

"Let's go." As he opened the car door for Kayla, she looked back at the condo, surprised to see a curtain flutter against the window. Had her grandmother been watching them? Was she simply worried, or was there something more going on? If she couldn't trust her grandmother, who could she trust?

* * *

It was almost ten o'clock that night when Kayla finally led Nick up to the attic of her house. They'd stopped for pizza and wine on the way back from her grandmother's condo, and after the initial awkwardness, they'd actually managed to converse about neutral topics like movies, books, and the weather, carefully staying away from the personal events of the past month. The breather had helped her get her head together. While she wouldn't say they were comfortable with each other now, she was feeling a lot less tense, although that might have had something to do with the wine.

She would have liked to put off going through the attic until the next day, when she would have had a chance to think about everything she had learned, but Nick was like a runaway train; he couldn't be stopped. He didn't seem to understand that she needed more than a few minutes to come to terms with the fact that the man she'd married had lied to her about the very basics of his identity. Nick just wanted her to get on with the task of finding Evan.

And she did want to find Evan, more than she wanted anything. She wasn't sure that a photograph would tell Nick what he wanted to know, but she suspected he needed something specific to focus on, something that would give him a way to fight back.

She entered the attic with some trepidation. It had been years since she'd come up here, and she vaguely remembered piles and piles of junk. She paused in the doorway to turn on the light, little more than a bare bulb hanging on a chain. The musty, dusty room was even more cluttered than she remembered, littered with old pieces of furniture stacked on top of one another and dozens of boxes that had accumulated in the last forty or fifty years.

"Well," Nick muttered, putting his hands on his hips as he surveyed the room.

"It's a mess, I know. My family has the nasty habit of cleaning up by throwing everything into one room and shutting the door. The albums could be in any one of those boxes. This search could take all night."

"We'd better get started then."

"Are you sure you don't want me to work on it and let you know what I find? You must be tired after your trip home. You probably haven't slept in days."

"I'm more interested in finding Evan than sleeping," he told her, a glint of determination in his eyes. "That watch is the only clue I have right now."

"It's a pretty small clue."

"Actually, we don't know how small it is," Nick corrected. "I know we're not working on the same page, Kayla. When you think of Evan, you see the man you married. When I think of him, I see the man who destroyed a lot of lives in the six months that I knew him, including my sister's. I know he's dangerous. And I don't think he's done with us yet. That's why he called you earlier. He wanted you and me to both know there's more to come."

She stared at Nick in growing alarm. She'd never considered Evan to be dangerous, but his voice on the phone earlier had sent a chill down her spine. There had been a wicked, nasty edge to his tone. She'd expected that if they ever spoke again, he'd say he was sorry about walking out on her, but he hadn't sounded sorry, more like triumphant, as if he'd won something. She wanted to believe that her instincts about him had not been completely wrong, but how could she? He'd lied about his name, his home, his job -- she had to accept the fact that she didn't know him at all.

"Evan left me two weeks ago," she said aloud. "He took what he wanted. He had the chance to take anything else. What more could he possibly want with me?"

Nick's gaze was hard and unyielding. "That's what we have to find out, before he catches us off guard once again. I believe that Evan is a sociopath. He has no conscience, no moral boundaries, no regrets."

"But he was so charming," she protested, still having a little trouble seeing Evan the way Nick saw him.

"Which is how he gains the trust of the people he wants to use."

And she'd trusted him completely, given herself to him, gone off with him alone. He could have killed her. Maybe she was lucky he'd just left. But the other side of her brain wanted to know why she was so willing to believe this man -- this Nick Granville. She'd known him for only a few hours. And while his story made sense, did she really have all the facts? Here she was again, alone with a strange man whom she'd freely invited into her home, into her attic, into a place where no one would find her for days if something were to happen.

Her gaze shot toward the door. She had the urge to run as far away from him as possible.

"Don't," Nick said abruptly. "Don't go."

"You're scaring me." Saying it out loud made her feel marginally better. Grabbing a nearby tennis racket off a pile of sports equipment made her feel even more in control.

Nick's eyes narrowed. "You're scared of me?"

"I don't know you any better than I knew Evan. You could be lying, too."

"I thought we'd gotten past that, Kayla."

"You reminded me that I made a terrible mistake when I trusted Evan. Why should I trust you?"

"Because you know Evan was in my house. You know he pretended to be me. He's the bad guy." Nick paused, blowing out a frustrated breath. "Look, I'm sorry if you're scared. I'm not going to hurt you. I'm also not going to back down. I want to find a photo of that watch. And unless you plan to hit me over the head with that racket, I'm going to start searching the boxes now."

Her fingers tightened around the handle of the racket. She felt torn between logic and her imagination, which was running amok in the shadowy, eerie light of the attic. "I could hit you if I need to. Just so you know. I can protect myself."

"Good, but I'm really not the one you need to be worried about. Now why don't you start on that side of the room, and I'll start here. Hopefully one of us will come up with a photo of that watch."

Kayla took the racket with her, keeping it nearby as she began to look for the photo albums. They worked in silence for a while. Nick made faster work of the boxes than she did. She kept getting caught up in old memories, the costumes she'd played dress-up in, the ceramic vase she'd made in art class. Then there was the scrapbook of plane tickets. "I forgot about this," she muttered, pulling it out to take a closer look.

Nick came over to her side. "Did you find a picture of the watch?"

"No, just an old album I made a long time ago."

His brow furrowed as he stared down at her page of ticket receipts. "You must have done a lot of traveling."

"Every other weekend for three years. I always went to the same place, San Diego. That's where my father moved after my parents divorced when I was ten years old. They shared custody of me, so I went back and forth, and then it stopped," she said with a sigh.

"Why?"

"My dad remarried, had a baby with his second wife. He thought it would be easier if I just came in the summer, and then eventually it seemed easier if I didn't come at all." She'd been so hurt at the time. She'd kept the plane tickets, thinking that one day she'd throw them in her father's face, and tell him how horrible it had been, and that he would actually care. But she'd grown up and realized that he'd never care the way she wanted him to. She tossed the tickets back into the box. "Are your parents still together?"

"No. They divorced when I was thirteen. My father had an affair. Unfortunately, when he moved out he didn't go far, just a few blocks away to his girlfriend's apartment. I would have preferred he'd gone to the other side of the world. I wanted nothing more to do with him, but my sisters had a soft spot for him. They used to cry when he didn't show up, which was a lot." His mouth twisted into an angry grimace, and Kayla caught a glimpse of pain in his eyes, but before she could comment he looked away. "Let's get back to work," he said gruffly. "Stay focused."

"Okay, I'm on it." She opened another box. It was filled with odds and ends that she vaguely remembered being in her grandmother's curio closet, old teacups, ashtrays, and vases, nothing of any value.

Nick opened the box next to hers. A moment later, he let out a low whistle. "I think I found something, Kayla." He pulled out two old albums. "Somebody's baby pictures."

He sat down on the floor, leaning against the wall with his legs stretched out in front of him. She scooted over next to him to take a look. "That's my mother," she said. "And my grandparents. I don't know if I've ever seen this album." They flipped through the pages together. Most of the pictures were of her mother and her grandmother. Her grandfather had probably been the one taking the photos.

"No watch," Nick said, closing the book.

She picked up the second album and leafed through the yellowed pages. "This must have been my grandmother's album before she married Grandpa." The photos were all black-and-white and showed her grandmother at various key moments in her life: first day of school, first Communion, cheerleading, going to the prom. Charlotte always had a sparkle in her eyes, even back then. "She looks so young," she said. "So full of life."

"She looked full of life tonight," Nick commented.

That was certainly true, Kayla thought with a frown. Not that she didn't want her grandmother to be happy, but poker, bourbon, cigarettes? Was she having some sort of midlife crisis a few years late?

"Hey, what's this?" Nick took a brown envelope from the back of the scrapbook. He pulled out several newspaper clippings, a couple of playbills, and an eight-by-ten photo of her grandmother in a fifties-style dance costume, short skirt, high heels, black mesh stockings.

"Good heavens. Is that Grandma?" she asked, snatching the photo from him. The sexy woman in the skimpy outfit did not look like the woman she knew.

"She was a dancer," Nick said, opening one of the theater programs. "She's listed in the chorus."

"I can't believe it. Give me that." She was convinced he was wrong until she saw her grandmother's maiden name -- Charlotte Cunningham. "She never told me she danced onstage. She said she was a secretary."

"Maybe a topless one," he suggested, handing her an ad from a newspaper highlighting the opening of a new strip club on Broadway featuring "Sweet Charlie" and "Dazzling Dana."

Kayla swallowed hard. She couldn't believe it. Her grandmother had been a stripper? She felt her stomach turn over. Was no one who they appeared to be? Did everyone have a secret life? "This is crazy and shocking," she muttered. "Why didn't she tell me?"

"Maybe she thought you'd be horrified," he said pointedly.

"Well, it is kind of horrifying, isn't it?"

"It was a long time ago."

"She's always lived such a respectable life. My grandfather was a banker. They went to church every Sunday. They were conservative. I just don't understand how she could go from stripping to that life." She paused. "I wonder if Grandpa knew about her past."

"Maybe he liked the fact that she had something to show off, you know?"

Kayla's jaw dropped. "I can't believe you just said that. She's my grandmother, for God's sake."

Nick smiled. "She stripped, big deal. She didn't kill anyone. And she was a young, single woman at the time."

"I don't think she'd like it if I were doing the same thing

now." Nick's gaze dropped to her chest and lingered there. She instinctively crossed her arms, knowing she was not nearly as well-endowed as her grandmother. "Hey," she protested.

"Sorry, male reflex," he said with an unapologetic laugh.

"Yeah, well, as you said a few minutes ago, stay focused." As she stuffed the clippings back into the envelope, she found another interesting photo. Her grandmother stood next to a tall, dark-haired man with a mustache. He had his arm around Charlotte, and she was smiling up at him with complete adoration. She looked like a young woman in love.

A glint of silver caught Kayla's eye. Her heart stopped. There, hanging out of the man's coat pocket, was a chain and a watch, a pocket watch -- her grandfather's watch, the same watch she'd given Evan. She couldn't believe her eyes. There had to be some mistake.

"Kayla? Did you find something?" Nick asked.

Swallowing hard, she turned the photo around so he could see it.

"Is that the watch?"

"Yes, but the man wearing it is not my grandfather. I've never seen him before. They look like they're -- friends."

"Or more than that," Nick said, as his gaze met hers. "I knew your grandmother was hiding something. Maybe this man is the reason she didn't want to talk about the watch."

"Maybe," she conceded.

"Do you mind if I take that photo home with me? I'd like to look at it under a magnifying glass."

"I guess," she said, a little reluctant to let it out of her sight. "I still don't know what Evan would want with a fifty-year-old watch, even if it did belong to someone other than my grandfather. It can't be worth that much. Can it?"

"I don't know yet." Nick tapped the photo in his hand. "I think this guy is important."

She gave a reluctant nod of agreement. Maybe her grandmother was right. Maybe nothing good ever came from looking back. It was too late now; they'd already opened the door to the past. And a stranger had walked through it. Who was he? She had to find out.

Chapter Four

Charlotte Hirsch opened the door Saturday morning and offered Kayla a resigned smile. "I had a feeling you would be back."

"We need to talk, Grandma." As she entered her grandmother's condo, Kayla saw no evidence of the poker game from the night before. The living and dining rooms were spotless. Charlotte was dressed in a pair of conservative black slacks and a navy-blue sweater. She looked like a grandma, not a chorus girl or a stripper. If Kayla hadn't spent most of the night going through the theater programs and scrapbooks, she might have been able to convince herself it was all a mistake. But there was too much hard evidence.

"I found an old photo album last night in the attic, starring you," she said as she took a seat on the red leather couch in her grandmother's living room. It occurred to her that red leather was not something her grandfather would ever have chosen. Her grandmother had changed since he'd died. Or maybe she'd just gone back to the person she'd once been.

"Oh, dear, I think I know where this is going," Charlotte said. "Do you want some tea?"

"No, I don't want tea; I want answers. No stalling, Grandma, and no kicking me out like you did last night."

"I had company."

"That's not the reason you wanted to get rid of me." Kayla patted the seat next to her. "Sit."

Charlotte sat, folding her hands in her lap, her expression both wary and annoyed. "What on earth were you doing in the attic?"

"Looking for photos of the watch."

"Why would you need a picture? You know what it looked like."

"Nick wanted to see one. He wants to trace the watch. He thinks it will lead us to Evan."

"I told you to let that go."

"I can't." Kayla let the words sink in and then said, "Grandma, I don't think you were being completely honest with me last night."

"The watch wasn't valuable, Kayla."

"But it also wasn't Grandpa's, was it?" She saw her grandmother flinch and knew she was right. "I found a photograph of you and another man. He was wearing the watch. Who was he?"

Charlotte didn't answer right away. Her eyes took on a faraway look, as if she were going back in time. A small smile played around her mouth, touched off by some distant memory.

"Grandma." Kayla nudged her.

"He was someone I cared about a long time ago," Charlotte said slowly. She drew in a breath from way down deep and slowly let it out. "I guess you could say he was my first love. And yes, it was his watch."

"I don't understand why you lied about it."

"I didn't want to have to explain whose watch it was and why it was special to me."

"Well, I'm sorry, but I think you have to explain. Not just about the watch, but about your life. You were in a chorus line. You danced professionally, and ..." She cleared her throat. "Sometimes you stripped, isn't that right?"

Her grandmother looked down at her hands, twisting her fingers together in agitation. "I should have cleaned out that attic myself. I'd forgotten there was anything up there. It was so long ago, so many years. It was a different life. I was a different girl."

"I'm not judging you," she said softly.

Charlotte's head lifted, relief in her eyes. "You're not ashamed of me?"

"How could I be? I know what kind of person you are today and what kind of grandmother you've been to me. I'm certainly in no position to judge anyone else's choices. I just wonder why you never said anything."

"In my youth some people would have called me wild or fast. I loved to dance and I was very comfortable expressing myself with my body." She let out a sigh that sounded like regret. "The stage spoke to me. I felt at home under the lights, the music playing, the crowds of people watching, applauding. It was a great feeling, exhilarating. I never felt so alive."

"Why did you stop?"

"A lot of reasons," she said, with a vague wave of her hand. "Your grandfather was very conservative, respectable. I wanted to honor him."

Kayla could understand that, but it almost seemed as if her grandmother were two different people, or that she'd changed drastically when she'd married. "Grandpa was so straight, so stern," she murmured. "Didn't you ever find life with him a bit constraining?"

"He took care of me. He was a good husband, an excellent father. I respected him very much."

"Respect isn't love."

"Then I should have said I loved him, because I did."

Despite her grandmother's vehement tone, Kayla wasn't quite convinced. "What about the guy in the photo? How did you feel about him? Was he part of your wild time?"

"Yes," she said after a moment. "He was part of that time and very special to me. He was a charmer, Kayla, so handsome and smooth he swept me off my feet. It was instant attraction. I fell head over heels before I even knew his name. And I couldn't think straight when he was around." She took a breath. "Some people thought I was a fool, but he was good to me. I had never met a man so passionate. When he was around me the air sizzled. I suppose that sounds silly, but that's the way it seemed to me. I was a young woman. I didn't know what to make of the feelings he stirred up in me."

Kayla cleared her throat, feeling a bit warm and uncomfortable by the candidness of her grandmother's remarks. It was a little too much information, and a part of her very much wanted to drop the whole subject, but she couldn't. If she didn't ask her grandmother the questions, Nick would, and this was her family business, not his. "What was his name?"

"Johnny. His name was Johnny."

"What happened to him? Why didn't you stay together?"

"He went away." Sadness filled her eyes. "It still hurts, even now, fifty years later. But he had to go, and I had to let him go. That was that, the end of our love story."

"Why didn't you go after him? Or why didn't he come back?" Kayla asked. It felt strange to be discussing a man other than her grandfather. But whom would it hurt? Her grandfather had passed on.

"It wasn't meant to be. After Johnny left I met Edward, and we got married and had your mother. I ended up with you as my beautiful granddaughter," she added with a smile. "I had a great life."

Her words were positive and cheerful, but Kayla could see a lingering sadness in her grandmother's eyes. Had it always been there? Had Kayla never noticed it before? They'd been close over the years, but not really confidantes, not until now. "But you didn't have a great life with your first love," she murmured. "You must have missed him."

"Terribly." Charlotte paused. "Johnny left the watch with me before he went away. He said he'd be back to get it, that it would remind me of him and of our love, and that I should never let it out of my sight. It would be a symbol of our future together. I was young, only twenty-three years old. When he said he'd come back, I believed him with all my heart. I thought he could do anything. I thought he could beat the odds." She drew in a long, shaky breath. "But years passed and he didn't return. I kept the watch tucked away in my panty drawer. I'm not sure why. Every once in a while I'd remember, and I'd take it out and look at it and think about him. After your grandfather died, and I decided to move out of the house and get on with the next stage of my life, I thought it was time to give up the watch, too. That's why I gave it to you. It was about love, Kayla, and I wanted you to give it to the man you loved."

"Well, that didn't work out too well." She felt even worse now that she knew the whole story. She hadn't just lost the watch; she'd lost the only thing her grandmother had left from her first love. "I'm so sorry. I should have waited, made sure Evan was going to last, that our relationship and our love were the real thing. I made so many mistakes." She hesitated, curious about something else. "I guess Grandpa didn't know about this other guy if you kept the watch tucked away?"

"He knew there was someone else before him, but not anything more. Edward didn't ask, and I didn't tell." She looked Kayla straight in the eyes. "Don't misunderstand, Kayla. I loved your grandfather. Edward was a wonderful man. I don't want you to think any differently about him."

She was relieved to hear that. She'd always held up her grandmother's long marriage as the kind of relationship she wanted to have. "Thanks for telling me."

"I do understand what it feels like to love the wrong man. You have to forgive yourself for doing that," she said, patting Kayla's leg. "It's in the past now, dear. Let it go."

"I don't move on as easily as you do."

"Try. You can't change what happened."

"But I can find Evan and get that watch back for you. Do you have any idea why the watch would have been important to Evan? I understand why it's important to you, but why would he care? What's special about it?"

Her grandmother hesitated a split second too long. "I don't know."

Kayla didn't believe her. "I think you do know. Where did the watch come from?"

"It was a present."

"Do you know what the inscription meant?"

"Johnny never said."

Kayla frowned. She was getting nowhere fast. "So you don't know anything about the watch? There's nothing you can tell me?"

"I think I already said that, Kayla," Charlotte replied, sounding irritated. "I don't know what you want me to tell you. Just forget about the watch. It's not important."

"It is important. If it weren't, you wouldn't be so evasive. You have to tell me what you're not saying. I'm not the only one involved, Grandma. Nick won't forget that Evan stole his money or that I helped him spend it. I owe it to him to try to help."

"You don't owe him anything. You were a victim, too."

"That may be, but I'm still involved. Nick will not give up this search. He's going to go after the truth until he finds it. And the watch is the only clue we have."

"I don't want to put you in danger," Charlotte said.

Kayla was surprised by her grandmother's choice of words. "How could you put me in danger?"

"By telling you too much. I think the watch was stolen, Kayla. That's why I don't want you to look into it. I don't know who the real owners are or what they'll do if someone goes looking for that watch. Will you stop now? Will you do that for me?"

* * *

Nick pulled into a parking spot behind his sister Jenny's beauty salon in Noe Valley and turned off the engine. He had debated whether or not to involve her in his search for Evan. In the end, he'd decided it would be better to warn her that Evan was back in his life rather than leave her vulnerable. He didn't want Evan to show up and catch her off guard -- if he hadn't done so already.

Nick found it odd that Jenny hadn't contacted him while he was away. They'd always kept in touch, at least sporadically. He hadn't worried about it. Instead, he'd been relieved not to have to worry about his family and just concentrate on work. Now he couldn't help wondering if he'd missed something. Not that Jenny would have helped Evan rob him. But he didn't know what she would allow Evan to do. Or what game he might be playing with her. Because if Evan hadn't forgotten about him in twelve years, Evan certainly hadn't forgotten about his sister.

Jenny was blow-drying a woman's hair when he walked into the shop. Her jaw dropped when she saw him. She shut off the dryer. "Nick, you're back. What are you doing here?"

"I came to catch up," he said.

"I'm almost done, if you want to wait."

He nodded and sat down in a chair. There were two other stylists working in the shop, both young women, and their chairs were occupied. There was music playing and a busy, energized air about the place. He knew Jenny wanted to open her own shop one day. She'd already approached him about investing, but he'd put her off. A part of him still wished she'd do something more with her life than cut hair. She'd been such a smart girl, such a good student, until Evan had sapped her confidence and her ambition.

Jen finished a few moments later and chatted with her client while the woman wrote out a check. Then she said good-bye and walked over to give him a hug. "Hey, there. Long time, no see."

She felt smaller, thinner, and he could see her bones above her low-riding blue jeans and small white T-shirt. "You've lost weight," he muttered.

"Wow. You know just what to say to a girl," she teased.

He looked into her hazel eyes, hoping to see a sparkle, but instead he saw tired shadows. Even her brown hair appeared limp. "What's going on, Jen?"

"Nothing. Jeez, you're back five minutes, and you're already interrogating me." She stepped back, wrapping her arms around her waist, which only emphasized her slender frame. "How was your trip?"

"It was fine, productive, successful, the usual. But I didn't come here to talk about me."

"Big surprise. So what are you doing here?"

"Can we go somewhere more private?"

Her eyes narrowed. "That sounds serious. No one is hurt, are they? Mom and Dee are on their way to Carmel for a few days. There wasn't an accident or anything-"

"No. It's nothing like that," he said quickly. "They're fine." He'd just spoken to his mother and had been relieved to learn she would be out of town with his other sister, Dee. He didn't want Evan anywhere near his family.

"All right. We can sit in the park," Jenny said. "My next client won't be here for a few minutes."

Jenny's salon was located on a street of boutiques and cafés adjacent to a small, grassy park. As they sat down on a bench, Jenny said, "So tell me what's wrong."

He wasn't sure how to start, but he'd never been one to mince words. "Evan."

Her skin paled, and her eyes glittered with some emotion he couldn't quite define.

"Evan? Good heavens, Nick. Why are you bringing him up after all these years?"

"Because he's back. He broke into my house while I was out

of town. It appears that he spent a number of weeks living there, impersonating me, helping himself to my money, my credit cards, all that." Nick was watching her so closely he could see her pulse jump in her throat, and the confusion and wariness spreading across her features. Confusion he could understand. Wariness made him suspicious.

"God, Nick, that's horrible. Are you sure it was Evan?"

"Positive." He let a moment pass before he added, "Aren't you going to ask me how I know?"

"You must be able to prove it. You seem certain."

"I am. I met someone who showed me a photo of the man who was in my house. It was Evan."

"I can't believe it. Why would he do that now -- after all these years?"

"I was hoping you had an idea."

She avoided his gaze, staring down at her hands, which were folded in her lap. "Why would I?"

"Because if Evan came back for me, I wouldn't be surprised if he'd contacted you. And to be frank, you look like hell. Your eyes are tired. You've lost weight. If it's not Evan causing your sleepless nights, then who is?"

"No one. I'm busy with work. I had a cold last week. I'm still recovering. Why don't you give me a break?"

"Why don't you give me an answer? Have you heard from Evan?"

She hesitated, then said, "I did receive some presents that were sent to me anonymously in the last few weeks, flowers, candy, a book, that sort of thing."

"And you thought they were from Evan?"

"Well, it wasn't the first thing I thought," she snapped. "I have dated a few other men in my life, you know. Anyway, the presents stopped, so that was that."

"You should have told me." It gave him chills to think that Evan had been stalking his sister while he was out of the country.

"You were in Africa," Jenny replied. "And we don't even know that Evan sent me the presents. It could have been anyone."

"You should have called the police."

"And told them I was scared of a few gifts? They would have laughed at me."

She was probably right, but he hated the thought of Evan watching her. "Why the hell didn't he stay out of our lives?" he murmured. He didn't wait for her to answer. "If he comes back, if he calls, if any more gifts arrive, you pick up the phone and call me. I already alerted the police. They're going to try to track Evan down. Until then, I have to figure out how to get myself out of the mess he got me into. You wouldn't believe what he's done to me."

"He probably thought he owed you," she said.

He heard a note in her voice that he didn't want to hear. "Jen, don't let yourself start thinking that Evan had a good reason for doing any of this, or that there's some good part of him that only you can see. He's a thief. He's a criminal. He always has been and he always will be."

Anger flickered in her eyes. "I'm not stupid, Nick."

He raised an eyebrow, fighting an urge to remind her that she'd been extremely stupid at one point in her life.

She put up a hand, reading his mind. "Okay, maybe I was naive once, but I was a kid then. I'm an adult now. I know that Evan is a thief. I also know that he has a weird code of honor that you couldn't possibly understand. And," she added with a touch of defiance, "not everything or everyone is as black-and-white as you would like them to be. Evan did have good traits. He wasn't all bad. He treated me very well at times. I think his childhood had a lot to do with the kind of person he became. It wasn't his fault that he was abused and abandoned, that he had to grow up on his own in a very tough world."

"You don't even know what his childhood really was," Nick argued. "Everything that came out of his mouth was a lie. How do you know what the truth is? He told you what he wanted you to believe."

"Not everything was a lie. I knew him better than you did, Nick."

"You think a man is going to tell you the truth just because he has sex with you? God, Jen, that's when most of the lies are told." He saw the hurt on her face and almost regretted his choice of words, but she was scaring him. Knowing that Evan was back in their lives, knowing how close he'd come to ruining her once, Nick couldn't bear to see it happen again. Jenny was weak where Evan was concerned. "You can be so smart about everything else; why can't you see Evan for who he is?"

"I think we're done," she said with a sharp, irritated edge to her voice. "You've made your point."

Before she could get to her feet, he put a hand on her shoulder. "One more thing, just in case you're thinking this is all some attempt by Evan to get back into your life. You should know that he married someone else using my name just two weeks ago, about the same time he started sending you gifts."

"What?" she asked. "What did you say?"

Nick frowned. Jenny seemed more surprised by this piece of news than by the fact that Evan had robbed him. "You heard me. Evan married someone using my name. He took her to Lake Tahoe and married her in a casino chapel. Her name is Kayla. At first I thought she was an accomplice, but I'm convinced now that she was just a mark, some pawn in Evan's game of revenge."

"Maybe she's not part of a game. Maybe he loved her," Jenny said slowly.

"He disappeared on their wedding night," Nick told her. "Does that sound like love?"

"It sounds like he got scared and ran away."

"Or he had another reason for marrying her." He waited a moment before saying, "Do you have any idea why Evan would be interested in an antique pocket watch?"

She blinked in confusion. "What?"

"The watch was the only thing he took from Kayla, and I feel sure it must mean something."

"I don't know. I don't know anything except that I have to get back to work. I just saw my next client walk into the salon." She tipped her head toward the shop.

"All right, but be careful, Jen, okay?"

"I will, but if Evan wanted to hurt me, he already had his opportunity. I don't think he's coming back."

"One more thing, Jen. You said Evan probably talked to you more than he ever talked to anyone. Did he ever tell you about a relative, a friend, someone he might know here in San Francisco who could help me find him?"

She thought for a moment and then shook her head. "I'm sorry. I can't think of anyone."

"If you do remember something that might give me a clue, call me, okay?"

"Okay."

Nick frowned as he watched her walk across the street. He had a feeling that despite her strong words, if Evan came knocking on her door, she might just answer. What was it about Evan that made ordinarily smart women do incredibly stupid things? Before he could come up with an answer, his cell phone rang.

"Hello?"

"Nick, it's Kayla. I spoke to my grandmother, and I got a little more information."

"Good," he replied. Things were beginning to break. "I was going to call you, too. I did some research, and I found a watchmaker in the city with the initials D.R. I'm on my way to check him out. Do you want to meet me?"

"Yes, where is it?"

"North Beach. Why don't we meet in front of that church in Washington Square? Do you know it?"

"Of course I know it. I'm a stained-glass artist. I've been in every church in the city, and St. Peter and Paul is one of my favorites."

"Good. Give me about twenty minutes to get there."

"All right. There's something you should know, Nick. My grandmother thinks the watch may have been stolen."

His spine began to tingle as he connected the dots... If the watch had gone from one thief to another, that couldn't be a coincidence. The watch had to be worth something. He'd bet his house on it -- one of the few things he had left.

* * *

Jenny walked into the salon, feeling unsettled by her conversation with Nick. She had a terrible feeling she was to blame for everything that had happened. Telling her client she'd be with her in five minutes, she pulled her cell phone out of her purse and went into the small bathroom at the back of the salon and locked the door. She dialed the number that was still on her phone. She should have erased it, but she hadn't. It probably wouldn't work anymore. Or maybe it was a pay phone. She had no idea. But she had to try.

"Hello, Jenny," he said.

Her heart stopped. Evan's voice was forever imprinted in her brain and in her heart. Nick would never understand that love wasn't always a choice. Sometimes it was a noose around your neck, or a cement anchor dragging you under.

"What did you do to Nick?" she asked abruptly.

"I think you already know or you wouldn't be calling me. I'm touched you kept my number."

"It was on my phone from when you called before." She leaned against the wall, feeling the need for support. "You stole Nick's money. You invaded his life -- why?"

"We have unfinished business. I thought it was time we finished it."

"Because I told you Nick was doing well." She remembered the brief conversation they'd had two months earlier, when Evan had called her out of the blue to wish her a happy birthday. "You wanted to take him down."

"I've always wanted to take him down. I was just waiting for the right moment."

"Why? Why can't you just leave us alone? We were done so many years ago."

"I never forgive. I never forget."

His cold, cruel tone sent a chill down her spine, reminding her that his personality had always had two sides: one light, one dark; one good, one evil. When she was young and foolish and madly in love with him, she'd believed she could change him, make him right and whole. But Nick had shown her that Evan was beyond her ability to fix. Nick had made her see the truth. He had broken them up, and he had sent Evan to jail. She had thought after a dozen years that Evan had moved on; she'd been wrong. He had just been waiting for the right moment to pounce.

"Leave Nick alone, Evan," she said "If you ever cared about me at all, do this one thing for me."

"I'd do just about anything for you, Jen. You've never appreciated how good I am at what I do, but I'm going to show you. I'm going to show everyone. I'm the best there ever was. You'll see."

"Evan, please listen to me."

There was nothing but silence. Evan had hung up.

Her hand shook as she closed the phone, and a wave of helpless fear ran through her. Evan wanted revenge. How far would he go?

Chapter Five

Charlotte Hirsch felt more than a little trepidation as she parked her car on Broadway between Columbus and Montgomery streets, not far from the strip club where she'd once worked. As she stood on the corner looking down the block at the neon lights, the billboards touting sleazy midnight shows, she wondered why it hadn't seemed so seedy back in her day. Or maybe she just hadn't seen it that way. She was older now, more mature, more conservative. In the fifties she'd been a young woman poised on the verge of her own life, and she'd wanted to have it all.

She didn't even remember now what having it all had entailed. She'd just known that she wanted more than the small-town farm-wife role her mother had settled for. At eighteen she'd left the garlic-growing town of Gilroy and headed north to San Francisco, determined to be a dancer or an actress. She'd auditioned, waited tables, worked as a grocery-store checker, and dreamed about being a star.

When the money ran out, she let a friend talk her into dancing at a small club on Broadway. The pay was great. The customers were rich, exciting, sometimes dangerous men. Before she knew it she was dancing on tables and answering to the name "Sweet Charlie." After the shows, she drank cheap wine, smoked pot, and listened to jazz with her friends. She was part of the beat generation made famous by Jack Kerouac, not that she'd known that at the time. She'd just been living her life as recklessly and joyously as possible.

She'd made mistakes, lots of them, one particularly big one. His name was Johnny Blandino. She'd fallen hard and fast for him. One lustful smile and she'd been his, no questions asked. Johnny had changed the course of her life -- some might say for the worse; some might say for the better. Who knew what road she would have gone down if she hadn't met him? She certainly didn't know. And looking back never got her anywhere.

Sighing, she wished now that she'd kept Johnny in the past, where he belonged. But when she'd given Kayla his watch, the watch she was never supposed to let out of her sight, she'd ripped a hole in the protective covering that had surrounded her for the past fifty years, hiding her secrets from the world. She had to find a way to make it right...or to make it stop. Which was why she'd come back to a place she'd been careful to avoid for decades.

Forcing herself to move, she walked down the street and entered the club, named simply Deception. It was quiet and nearly empty, not surprising for a Saturday morning. She paused in the dim light to get her bearings. The bar was on her left. A raised stage surrounded by tables took up most of the room, with two shiny gold poles on each front corner of the stage. Several private booths ran along the far side of the room. She wondered just how far the dancers went these days; she suspected farther than she'd ever gone.

"Can I help you?" a young man asked, coming up behind her.

"I'm looking for Dana," she said, feeling suddenly nervous. It had been a long time since she'd seen the woman who had gotten her into the business, and she wasn't sure of her reception. She'd turned her back on Dana and everyone else after she'd married Edward.

"In the office. Down the hall, first door on your left," he said, waving in that direction.

Charlotte walked down the back hall, the smell of cigarettes and pot lingering in the air, stirring up old memories. Those memories came to life as she stopped to look at the photographs on the walls. In one picture, she was astonished to see herself sitting on a man's lap. Her arm was flung around his shoulders, her breasts practically bursting free of her skimpy costume, her legs encased in fishnet stockings, her feet in stiletto heels. The man wasn't Johnny but another club regular, Peter Harrison, a local writer for the newspaper who always proclaimed he was doing research. Peter, like so many other men who came to the club, had a good explanation for why he was there. Not that she'd cared, not that any of the girls had cared. The men were customers. They spent money. It had all seemed so simple back then.

She put a hand to the photo, tracing the wide smile on her own face, hardly remembering that girl. She was laughing uproariously at something. The rest of the party seemed in equally good spirits, including Dana, a stunning redhead with the longest legs and the biggest breasts Charlotte had ever seen. There was a birthday cake on the table, as well as empty bottles of booze and more glasses than she could count. Maybe the alcohol had had something to do with their good spirits.

"Are you looking for someone?"

Charlotte turned at the sound of a female voice. Her stomach clenched as she realized it was her old friend Dana. She was seventy-two years old now, but she looked more like fifty. Her hair was still red, her face expertly made up, and while she was wearing black slacks and a conservative jacket over her camisole top, her breasts still took center stage, the way they always had.

Dana was giving her the same once-over, recognition flitting through her eyes. "Charlie? Is that you?"

"It's me."

Dana gave a deep, throaty laugh and shook her head in disbelief. "I can't believe it. I never thought I'd see you again, and certainly not here." There was a hint of censure in her voice that Charlotte couldn't ignore.

"I know I said I'd never come back, but I guess never is a long time."

"You're a little old to want a job, so what are you doing here?"

"I need to talk to you. Can we go somewhere more private?"

Dana hesitated and then waved her into the office. It was a small room, barely big enough for a desk, two chairs, and a couple of filing cabinets. Dana sat down behind the desk. Charlotte perched on the edge of a hard wooden chair. "So you run this place now," she said. "You always said one day you'd be the boss."

"I had to do something once gravity took over, and I've always been a good businesswoman."

"That's true. You look good," Charlotte said.

"You look like a church lady."

Charlotte smiled. "That's nicer than what I thought you'd say."

"Why are you here, Charlie? It's been more than a few years."

"It seems like yesterday now. I can't believe you still have our photos up on the wall."

"Not everyone is ashamed of their past," Dana replied. "And those were the good old days, for some of us anyway."

Charlotte ignored that comment. She hadn't come here to fight. "Speaking of the past, I need your help."

"And what makes you think that after fifty years of silence you have a right to ask me for help? You turned your back on me, Charlie. You went off to live in your rich house with your rich husband. You were too good for me."

"No, it wasn't like that. I found a way out and I had to take it. I couldn't come back because...Well, I couldn't."

"Sure, I know. I understand," Dana said, bitterness in her eyes. "We were your secret past. You were ashamed of us. You forgot that you used to be one of us."

"I never forgot. I just moved on. At least, that's what I thought. But now I'm terribly afraid that my secrets are about to be completely exposed."

"Why should I care?"

"Because they're your secrets, too."

Dana's eyes narrowed. "Do I look like I have something to hide? I run a strip club. Everyone knows who I am, where I come from. I'm famous around here, and I like it that way."

Charlotte shook her head. "I'm not talking about our days as dance hall girls, or this club. I'm talking about Johnny."

Dana drew in a sharp breath. "What about him?"

"Do you remember the watch he used to wear?"

A light flickered in Dana's eyes. "Of course I remember," she said evenly.

"I gave it to my granddaughter, and now it's missing. Someone stole it two weeks ago." Charlotte saw Dana's eyes narrow and the pulse in her throat begin to jump. "It was the only thing they took," she added. "It wasn't a random theft. Someone knows the value of the watch. I need your help to find out who."

Dana looked down at the desk, then back at Charlotte. "I can't help you."

Charlotte gazed into her old friend's eyes and saw fear. "Can't or won't?"

"It's all the same."

"You heard something. What?" Charlotte leaned forward. "I have to know, Dana. I have to protect my family."

"So do I," Dana said. "You need to leave."

Charlotte gave her a long, hard look. "I'll go, but think about this: If they know about me, then there's a very good chance they know about you."

"I was smarter than you, Charlie."

Charlotte smiled. "No, you just liked to think you were."

* * *

Kayla walked through the front door of St. Peter and Paul Church in Washington Square and immediately felt a sense of peace wash over her. She loved churches, and this one was particularly magnificent with its forty-foot altar made from Italian marble and North African onyx. It had been carved in Italy by master craftsmen, then carefully shipped to San Francisco in pieces and reassembled in the church. For a few moments Kayla stood still, absorbing the beauty of the cathedral, the light streaming through the stained-glass windows that were superbly done. Here in this beautiful church everything seemed to be exactly as it should be. She could almost forget that her life was in complete chaos. Almost...

The sound of footsteps drew goose bumps down her arms, and the serenity in her soul turned to uneasiness. She whirled around, ready to confront whoever was behind her. It was a nun dressed in full habit, black gown, white head covering, a cross hanging on a chain around her neck. A pair of thick glasses sat on the end of her nose. As she came closer, Kayla looked up and saw a pair of sharp blue eyes. She sucked in a breath. She had the weird feeling she knew those eyes.

The nun smiled and murmured, "Bless you," as she moved past, heading down the aisle toward the altar. She was a tall woman, and she walked with a long stride. Kayla's body tightened.

Her instincts told her something was off. The nun disappeared through a side door in front of the church. There was no one else in the cathedral, but now it was too quiet. The silence was too tense. She turned to leave; she had the urge to get out of the building as quickly as possible. The sudden sound of organ music caught her off guard, made her pause in the middle of the aisle. She looked up at the balcony just in time to see something come hurtling down toward her head.

A moment later she was on the ground, flat on her back, looking up at the vaulted ceiling, stars spinning in front of her eyes.

"Kayla?" Nick's face came into view as he knelt beside her.

Where had he come from? She tried to ask, but she couldn't catch her breath. Her chest was too tight.

"What's wrong? What happened?" he asked, his eyes worried.

She opened her mouth but no words came out.

"Take your time," he said, stroking her forehead with his fingers. "You got the wind knocked out of you."

A priest appeared behind Nick, an older man with white hair and dark brown eyes. "Are you ill, dear? Shall I call for an ambulance?"

"No. Something...something hit me on the head." She sat up, putting a hand to the top of her head. She could feel a bump beginning to swell.

The priest picked up a Bible from the floor next to her. He looked up at the balcony overhead. "This?"

"I guess."

"I wonder how that Bible just happened to come down on your head," Nick said. "There's no one around."

"I saw a nun earlier. She walked by me. Then the organ began to play. I looked up, and the next thing I knew I was on the ground," she said.

"A nun? There aren't any nuns here at the church," the priest said in surprise.

"But I saw her. She was wearing a habit."

"Perhaps she was visiting," he said. "I'll check the balcony to see if anyone is up there."

"Thank you."

Nick helped her to her feet. She felt a bit wobbly and had to hang on to his arm. "Okay?" he asked.

"Getting there. It was just an accident, right? A freak accident."

"Why would you think it was anything else?" he asked, his expression speculative as he surveyed the church.

She didn't want to say the words out loud. They sounded foolish in her head. "There was just something about that nun. She was so tall, and her eyes seemed familiar." She stopped abruptly, remembering another odd detail. "Her shoes. She had on running shoes."

"What are you getting at?"

How could she answer that question? The thought going through her head was ridiculous. "It's nothing. Never mind."

"Just say it -- whatever it is. Trust your instincts."

"My instincts have been wrong before."

"Maybe not this time."

"Fine. I think the nun had Evan's eyes. And she was about the same height. See, I told you it was crazy. Evan isn't dressing up like a nun, following me around town." She waited for Nick to agree with her, but he was silent. "What? Do you think it's possible?"

"Evan always liked disguises. I told you about the time he pretended to be a college professor. That was just one instance. Another time he put on a wig and women's clothes and faked his way into the locker room to take photos of girls getting dressed. He was always doing crazy stuff like that."

"Okay, you're not making me feel better. Can we get out of here?"

"Sure."

When they reached the sidewalk in front of the church, the warm sunshine began to take the chill out of her bones. It was a nice day, a beautiful one, in fact. There was nothing to be afraid of, Kayla told herself firmly. Someone had been up in the loft playing the organ. They'd knocked the Bible off by accident. It was probably a child or a teenager. And the nun was just visiting the church. There was a rational explanation for everything that had happened.

"Where's the jewelry store?" she asked, trying to focus on what they'd come here to do.

"Down the street," Nick replied, his sharp gaze perusing the area around them.

She followed his glance and saw nothing out of the ordinary. If her head weren't aching, she could probably convince herself she'd imagined the entire incident. She put a hand to the swelling bump and winced.

"Maybe we should get you some ice," Nick suggested.

"No, it's fine. Nothing serious."

"Not this time," Nick said with a somberness that did nothing to improve her mood.

"What does that mean?"

"I don't like it that someone threw that book at you."

"We don't know that's what happened. It had to be an accident. It was on the railing. Someone brushed by it, knocked it off."

"Just when you happened to be standing right in its path."

"Still, it was just a Bible," she argued. "No one tried to shoot me or anything."

"Not this time," he repeated.

"Stop saying that. You're making me nervous. Let's just go to the jewelry store and see if we can get some more information on the watch."

"Fine."

They set off down the street, but they hadn't gone far when Nick said, "So, tell me about your conversation with your grandmother. Did she identify the man wearing the watch in the photograph?"

"Yes, she said he was her first love. His name was Johnny, and apparently he had to go away, but he gave her the watch before he left. They never saw each other again. I guess she didn't want to tell anyone about him, so she pretended the watch was from my grandfather."

"And why did she think the watch was stolen?"

"She didn't say," Kayla replied, remembering how evasive her grandmother had become. After proclaiming that the watch might have been stolen, she'd completely shut down the conversation. "She asked me to drop it. She said she didn't want me to follow up on the watch because she's afraid that the theft will come back to haunt her or me or whoever. I'm not quite sure. I have to admit I feel a little guilty following up in the face of her very strong objections."

"If it was stolen, it happened fifty years ago, right?" Nick asked. "That's a long time for anyone to hold a grudge. If the watch does belong to someone else, maybe that will clue us in to what Evan's long-term plan is."

"I agree. That's why I'm here. I have to see this through. I have to find a way to make things right for myself, and for you, too."

"I appreciate that."

"I am sorry about whatever part I played in robbing you."

"I don't hold you responsible."

"Thanks, but I'm not letting myself off the hook that easily." She paused, seeing the sign for Ricci Jewelers. "Is this it?" The small jewelry store was located between an Italian café and a card shop very near the Broadway strip, which reminded Kayla of her grandmother's foray into taking off her clothes, something she preferred not to think about.

Nick pointed toward the *D*-and-*R* logo on the glass window. "Look familiar?"

"Yes, it's the same initials as on the watch." Excitement surged through her. Despite Nick's conviction that the watch would lead them to Evan, she'd thought it was a complete long shot, but maybe not. Maybe they could find out more about the watch and why Evan might have wanted it.

As they entered the store, an older woman looked up from behind the cash register. Her hair was peppered with gray, her eyes almost black, and she appeared to be in her fifties or sixties. "Can I help you?" she asked.

"We're looking for the manager," Nick said. "Or someone who has worked here for a long time."

She smiled. "That would be me. I'm Delores Ricci. My grandfather opened this store at the turn of the century. My father, Dominic, ran it for a long time, and now I run it. What can I do for you?"

"We're trying to find out the history and the value of a pocket watch like this one." Nick took two pieces of paper out of an envelope. One was the original photo Kayla had given him and the other was an enlargement of the watch. He pushed the enlargement across the counter. "The watch is silver, and there is some engraving on the front that we can't decipher, although it appears to be the front of some particular building. On the back, there's an inscription, just a few words: 'of Heaven Await.'"

Delores's hand shook as she picked up the enlarged photograph of the watch. She cleared her throat. "What did you say was the inscription?"

" 'Of Heaven Await,'" Nick repeated. "Do you recognize the phrase? Or does it mean anything to you?"

Delores rubbed her temple and glanced over her shoulder at a door leading into the back room. Then her gaze returned to them. "I think it's from the Bible."

Well, that wasn't much help, Kayla thought. But Delores knew something. Her entire demeanor had changed once she saw the photo.

Delores slipped on a pair of glasses and studied the photograph. The pulse in her neck seemed to be beating double-time. Every thirty seconds or so, she took another look over her shoulder, as if expecting someone to appear. The air in the store grew tense. Kayla told herself to get a grip on her imagination. The woman was probably just waiting for another clerk or trying to remember if she'd ever seen the watch.

"You said the watch was silver?" Delores asked.

"Yes."

"And you own it?" She looked from Nick to Kayla.

"I do," Kayla said, lying for the moment. This woman was asking more questions than she was answering. "It belonged to my grandmother. She recently gave it to me."

"I see. What was your grandmother's name? Maybe I could check our records. We have records on everything we've ever sold, although some of them are in storage."

"The watch didn't actually belong to my grandmother, but to a man she knew, the man in the photograph," she said, as Nick handed the original photo to Delores that showed not just the watch, but also her grandmother and her first love. "I think his name was Johnny."

Delores's face turned white, and her eyes glittered.

"Do you know him?" Kayla asked.

"Johnny Blandino," she muttered, as if she were talking to

herself.

Kayla's pulse quickened with this piece of information. She now had a last name to go with the first. "Was he a friend of your father's? A customer?"

Delores cleared her throat. "I'm not sure it's even the same man. The photograph is not very clear. Why don't you give me your name and number? I'll check our records and see what I can learn."

Kayla wrote the information down on a piece of paper. "Whatever you can tell me would be greatly appreciated. It's very important."

"It is a beautiful timepiece," Delores said, running her finger around the edges of the watch in the photograph. "Why didn't you bring it with you?" She looked at Kayla with dark, questioning eyes.

"I didn't want to lose it," she lied. For some reason, she didn't want to tell Delores any more of the story, not until she revealed whether or not her father had made the watch.

"Are pocket watches such as these valuable?" Nick asked. "In today's market?"

"I doubt it's worth more than a few hundred dollars," Delores replied. "When can you bring it in?"

"When can you check the records?" Kayla countered.

"I can take a look later tonight."

"Great. Why don't you call me, and if you have the records, I'll bring the watch in," Kayla suggested.

Delores nodded. "I'll do that. May I keep the photograph until then?"

"We'll hang on to the photo. You can keep the enlargement." Nick handed the original photo back to Kayla. "I'm sure you don't want to lose that."

"No, I don't," she murmured as they said good-bye and left the shop.

Nick paused on the sidewalk outside the store. "She recognized the watch and the man wearing it."

"I agree. And she gave us his last name, Blandino, which my grandmother neglected to mention."

"I don't understand why your grandmother is being so secretive. Her husband is dead. Who's going to care about a man she dated so long ago?"

Kayla wished she had a good answer. "I don't know."

"The watch has to be worth something," Nick said. "That's why everyone is acting so strangely about it. By the way, how are you planning to produce it when Delores calls you tomorrow?"

"I'll worry about that then. I had the feeling that if she knew we didn't have it she wasn't going to check the records. Let's see if she comes up with anything. We'll go from there."

"I'll walk you back to your car. I'd like to get on the Internet and see what we can find out about Johnny Blandino."

"Sounds like a good idea." As they started down the street, Kayla's stomach began to grumble, her senses tickled by the wafting smell of garlic. "Uh, Nick," she said, stopping abruptly.

"What now?" he asked, glancing quickly around.

"I'm starving. And it smells like heaven in there." She pointed to the nearby café. "Have you eaten lunch?"

"No, but--"

"But what? You have to eat. You'll be able to think better after a delicious plate of lasagna; I'm sure of it."

A small, reluctant smile curved his lips for the first time all day, and she was struck by how attractive he was when he wasn't scowling or frowning. She had the irresistible urge to try to keep that smile on his face.

"All right, you sold me," he said. "Lunch it is."

* * *

The Italian café was crowded, obviously a neighborhood favorite. Once Nick had taken a look at the menu and seen the bowls of minestrone soup going by, he'd become aware of how hungry he was. He was glad Kayla had called for a break. They could both use a good meal.

He watched as she pulled her long brown hair back into a ponytail, then swept it up on top of her head with a band. She had a gorgeous face, with beautiful skin that had a natural pink glow. A pair of colorful, funky earrings dangled from her ears. Her short floral skirt showed off her great legs, and her hot pink top was... well, quite frankly hot. It was no wonder Evan had decided to romance the watch out of her. If she'd been an ugly old hag, he suspected Evan would have taken the watch and run.

While he wasn't surprised Evan had chosen to seduce her, he was still amazed that Kayla had fallen so hard and fast for him. She wasn't a flaky bimbo. She seemed to have a good working brain. And she couldn't be lacking for dates. So why had she let herself get swept up in a speedy marriage?

He'd probably never understand women. His conversation with Jenny earlier had left him just as puzzled. Evan had ruined her life, yet she still seemed to have a soft spot for him. Why?

Evan must have been really good at making each of them believe they were going to get everything they wanted. Desire was the vulnerable point. Once a person wanted something, they became a target for all those who would give it to them.

"What are you going to get?" Kayla asked, taking a sip of water.

"Well, we had pizza last night, so I'm thinking cannelloni."

"That's right. We're on an Italian streak," she said with a smile. "But North Beach does have the best Italian food outside of Italy."

"Have you been to Italy?"

"Yes, Rome and Florence. They have some of the most beautiful churches and stained-glass windows in the world."

"You think you'll still be a fan of churches after today?"

"I'm sure it was just an accident. My imagination has been in overdrive the past few weeks. I really need to get a grip."

"Don't dismiss your instincts," he told her. "If your gut tells you something is wrong, you should listen."

"I'll keep that in mind." She paused as the waiter came to take their orders, then said, "There is something I want to ask you to promise me, Nick. And think about it before you say anything."

His body tensed at the serious note in her voice. He hoped he could do what she was going to ask. But if it meant taking it easy on Evan, there was no way in hell he could agree to that. "What is it?"

"Tell me the truth -- always, no matter what, no matter how ugly or painful or whatever it is. I can't take any more lies. I have to be able to trust what you say." She extended her hand. "Deal?"

He took her hand and gazed into her beautiful brown eyes and completely forgot what he was going to say. Touching her kicked off a connection between them of pure, unadulterated lust. *Shit!* Where the hell had that come from? He wanted to snatch his hand away, but he also didn't want to act like a fool. "Deal," he said, forcing himself to focus. "No lies between us."

"Good." She pulled her hand free and licked her lips.

The tiny gesture almost undid him. He did not want to be attracted to her. Hell, she was the last woman on earth he wanted to be attracted to. She'd married Evan, his enemy, for God's sake. He shouldn't even like her, much less be feeling anything else for her.

The only problem was that he did like her -- too much. She was getting under his skin. *Damn.*

"Is something wrong?" she asked quietly.

"No, everything's great." He took a swig of ice water, hoping it would cool him down from the inside out.

"There's something else we should talk about," Kayla began.

God. What now?

"Our marriage," she continued.

Her words stirred up an image in his head of Kayla in white silk lingerie beckoning him into their bed. He cleared his throat and blinked his eyes. What on earth was wrong with him? "Our... our marriage?" he asked.

"Don't panic. I just mean that we should probably talk to a lawyer about how to undo it. I'm sure the last thing you want to be is married to me," she said with a joking smile.

He wanted to tell her that he absolutely agreed that would be the worst thing in the world, but for the life of him he couldn't get any words out. He took another drink of water, hoping to clear the knot from his throat.

"Here I was thinking you were the kind of guy who wasn't scared of anything," she mused. "But you just about flipped out when I mentioned the word *marriage.* You're one of those men who is scared of commitment, aren't you?"

"Well, I can't see myself marrying someone after three weeks," he snapped.

"Ouch."

"You started it. And for the record, I'm not scared of anything, especially commitment. I just choose to live my life alone. I've had enough of family responsibility to last me a lifetime. I don't need another demanding female in my life."

"Is that how you see your future wife? As a demanding female?"

"I've never met a woman who wasn't demanding."

She frowned at that and sat back in her chair. "That sounds pretty cynical."

"I prefer realistic. I call it the way I see it."

"Since we're being frank, I've never met a man who didn't want to be in charge. All that macho crap can be really irritating."

"So why the urge to marry, Kayla? Why not just stay single, in control of your life, your house, your remote control?"

"Believe me, that idea has been growing in merit the past two weeks." She glanced down at the ring on her finger and, after a momentary hesitation, she twisted it off her finger and handed it to him. "Why don't you see if you can get your money back on this?"

The metal was warm from the heat of her skin. His palm tingled. He was glad she'd taken off Evan's ring, but at the same time he wondered if it wouldn't be easier to have that gold band between them. "Are you sure?" he asked, testing her resolve.

Her gaze didn't waver. "I'm positive. From here on out, I'm never again going to think of myself as Mrs. Nick Granville."

"That's a good idea," he said, feeling unsettled by the words *Mrs. Nick Granville.*

"It's back to being Kayla Sheridan." She raised her water glass. "Here's to getting Evan Chadwick out of our lives once and for all."

Nick picked up his glass. "I'll drink to that."

Chapter Six

By the time they returned to Nick's house it was almost four o'clock. Kayla couldn't believe the afternoon had passed so quickly. After they'd toasted Evan's eventual demise, the conversation had veered into more neutral topics, and she'd actually enjoyed their time together. Nick was smart, well-read, and had a dry sense of humor that became more apparent when he wasn't caught up in chasing down Evan. He'd told her about his job, and his passion for what he did had come through in every word. For a while she'd forgotten why they were together and just let herself relax.

Unfortunately, her tension had returned the moment they'd returned to Nick's house. She grew more uncomfortable as she followed him up the stairs and into his bedroom so they could access his computer. She kept looking at the bed, remembering the last time she'd been in this room...in that bed.

Evan had followed her upstairs after she'd spilled wine on her blouse. She'd wanted to rinse it out. They'd started fooling around, kissing, touching, caressing, falling onto the bed.... She could see it in her mind in glorious, colorful, and now somewhat embarrassing detail. She desperately wished she could erase every minute that they'd spent together.

"Something wrong?" Nick asked, drawing her attention back to him. His jaw tightened as his gaze moved to the bed. "Memories, huh?"

"I don't want to talk about it."

"Good, because I don't want to hear about it." Nick sat down in front of the computer and waved his hand to the nearby armchair. "You can pull that up, if you want."

She did as he suggested, looking over his shoulder as he entered Johnny Blandino into the search engine. A moment later a page of entries came up. There appeared to be a lot of Johnny Blandinos in the world. "Narrow it down to San Francisco," she suggested.

A second later they had a batch of new listings. Nick let out a low whistle. "Would you look at this?" He pointed to the first entry. " 'Johnny Blandino, escape attempt, Alcatraz.'"

"That can't be the same guy," she said in disbelief.

"Let's check it out."

He clicked on the link, which led them to an article in the *San Francisco Tribune* celebrating the anniversary of one of Alcatraz's most famous escapes and the release of a new book, titled *Tales from the Rock.* Nick continued reading, " 'One of Alcatraz's most infamous escape attempts occurred in 1960, when a famous band of San Francisco bank robbers, Johnny Blandino, Nathan Carmello, and Frankie Damon, disappeared from the island prison,'" Nick read. " 'Three days later, Frankie's body washed ashore. The other two men were never found but were believed to have drowned in the dangerous currents around the island. Their escape remains one of Alcatraz's unsolved mysteries.'" Nick glanced at Kayla. "What do you think of that?"

She didn't know what to think, but she felt cold, shivery. Her grandmother had told her that Johnny had to go away -- had he gone to jail? "I don't want to believe it, yet I think I do." She continued reading where Nick had left off. " 'The three men, former altar boys at St. Basil's Church in North Beach, terrorized San Francisco businesses for almost five years. They were finally caught a month after stealing a fortune in rare gold coins from the U.S. Mint in San Francisco. During the course of the robbery two security guards were killed. The gold coins were never recovered. The men were captured and sentenced to life in prison at Alcatraz but had served only five years of their sentence when they made their escape.'" Kayla drew in a breath, shocked by what she'd just read. "This can't be the same guy. Grandma could not have been in love with a murderer." She saw the truth in Nick's eyes, a truth she didn't want to accept. "It's not possible."

"It explains why she was so reluctant to tell you anything about him. What interests me even more is the treasure in missing gold coins. That sounds like something Evan would want to pursue." Nick sat back in his chair, rubbing his jaw as he pondered the situation. "It's a leap, but I'm guessing the watch that once belonged to Johnny has something to do with that missing treasure. Plus, this article appeared in the newspaper just after the New Year. When did you meet Evan?"

"Middle of January. But how would he know about my grandmother or me?"

"I don't know, but he first made contact with your grandmother just after that article came out. You said he toured her house to give her an appraisal, which would have provided him with plenty of opportunity to look for the watch there. Then he met you."

"And he took a tour of my house," Kayla finished. "He asked me about the history, who had lived there, for how long, that kind of thing. I told him my grandmother had moved in just after she got married and had stayed there until two years ago. I think I even complained to him that she'd left everything behind, and that I didn't understand how she could not want to take the things from her past with her." She took a breath, trying to recall their conversations. "At some point we started talking about antiques, and the conversation must have turned to jewelry."

"And none of this made you suspicious?"

"Well, it didn't happen right away," she said defensively. "I'm just giving you the condensed version."

"Your whole relationship lasted less than a month. That's pretty condensed already."

She frowned at his sarcasm. "You're not helping."

"Fine, go on."

"I'm trying to remember when I first told him about the watch." She paused for a moment. "I remember we were shopping at an antique store. When we got back that night, he asked if I had any antique jewelry from my grandmother. I mentioned that I had my grandfather's pocket watch. I showed it to him, and he was very interested in it. He said it had great craftsmanship. He spent a long time studying it."

"Did he ask if he could buy it?"

"How did you know?"

"It seems like a reasonable next step." He paused. "Did you tell him you couldn't sell it because it was a family heirloom?"

"Yes." She could see in Nick's eyes that his brain had already made it to the next step. She had only to confirm it. "I told him I was going to give it to the man I married. That it would be his wedding present."

"And the next day he asked you to marry him."

"No, it was at least a few days later. I don't think the conversation was still in my mind at the time. I know it seems clear now, but it wasn't as if we were talking about a diamond necklace. I didn't think it was a big deal."

Nick didn't say a word for a long moment. She didn't need to ask what he was thinking; she already knew. She was an idiot who'd overlooked obvious red flags, caught up in a whirlwind of romance and promises. And now there was nowhere left to look but at herself. She'd let Evan into her life. She'd helped him ruin Nick. But the past was done. She could kick herself all the way across the city and it wouldn't change anything. She had to concentrate on the present and the future.

"It says that the author of *Tales from the Rock* will be doing a book signing on Alcatraz in a few days. We should check that out, see what he knows about Johnny Blandino," Nick said. "But in the meantime you need to talk to your grandmother again. Tell her we know about Johnny. Find out more about the watch."

"You're right. Maybe she'll stop trying to protect me if I confront her with what I now know."

"Didn't she tell you that she thought the watch was stolen?"

"Yes, she did," Kayla replied, latching on to that little fact. "Maybe that's the key. Maybe the watch never belonged to Johnny, and the true owner is important in some way."

"It will be interesting to find out if Delores Ricci can tell us if Johnny Blandino bought that watch from her father."

"Or maybe he robbed the jewelry store." She blew out a weary breath. "It's a lot to take in." Before Nick could reply, the doorbell rang. "Are you expecting someone?"

"No, but it could be one of my sisters or my mother. They love to drop in unannounced."

Kayla hesitated as Nick stood up. Not particularly wanting to get caught in his bedroom by his mother or his sisters, she followed him down the stairs. When he opened the door she saw a package on the front step. There was no one in sight.

"What's this?" Nick muttered, bringing in the white box tied with a silver ribbon.

He held up the card and her heart skipped a beat. The envelope was addressed to Mr. and Mrs. Nick Granville.

"Do you want to open it?" Nick asked in disgust. "It looks like a wedding present."

"Who would send a wedding present here? My friends never had this address."

Nick opened the envelope and pulled out a card. " 'Welcome home, Nick,'" he read. "'Hope you enjoy your new wife. It was the least I could do. Evan.'"

The note was stunning and cruel in its simplicity. Kayla thought for a moment that Nick had read it wrong. There was no way that Evan had married her and left her for Nick as some sort of...consolation prize? He wouldn't have done that. She put a hand to her mouth, feeling sick at the thought. "Do you think Evan rang the bell?" she asked.

Nick met her gaze, then threw the note on the table and ran to the front door.

She was right on his heels.

Had Evan been standing just outside the door a few minutes earlier? Had he personally left the present for them?

Nick jogged down the steps to the street, looking in every direction. A car passed by. Kayla caught her breath and then let it out when she saw an older man and woman sitting in the front seat. It wasn't Evan. He must have left. Or had he?

There were lots of cars parked on the street. It was the weekend. Everyone was home. He could be in any one of those cars, watching them right now. And he probably was, she thought. He'd left the present for a reason. No doubt he'd stick around to see their reaction.

Nick joined her by the front door, his expression grim. "If he was here, he's gone."

"I don't think so."

"What do you mean?"

"He wants a show," she said. She felt an intense burst of anger as she remembered his callous words, *Hope you enjoy your new wife.* "Let's give him one."

"What are you talking about--"

She threw her arms around Nick's neck and kissed him hard on the lips before she could think twice about the wisdom of such a move. Rage and frustration drove her over the edge, and she thrust her tongue into his mouth, taking advantage of his surprise. After a moment Nick kissed her back, wrapping his arms around her body, pulling her up hard against his chest, meeting her kiss with demands of his own.

Suddenly she wasn't leading anymore; Nick was. His restless, eager hands roamed her body, cupping her buttocks, pulling her into the hard cradle of his hips. He completely erased all rational thought from her brain. She just wanted to taste, touch, and kiss her way into mindless oblivion. She thought Nick was willing to go with her, but suddenly he wasn't there anymore.

Kayla reached for him, but he took a step back, his breath coming fast and ragged. His gaze burned into hers with a question she didn't want to answer.

"What the hell was that?" he asked.

"I'm not sure," she muttered, running a hand through the hair he'd tangled with his fingers.

"Get in the house," he ordered.

She didn't like his tone, but she moved inside anyway. Nick shut the door and leaned against it, crossing his arms. His gaze was sharp, penetrating, and still glittering with desire. She had the terrible feeling she'd just awoken the beast. She wanted him to say something, and yet she was afraid of what he would say.

"I'm sorry," she said, unable to stand the tension a second longer. "I thought maybe Evan was watching."

"He probably was."

"I didn't want him to think he was in control. I didn't like his note. He acted like he'd left me for you. It made me mad. I didn't think."

Nick slowly nodded. "Got it," he said, his voice clipped.

She didn't think he *got it* at all.

"Let's see what else is in the box," Nick said, brushing past her.

Kayla wasn't sure she wanted to know. "It can't be good," she murmured. She was right. Nick pulled out a picture. He turned it around to show her. She swallowed hard. It was a picture of her and Nick having lunch together a few hours earlier. Across the print Evan had scribbled the words, *The happy couple.*

"Evan was there. He was watching us," she said, stating the obvious.

"Maybe he was in the church, too," Nick said.

"And at the jewelry store. He must realize we're trying to find out about the watch. But why is he following us? Why isn't he doing whatever he wants to do with that damn watch?"

"That's a good question. I'm sure part of his enjoyment comes from watching me try to squirm out of the ropes he's tied around me."

"And I'm one of those ropes." She wanted Nick to deny it, but he simply shrugged. She let out a sigh, feeling suddenly overwhelmed and exhausted. She'd gone through so many emotions in one day, her head was both pounding and spinning. "I have to go, Nick. I have to get out of here."

"Kayla, wait," he said, as she headed toward the door. "Where are you going?"

"Home. I'm going to lock myself in my studio and concentrate on my work and try to forget the past several weeks."

"You can't bury your head in the sand."

"I can try." She grabbed her purse off the table and then stopped. "Do you think he's still out there?"

"I don't know. But I don't think you should go home alone. I'll follow you in my car and make sure you get into your house okay."

"He's not going to hurt me. At least not physically," she said, not completely sure she was right.

"You don't know what he's capable of doing." Nick waved the photo in his hand. "Does this look like the work of a man who is totally sane?"

Her heart skipped a beat. No, it didn't, bringing home to her the fact that she'd married someone who might be crazy, cruel, and diabolical. Had Evan disguised himself as a nun? She could still see those blue eyes behind the clear glass frames. The familiarity of his gaze had kicked her in the stomach, but she hadn't wanted to acknowledge the truth. What did he want? Why was he still hanging around? What was left for him to do?

"Don't you think he's done his worst?" she asked.

Nick slowly shook his head. "You asked me to always tell you the truth. I'm sorry, Kayla. I think the game is just beginning."

She almost wished he'd lied, but she had to face reality. "If you want to follow me home, I won't say no."

"Then I'll follow you home."

Kayla was glad for Nick's presence when they walked outside. She got into her car and locked herself in while Nick pulled the Porsche out of his garage. She searched the street for something unusual but found nothing. She felt as if every nerve in her body were strung so tight it was ready to snap. She didn't think she'd be able to relax until she got home.

Nick stayed close behind her on their drive across town. She occasionally checked her rearview mirror for some other car, but nothing seemed out of the ordinary. At her house she pulled into the driveway and parked there. Nick met her on the porch. She dug through her purse for her house keys.

The porch light was off, and she was glad to have Nick's solid body behind hers. She tried to insert the key in the lock and was shocked when the door pushed open before she'd unbolted it. Had she somehow left it open?

Nick grabbed her arm. "Wait? You didn't lock your door?"

"I thought I did."

"Someone could be inside," he said.

Her breath caught in her chest. Had Evan come to confront them? Was he here waiting, knowing she'd return eventually? "What should we do?" she whispered.

"I'm going inside. Stay here." Nick pushed open the door and stepped into the entry. "Where's the light?"

"On the wall to your left," she replied.

He fumbled for the switch. When the light went on, he moved down the hall and into the living room. She heard him swear.

"What's wrong?" she called.

"Someone has been here," he said, reappearing in the hall. "The living room is a mess."

"Someone robbed me?" she asked in astonishment. No one had ever broken into this house, not in the fifty years that her grandparents had lived here.

"Or someone was looking for something," Nick replied soberly. "And they could still be here. I'm going upstairs. Where's your bedroom?"

"First door on the right. Be careful." She grabbed an umbrella from the stand next to the front door, just in case she needed a weapon. It wasn't much, but it was better than nothing.

Nick dashed up the stairs. She saw him go into her bedroom. "What did you find?" she asked when he didn't immediately reappear. "Nick?" she called again. She heard a loud bump. God, had someone confronted him? "Nick, answer me."

Her nerves jumped; her blood raced. Should she go upstairs? Should she call the police? A dozen ideas collided in her brain. Then she heard a step behind her.

Someone was on the porch.

She whirled around.

A dark, tall shadow loomed over her. Adrenaline shot through her veins. She swung the umbrella at his head, praying it would stun him long enough for her to get away.

Chapter Seven

The shadow was quicker than she was. The man caught the other end of the umbrella with a sure, swift hand. Kayla tried to wrestle it away from him, but he was strong and big. She kicked out at him; her boot connected with his shin. He slammed her up against the wall, his forearm against her throat.

For the first time she could see his face. He had dark brown, ruthless eyes. And he wasn't Evan. Who the hell was he? And why was he trying to strangle her?

Nick came out of nowhere, pulling the man off of her. She grabbed her throat, still feeling the imprint of his arm against her windpipe. Nick smashed his fist into the intruder's face. The man stumbled, but bounced back quickly. He shoved Nick up against the wall next to her and yelled, "What the fuck is wrong with you, Nick?"

Kayla gasped. How did this guy know Nick's name?

Nick looked just as stunned.

For one tense moment, all she could hear was the sound of their ragged breaths beating in time to the grandfather clock nearby. She wasn't sure how many seconds had ticked by before Nick said in bemusement, "J.T.?"

"That's right," the man ground out. He let go of Nick and stepped back, putting a hand to his rapidly swelling face. "Hell of a way to greet an old friend."

"I thought you were attacking Kayla."

"She swung an umbrella at my head," he said with a scowl.

"You tried to strangle me," Kayla countered.

"I was trying to stop you from kicking me in the balls."

"I thought you had broken into my house. You came up behind me. You startled me. Who are you, anyway?"

"My name is J.T. McIntyre. I work for the FBI." He pulled an ID out of his pocket and flashed it at her. "I'm assuming that you're Kayla Sheridan, the one who married Evan Chadwick?"

"Yes--"

"FBI?" Nick interrupted, shock in his tone. He grabbed the I.D. from J.T.'s hand. "Are you kidding me?"

"No. I work in the fraud division, and I've been following Evan off and on for the past four years. I understand he took you for a ride, Nick."

"He stole everything from me while I was out of town," Nick said. "He even lived in my house for a few weeks."

"Excuse me." Kayla felt like she was out of the loop. "How do you two know each other?"

"We went to school together," Nick answered. "In fact, J.T. lived with me and Evan."

Another Evan connection? She was stunned. She took a good look at J.T. Like Nick, he appeared to be in his early thirties. He had short, spiky, sandy-brown hair, dark brown eyes, a slightly crooked nose that looked like it had once been broken, and a five-o'clock shadow across his cheeks. He wore blue jeans, a polo shirt, and a brown leather jacket. And he was returning her gaze with a leisurely arrogance that put her back up. She had no idea what he knew about her relationship with Evan, but judging by his expression, he didn't think much of her.

She dug her hands into the pockets of her jeans. "So you're here because of Evan?"

"Bingo."

"That's surprising. When I went to the police, they seemed completely uninterested."

"Before they knew you were talking about Evan." J.T. paused. "Why don't we sit down? We have a lot to discuss."

Kayla moved toward the living room without thinking. She stopped just inside the doorway. The room was in a shambles. The couch cushions were scattered about. Several of her grandmother's glass figurines had been broken. The drawers in the end table had been opened and tossed on the floor. Her knitting yarn was all over the couch. With J.T.'s arrival, she'd forgotten that someone had been in the house. Now, the seriousness of what had happened was sinking in.

"Who did this?" J.T. asked, moving into the room, his sharp eye absorbing every detail.

"We don't know. We got here a minute before you," Nick said. "I checked the upstairs. There's no one there, but Kayla's bedroom looks even worse than this room."

Kayla walked over to the piano and picked up a family photograph, setting it upright.

"Don't touch anything," J.T. said quickly. "The cops will want to look for fingerprints."

She stopped abruptly. "Right. I didn't think. I don't even know if anything was taken. I guess I should check all the rooms."

"In a minute," J.T. said in an authoritative voice. "First, I'd like to know a little more about your relationship with Evan other than what I read in the file."

"I doubt there's more to know," she replied. "We knew each other for a few weeks, got married, then Evan disappeared. He took with him my grandfather's pocket watch that I gave him as a wedding present. That's it."

J.T.'s eyes didn't give away a thing. She had no idea what he thought of her very short story.

"And you haven't heard from him since he left you in Tahoe?" J.T. asked.

"Not until yesterday, when he called here, and again this afternoon, when he left a present for us at Nick's house. It was a photo he or someone else took of me and Nick at lunch today."

J.T. nodded. He glanced over at Nick. "Do you want to add anything?"

"Yes. The pocket watch is connected to a famous criminal from the fifties and a missing cache of gold coins. My gut tells me that that's part of Evan's interest in the watch."

"Well, that's a twist."

"Maybe you can get more information on the old con, a man named Johnny Blandino."

"I'll check it out. Anything else?"

"Not yet. Except that I can't figure out why Kayla and I have been grouped together in this con."

"Knowing the history between you and Evan, I suspect at least your part is personal, Nick. We'll have to figure out the rest."

Kayla felt renewed confidence at J.T.'s calm, deliberate statement. If the FBI was involved, surely they could find Evan and get the watch back.

"What can you tell us, J.T.?" Nick asked. "You said you've been on Evan's case for a number of years?"

"Yes, he's gotten very good, better than when he was in college. No one has been able to catch him. We're always one step behind. Evan has a way of convincing ordinarily smart people to give him their life savings, their jewelry, their homes, and anything else they have. Unfortunately, he's also gotten more dangerous. Last year he took over the identity of a man who had been killed in mysterious circumstances three weeks earlier. Evan managed to fool the man's family. They hadn't seen their son in fifteen years, and somehow Evan convinced a mother and father that he was their long-lost son. It's possible that Evan killed the man and then took over his identity, although we don't have proof of that."

"How could he do that?" Kayla asked in amazement. "How could Evan convince parents that he was their son?"

"Like I said -- he's good," J.T. replied, holding her gaze. "He told them what they wanted to hear, and they saw what they wanted to see."

Which was exactly what she had done, she realized. "I still can't believe he would kill anyone. But that's what you're implying, isn't it?" Could she have married a killer? Her heart stopped at the thought.

"It's definitely a possibility," J.T. replied. "I'd like to go over everything that happened since the day you met Evan," he said, then turned to Nick. "Then we'll discuss your situation. First we need to report this break-in to the local guys, not that I expect them to find anything. Evan is too smart to leave fingerprints."

"So you think Evan did it?" Kayla asked doubtfully. "He was here many times when we were dating. He had plenty of opportunity to steal whatever he wanted."

"She's right," Nick put in. "It's not logical. Or smart. And we know Evan is both."

"Then we'll have to figure out who else is in the game," J.T.

replied.

Kayla's stomach rolled over at the thought of someone else being involved. The situation got worse by the minute. Feeling the need to take some action, she said, "I'll call the police. I'm going to use the phone in the kitchen, if that's all right."

"Just don't touch anything else."

After reporting the break-in, she was told an officer would arrive shortly. She hung up the phone and walked around the kitchen. All the drawers were either half-open or all the way open, as if someone had quickly gone through the room. The back door was ajar. Had she left it unlocked? She started toward the door as Nick called her name.

"Where are you going?" he asked.

"The police are on their way," she said. "I need to check my studio, in the garage."

"I'll go with you. J.T. is making some calls."

As they walked down the dark path to her studio, Kayla stayed close to Nick, grateful to have him with her. She'd been down this path at night a thousand times, but tonight the shadows seemed far more menacing. When they got to the door she realized that the glass panel over the knob had been broken, the pieces scattered on the ground.

"Careful," Nick said. He pushed the door open. They paused on the threshold.

Kayla strained to see in the darkness. Nothing moved. Finally she reached out and turned on the light. The studio looked almost exactly as she'd left it. She felt tremendous relief that the burglar hadn't done anything more than open drawers and cabinets. "What on earth was he looking for?" she muttered.

Nick shook his head. "Obviously something small enough to fit in a drawer."

"That could be anything."

Nick walked over to her worktable and stared down at the glass. "What is this?"

"A window I'm restoring for a church."

"There's a lot of little pieces," he commented. "It must take hours."

"Painstaking hours and days, sometimes weeks," she replied.

"You have a lot of patience then."

"You sound surprised."

He shrugged. "You did get married after less than a month."

She made a face at him, not happy about the reminder. "I know. It was crazy, and you may not believe this, but not at all like me. I think I was temporarily insane."

"And when you kissed me earlier, was that temporary insanity, too?"

She was startled by the change of subject. "No. I mean, yes. Hey, you kissed me back. What was your excuse?"

He took a step closer, his breath fanning her cheek. "I liked kissing you."

She swallowed hard, wondering if he was going to kiss her again. His gaze was fixed on her mouth, and he was close, so very close. Her breath caught in her chest. She didn't want him to kiss her, did she? She put a hand up, not sure what she intended to do. Certainly not touch him, but somehow her palm came to rest on his chest. He covered her hand with his, taking another step forward, trapping her between the worktable and him.

The door opened and J.T. walked in.

Kayla pushed Nick away, sure she looked guilty of something. Her face was hot, and her heart was pounding. J.T. gave her a curious glance but simply said the police had arrived and were waiting in the house.

Kayla headed for the door. She needed to put some space between her and Nick, take a breath, think. Too much was happening too fast, and she did not want to make any more mistakes.

* * *

An hour later Nick opened the refrigerator door in Kayla's kitchen, disappointed to find nothing but diet soda and juice. He could have used a beer, but at this point he'd settle for anything cold. He took out two cans and set one down on the counter in front of J.T., who was finishing up a call on his cell phone. The police had left a few minutes earlier, and Kayla had gone upstairs to clean her bedroom.

Nick popped the top on his soda and took a long sip, then pulled up a stool at the counter next to J.T. "That your boss?" he asked as J.T. ended his call.

"An associate," he said. "I'm finishing up a case. I have to be in court in LA on Monday." He picked up the can and frowned. "Diet Coke, huh?"

"It's all she has."

"I'll take it."

J.T.'s right eye was black-and-blue now, his cheek swollen. Nick felt a momentary twinge of guilt that he'd hit him so hard. He got up and walked over to the freezer, pulling out an ice pack. He tossed it on the counter in front of J.T. "You'd better put that on your face."

J.T. scowled at him and let the ice sit. "It's fine. You hit like a girl, Granville."

"Maybe you should look in the mirror before you criticize my technique." Nick glanced down at his knuckles, which were still stinging. "I can't remember the last time I hit anyone."

"Well, next time, you might want to take a look at who you're hitting."

"All I saw was Kayla struggling against you. I thought you were Evan or whoever broke into her house."

"Which raises another interesting question." J.T. sent Nick a speculative look. "Why are you so friendly with the woman who helped Evan rob you?"

"Because Kayla is a victim. She believed what Evan told her. She didn't know his history. She didn't understand that he cons people for a living."

"Are you sure Evan didn't clue her in on any of it, maybe offer her a cut of something? She married the guy after a few weeks. Who does that for real?" he asked, sounding skeptical.

"Women do that," Nick replied. "And don't ask me why."

"Good point."

"So what's your story, J.T.? Last I heard, you were going after a pro football career."

"Yeah, well, things changed," J.T. replied, turning somber.

"I still can't believe you're with the FBI. You used to hate authority figures. You said you'd never wear a suit and work a nine-to-five job. What happened?"

"A lot. Too much to go into now."

Nick detected a hint of pain in his old friend's voice, but it was obvious he didn't want to talk about it. And Nick had never been one to stick his nose into other people's business. "Does Evan know you're following him?" he asked instead.

"Oh, yeah. He actually personally invited me into his games a few years back."

"What do you mean?"

"He owed both of us, Nick." J.T. sent him a pointed look, letting the words sink in.

"Right. What did he do to you?"

"He ruined my father a few years back. Dad was a gambler, always thought he was going to make his fortune on one lucky roll of the dice or a Pick Six at the racetrack. Evan offered him better-than-even odds, some investment scheme that he'd concocted. I didn't know about it until it was over, until my father lost everything, including his house. My mother blamed my father, said he was weak, and she was done with his foolish dreams. She left, moved into her sister's house." J.T. stared down at his can of soda as if it held the answer to life. "Three weeks later my father killed himself. Evan didn't pull the trigger, but he might as well have." When J.T. lifted his head to meet Nick's gaze, his eyes were brutally cold. "I'm going to put Evan away if it's the last thing I do."

Nick's stomach clenched at the horrific story. J.T. had always had a conflicted relationship with his dad, who'd also been his football coach. That sometimes made a volatile combination. But despite their many arguments, Nick knew that J.T. had loved his father more than anyone else. Evan had known it, too. *Damn him.*

"I'm sorry about your father. I'm going to help you nail Evan," Nick said. "He'll pay for what he's done."

"Yes, he will," J.T. said. "Speaking of family, how's Jenny?"

Nick didn't like the question. J.T.'s story had reminded him that Evan's revenge knew no boundaries. "I talked to her earlier today. She said she hasn't spoken to Evan in years, but a while ago she began receiving anonymous presents in the mail, and she admitted that she thought it might be Evan behind them. I can't stand the idea that he's watching her. And it irritates the shit out of me that she still doesn't hate him, after everything he did to her. At least Kayla is angry now. She sees what Evan is really about. Why can't Jenny get real?"

95

"She fell hard. First love and all that shit. You know how that goes."

Nick wasn't sure he did. He'd had relationships, but he'd never known a woman he'd wanted to die over, one he couldn't live without. He'd also seen firsthand with his parents and with Jenny just how bad love could get. As far as he was concerned, the emotion was highly overrated.

"What's Jenny doing now?" J.T. asked.

"She cuts hair."

"Is she married?"

"No. She dated one guy for a few years, but he's not around anymore. I'm not sure why." Nick thought back to how much promise his sister had had. "She could have been anything, you know? She was so smart, so good in school. I remember when she wanted to be a doctor. If she hadn't had to drop out, if Evan hadn't ruined her life, things would have turned out differently."

"Is that what she says?"

"She says she's happy." Nick shrugged. "She doesn't complain, so I'm not sure if that's true, or just her nature."

"I think I'll drop in on her, have a chat."

Nick nodded. "Do you think she's in danger?"

"Absolutely," J.T. said bluntly. "Anyone around you is in danger. If Evan wants to completely destroy you, he's not just going to hit your wallet."

"You said you've been tracking him for years. Why haven't you caught him?"

"So far he's played a better game," J.T. admitted, "but now that it's turned personal, he may have made a critical mistake."

"What's that?"

"Sticking around to watch you and Kayla twist in the wind."

"Or maybe he's still around because he has something else in mind. Or he didn't get what he was after. That's why he trashed this house."

"I don't know if he did this. It doesn't look like his handiwork."

"You think it's a random burglary?" Nick asked in disbelief.

"No, I think it has to do with Evan. Someone else is in the game. We have to find out who."

"Maybe a partner in crime," Nick suggested. "What else have

you learned about Evan? I haven't seen him in years. You're obviously more up-to-date."

"His real name is Evan Jones. He took Chadwick when he was a teenager. Thought it made him sound more important. No known father of record. Mother died of a drug overdose when Evan was eight. He got shuffled around the system, ended up on the streets at fifteen, where he survived by pulling cons and stealing. He changes his name, wears disguises, and becomes who he wants to become."

"He didn't disguise himself this time. Kayla has a photograph of the two of them together. That's how I identified him. I still haven't figured out exactly how what he did to me is related to what he took from Kayla."

J.T. rubbed his jaw. "I do find it interesting that there's an old treasure involved with this watch Evan took."

"Apparently the original owner of the watch, Johnny Blandino, was part of a gang that terrorized San Francisco in the late fifties. He was sent to Alcatraz. And get this: He and his buddies attempted an escape five years later, and only one of their bodies ever washed up -- not Johnny's. No one has seen him since. And no one has seen the gold coins."

"I'll check it out. Those coins could be worth a lot of money today."

"Exactly. Which leads me to believe that Evan thinks he knows where the coins may be, because I don't think he went to all this trouble to get himself a silver pocket watch from fifty years ago. I just don't know how a watch could lead him to the coins. Although," he added, drawing a breath, "there is an inscription -- 'of Heaven Await.' It could be some kind of code or a clue to something else."

"It's definitely worth looking into. However, I wouldn't completely discount the theory that Evan wanted the watch for itself. He likes family heirlooms. He's taken those before from other people, and they haven't led to any hidden treasure. He especially likes items with engravings or initials. I'm not a shrink, but a profiler told me that Evan has probably always felt like an outsider. Taking on new identities, becoming different people, feeds on his fantasy of belonging somewhere. Owning family heirlooms completes the picture in his brain."

Nick thought about that for a moment. He supposed it made sense in an odd way. Not that he gave a damn about the fact that Evan had no family. Not every orphan turned to a life of crime. Evan had to be held accountable for his actions. But was it possible that he was jumping to assumptions that weren't true? Had Evan just wanted the watch?

Despite his rationalization, his gut told him that didn't track. The scheme had been too elaborate, too complicated -- and why would Evan still be hanging around if that were all he'd wanted?

"You know, Nick, I can't believe you didn't safeguard your accounts better," J.T. said, interrupting his thoughts. "I thought you were supposed to be the brain of our group. Have you never heard of passwords?"

Nick didn't appreciate the reminder. "I live alone. I didn't think I needed to lock up my computer. Believe me, I've learned my lesson."

"So what have you been doing the past few years? I take it that means no one has been able to get you down the aisle."

"Nope. What about you?"

"I was married for a couple years. Things got bad and then they got worse." A shutter came down over his eyes. "Anyway, it ended. I'm a free man. It works better with my job."

Nick liked his freedom, too. At least, most of the time he did. Now that his savings had been wiped out, he was beginning to realize he'd never fully appreciated the security that he'd built, which had allowed him to travel without any worries. He had to find a way to get that back.

"I have to take off," J.T. said, rising to his feet with a sigh and a stretch. "I have to catch a plane to LA. But rest assured I will be working on the case. And I should be back here on Tuesday, at which time you will have my undivided attention." He pulled out a business card and held it out to Nick. "You can reach me at that number any time of day or night." Nick reached for the card, but J.T. moved it away from him. "One more thing. I want you to stay out of this, Nick. Don't try to track Evan down on your own. He's not a nineteen-year-old kid anymore. He's dangerous. His brain is wired wrong. I'm not sure any of us knows what he's capable of doing."

"I appreciate your concern, but I won't sit by and do nothing while Evan spends my money."

"Think about what happened the last time, Nick. You tried to be the hero, and you almost got Jenny killed."

Nick burned at the memory. He had rushed in stupidly, recklessly. And Jenny had been hurt because of his actions. He'd blamed himself for that for a long time. "That won't happen again," he promised.

"Let me take care of it. This is my job. It's what I do. I catch the bad guys."

"Maybe you can use my help. He's evaded you so far," Nick couldn't help pointing out.

J.T. scowled at him. "I will catch him -- if it's the last thing I do. I just don't want it to be the last thing *you* do, Nick."

* * *

The Pagoda Dragon was a popular restaurant in Chinatown. Evan bypassed the main restaurant, heading up the stairs to the private dining room. Two men in dark suits met him at the door. One quickly moved in front of him.

"This is a private party," he said.

"I'm invited. Evan Chadwick. Go ahead, ask."

One of the men slipped into the room, while the other gave him a hard stare. Evan wasn't intimidated. He'd never been afraid of the muscle. In the end, brains always won out. The first man returned to the hall. "You can go in," he said, holding the door open.

Evan had expected nothing less.

The room was shadowy, lit by candles. Incense burned. Thick drapes covered the windows. So pretentious, he thought, as if anyone cared who was using the room. She was not only rich; she was paranoid. It was that element of madness in her personality that he liked. The rest of her drama bored him. But she had presented him with a challenge, a dare, and he'd never been able to resist a gamble such as this one.

There were two other men at the table. When he moved across the room, they got up and left without saying hello, without offering an explanation. She'd always demanded obedience from her men, but he wasn't one of her men.

He waited until they were completely alone. He didn't bother to sit down. He had no intention of lingering. "Someone broke into Kayla Sheridan's house." He watched carefully for her reaction. There was none, except bored disinterest. Was it feigned? Or was it real?

She picked up her wineglass and took a sip. "And why should I care?"

"Because it wasn't me." Evan paused. "Nick and Kayla went to Ricci's earlier. They know about the watch."

"You were a fool. You should have taken more from her than the watch, so she wouldn't know your true intention. If you'd taken her other jewelry, even her cash, she would have had nothing to go on."

No one called him a fool. He'd had his reasons, and he wouldn't explain them.

"I know what I'm doing," he said, keeping his temper in rein. He would wait until the right moment to exact penance for that remark. "I won't have you interfering. If you sent someone else-"

"Then that would be my choice."

"No, that would be your end," Evan said flatly.

She laughed. "Do you think you call the shots? How sweet and very naive."

"I do call the shots. And you need me -- far more than I need you. We do this my way, or we don't do it at all. You already sent me on one wild goose chase."

"It was a necessary move. We had to rule out that side of the family."

"It was a waste of time. From now on, I follow my instincts, not yours. Now, I want an answer to my question."

A tense silence lengthened between them. And then came her words, slow and deliberate. "I didn't send someone else."

Evan didn't particularly like the answer. If she hadn't made a move, who had? Who else was in his game? "Then I'll find out who did."

"Do that. Time is running out. And make no mistake: If Nick Granville and Kayla Sheridan get in my way, I will eliminate them, with or without you."

Evan didn't bother to reply. Nick and Kayla wouldn't get in the way. They were his puppets. He called the tune. If he wanted them to dance, they would dance. And if he wanted them to die, they would die.

Chapter Eight

It was almost one o'clock in the morning, and Kayla could not sleep. She'd tidied up her house, in particular her bedroom, but it was impossible to forget the chaos she'd found earlier. Her dresser drawers had been emptied into a large pile of clothes on her bed. Her jewelry box had been ransacked, yet surprisingly nothing had been taken. Her closet, her desk drawers, even her laundry hamper had been dumped out on the ground. She couldn't imagine what anyone was looking for. Evan already had the watch. What else could he possibly want?

She ordered herself to forget about him. She needed to relax, unwind, get some sleep. Tomorrow was a new day. She could start again, figure things out.

She wondered if Nick was sleeping. He'd refused to leave her alone in the house, and while she'd put up a halfhearted argument, secretly she'd been relieved to let him stay. She was more than a little scared. Her home had been violated, her privacy invaded. Someone had gone through her underwear drawer, touched her things. She shivered at the creepy thought, feeling more uncomfortable by the moment. Shadows from the moonlight slipping through the blinds danced like scary monsters on the walls. A clock on the bedside table ticked off the minutes like a time bomb. Every little creak made her think of footsteps. Was Evan just outside the door?

She kicked at the covers with restless legs and moved onto her back, staring at the ceiling. Her thoughts turned from Evan to Nick and J.T. The three men had lived together in college and now had been brought back together again. That couldn't be a coincidence. She should have asked Nick if there was anyone else, any other roommates about to come out of the woodwork. She should have asked him more about what had happened in college. She needed to know exactly why Evan wanted revenge, and how far he would be willing to go before he was satisfied. And she needed to know why she was in the middle of their old feud.

Was she just a consolation prize? Had he married her to tie her to Nick, to give Nick another rope around his neck? Did Evan even care about the watch? Maybe he'd just liked it and kept it. He certainly hadn't kept his wedding ring. He'd stuffed that in the pocket of the jacket that he'd thrown into the casino garbage. He could have pawned it, not that it would have been worth much, but something. Or was a simple gold band too low-class for Evan?

How could she know? He was a stranger to her. It was hard to believe how quickly she'd gone from love to hate. They really were two sides of the same coin. Of course, lies and betrayal had a way of flipping that coin. And somewhere along the way, anger had replaced sadness and worry. She didn't care about Evan anymore, because he'd never been real; he'd just been an illusion. He'd become her "dream guy." She could see that now.

She'd mentioned things she liked and suddenly he was giving them to her. At the time it had been subtle, but in retrospect blazingly clear. She couldn't have created a better man if she'd waved a magic wand.

Well, it was done, over, finished. She wanted only two things now: to get her watch back, and to put Evan in jail. Then she could truly move on with her life.

She rolled over on her side. She heard a loud thump next door. Was it the bed frame hitting the wall, or something more ominous? Next came a voice -- Nick's? Was he talking on the phone to someone in the room? Her stomach churned. She wondered if something else was wrong. She stared at her closed bedroom door, wishing she'd locked it.

It was nothing, she told herself, holding her breath until all was silent again. Her imagination was just working overtime. She had to sleep.

Forcing herself to close her eyes, she tried to think of a happy place. She'd always loved the beach at sunset, all those glorious colors -- the sky, the ocean, the sun -- mixing together. She could see it in her mind, the yellows turning to oranges and reds, the water glistening in the fading light, the heat humming through her body as Nick's mouth came closer... Wait, that wasn't the way it went. She tried to focus on the ocean, the sunset, but she couldn't stop the memory of their kiss, that foolish, impetuous, angry kiss that had ignited a flame she couldn't quite put out.

It was just the rush of adrenaline, the fear of the unknown that was heightening her senses. It wasn't Nick. It wasn't her. It was just the situation, she told herself firmly. She just had to go to sleep...

* * *

Nick tossed and turned, the dream taking over his brain. He didn't want to go there. He didn't want to remember that night, but Evan's mocking blue eyes were pulling him back.

He was striding down the stairs to the basement of their apartment building, to the storage room, where he knew Evan was running a card game. Tonight he would prove that Evan was a liar and a thief. He had to save Jenny from herself. She hadn't believed him when he'd told her that Evan was working so many schemes Nick didn't know how the guy had time to sleep. Evan had organized a female cleaning service, sending supposed maids to dorm rooms, only they were doing a lot more than cleaning, and Evan was pocketing the money.

Jenny hadn't believed him when he'd told her about the call-girl ring or the pyramid scheme or the test selling or the drug running. She'd sworn he was making it up, that he would say anything to tear them apart.

Jenny didn't know the man she was sleeping with. She was a sweet, innocent girl who thought Evan was good, but Nick knew now that there was nothing good about the bastard he'd been calling a friend for the past six months.

He'd told Evan to stay away from Jenny. Evan had laughed in his face. Jenny had told him to stay out of her life.

Nick had no choice but to take Evan down. He'd called the police. They said they would investigate. He couldn't wait that long. He opened the door and saw six guys sitting around a card table. A pile of money and chips showed Evan to be winning. Not for long.

Evan smiled when he saw him, as if they were friends. They weren't.

"He's cheating," Nick said. "The cards are marked. I can prove it."

Everyone started talking at once, everyone but Evan. Their eyes met. Evan got to his feet.

Jenny came into the room, demanding to know what was going on. One of the other guys jumped up. "Evan is cheating, stealing our money," he said, his eyes wild from whatever he'd been drinking or smoking.

Nick saw the knife at the same time he saw Jenny step in front of Evan.

He cried, "No!" as the knife came down on her.

By the time he'd reached her side, she was on the ground. Her shirt was covered in blood, her eyes wide and shocked.

"Hang on," he told her. "Call nine-one-one," he yelled, but everyone was running from the room, including Evan. He stopped to offer one last taunt.

"You did this to her," Evan said. "It's your fault."

Nick turned back to his sister, desperate to save her. Her eyes fluttered closed.

"No!" he screamed again. "You can't die. Don't die." He looked around wildly but the room was empty. "I need help. I need help." Everyone was gone. His sister was hurt, and it was his fault. He tried to get up, tried to get to the door. He couldn't seem to move. He was stuck, trapped, and Jenny was dying. He screamed in frustration. He had to save her life. He had to.

* * *

Kayla thought someone had broken in and was attacking Nick, but he was dreaming, wrestling with the covers as if he were fighting for his life. She put out a tentative hand. He knocked it away.

"Nick, wake up," she said loudly.

"Gotta get help. Get help," he muttered, trying to get out of bed.

She put a hand on his shoulder. He wasn't wearing a shirt. His skin was hot and clammy, his breathing coming hard, as if he'd run a marathon in his sleep. His brown hair was tangled and matted with sweat. She gave him a shake. He blinked and grabbed her arms as he sat up fast. "Don't," he said wildly. "Don't try to stop me."

"Nick, you're dreaming. It's me, Kayla."

"Jenny's dying."

"Jenny's not here. It's just me. Come on, Nick, wake up."

The clouds in his gaze slowly began to clear. "Kayla," he muttered. His hands burned on her arms. She would have pulled away, but she didn't want to startle him again until he was all the way back to reality.

"What were you dreaming about?" she asked quietly.

He thought for a moment. "Jenny. God. It was Jenny. I thought she was dying."

"Jenny is your sister, right?"

He nodded. "She wasn't supposed to be there that night. She wasn't supposed to get hurt. I was going to take Evan down, not her. But she stepped in front of him. She took a knife in the chest. She lost so much blood. I had it all over me, my hands, my shirt, my jeans." He paused, lost in thought. "She almost died. It took forever for the ambulance to come."

"But she didn't die, right?" Kayla said, wanting to remind him of that important fact.

Nick swallowed and cleared his throat. "No, she didn't die, but she could have. I blew it. I didn't protect her. I was her big brother. That was my job. I failed."

She heard the bitter condemnation in his voice. Nick was a man who hated to fail, and also a man committed to his family. She admired that. "You tried. That's more than most people do."

"I'm not most people. Tried isn't good enough."

"Sometimes it has to be." As she gazed into his eyes, she saw something change. He'd lost that dazed look of the past. He was in the present now. His hands were stroking her arms. His hard, muscled chest, covered with a smattering of dark hair, was just inches from her breasts, breasts that were spilling out of her camisole top. She'd been in such a rush to get to him, she hadn't even put on a robe, and she was suddenly very aware of her skimpy shorts and clingy shirt.

Nick's gaze slid down her face to her throat, her chest, zeroing in on her breasts. She felt her nipples pucker in response, and a shiver ran down her spine, but it wasn't from the cold; it was from the heat. She tried to look away, but no place was safe. She loved the little hairs on his chest, the way they tapered down to his flat abs, disappearing beneath his boxers, shorts that were showing a definite and impressive bulge.

"I...I have to go," she said hastily.

His hands tightened on her arms. "Do you?"

Did she? Dear God, why did the question seem so difficult to answer?

"Stay," Nick murmured. "We can...talk."

"You should go back to sleep."

"The last thing I want to do right now is close my eyes."

He leaned forward so slowly she had plenty of opportunity to move, plenty of time to weigh her options, to say no if she wanted to. But she couldn't think with her body tingling in anticipation.

He kissed the corner of her mouth, then slid his tongue across her lips to the other corner. It was a teasing touch that only made her want more.

Just a kiss, she told herself. What was the harm in that?

His lips were hot and sensuous. She felt herself melting inside. He put a hand on the back of her neck, bringing her closer, wrapping his fingers in her hair as he tasted her again and again with his mouth. Each time she wanted to pull away. Each time she went back for more. She didn't want to think. Thinking was highly overrated. Feeling was so much better.

His mouth left her lips and made a slow journey across her cheek. His tongue swirled around the shell of her ear, then the sensitive point on her neck, drifting down to her throat, to the pulse that was hammering wildly. He pulled her skin gently between his teeth, a mark of passion. She could feel the tension building within him, within herself.

Her senses were screaming contradictory commands: *Hurry, go slow, hurry.* She told herself she didn't want this, but she did. She wanted all of it.

His hands cupped her breasts, kneading and plumping,

running his fingers across her nipples. His mouth dropped lower. He slid his tongue along the edge of her camisole. She ran her fingers through his hair as he pushed down her camisole and put his mouth to her breast. He took his time there, attending to one breast and then the other, his heat shooting through her until her nerve endings were on fire.

He rolled her onto her back on the bed. His gaze met hers in a question she answered only with a nod. He lifted the edge of her top. She helped him pull it over her head, then fell against the pillows as his mouth returned to her breasts before moving down to her navel, his tongue swirling around the edge. His hands were on her shorts, teasing at the waistband for one long second. She wanted him there. She wanted him everywhere.

And she wanted to touch Nick as he was touching her, but he shifted away, pulling down her shorts as he moved between her thighs. He cupped her buttocks. His breath blew on the soft curls he found there. She caught her breath in an agony of anticipation. And then his tongue was on her, his mouth, his fingers.... Her body trembled and shook. She felt the pressure building inside her, and she tossed her head on the pillow, begging him to stop, begging him to keep going.

He tasted her until the tremors ran through her, until she called his name, and then he was sliding back up her body, settling his hardness between the soft, wet heat of her thighs, kissing her hard on the mouth. She pushed at his boxers, wanting nothing between them but skin and muscle. He trapped her face with his hands, his eyes burning with desire. She saw a question in them.

"Don't ask," she murmured. "Don't say anything."

"Do you want to think about this?" he asked, ignoring her plea.

"I definitely don't want to think."

"You're sure?"

"Yes. Just make love to me, Nick."

He moved away from her. She tried to grab his arm. "Where are you going?"

Nick reached for his jeans on the chair, pulled out a condom. *Protection. Good, at least one of us is thinking.*

He quickly rolled on the condom, returning to the bed, pushing her back against the pillows, sliding inside before she had a second thought. Her gaze met his and she saw nothing but desire, want, and need. It was enough, more than enough. He stole her breath away with another kiss. They moved as if they were one, each thrust deeper and harder than the last until she didn't know where she ended and he began. She wrapped her legs around his waist, her arms around his neck, loving the power of his embrace, the intensity, the passion, and when they came together, she cried out in release -- blessed, mindless release.

For a few moments they held each other tight, and then Nick slid out of her and onto his side, draping his arm around her shoulders. With her head against his heart, she could hear the solid, pounding beat. Kayla closed her eyes, feeling as if she were in a warm, safe cocoon. Finally, she could sleep.

* * *

Nick awoke to the ringing of the telephone Sunday morning. It took him a moment to register the fact that he was in Kayla's guest room, Kayla's bed, but where was Kayla? The covers were tangled, evidence of their passion, but she was gone, her side of the bed already cold. He got up and reached for his jacket on a nearby chair. He pulled out his cell phone. "Hello?" he barked.

"It's Jen," his sister said.

His mind sharpened at the tone in her voice. His heart began to pound. "What's wrong?"

"Nothing. I was thinking about Evan and his family, his background -- trying to remember something that might help, the way you asked me to," she added defensively.

He drew in a breath and sat down on the edge of the bed. "Go on."

"Evan took me to the racetrack at Golden Gate Fields one day. He introduced me to a guy named Will. Evan told me that Will took him in when he was a kid and living on the street, and that Will was the only person who'd ever given a damn about him. He'd taught Evan everything he knew. Does that help at all?"

"Do you remember the guy's last name? What he looked like?"

"He had tattoos on his arms. He was overweight, not dressed very well, looked like someone down on his luck, you know. He had a red face, like someone who drank a lot. That's all I remember. He was nice, though. He gave Evan a big pat on the back, told me how great Evan was. There seemed to be a friendship between them."

"Name, Jen?" he prodded.

"I don't remember his last name. But he had a nickname -- Lucky Seven. Supposedly he always won the seventh race. Evan said he was a legend at the track."

Nick wasn't sure what he could do with the information. The facts were twelve years old. How was he going to find an old guy named Will at a racetrack? The odds were definitely against him. Then again, Will was a gambler with a nickname. Maybe someone would know him.

"So, was I right to call you?" Jen asked. "Or was this just a piece of worthless information?"

"Of course you were right to call. I appreciate it."

"Have you learned anything else since yesterday?"

"J.T. McIntyre showed up. Remember him? Did you know he works for the FBI now?"

"Are you serious? J.T.? Mr. Rebel-without-a-cause?"

"That's the one. Apparently, his cause is now Evan. He's been trying to catch him for a couple of years, but Evan keeps changing his aliases and his identities. By the way, J.T. asked about you."

"Right. He probably wanted to know if I'd fallen sucker to Evan again, right?" she asked bitterly.

"You almost died because of him. Last night I dreamed about that moment when you stepped in front of the knife. Evan left you there bleeding."

"He called nine-one-one."

"I doubt that."

"He did," she said firmly. "I know. I asked him."

"He probably lied. He was trying to get away, protect himself."

"He knew you would take care of me, and you did," Jenny said. "But I don't believe he meant for me to get hurt. I wasn't supposed to be there that night. I was looking for you. And I had a feeling you were trying to prove something."

Her words reminded him of how reckless he'd been. "I should have waited for the cops."

"Probably. But it was over a long time ago."

"That's what I thought, but I was wrong."

"I have to go to work. Let me know if you find out anything." She paused. "Be careful, Nick. I may have once thought that Evan had a good side, but I'm older now, and... well, as much as I don't think Evan would ever physically hurt me, I'm not so sure about you."

"Don't underestimate Evan where you're concerned either, Jen. If he calls you, makes contact, let me know, all right?"

"Good-bye, Nick."

Nick hung up the phone, feeling distinctly uneasy. It occurred to him that Jen hadn't made the promise to call him if she heard from Evan. He hoped she didn't make the mistake of thinking she could stop him on her own. Letting out a sigh, he contemplated his next move. He needed to shower and get dressed. Then he needed to find Kayla. He had no idea what she was thinking about last night, but as he glanced back at the bed, his body tightened with pleasure. It had been damn good, but what the hell had he been thinking?

The problem was that he hadn't been thinking. Neither had she.

Or was he wrong about that? It suddenly occurred to him that Kayla had first kissed him to get back at Evan, to prove something. Was that why she'd had sex with him? To show Evan? The thought left a bitter taste in his mouth.

He had a feeling he'd just added one more complication to the chaos that was his life.

* * *

The car was too small, too quiet, and far too intimate. Kayla was acutely aware of the man at her side, his musky scent, his minty breath, his incredible body -- the same body she could still see naked and magnificent in her mind if she closed her eyes. Only she didn't have to close her eyes, because he was sitting right next to her. She wanted to focus on where they were going, what they were planning to do, but all she could think about was the night they'd spent together, the reckless, impulsive, passionate night. She couldn't believe she'd made love to him. Not that it was love.

It was sex. Right?

It had all seemed so simple and straightforward the night before, but now she was feeling more than a little confused, even a little frustrated. She had the urge to put her hand on his hard, muscled thigh, to slide her fingers toward his crotch, to lean into his body and steal a kiss.

She clenched her hands into fists, her brain battling her body. She really had to start thinking logically, rationally, unemotionally. She let out a sigh. Unfortunately, the sound drew Nick's attention to her. She quickly looked away from his sharp gaze, afraid of what she would see in his eyes -- even more afraid of what he would see in hers.

"All right?" he asked.

"Fine."

Nick tapped the steering wheel with impatient fingers as they came to a light. They'd taken her practical and not-so-sexy Honda CRV today, leaving the Porsche in Nick's garage. She felt more comfortable in this car, and she suspected Nick did, too. The Porsche was definitely more of an Evan car. Since she didn't care all that much about driving, she'd let Nick do the honors. She had enough on her mind without having to worry about traffic.

"You don't have much to say," he commented.

"I'm surprised that bothers you."

"I'm surprised it does, too," he admitted, casting a quick sideways glance in her direction. "And curious."

"I don't want to talk about last night." She was afraid of what a conversation between them might reveal. In the cold light of day, she'd considered the fact that he might have made love to her to get back at Evan. She hated to think that was true, but maybe it was. And if it was, she really didn't feel strong enough to hear it.

"All right," he agreed. "We won't talk about it."

"Good, let's talk about your sister."

He frowned. "What can I say? Jenny is a mystery to me, especially where Evan is concerned. She can't seem to accept the fact that he's a bad person."

"So, she's not cynical like you?"

He tipped his head. "No, she's more of an optimist. Women tend to be that way."

"Well, that's a sweeping generalization."

"In my experience women have their head in the clouds where men are concerned. After my father walked out, my mother spent years thinking he'd come back. Why she'd want to take his cheating ass back, I don't know. Jenny mourned Evan for months, maybe years, after they split up."

"What exactly happened after she got stabbed?"

"The police caught Evan. J.T. and I were the chief witnesses who testified against him. There were numerous charges. He was running a lot of scams. He was expelled and sent to jail for around two years. I think he got out about the same time we graduated."

"That's an interesting coincidence. He must have felt you cheated him out of that moment."

Nick uttered a harsh laugh. "He didn't deserve that moment. He'd conned his way into college on fraudulent transcripts. Nothing about him was real."

"Why did he do that? I mean, why go to college at all, especially if he had no interest in actually learning anything?"

Nick didn't answer right away. "I suspect he just wanted to have the experience. J.T. told me last night that the profile they have on Evan is that he's always felt like an outsider, the kid looking through the window at the happy family inside. Sometimes he finds a family to put himself into."

"Or situations like college and fraternities," she said. "It makes sense. Who's this man that your sister remembered?"

"Some old guy who supposedly took an interest in Evan when he was a kid. He sounds like a loser, too, and it's definitely a long shot that we can even find him."

"At least we're doing something. It's the waiting that's the worst. After Evan disappeared, I spent two weeks waiting for the phone to ring, or the door to open, or a letter to come in the mail. I was sure there had to be a good explanation." She smiled to herself, realizing what she'd just said. "I guess I am like the women you know -- far too optimistic when it comes to men."

He shot her a quick, intimate gaze that took her right back to the night before, when they'd been naked and tangled up in each other. Did he think she was looking for something from him? She suspected he did. But she wasn't. Was she? She shook that thought out of her head.

He glanced away, then a moment later said, "Why Evan?

What made him right for you?"

"Everything. I realize now that whatever I said, he did. I dropped clues, and he picked them up. I thought he was just being attentive, paying attention. He was playing me. Giving me exactly what I wanted, so he could take what he wanted. I don't know why I didn't see it."

"Because you weren't looking. You can't defend against an enemy you can't see. I did the same thing, leaving my accounts vulnerable, because I didn't anticipate anyone coming. And I should have. Evan swore that one day he'd get his revenge."

"I'm sure you expected it a little earlier."

"I got lax," Nick agreed. "I forgot. That won't happen again."

She heard the ruthless resolve in his voice and knew he was determined to nail Evan, to exact his own revenge. She wondered how far he was willing to go to get it.

"We're here," Nick said, turning off the freeway. He pulled into the parking lot behind Golden Gate Fields and turned off the engine. "So, are you feeling lucky?"

When Nick focused that high-watt smile on her, she definitely felt something, but it had nothing to do with luck and everything to do with that other *L* word. And she wasn't talking about *love*.

Chapter Nine

The grandstand at Golden Gate Fields was huge and comprised of several levels starting with standing room only, leading up to cheap seats in the sun, and finally the clubhouse and turf club sections that offered fancy dining and private betting rooms. Deciding that anyone with the nickname Lucky Seven was most likely to be found in the grandstand, they'd bought the cheap tickets and were now walking around the main betting area, where gamblers lined up at windows or placed their bets electronically.

As they moved outside, they saw the horses being saddled up in the paddock area in front of the grandstand. A crowd of people lined the rails. Some were making notes in their programs. Others were holding their kids up to see the horses. Music played in the background. The scene was festive, filled with energy and excitement.

Kayla moved closer to the rail to get a better view. It was a beautiful spring day with a gusty breeze. Her hair blew against her face. She tried tucking it behind her ears, but strands kept escaping. She noticed Nick's gaze on her and started to say long hair was a pain when the look of desire in his eyes stopped her. Her stomach did a little backflip. She wanted to glance away, but she couldn't quite make herself do it.

He reached out and moved a lock of hair away from her face; then he leaned in and kissed her on the mouth. It was barely a touch, a feathery caress that made her want to take another taste, but she knew she shouldn't. *Look away,* she told herself firmly.

Think of something else. She forced herself to turn her attention back to the horses. She was thankful when Nick moved down the rail, putting some space between them as if he regretted that kiss, too. *Good.* She needed him to fight against their attraction as well. She couldn't do it all by herself.

Last night had been a mistake. They'd gone too far too fast. She couldn't pretend that he'd talked her into it. She'd wanted to make love to him. Only now it was the next day, and she had to face the fact that their relationship was more than a little confusing.

She told herself not to do this, not to get crazy, over-analyzing, overthinking. She didn't need to figure anything out. Last night was last night. For the moment she was just going to let it be.

Drawing several deep, calming breaths, she watched the horses move into the walking ring. At various points the jockeys would hop aboard, and then the horses would turn onto the main track. Kayla had to admit that the thoroughbreds were beautiful, powerful creatures. Some looked nervous, prancing and pulling away from their handlers. Others seemed calm, almost bored, as if they'd done this a hundred times already.

"Which one do you like?" Nick asked her.

She was grateful for the casual conversation. "I don't know what to look for. Do you?"

He shrugged. "No idea whatsoever. I'm sure there are techniques for picking winners, but it all seems too much of a gamble to me. I like to bet on things I can control."

She could understand that. Nick didn't like to put his life into anyone else's hands. "I don't think it's considered a gamble if you have control," she pointed out. "The element of risk is what makes it exciting."

"So you find the idea of betting on the horses exciting?" he drawled.

The wicked light in his eyes thrilled her far more than the horses, but she wasn't about to tell him that. "It could be fun," she said lightly.

"Which one would you pick?"

As the horses paraded up and down in front of the crowd, she decided she liked number eight. "That one." She pointed to the only gray horse in the race. "Because she isn't as pretty."

"Maybe she isn't as fast either." He picked up a discarded program on the ground and flipped through it. "She's not a she either," he said with a laugh. "Guess what? The horse you picked is named Mr. Right."

"No way." She grabbed the program out of his hand. Damn, it was true. "I'm changing my pick. This one -- Pat's Mink Coat. I like that. It sounds like a strong, independent woman."

"That horse is also a colt," Nick pointed out.

"Fine, then Pat can buy me a mink coat when he wins."

Nick's smile was filled with amusement. "How much do you want to risk?"

She dug into her wallet. "Five bucks?"

"Ah -- the last of the big-time spenders."

She made a face at him and walked over to a ticket machine. A minute later she had a ticket in hand. "I think I am feeling lucky," she said. It was hard not to get fired up. The air was filled with the hopes and dreams of hundreds of people believing that today they might just beat the odds. Maybe she could, too.

"Good, let's hope your luck helps us get some information on Evan's old pal."

They walked over to a nearby bar concession and waited for a middle-aged woman to finish filling the order before them. She was a hard-looking woman in her late forties with a lined face and a tattoo of a boat anchor on her wrist. Her name tag read "Cass."

"Hi, there," Nick said, flashing Cass a disarming smile. "We're looking for some horse experts. The guys who hang out here every day of the week rain or shine and never seem to win as much as they lose."

"Sweetie, you just described half the men at the track," she said with amusement.

"One of the guys goes by the nickname Lucky Seven. Does that ring a bell?"

"Sure, I know Lucky. Haven't seen him around in a while, though. You should talk to Roger. He and Lucky always hang out together. They swear they have a secret system for picking horses. They claim the jockeys are sending them signals from the paddock." She tipped her head to two men sitting at a corner table nearby. "That's Roger, the one with the cap. Do you want a drink?"

"Thanks anyway," he said, sliding a ten-dollar bill across the counter.

"You come back anytime now."

Nick smiled at Kayla as they moved away from the bar. "Looks like your luck is holding so far."

"Or yours." She gazed at the men Cass had pointed out.

Roger appeared to be in his mid-sixties and wore a cap on his balding head. His companion looked to be even older, his face weathered, his hands a bit shaky as he raised his beer glass to his lips. Several newspapers were spread out in front of them, as if they were doing some serious handicapping.

"Excuse me, are you Roger?" Nick asked, as they walked over to the table.

The man looked up, wariness in his eyes. "Who said I was?"

"The bartender, Cass."

"Oh, well, if you're a friend of that doll, then you can sit." He kicked out the chair next to his.

"Great. I'm hoping you can help me find someone," Nick said, as he and Kayla took the seats. "His name is Will, and he goes by the nickname Lucky Seven. Do you know him?"

Roger exchanged a look with the man next to him. "Of course I know Lucky. Everybody does. He's a legend around here. Always wins the seventh race. I swear, sometimes I thought he had the jockey in his pocket."

"Is he here today?" Kayla asked.

"Nah. Lucky hasn't been here in a few months, I don't think," he said. "Had a stroke a while back, and he ran into some bad luck."

Kayla's heart sank. Great, just when she'd thought they were getting somewhere.

"Do you know where to find him?" Nick asked. "Where he lives?"

"What's the name of that hotel?" Roger asked his friend. "Where Lucky is?"

The other man frowned. "Something with a bird in it."

"Pelican, that's it," Roger said with a snap of his fingers. "Off Sixth Street in San Francisco. What do you two want with old Lucky?"

"We just want to speak to him about one of his friends."

Roger let out a loud guffaw. "Lucky don't have no friends. The man's full of shit, always has been. He'd steal from his own mother, you know?"

That sounded like one of Evan's friends, Kayla thought. Maybe they were on the right track.

"I wouldn't believe a word he says," Roger continued. "Lucky don't know a lie from the truth."

"Thanks, we'll keep that in mind," Nick said, getting to his feet. He paused. "You don't happen to know a friend of Lucky's named Evan -- a tall, blond guy?"

Roger shrugged. "Don't think so."

"What about Lucky's real name?" Kayla asked.

"Will Jacobson," Roger replied.

Kayla stood up as well. "Thanks for your time."

"What do you think?" she asked Nick as they walked away from the table.

"I think we should try to find a hotel off Sixth Street with the word *Pelican* in it."

"Another long shot," she pointed out.

"So far so good. Hey, I think your horse is running."

They rushed back out to the rail. Kayla caught her breath at the magnificent sight, the flying hooves and flowing manes, the jockeys battling for position, the excitement of the crowd screaming for their favorites. The gray horse was out in front...Mr. Right. Wouldn't it figure that the one time she didn't go for him, he'd probably win.

"Looks like we should have gone with the long shot," Nick murmured.

"Where's Pat's Mink Coat?"

"Close to the back, I think."

She stood on tiptoe, trying to get a better view of the far side of the track. "I think he's making a move." Sure enough the announcer followed with, "And now moving into second is Pat's Mink Coat."

Kayla gripped the rail as the horses made the final turn. They pounded down the stretch, the jockeys using their whips, the horses straining with each movement. Pat's Mink Coat suddenly made a dash for the lead.

"Go!" she screamed. Pat's Mink Coat crossed the finish line

first by a nose. "We won. We won." She jumped up and down, and suddenly she was in Nick's arms. She didn't know who kissed who first, but the lingering sparks from the night before suddenly roared again. One kiss turned into two, then three. Finally she pulled away to catch her breath, to neaten her hair, to get her wits about her.

"Let's collect our winnings," Nick said, an odd note in his voice. "And then we can decide what to do next."

His words sounded strangely ominous. But he wasn't talking about what to do next in a personal way, she told herself firmly. Their next move would be to find Will, then Evan. Nick was with her only until they found Evan. After that they would be finished.

* * *

Nick's nerves were jumping as they left the track. He feared his latest adrenaline rush had little to do with the information they'd dug up or Kayla's winning horse. His heart was pumping faster because of Kayla, because he couldn't stop thinking about her, couldn't stop wanting her. He had the terrible feeling he could get lost in her big brown eyes, in her lush, soft body, and he'd never find his way out.

He had to focus, concentrate. *Stop touching her.*

First things first -- he had to find Evan. Nothing else was as important. His brain knew that for a fact. Unfortunately, his body was having a little trouble reprioritizing.

They didn't say anything as they got back on the freeway. Kayla spent an inordinate amount of time trying to pick a piece of lint off her jeans. Of course, glancing at her jeans only reminded him of how great her ass was. He cleared his throat and turned on the air conditioner. He needed to cool down fast.

He pushed his foot down on the gas pedal, eager to get to their destination. "Damn this traffic," he muttered. "Has the Bay Area gotten more crowded since I've been gone? It's Sunday. Why isn't anyone home?"

"It's too nice a day to stay inside. And it was a long winter. Spring fever is setting in."

Maybe that was his problem, he thought, as her smile drew his gaze to her soft mouth, her sweet, delicious lips.

"Nick, you have to stop looking at me like that," she

whispered.

His hands jerked on the wheel, and he swerved, hitting the bumps along the lane dividers. He immediately corrected, turning his gaze back to the road. Kayla was right: He did need to stop looking at her like that. He needed to find Evan and move on. And Kayla needed the same thing. What *else* they both needed he wasn't going to think about.

As they drove off the Bay Bridge back into San Francisco, Kayla shifted in her seat, relieved that she now had something else to think about besides Nick. They needed to find the hotel and hopefully Evan's old friend. Sixth Street ran for many blocks, but it grew seedier as they entered the part of San Francisco known as the Tenderloin. Homeless people and ragged-looking panhandlers were everywhere, some standing at intersections with signs, begging for food, others sprawled in doorways or on steps, one drunk lying half on the curb, half off. Kayla wasn't sure if he was alive or dead.

"I haven't been down this way in a while," she muttered. "It's pretty bad."

"Maybe I should take you home."

"Don't be silly. I'm a big girl, and it's broad daylight."

"This isn't your pretty world of stained glass."

"It's not your world either, Nick, but it exists and I'm not afraid of it. If anything, I'd like to do something to help. I've been so self-involved the last few weeks I've forgotten about the rest of the world." She suddenly realized how completely engrossed she'd been in the fantasy world she'd created with Evan. It was as if she'd entered a twilight zone, a different dimension where nothing was real. But now she was back.

"I think that's it." Nick pointed down the street to a four-story building in disrepair, a sign swinging off one nail that claimed they'd reached the Grand Pelican Hotel. There was nothing grand about the hotel or the pelican statue that sat out front and was currently being used as a urinal.

Kayla grimaced as a man zipped up his pants and stumbled on his way.

Nick found a parking spot not too far away. He took her hand in his as they walked down the sidewalk together. A few bums approached them for spare change, but Nick brushed them off.

She'd appease her conscience later by making a nice donation to a homeless shelter, she told herself.

The Grand Pelican was a low-income residence hotel, Kayla realized, as they stepped inside the dark, murky interior that smelled of booze and other odors she didn't particularly want to identify. After they asked for Will Jacobson, the bored clerk watching a rerun of *Jeopardy!* muttered, "Sixty-two, sixth floor."

Relieved that they were getting somewhere, they boarded the elevator and got off at the sixth floor. The door to number sixty-two opened at the first knock, and they found themselves face-to-face with a disheveled old man who appeared to be in his sixties. His hair was white and rose in unkempt tufts across his head. His cheeks were unshaved, his whiskers gray. He had a large, bulbous nose, a red face, and bleary blue eyes. He wore an old T-shirt and a pair of pajama bottoms.

"Who are you?" he asked, his expression confused. "You're not Candy. Candy said she was coming by to bring me lunch. Where's my lunch?"

Kayla didn't know how to answer. She drew a little closer to Nick, not sure why she felt so unsettled. This man wasn't going to hurt them, but the whole building felt a little spooky.

"Candy's coming along later," Nick said. "We want to talk to you, Will. Are you the same guy they call Lucky Seven?"

His mouth suddenly widened, and his eyes sharpened. "That's me. Who told you about me? You brought old Lucky a tip?"

"Your friend Roger said we could find you here," Nick told him. "Can we come in?"

Will moved back and waved them into the crowded, messy room filled with old furniture and lots of newspapers. He shut off the loud TV and threw a pile of clothes on the floor so they could sit on the lumpy couch.

Kayla had never seen such a dumpy apartment. Everything in it was old, broken, chipped, or faded. Except... it suddenly occurred to her that the television was new, and Will had a DVD player, too. She'd always been better at the details than the big picture. Suddenly those details jumped out at her -- the cell phone on the table, the new blanket on the back of the beat-up couch.

Will wasn't completely down-and-out. He had to be getting money from somewhere. From Evan? Her heart began to beat faster. Maybe they were getting close.

"Who are you again?" Will asked. "More reporters? I'm not saying nothing until someone pays me for my story."

"What story is that, Will?" Nick asked easily as he sat down on the couch.

"How to find the money," he said, leaning forward as if he were afraid they'd be overheard in his own apartment.

Kayla caught her breath at the fervor in his voice. What money was he talking about? If he knew how to find some money, why was he living in this dump?

The old man sat back in his seat and gave them an eerie grin. "But I ain't going to tell you. I'm not stupid, you know. I don't know you. And Eric says I shouldn't talk to no more reporters. Eric is smart." He tapped his own head. "Smart as a whip. Nothing gets past him."

Eric? It was close to Evan, but it wasn't Evan. Or was it? Was this his real name – Eric -- or one of his many aliases?

"I wouldn't expect you to tell me," Nick said evenly. "Did the other reporters want to know where the money is, too?"

"Nah, they wanted to know about the island," he said with a wave of his hand. "Old Joel wrote himself a book talking about all the escapes. He never gave me credit for stuff I told him. Now he's going on TV acting like an expert, and between you and me, he don't know nothing. He was a two-bit guard back then."

"What island are you talking about?" Kayla asked.

"Alcatraz, of course."

"Alcatraz?" Kayla and Nick echoed together. They exchanged a quick look. They'd come to ask Will about Evan, but now it seemed he was taking them back to Alcatraz.

The old man turned his head to look at her, his eyes suddenly confused. "You ain't Candy. Candy has red hair. I always did like red hair on a woman. Rose, she had red hair. My red, red Rose." His eyes watered.

Kayla wondered if Will was drunk or just old and sick. He seemed a bit dazed. "I love stories about the island," she said. "I bet you know all the good ones."

He nodded, his expression easing. "Sure do. I was there almost two years. Coldest place I ever lived. The boys there were bad. Meanest sons of bitches you'd ever meet. I was lucky to stay alive.

I shouldn't have been there, you know. I was innocent. I just drove a car. I didn't know anyone was robbing a bank."

"Did you know Johnny Blandino?" she asked. If Will was at Alcatraz at the same time her grandmother's former boyfriend was there, maybe this was all beginning to tie together.

"Sure did. But Johnny didn't have much to say. I was better friends with Nate. He was more of a talker." Will gave a long, choking cough and cleared his throat. "Nate told me everything about their plans, you know. He couldn't stay quiet for two seconds. That's how I found out about the money. Those boys had a fortune waiting for 'em when they took off. And other stuff, too, stuff no one else knew about. I know more than most people think." He tapped his head again. "I got a lotta stuff in this head of mine. A lotta stuff. Can't keep track of it sometimes, that's all."

"So is Eric going after the money?" Nick asked. "It was a long time ago. It could be gone by now."

"Somebody would have said something if it was found." Will frowned and scratched his jaw. "At first, I thought maybe the boys made it out, you know? They were clever and strong. Nate was a good swimmer. He used to swim in the bay when he was a kid. He knew the currents. Then poor old Frankie's body washed up on shore. They laid him in the yard for all of us to see. An example, he was." He took a breath. "But Nate and Johnny might have made it out."

Kayla wondered if the men could have survived. Then again, Johnny had never attempted to find her grandmother or tell her he was alive. And why wouldn't he have asked for his watch back if it had been that important? If he were alive, wouldn't he have gotten the treasure? She had too many questions. She needed more answers.

Will's mouth turned down. "Eric was supposed to call me. Do you know where he is?"

"We were hoping you did," Kayla said.

"Eric's a good boy. He comes back, takes care of me. Rose always said he was special, smart."

"It sounds like you haven't seen Eric in a while," she said. "What if he's hurt or sick? Maybe we should look for him -- for you," she added, feeling as if she were the worst liar in the world.

Fortunately, the old man seemed too out of it to notice. "Eric's a good boy," he repeated. "He just has to get the other watches. Then he'll come back. Where's Candy? Can you find Candy for me?"

Kayla's heart stopped when she realized he'd said *watches* -- as in more than one. How could that be? "Watches?" she asked sharply. "There's more than one watch?"

He suddenly stiffened and his mouth drew into a taut line. "I ain't saying nothing. You gotta go. You gotta go." He stood up and marched toward the front door, repeating over and over again, "You gotta go."

The man was getting increasingly agitated. Kayla was sorry she'd jumped in so abruptly, but he'd shocked her with the mention of more than one watch.

"It's okay," Nick told him. "Calm down. We're leaving, Will. It's okay. Candy will be here soon."

"Candy's coming," Will said, shaking his head up and down. As soon as they'd left the apartment, he slammed the door behind them.

Kayla let out a breath as she grabbed Nick's arm. "Oh, my God! There's more than one watch. What does that mean?"

"It means we have another clue," he said, his eyes shining. "And a trail to follow. Evan must be looking for the other watches."

"They had to belong to the men who went to prison with Johnny," she said, putting the clues together.

"I think so, too." He punched the button for the elevator. The doors opened almost immediately, and they stepped inside. "I knew your grandfather's watch was important. I knew it."

"Don't get too excited. We don't know much more than we did before."

"We know enough," he said.

"I thought you were supposed to be the pessimist."

"Not today," he said with a smile. He leaned forward and kissed her hard on the lips.

The ground jerked beneath her feet. For a moment she thought she was simply reacting to Nick's kiss; then the elevator jerked again. She gasped. Nick caught her in his arms as they came to a grinding halt. "What happened?"

"I think we're stuck," he said, his smile fading.

"We can't be." She felt a twinge of ensuing panic. She didn't like elevators on a good day, especially not old, smelly, cramped elevators in run-down buildings.

"Take a breath, Kayla. We're okay. I'm sure the elevator will start moving again in a minute."

"You're sure?" she echoed. "Did you take a look at this building when we walked in the door? I can't imagine there's been an inspector anywhere near this elevator in the last ten years. What if no one even knows it's broken?"

"The residents who live here will notice if the elevator doesn't work, and the clerk at the desk will get help," he said logically. Nick stroked her arms and offered her a reassuring smile. "We're going to be all right."

"I don't have a good feeling about this." She looked around the elevator. There was a red alarm button, but not an emergency telephone. She pushed the button but didn't hear a thing. "Do you think it's broken, too?"

"I don't know."

She shot him an irritated look. "I would have preferred a comforting lie."

He smiled. "You're claustrophobic."

"Huh. You think? It's not so much the small space that bothers me as the idea of being suspended in midair by a few cables that are probably about to snap, sending us plummeting to our deaths."

"Okay, that's not what I wanted to hear." He put his arms around her and pulled her into a tight embrace. "I'm not going to let anything happen to you, Kayla."

She buried her face against his chest and drew in a deep breath. She felt better in his arms, his strength surrounding her, supporting her. She knew he would do his best to protect her, but he wasn't Superman...or an elevator repairman, for that matter.

The elevator jerked again, dropping another foot. She hugged Nick tighter. "Oh, God," she murmured. "I don't like this. I really don't like this."

"Think about something else."

"Like what?"

He lifted her chin with his hand and kissed her again.

"That's not going to work," she muttered, the tension still building inside her.

"Give me a chance," he murmured, smiling against her mouth before he deepened the kiss.

With his tongue dancing around hers, his hands moving down to her butt, her breasts began to tingle, and her body let go of the panic and embraced the desire. All she could smell was the musk cologne he wore. All she could hear was his breathing in her ear. All she could feel was his heat.

And then the elevator took another nosedive. She screamed and grabbed onto Nick's arms as they started to fall.

Chapter Ten

Evan laughed at the sound of Kayla's screams. Some things were just too easy. He threw the lever forward, bringing the elevator to an abrupt halt. It was now suspended just below the third floor. He walked back out to the front lobby. The clerk was still gone, as he'd expected him to be. Old Henry never could resist a drink or a crisp twenty-dollar bill. He'd headed for the nearest bar without a second thought. Taking a piece of paper off the desk, Evan scribbled on it *Out of Order.* He then taped the note to the front of the elevator.

Jogging up the stairs to the third floor, he moved in front of the elevator and jacked the doors open about six inches. The top few inches of the elevator were at his floor level. He knelt down so he could see them through the small opening. Kayla was in Nick's arms. Her face was white, her eyes stricken. But Nick didn't look scared at all, just extremely pissed off, especially when he realized who was in charge.

"How you doing?" Evan asked.

"Evan," Kayla breathed in shock.

"You son of a bitch," Nick swore, moving away from Kayla. "What the hell are you doing?"

"You've been looking for me. Here I am." Evan could see that Nick was searching for a way to get out, probably so he could strangle him. But there was no way out. Evan had made sure of that. This was his game. "It's nice to see you again, Kayla."

"It's not nice to see you," she snapped. "Why did you lie to me? Why did you marry me? Why did you disappear without a damn word?"

"So many questions," he mocked. He'd figured she'd be angry, but he had to admit he was surprised by the fire in her eyes. She'd changed in the past few weeks. Because of him? Or because of Nick?

"Dammit. Answer me. I deserve the truth."

"We had a good time. It was over. Simple as that."

"You bastard. You played with my feelings. I could kill you."

"Now, Kayla, that isn't nice. I'm rather hurt. I thought you might be missing me just a little."

"Miss you? I don't even know you," she replied. "You're not the man I thought you were."

"No one could be, sweetheart. That man couldn't possibly exist. You have very high expectations."

"Don't call me sweetheart. And obviously I settled far too low with you."

"Ouch. You know how to hit where it hurts. But the truth is, I gave you everything you wanted, and all I took in return was a small token of your affection."

"What is it you're after, Evan?" Nick interrupted. "You already took everything from me."

Evan smiled. "Not everything, Nick. I'm just getting started."

"Why wait until now to come after me?"

"You have more now," Evan said simply. "And we had some unfinished business, didn't we?"

"We still do," Nick said, deadly purpose in his voice. "You're not going to get away with this. I will stop you."

"You'll try," Evan said with a laugh.

"We know everything," Nick said. "Will told us what you're after."

"You're not trying to con a con, are you?" Evan asked. He doubted Will had told them much of anything, although he was a little annoyed they'd connected him to Will. Jenny must have talked to Nick. He frowned at that thought. Jenny had betrayed him. He would have to speak to her about that. "Will is an old man," he said. "He lost his mind years ago. He talks a lot of nonsense now."

"Will seemed lucid to me," Nick said.

"Well, I'd love to stay and chat, but I have things to do, people to see, all that shit." He pulled out a box of See's Candies, dark chocolates with soft centers. He tossed it into the elevator. "Your favorite, Kayla."

She caught the box in one hand, staring at it as if it were a bomb. "What's this?"

"In case you get hungry," Evan said. "See, I'm not such a bad guy." Without waiting for a reply, he let the elevator doors close. He stood up and walked down the stairs and out into the bright sunshine.

* * *

Nick's body shook with intense rage. He hadn't wanted to let Evan see his emotion, but now he had to let the anger out. He hit his fist against the wall. The pain that ran from his knuckles down to his elbow did nothing to relieve his tension. He looked over at Kayla. She stared down at the box of candy, her dark eyes huge, shocked.

She was trembling, and her face was ghostly pale. He moved over to her, taking the box out of her hand and tossing it on the ground. "You don't want that," he said. She leaned back against the wall, wrapping her arms around herself as if she were cold.

"You okay?" he asked.

"No. Evan looked so...normal. But he sounded so...evil." Her voice shook as she got out the words. "He didn't sound like that before. He didn't act so cold, as if he had no heart. I didn't know it was a game. I didn't know it was pretend. I thought it was real. I was so stupid. He didn't care about me at all. And just now when I was looking at him, it was as if I were looking at a stranger. I didn't recognize him."

Nick let her talk. She had to sort things out for herself, and he knew she would. She was already halfway there. He liked the way she'd stood up to Evan, especially since they'd been at a distinct disadvantage with Evan towering above them, obviously having been the one to trap them in the elevator. Which begged the question, How were they going to get out? He suspected it might take a while. At the moment Kayla was distracted by her thoughts. But eventually she would come to realize that they were still stuck.

He reviewed the brief conversation in his head. Evan had admitted nothing. But the fact that he had known that they had met with Will told him that Evan was sticking close to them. He had probably followed them to the track.

Nick should have been more aware, checked his rearview mirror more often. Done something.

Evan was wrong about him. He was smart enough to play the game; he just had to start playing it. He had to find a way to get ahead of Evan instead of trying to catch up. Maybe Evan hadn't found all the watches yet. Maybe there was still time. Because if Evan cared enough to slow them down, they had to be getting close to something.

"What are we going to do?" Kayla asked.

Nick frowned when he saw her shivering. "You're cold."

"I shouldn't be. It's warm outside."

"We're not outside. I think you're in shock."

"Evan trapped us in this elevator."

Nick nodded. "I think he wanted to put us out of commission for a while."

"He succeeded." She tried to drum up a smile but fell considerably short. "How long do you think we'll be here?"

"I don't know." He wished he had a better answer. He could see that she was terrified.

"He could have planted a bomb in the elevator shaft," she continued. "Maybe he's going to just step outside and push a detonator button."

That thought had not occurred to him, but he couldn't discount the possibility that Evan intended to kill them. He had said he was just getting started. Still..."I think blowing us up would end the game," Nick said. "And I don't think Evan is ready to do that yet."

"Well, that's comforting," Kayla said.

Nick was pleased to see the color returning to her cheeks. She was bouncing back. "We must be on the right track or Evan wouldn't have bothered to slow us down. That's the good news."

"Great. Here I was thinking there was no good news and now I know there is. I feel so much better."

"I can tell." He put his hands on her shoulders, gazing into her eyes. "We're going to be okay."

"Maybe today. But this was a warning."

"Yes, it was. You don't have to do this, Kayla. You can back out anytime you want. I wouldn't blame you if you did."

"What about you?"

"I'm going to put Evan back in jail."

She gave him a long, searching look. "You sound so confident, but look where we are. Look where Evan is. He's in control, not us."

"That can change. It will change." He paused. "Trust me, Kayla."

She shook her head. "That's a lot to ask right now."

"I guess it is." He wished he could erase the suspicion from her eyes, but he knew she'd have to do that herself.

"Do you think there's any way out of here? Can I squeeze through that opening?"

"It's only open a few inches. I don't think you can fit," he replied. She looked up at the ceiling. "Isn't that a trapdoor?"

It was, but he didn't think he could get up there with a jump, and there was nothing in the elevator to get leverage on, not even a handrail. Their only hope would be for Kayla to get on his shoulders and try to pull herself through the trapdoor. But then what?

"It has to be me, doesn't it?" Kayla asked, reading his mind.

"I think we should stay put. Someone will come along and get the elevator going again. People live here."

"Drunks and bums and people no one cares about," she said. "We could be here for hours." She drew in a deep breath, and he saw a light of determination flare in her eyes. "I'll do it. We know we're close to a floor. We can see it."

"You probably won't be strong enough to pry the doors open."

"Well, I can try, right? Give me a leg up."

They moved to the center of the elevator. Kayla put her hands on his shoulders and braced her foot against his intertwined hands. She pushed against the top panel. It moved easily, revealing a gaping hole. He pushed Kayla up so she could get her hands on the roof of the elevator. She pushed and kicked and he lifted her as high as he could, until she scrambled out.

"What do you see?" he called, feeling helpless and frustrated that he wasn't the one risking his life.

"It's dark, but I can see the doors of the elevator. It's right next to me. I'm going to try to open them all the way up so I can get through."

"Be careful." He heard her moving around, grunting and swearing. "What's happening?"

"I can't get the doors to move."

A moment later her face appeared. "What should I do?"

Before he could answer he heard the whir of a motor.

Kayla gasped. "Oh, my God, it's moving."

"Jump," he ordered.

"I don't think I can."

"You have to. Jump. I'll catch you. Hurry."

Her body slammed into his as the elevator went down. He wrapped his arms around her, keeping her on top as he fell backward onto the floor. He had no idea how far they had to fall and was shocked when the elevator stopped a moment later. The doors opened. The old man from the front desk looked at them and shook his head in disgust.

"You wanna have sex, you gotta buy a room." He pulled a piece of paper off the door that said, *Out of Order*. "Now go on, get out of here."

Kayla had never been so relieved to see the street, the city, even the bums. She stopped to take a deep breath. Nick put a hand on her shoulder.

"Are you all right?" he asked.

"You caught me."

"I said you could trust me."

"Yes, you did." She moved forward and gave him a grateful kiss. "Thank you. It feels good to be outside."

"Yes it does. Ready to go?"

"Absolutely. I don't ever want to go back there."

"Hopefully, we won't have to."

They walked to her car as quickly as possible. As Kayla fastened her seat belt, she took a quick look around, wondering if Evan was still watching them. Nick followed her gaze. "Do you see anything?" she asked.

"No, but from here on out we have to be smarter." He started the engine, then paused. "I'll take you home now."

She didn't like the sound of that. "Where are you going?"

"To see if I can find out more about the existence of the other watches."

"Then I'm going with you."

"Are you sure? You look a little shaken up."

"I'm fine. As long as we don't have to step into another elevator anytime soon, I'm good."

"I think we should go back to the jewelry store," Nick said. "And talk to Delores."

Kayla nodded. "Good idea."

"After that, I think we should have another chat with your grandmother," Nick added as he pulled out into traffic.

Kayla knew he was right. Her grandmother had to know more about Johnny than she'd originally said. Who was she protecting? Kayla? Herself? Johnny's memory? Kayla was beginning to think that her grandmother had asked her to leave it all alone for her own personal reasons that had nothing to do with Kayla.

"Did I mention how impressed I was with you in the elevator?" Nick asked.

She looked at him in surprise. "Impressed? With what?"

"With the way you volunteered to try to rescue us."

"I didn't succeed."

"You tried. Even though you were scared."

She was touched by the admiration in his eyes and felt oddly emotional. The stress of the last hour had left her near the breaking point. "Don't say anything else. You're going to make me cry."

"Now?" he asked in amazement. "Now you want to cry?"

She gave him a watery smile. "It's a girl thing. But thanks for the compliment. In the end, all we really had to do was wait. Next time I'll be more patient. When that elevator started to move, I thought I was going to die. I don't think I've ever been that scared."

"Don't think about it anymore."

"I won't." She paused. "Do you think you should call J.T.? Tell him about Will and Evan?"

"Right. J.T. He went back to LA, but he did leave me his cell phone number. I'll call him after we talk to Delores. Maybe she'll be able to give us more information."

When they reached the jewelry store, Kayla was surprised to find a "closed" sign on the door. "That's odd. The hours say they're open on Sundays."

"There's someone inside," Nick said, tipping his head toward the window. "Maybe she just forgot to turn the sign. Try the door."

Kayla twisted the knob. It was locked. She knocked on the glass. A young woman came over, took a look at them, then opened the door. Her eyes were red and puffy, as if she'd been crying. "We're closed," she said.

"Oh, I...we were just looking for Delores. We don't want to buy anything," Kayla said. "We want to talk to her. Is something wrong?"

"My aunt Delores was in an accident this morning," the young woman replied. "She's in the hospital and she's unconscious. I'm sorry, but you'll have to come back another day."

"What happened to her?" Kayla asked, truly shocked by this latest piece of information.

"No one knows. She came to the store early this morning and must have interrupted a burglary. She was knocked out."

"Oh, dear. I'm so sorry," Kayla said.

"Thank you. I don't know how long she'll be off work. You'll have to come back." She closed the door and turned the dead bolt.

Kayla's stomach began to churn.

"Evan was here before us," Nick said with a certainty she couldn't deny. "He wanted those files or whatever information Delores had."

She felt terrible. "We caused this. We got her hurt."

Nick frowned. She knew he was thinking the same thing and not feeling good about it.

"You're right," he agreed. "We led Evan to her."

Even though she felt extremely guilty, she could see that Nick was taking it even harder. He always felt so responsible for the people around him, even people he didn't know. She wanted to ease his guilt. "It's possible that Evan could have found her on his own, Nick. He has the watch. The initials D. R. are on it. Maybe he would have come here anyway. Why don't we ask J.T. to check with the police, find out exactly what happened, if anything was stolen, if her files were searched, that kind of thing?"

"I'll call him from the car. I don't want anyone to overhear us."

Kayla kept an eye out for Evan as they returned to the Honda. She didn't see him, but that didn't mean he wasn't there. He seemed to be everywhere. Was he in this alone? It seemed difficult to believe that one person could be responsible for breaking into her house, knocking Delores on the head, and trapping them in an elevator, all within twenty-four hours. So who else was involved, and why?

* * *

Charlotte stared at the silver tea service that Elizabeth Pasano had just placed on the coffee table in front of her. The service must have been a hundred years old. It was beautiful, grand, impressive, just the way Elizabeth liked it, she was sure. Elizabeth took pride in the fact that she was rich, married to a successful businessman, living the good life. She'd always wanted to be someone, and she'd certainly achieved that.

"Sugar?" Elizabeth asked, her dark eyes cool, not particularly welcoming. She was so polite she hadn't said a word of reproach when Charlotte had appeared on her doorstep without an invitation, but Charlotte doubted Elizabeth was happy to see her. They'd known each other at a time in their lives they would both prefer to forget.

"No, thank you." She took the cup from Elizabeth's hand and set it down on the sterling-silver coaster. She wasn't thirsty or hungry; she was worried. She wasn't sure she should have come, but it was too late now.

Elizabeth sat back in her chair, crossing her slender legs. In her late sixties, she was dressed in a beautiful, rose-colored Armani suit, her skirt demurely touching her knees, her stockings pale, her pumps conservative but expensive. She fit so well in her elegant two-story mansion that no one would ever guess she had come from the other side of the tracks.

"How have you been, Charlotte?" Elizabeth asked politely. "I understand you're a widow now."

"Yes, Edward died two years ago."

Elizabeth nodded. Her husband, Robert, had done business with Edward over the years, and at times their social circles had crossed. They'd never exchanged anything but small talk during those rare moments, but that was about to change.

"Someone stole Johnny's watch," Charlotte said bluntly,

abruptly.

Elizabeth barely blinked. "I don't understand."

Charlotte didn't drop her gaze. "I think you do."

Elizabeth frowned. "Why did you come here? Johnny died years ago, along with the rest of them. I don't want to talk about the past."

"I'm here because I suspect someone is looking for the other watches. And the last time I saw Nate's watch, you were putting it down your blouse. It was at Nate's birthday party, remember? You were joking that he had so many presents he had to give you something."

Two bright spots of red burned on her cheeks. "Nate retrieved the watch later," Elizabeth said, with a touch of the acidic spark she'd never bothered to hide when she was younger, when she was stripping onstage with the rest of them.

Charlotte wasn't sure she believed her, but for the moment she would go along. "Do you know what happened to the watch after he went to prison?"

"I have no idea. Maybe he gave it to his sister, Janine. She seemed to have everything else of his. Of course, she's dead now, died about five years ago, lung cancer. She couldn't stop smoking."

Charlotte was sorry to hear that. She'd always liked Janine. "What about one of his other sisters? You knew Nate pretty well. If he was going to give that watch to someone for safekeeping, who would he have given it to? Dana?"

"God, no! He didn't trust Dana for a second. She might have thought he did, though. Just because he slept with her didn't mean he couldn't see her for the conniving bitch she was."

Charlotte had forgotten that there was no love lost between the two women. They'd often fallen for the same man, and Nate had been one of those men.

"Are you trying to find the money, Charlie? After all these years? Do you think it still exists?"

Charlotte frowned, not liking the light in Elizabeth's eyes. Not for the first time she wondered just where Elizabeth had acquired her wealth. Had it all come from her husband's side? Or had she somehow gotten her hands on the coins? "I'm not looking for money. I'm trying to protect my family," she said. "My granddaughter got involved with a con man who was after Johnny's watch. I suspect he's looking for the coins, and he may be working with someone else."

"Well, if he already has Johnny's watch, what are you worried about?"

Charlotte hesitated. She couldn't tell Elizabeth the truth. She didn't trust her. "I'm just trying to figure out what's going on. We all have pasts we'd like to protect. If someone discovers the money, who knows what else they'll dig up?"

"Certainly not the spoils of other robberies," Elizabeth said, looking Charlie straight in the eye. "You and Dana made sure of that, didn't you?"

"Your husband is still alive. Do you want him to know just how involved you were with Nate before he went to prison?" Charlotte countered.

"I don't think you're worried about me at all," Elizabeth replied. "I think you're worried about yourself. Everyone always wondered how the men got away from the mint so quickly, so easily. They disappeared as if into thin air. If they hadn't been stupid enough to show their faces to those witnesses, they might have gotten away with it. But they were too famous for their own good."

"I'm not sure what you're accusing me of," Charlotte said sharply. "But I can assure you that I had nothing to do with that robbery."

"Oh, you can assure me all you want," Elizabeth said with a dismissive wave of her hand. "I won't believe you. You may have grown a conscience, but you didn't have one back then. In fact, I always thought you had the money. Or Dana did. How else could she finance three nightclubs? She wasn't that good a stripper."

"Dana owns three nightclubs? I thought she just owned Deception."

Elizabeth smiled. "She owns a new club south of Market and another one off Broadway. She's very wealthy now." Elizabeth paused. "We all made it, didn't we? Who would have thought the three of us could climb out of that dark club and make something of our lives? Not that Dana went far."

"So you really don't have Nate's watch?"

"I really don't." Elizabeth paused. "Is it the watch you want --

or the map?"

"The map?" Charlotte echoed, unable to keep a nervous twinge from her voice. She cleared her throat. "What are you talking about?"

"Nate used to talk a lot after sex. He said Dominic's brother had drawn him a map and it was going to make them all a lot of money. I laughed about it. Asked him to show it to me. But of course he couldn't."

"I don't know anything about a map."

"You wouldn't tell me if you did. Why are you here, Charlie?"

"I wanted to warn you that if you have the watch, you should be careful."

"I don't have it."

"Then I'll leave," Charlotte said, getting to her feet. "Unless you can tell me who else might have the watch."

"Maybe you're walking down the wrong side of the street, Charlie. We were the bad girls those boys had for fun. There were good girls, you know, one for each of them. And Nate had one in particular."

Charlotte started, Elizabeth's words bringing back an old memory. They'd stopped at the flower shop down the street from St. Basil's. Nate had run inside. He came out blushing like a schoolboy. Johnny teased him about Anne Marie. Nate said it wasn't funny. Her parents hated him. He'd never get a girl like that.

"You know who I'm talking about, don't you?" Elizabeth asked. "I can see it on your face."

"No, I can't remember," she lied. "It was so long ago. I should be going. Thanks for seeing me."

"Of course."

"Be careful, Elizabeth. Even though you don't have Nate's watch, someone might think you do. And we both saw firsthand what greed can do to men."

"And to women," Elizabeth added. "I'm always careful, Charlie. That's the one thing I learned from you and Dana -- how to protect myself. I might have learned that lesson better than either of you." She waved her hand toward the front door. "I'll see you out."

* * *

Charlotte would have liked more time to get her thoughts together before she spoke to Kayla again, but when she got home she found her granddaughter waiting on her doorstep, looking more than a little determined and quite a bit annoyed.

"I didn't know you were coming over, Kayla," Charlotte said quickly, cheerfully, trying to pretend this was just a social call. Kayla was having none of it.

"We need to talk -- again," Kayla said. "And this time you're going to tell me what you didn't tell me the last time."

Charlotte set down her purse and walked into the kitchen. She took a bottle of bourbon off the shelf, filled two glasses with ice, and poured in liquor to the brim.

She handed one to Kayla and walked into the living room.

"Am I going to need this?" Kayla asked.

"I think so." Charlotte sat down in the armchair while Kayla took a seat on the couch. Her granddaughter set her drink on the coffee table. Charlotte took a long, reinforcing sip of courage.

"You're scaring me, Grandma," Kayla said. "I've never seen you drink like this in the middle of the day. You have to talk to me. Whatever you're holding inside is obviously eating you up. I know a lot more today than I knew yesterday, a lot you could have told me that you didn't, like that Johnny Blandino, your old boyfriend, was a thief and a murderer, and he served time in Alcatraz."

One of her biggest fears had just come true. Her granddaughter knew Johnny's true story. All these years Charlotte had tried to hide the truth from her family, and now to hear it said in such a bald, blunt fashion was shocking. Her heart began to beat too fast. She took another sip of bourbon.

"Grandma," Kayla said again, her eyes expressing both impatience and concern. "What's going on? Why is the watch important? And is there more than one watch? If so, who has the others?"

She caught her breath again at the questions. Kayla knew so much already. "All right, it's true -- everything you just said about Johnny."

"And the watches? There is more than one watch, isn't there?"

"Johnny and his friends each had a watch. I don't know what

happened to the others. I assume they were passed down within the families."

"Do they connect to a missing treasure of coins stolen from the U.S. Mint?"

Charlotte cleared her throat. She really did not want to discuss that last robbery. "I don't know where the coins are, Kayla, or even if they still exist." At least that much was completely true.

"Grandma, please, you can't keep beating around the bush," Kayla said firmly. "My house was broken into last night."

"No!" Charlotte gasped.

"Yes. Someone was searching for something, but nothing was taken, not even cash I had in my dresser drawer. What would they be looking for?"

She stared at her granddaughter for a long moment, searching her face for signs of harm. She had never meant to put Kayla in danger. "Are you all right? You weren't hurt?"

"No, I wasn't there at the time. I came home and found the place trashed."

"You can't stay in the house. You'd better move in here, or go to your mother's place."

"I think it's safer to stay where I am, since whoever searched it has already been there. Besides, Mom has her own life with her second family. We barely speak."

"I know she still loves you in her own way," Charlotte said firmly.

"When it's convenient. It's okay, Grandma. I've given up trying to make her into the mother I want, and I suspect she's given up on changing me into the daughter she wants."

It saddened Charlotte to hear the bitterness in Kayla's voice when she spoke of her mother, but that was an estrangement that would take years to undo. "I don't think that's true," she said, "but we'll leave it for another time."

"Good, because I have more to tell you. I saw Evan today."

Charlotte felt her heart drop. "What happened? Did he try to hurt you?"

"No, in fact, he was smiling, mocking me and Nick. He said something about the game not being over yet. If you know what the game is, you really need to tell me, because I think I could get into a whole lot of trouble trying to find out on my own."

Charlotte nodded, knowing it was time to put more cards on the table. "All right. I'll tell you what I know. As I mentioned before, Johnny was my first love, and deep down he was a good man, but he made some mistakes in his life. You have to understand that he had a rough childhood. His father killed himself when Johnny was only eight years old. He hanged himself in the master bedroom with a belt. They found him there."

"That's horrible," Kayla whispered.

"It was," Charlotte said. "Johnny's mother had her hands full with five children to raise, and Johnny was the only boy. He needed a father. He didn't have one. He turned to his friends for comfort. They didn't turn out to be good people."

"They turned out to be a gang of criminals," Kayla said brusquely. "That's public record, Grandma. I don't know why you didn't just tell me before."

"I was hoping I wouldn't have to. I want you to understand that it wasn't as sordid as it looks now. Yes, Johnny did some bad things. But he didn't do the worst of it. Two guards were killed during the robbery, but that was Frankie's fault. Frankie was always excitable. He got nervous. He panicked. He used the gun when he didn't need to. It was supposed to be clean, safe, simple."

"Is that what Johnny told you?"

"Yes."

"Grandma, how could you believe him? He had just robbed the U.S. Mint. There's nothing clean, safe, or simple about that."

Charlotte frowned, not getting the reaction she wanted. "Are you going to listen, or are you going to judge?"

Kayla sat back on the couch and folded her arms. "I'm going to listen."

"I know I've told you that my parents were strict and very religious, but I want you to know the whole story of my past, so you can understand where I was coming from. I grew up in a small farming town. I wasn't allowed to date. I couldn't wear makeup or have my friends over. All I was allowed to do was go to school and to church and occasionally help out at my father's grocery store. I wanted more -- a lot more. So I rebelled." She took another drink, then continued.

"After high school, I ran away to San Francisco. I wanted to be a dancer. I was good, but it was harder than I thought." She paused, remembering those wild and crazy days of living for a dream. "To make a long story short, I did whatever I could to get bit parts onstage, and I worked odd jobs. I met Johnny when I was twenty-one years old. I thought he was the handsomest man I'd ever seen. He had money, and he treated me well, and I was tired of being poor and struggling to make ends meet, to find a hot meal. It wasn't like that," Charlotte added quickly, seeing the distaste on Kayla's face. "I didn't sell myself to Johnny. I was in love. Johnny was, too. But he traveled a lot. I didn't know what he was doing at the time. I didn't ask questions. I think deep down inside, I knew he was doing things that were wrong. Then again, so was I. When the money got tight, I met someone who told me where I could make more cash. All I had to do was take off my top. She said I had great assets and I could use them."

"Oh, Grandma," Kayla murmured.

Disappointment once again flashed in Kayla's eyes. Charlotte squared her shoulders and continued. "I was desperate. I couldn't pay the rent. I couldn't go home. My parents had made it clear that I was dead to them. So I took a job stripping at a club on Broadway. It was hard the first time. I was shy. Embarrassed. But then I concentrated on the dancing part. I lost myself in the music. I didn't look at the audience. I went inside of myself and performed. I was a different person on the stage. I wasn't Charlotte anymore; I was 'Sweet Charlie.' And Sweet Charlie was sexy and very popular." She drew in another deep breath and let it out. "When Johnny came into the bar, he treated me like a queen. In fact, he wanted me to quit. He said I was too good for the joint, as he called it. He said he wanted to marry me."

"You were engaged to him?" Kayla queried.

"It never quite came to that. But just knowing that he wanted to marry me made me feel good. It was the fifties, Kayla. There was a clear distinction between good girls and bad girls, and I had definitely crossed the line. No respectable man would marry me. I wasn't about to question Johnny's intentions. Then everything went bad -- really bad. Johnny was arrested for the robbery at the mint and tried for murder. I was devastated. I couldn't believe he'd committed such a terrible crime. Even though Frankie had pulled the trigger, I knew that Johnny was also responsible for those men being dead. I wasn't completely stupid, you know. I knew Johnny was going away to jail, probably forever, and it almost destroyed me."

"Is that it, Grandma? Is that the whole story?"

"No. There's a little more. I want to explain to you why I gave you the watch."

"I know why. You wanted to start over in your life. You left everything behind. I don't really understand it, because I like to keep the things of my past close. But you don't. We're different that way."

"That is true, but that's not all of it." Her hand shook as she set down her drink. "I'm not sure I should tell you this. It will change everything. But then, I think I'm old, and I don't know how much longer I'll be around. Now that the watch is missing and people are following you...I can't let you get blindsided."

"Just say it, Grandma, whatever it is. I'd rather know the truth than hear any more lies."

"I hope you'll feel the same way in a moment." She closed her eyes, drawing on all of her inner strength. Then she opened them and fixed her gaze on Kayla's face. "When Johnny went to Alcatraz, I wasn't just devastated; I was also pregnant."

"What?"

"Your mother..."

"Oh, my God!" Kayla jumped to her feet.

"Johnny is your grandfather, your mother's biological father."

Chapter Eleven

Kayla couldn't breathe, couldn't speak, couldn't do anything but stare at her grandmother in disbelief. She'd come over expecting to learn something more about Johnny or the watch -- but she'd never imagined a secret like this. "Are you... are you sure?"

"Positive," Charlotte said gently. "I was three months pregnant when Johnny was convicted."

Kayla paced around the living room, her brain spinning. She had a lot of questions. She didn't know which one to ask first. "What about Grandpa?" she asked finally. "Did he know he wasn't Mom's father?"

"Edward knew I was pregnant," she said in a quiet voice.

"And he married you anyway?"

Charlotte nodded. "We were friends. I knew one of his cousins. We had spent time together -- away from my other life. He didn't know me as Sweet Charlie. He knew me as Charlotte. He was a solid and kind man. He found me crying one day and asked me what was wrong. I wound up blurting out the whole sordid story. I thought he would judge me, hate me, knowing that I danced topless and had sex when I wasn't married -- both very bad things in those days. But he didn't criticize me. He just listened. And he gave me a shoulder to cry on. I wasn't expecting anything else from him. When he suggested we get married, I was shocked. I said no, of course. It wouldn't be fair to ask him to raise another man's child, but he insisted that it was the right thing to do."

She took a breath and continued. "It was a different time back then, Kayla. I didn't think I could raise a baby alone. I didn't want to give up my child for adoption, but I knew I couldn't continue with my job as a dancer. I had to think of a way to take care of the baby and myself."

Kayla could understand how hard it must have been. Even now, the desperation her grandmother had felt was showing in her voice, in the tight lines around her eyes.

"Edward kept asking," Charlotte added. "And finally I said yes. We got married the next week."

A long silence followed her words. Kayla knew she was supposed to say something, but what? She still couldn't believe that the grandfather she had loved her entire life was not really her grandfather. "This is unbelievable."

"I know you need some time to take it in."

"Time? I don't think there's enough time in the world."

"It sounds bad, I know." Charlotte twisted her wedding ring around on her finger.

Kayla stared at the ring. She remembered when her grandfather had given her grandmother the two-carat diamond ring on their thirty-fifth wedding anniversary. He'd said that the simple gold band she'd always worn wasn't enough. Now she knew that the first band had been given in haste. And what had it symbolized? Love? Friendship? Duty?

"Why? Why did he ask you to marry him?" Kayla asked. "He could have given you money, helped you out. He didn't have to give up his whole life for you and the baby."

"Edward wanted the baby to have a name, his name. And he wanted to take care of me. He was almost ten years older than me. He was ready for marriage and children. Eventually he convinced me that we could make a marriage work. We could start with friendship and see where we ended up."

"So you never loved him. You married him because you were pregnant, and not even with his child." Kayla shook her head in bewilderment. "I don't understand. Why did you stay with him for so long?"

"Because I fell in love with him," Charlotte replied. "Just like he said I would. He was always so sure of that. Edward told me years after we married that he'd loved me all along, but he hadn't wanted to scare me off. I was lucky that he had such a generous spirit, that he was willing to take me in, as tainted and flawed as I was." She cleared her throat. "I'm not proud of any of this, Kayla. I lived a different life back then, as I told you before. But the one true thing in my life was always Edward."

Kayla wanted to believe her, but how could she? Her grandmother had lied about something important, something vital to their family history. How could she trust her now? "Does Mom know?" she asked, suddenly aware that there was someone who had even more at stake in this story.

"No, she doesn't. I never wanted to tell her. I still don't."

"But you have to. She has a right to know. You should have told her years ago, when it wouldn't have been such a big deal, such a big lie."

"It wasn't really a lie," Charlotte began.

"Oh, please, Grandma, you're not going down that road, are you?"

Charlotte pursed her lips together. "Edward was a wonderful father to Joanna. That wasn't a lie."

"But he wasn't Mom's biological father."

"Blood isn't everything," Charlotte argued with a touch of steel. "Edward was there in the middle of the night when Joanna cried. He picked her up and gave her a kiss when she skinned her knee. He was at her high school graduation. He gave her away in marriage. That's what a father does."

Kayla sat back down on the couch. She knew deep in her heart that her grandmother was right, but it still felt so wrong not to share her grandfather's blood. And Edward wasn't here to give his side of the story. She had only her grandmother's word -- a grandmother she barely recognized anymore.

"What about the stained glass?" Kayla asked abruptly. "Grandpa said I inherited the family gene. But I didn't, because I never had that gene. I wasn't really his granddaughter. He lied when he said that, because he knew I couldn't have inherited anything."

"Kayla, stop. Don't make it sound so bad," Charlotte pleaded. "Don't go over every conversation you ever had with your grandfather and turn it into a lie."

"It is bad. I'm the granddaughter of a murderer. God! A

murderer. That's the blood I have running through my veins."

"Don't call Johnny that," Charlotte said sharply. "Don't ever call him that."

"Why not? It's true, and you're the one who is suddenly so big on the truth." Kayla felt her chest squeeze into a tight knot. She could barely breathe. "Why? Why did you tell me now?"

Charlotte looked at her for a long moment. "Because of the watch. I gave you the watch because it belonged to Johnny, and I wanted you to have something of his, even though you didn't know it. I thought it was all right now. So many years had passed. The watch couldn't be important anymore. But it seems I was wrong."

"Yes, it seems you were."

"I realize that the watch has led you into trouble. I don't want you to be blindsided, in case you meet up with anyone who might suspect that you're Johnny's granddaughter."

"Why would that matter?"

"I'm not saying that it would, but-"

"But?"

"Johnny's band of friends was like its own family."

"You mean like a mob family?"

"No, I mean like a real family, like brothers. They were loyal to one another. They grew up together in North Beach. They were altar boys at St. Basil's. They had their own code of honor. But they could also be ruthless. If by chance one of them survived the escape from Alcatraz, it's possible he might want to make sure that no one else has a claim on whatever treasure was hidden away."

"So you know that something was hidden away," Kayla said, determined to get to the truth. "Because you said before that you didn't."

"I said I didn't know, and I don't. Johnny wanted to protect me. The less I knew about his business, the safer I was."

"I can't believe you would keep this secret all these years. There must have been some time in the last five decades when you considered telling the truth, like maybe when Mom was pregnant with me, or we needed some medical history."

"Fortunately, everyone has been very healthy," Charlotte said. "I did toy with telling you both at various times, especially your mother. But she was so close to her father. She was always more Edward's daughter than mine, which is the true irony. They had similar personalities, dreams, and goals. He understood her drive for success. He encouraged her ambition. Edward was your mother's hero. She admired him. Respected him. And she wanted to be just like him. How could I take that away from her?"

Kayla didn't know. Her grandmother had a point, but still...Didn't her mother deserve to know? "What are we going to do, Grandma? Are we going to tell her now?"

"Do we have to?"

"I think so." But Kayla wasn't excited about that prospect. Her grandmother was right: Her mother would be devastated by the news. It would rock her foundation. It would cause her so much pain. And what good would it bring?

"I think we should wait," Charlotte said.

"That's because you're afraid. You know Mom will be furious."

"Maybe you should tell her."

"Not on your life. This is your secret. I just wish I knew what was the right thing to do. It used to be so easy to know right from wrong, black from white, but everything is all mixed-up-complicated."

Charlotte nodded, understanding in her eyes. "My life was very complicated before I met Edward. He straightened me out. When I married him I left all that emotion and drama behind. Edward was so good to me, Kayla. It wasn't hard to love him. He didn't demand it. He just made himself so indispensable that I never needed anyone else. Love grew between us. I don't know exactly when or how, but the friendship we had blossomed into love. I don't regret marrying him. I could have gotten divorced over the years. Times changed. No one would have cared. I didn't stay with him because of Joanna. I was never that noble. I stayed with him because after spending so much of my early life in turmoil, it felt good just to be safe."

"Safe doesn't sound like passionate love. It sounds like you settled." The thought disappointed her.

"Then I'm not explaining it right, because that's not the way I feel. There are different kinds of love that we experience at different times in our lives. You loved your old boyfriend David for a long time. Then you loved Evan. They were both different."

Kayla didn't like the turn of the conversation. "They were

both bad choices, and let's leave my pathetic love life out of this."

"I'm just saying that what we want -- who we want -- changes, depending on how we grow, who we become."

"If Johnny hadn't gone to jail, you might have married him."

"I thought that for a time. But as I grew older, I knew that wouldn't have happened. Johnny wasn't the marrying type."

"Did he know you were pregnant?"

"Yes, I told him right before he went to jail. He was really happy. He said he'd find a way for us to be together."

"Excuse me? Didn't he have a life sentence, Grandma?"

"Yes."

"Then how was he going to get out? How would you be together?" Kayla saw her grandmother flinch. "You knew he would try to escape, didn't you?"

"I didn't know for sure. I didn't even think it was possible, but he was adamant when he told me that someday he'd come back. I said I wouldn't wait. I had to do what was right for the baby. He told me he understood, but he promised that one day he'd show up again."

Kayla felt a chill run down her spine. Was it possible that her grandfather was still alive? His body had never been found. But if he was alive, why hadn't he come back?

"Now, will you do what I asked you to do before?" her grandmother asked. "Will you stop looking for the watch?"

"I can't. And I'm not just looking for Johnny's watch. I'm looking for all three, because they're connected, and they're the reason Evan messed up my life, and the only way Nick and I are going to catch him."

"Nick and you?" her grandmother echoed. "You barely know the man. His problems are not your problems."

"They are now, because we're tangled up together. You did what you had to do, Grandma. Now it's my turn."

Charlotte gave her a long look. "All right, then I'll try to help. I've been thinking about where the other watches might be. The one thing each of the men had in common was that they weren't close to their families. They trusted their friends more than their relatives. I think that's why Johnny gave the watch to me and not to one of his sisters or his mother."

"Okay, that makes sense. What about the other guys?"

"Nate had a lot of women friends. He was very personable, very charming. He hung out at the club with Johnny and Frankie, and the girls were always swarming around."

"So maybe Nate gave it to one of his girlfriends," Kayla said.

"I asked two of them. They both said they don't have it. I believe them. I don't think either woman is particularly trustworthy, but one of them reminded me of something important. We were the bad girls. The men also had their good girls. One of them was a girl named Anne Marie Davis. She was younger than us, barely eighteen. She worked at her family's flower shop in North Beach. She was pretty, blond, a perfect white rose, Nate said, the kind of girl a man would marry."

"Do you have any idea what happened to Anne Marie?"

"I know the flower shop is still there. It's called the Flower Boutique, and Anne Marie's daughter, Connie, runs it. I called earlier. I don't know if Anne Marie is even still alive; the woman who answered the phone was just a part-time worker. I was going to go by myself, but maybe you want to do it."

"Why were you going to go there? You've been telling me to drop this search from the beginning," Kayla pointed out.

"I had a feeling you weren't going to listen to me. And I don't want you to get into trouble. I'm an old woman. No one will bother me."

"Maybe that's not true. You know far more about the past than I do. You lived it. Maybe you know something you shouldn't."

"If I did, I suspect someone would have come after me a long time ago."

"I don't know about that, Grandma. Something obviously changed, made someone want to go after the watches, the coins. They have to be what everyone wants, right?"

"I don't know *who* you're referring to," Charlotte said. "But missing treasure has a way of bringing out all the fortune hunters. Many people have tried to find the coins over the years. No one has succeeded."

"All right," Kayla said, feeling extremely weary. "I guess I should go."

"Wait. There's one more thing I need to show you."

"Really? One more thing?" Kayla asked in disbelief, afraid of what she would hear next.

Her grandmother walked over to a small desk. She pulled out a ring box and opened it.

Kayla expected to see a ring. Instead she saw a tiny key. "What's that?"

"It was in the watch. There was a compartment within the case. I think whoever searched your house last night was probably looking for this."

Kayla stared at the small piece of metal, her mind whirling with the implications. "I never saw any hidden compartment."

"There was a special way to open it."

"I wonder if Evan knew the watch held a key. What about the inscription? Did the other watches have different inscriptions?"

Charlotte shrugged. "I think they did, but if I ever knew I can't remember now. I'm sorry."

"Is this it, Grandma? Is this all there is to know?"

If Kayla hadn't been looking so closely, she would have missed the flash of indecision in her grandmother's eyes, but she saw it, and it made her nervous.

"I've told you everything I can," Charlotte said.

Her words seemed deliberate, as if she were trying to avoid a direct lie. "If you haven't, I'll be back," Kayla warned.

"Come back anyway, Kayla. You're my granddaughter. I love you. Whatever else you think, I hope you won't ever forget that."

Kayla knew she should go home, but she was afraid of what new horror she might find there. She couldn't go to Nick's house either. She'd have to rehash everything her grandmother had told her, and the information was too fresh, too raw to be put through the microscope. Nick would have questions. He would want to know everything, the way he always did. He would push her to move forward, and she didn't have the strength right now to take one more step. Her whole family history had changed in the past hour. She wished she could turn back the clock to the day she'd met Evan, and instead of saying yes to his offer of coffee, she would have said no. She would have walked away, never seen him again.

He probably would still have found a way to get the watch, but it wouldn't have been so personal, so cruel, and maybe she never would have known that that was all he wanted. Maybe she wouldn't have had to talk to her grandmother and stir up all the old secrets, the skeletons in the closet.

No, she couldn't go home, so she drove and drove until the gas tank was nearly empty and the clock struck midnight. The day was over. She'd made it through. For some reason that seemed important, as if she'd passed a milestone.

When she finally returned to her house, she saw Nick pacing on the porch. He ran up to the car before she'd turned off the engine, and yanked open the door.

"Where the hell have you been? Why didn't you call me back? I left you a dozen messages." His angry words spilled out in a rush. His hair was standing on end, as if he'd run his fingers through it a dozen times.

She unhooked her seat belt. It had barely snapped back in place when he grabbed her hand, and she stumbled out of the car. He caught her by the shoulders. "What's wrong, Kayla? What's happened? Did you see Evan again? Did he hurt you?"

His questions hit her like bullets from a gun. She didn't know which one to answer first. She didn't honestly know if she could answer any of them. Her breath was locked in her chest.

"Dammit, Kayla, talk to me. You're scaring me. I can see by your face that something is wrong."

"Give me a second," she said finally.

He bit back another question, but he didn't let her go.

"You're hurting my arms," she said.

His grip eased slightly. "Start talking. I went to your grandmother's house. She said you left hours ago. And she looked as bad as you do now."

Kayla shouldn't have been surprised he'd gone there. Nick was always more comfortable taking action than doing nothing, and she had promised to call him. It hadn't been fair to leave him hanging for hours. Then again, the past few days had reminded her that life was never fair.

"What else did my grandmother say?"

"She said I had to ask you. So I'm asking."

"Let's go inside. I can't do this out here. Evan could be watching us."

Nick followed her up the path. She unlocked the front door and stepped into the hall, relieved to see that the house appeared to be as she'd left it. It was still messy, but not a new mess. She really needed to finish cleaning up. She should have done that instead of driving around town for hours. She should have been more productive. She picked up her knitting needles, realizing that most of the yarn had come off. She'd have to start over on the sweater she was making. So much of her life she would have to start over.

Nick grabbed her arm when she went to pick up something else. "Leave it," he said quietly.

She gazed into his green eyes and saw not only impatience but also concern. She wasn't being fair to him. He deserved to know what she knew. "I'm sorry I didn't call you back. I needed time to think."

"I thought something had happened to you. I even called J.T."

"Now the FBI is looking for me?"

"No. He said to call back if you didn't show up by midnight. You made it by two minutes."

"The clock in my car must be fast. I thought it was already midnight. I thought if I came home and it was a new day, maybe everything would be different." She blinked back a tear, startled that her eyes were so moist. She wasn't going to cry. She really wasn't. But her lips were trembling, and she couldn't stop a sniff.

"Kayla, what happened?"

"Just hold me," she whispered. "Please."

Nick hesitated. "I don't know if that's a good idea. Whenever I touch you, I tend to get carried away."

"Do it anyway."

Nick opened his arms, and she slid into his embrace. She rested her head against his chest and closed her eyes. For the first time in a long while she felt safe, as if nothing else could go wrong. He seemed to sense her need for security, and his arms tightened around her. For long minutes they just stood there. Then his voice cut into her comfort.

"Kayla. We still need to talk."

"I can't. Not now," she muttered. She lifted her head to look at him. "It's too much."

She could see that he wanted to argue, but something made him back down.

"Will you tell me later?" he asked.

She nodded. "I promise. But it will be..." Her voice trailed away as she licked her lips, her gaze dropping to his mouth, her mind latching onto a happy, distracting memory.

"It will be what?" he prodded.

She tried to recapture her train of thought. Her mind was shutting down. Her senses were taking over. She was in Nick's arms. She didn't have to think anymore. "Much later," she murmured. "We'll talk much later." She tried to kiss him, but he held her away from him.

"Why?" he asked.

"I want you," she said simply, matter-of-factly.

"You don't know what you want, Kayla."

"Maybe not about anything else," she agreed, "but I don't have any doubts about this."

"Don't you?"

She placed her hands at the back of his neck, her fingers lacing through the wiry strands of his hair. She gave him a second just in case he wanted to argue, but he didn't seem to have anything else to say. So she pulled his head down and kissed him, not letting up until he opened his mouth and took her inside, which was just where she wanted to be.

"God, Kayla, you drive me crazy," Nick murmured against her mouth. "Part of me suspects you're just stalling so you don't have to answer my questions. Or maybe you just don't want to think anymore. You're using me to distract you."

"And the other part of you?" she asked, not willing to admit that anything he had just said was true.

"The other part of me doesn't give a damn why you're kissing me. I just don't want you to stop."

"Let's go with that part." She grabbed his hand, pulling him toward the stairs.

"Later you're going to tell me everything I want to know," Nick warned as they ran up the stairs.

"First I'm going to do everything you want me to do," she said with a reckless laugh as they entered her bedroom.

She stopped in the middle of the room and put up a hand when he started to move closer. "Wait," she said. She paused another second, then slowly pulled her sweater over her head and tossed it on a nearby chair. Then her hand moved to the front clasp of her bra. Nick's gaze followed her every move. She hesitated again. "No more questions. No more thinking, Nick. Okay?"

"If you take off your bra, that's pretty much a given."

She opened the clasp and let the bra slip from her shoulders. Nick stared at her for a long moment, his intense gaze making her feel wanted, desired, and very female. She had to fight the urge to cover her breasts with her hands, to give in to self-consciousness.

Nick must have read her mind because he said, "Don't."

"Don't what?"

"Stop."

Her hand dropped to the snap on her jeans. She flicked it open and slowly upzipped. Then she pushed down her pants, taking her panties off at the same time. She heard Nick catch his breath. Good, she liked him breathless and speechless. There were other things she wanted him to do with his mouth that didn't involve breathing or speaking.

"You're beautiful, Kayla."

"You're too far away."

"I can change that." He moved over to her, his hot gaze sweeping her body from head to toe, making every nerve tingle, and he hadn't even touched her yet. He stopped just inches away from her. She waited for his kiss, his touch, surprised and a little nervous when none came.

"You're staring," she said.

"I can't take my eyes off you."

She caught her breath at the deep emotion in his voice. "I feel the same way. But you have too many clothes on."

"You're right." He pulled his T-shirt over his head and tossed it on top of her pile of clothes. She swallowed hard at the sight of his naked, muscled chest. There wasn't an ounce of fat on him. She could see the ripple of his abdominal muscles. And when he stepped out of his jeans, kicking them away, she was struck by how utterly gorgeous he was -- and how utterly aroused.

Instead of reaching for her, he stepped to one side, surprising her again. He sat down on the edge of the bed and held out his hand. "Come here."

She took his hand and he pulled her toward him. His hands cupped her buttocks as he kissed her navel, running his tongue around the edge, driving her mad with the need to have his mouth on every inch of her body. But she didn't want to lose control. She wanted to do this her way. She put her hands on his shoulders and pushed him back on the bed.

He fell against the pillows, laid out before her like a feast. And that was what she wanted to do: enjoy, savor, make every second last. "My turn," she whispered.

His eyes darkened as she cupped him, stroked him, then replaced her hand with her mouth. His groan excited her. The way his hands gripped her head drove her on. She wanted to take him all the way over the edge, but he moved suddenly, pulling her away.

"With you," he muttered, urging her to straddle him.

She took him inside her body, the way she'd taken him inside her mouth. He filled up all the empty spaces with a delicious, impatient heat that made her nerves sing. They moved together until they were both mindless, both crazed with passion, both spent.

It was a new day, a new beginning. They would face it together. Kayla just hoped it would be a better day. It certainly couldn't be worse, could it?

Chapter Twelve

Jenny opened the door to her apartment and flipped on the light in her living room. Her heart came to a crashing halt. Sitting on the couch as if he belonged there, as if he had every right to be there, was the man who'd stolen her heart more than a decade earlier. Tall, tan, blond, with brilliant blue eyes, and a sexy mouth that told more lies than truths, Evan was exactly as she remembered him. He was older, though. There were lines across his forehead and around his mouth. His features had filled out. He'd gone from a boy to a man. There was more than youthful mischief in his eyes now.

As he slowly stood up, her pulse began to race.

Why on earth had he come here? What could he possibly want from her now? She was afraid to ask either question.

"Hello, Jenny." His voice took her back to a time when she'd longed to hear it just about every second of the day. He was her first love, the first man she'd ever slept with, the first man she'd trusted, the first man she'd hated. She had to remember the hate, she told herself firmly. She had to remember the lies.

"How did you get in?" she asked.

He shrugged. "Does it matter?"

"What do you want?"

"You told Nick about Will, didn't you?"

He took a step closer to her. She couldn't help but back up. She hit the door with her palms, and for a split second she contemplated the wisdom of trying to run. He would probably catch her. It might make him angry. Maybe it was better to stay put, to act as if he didn't bother her, to play along.

"You never used to be this nervous around me," Evan commented, his eyes shadowed with disappointment and a bit of anger. "Nick brainwashed you."

"You gave him good reason to do that, not only twelve years ago, but this past weekend. You took his hard-earned money. You ruined him."

"Not yet," he said.

She didn't like the implied threat. "Why can't you leave him alone? Leave us alone? Isn't it enough that you stole his money, that you broke my heart?" She felt it was important to remind him of that fact.

His gaze softened. "You were always so sweet, so innocent, so beautiful." He ran his finger down her cheek.

She tried not to flinch, but he must have noticed the slight stiffening of her muscles, because his hand dropped to his side, and his voice hardened as he said, "You've changed."

"So have you, I'm sure. We've both grown up."

"You never would have betrayed me before, telling Nick my secrets." He paused for a long, tense moment. "Don't do that again, Jenny. Don't make me mad."

She had the terrible feeling he was already mad, that he'd fallen off the thin line he'd always walked between sanity and insanity. She'd known he had a dark side, but it wasn't until all the lies came out that she saw how dark that side really was. "You were your own enemy, Evan. You ran the scams. You did the crime. If Nick hadn't caught you, someone else would have. It was only a matter of time."

"He caught me because of you," Evan said. "You let things slip."

She shook her head. "No, I defended you. I trusted you. I never knew you were doing the things he'd accused you of doing. I thought Nick was wrong, and you were right. He didn't change my mind about you -- you did that yourself by your own actions."

Evan blinked as if he were confused. Was there a chink in his armor? Was there a way to get through to this very slick, very cold man?

"Don't you remember how in love I was with you?" she

pressed on. "I would have died for you. I almost did."

"I never meant for you to get hurt. That was Nick's fault, too."

"It happened a long time ago. Let it rest, Evan. Leave Nick alone. Leave me alone."

"I can't do that. You have to know how good I am."

"Why does it matter?"

"Because it does," he said cryptically. "Because you're the only one who ever mattered."

She sucked in a quick, sharp breath and shook her head in denial. "Don't say that."

"It's true, Jenny."

"No, it's not. You don't have a heart. If you did, you would leave Nick alone."

"I can't do that, and it's not because he got me thrown out of school or because he testified against me. It's because of what else he took from me." His gaze bored into hers, daring her to admit the truth.

"I don't want to talk about that."

"Nick doesn't know, does he? All these years, you've kept our little secret."

"I want you to leave," she said.

Silence followed her words. She turned the doorknob behind her and opened it, stepping away from the door. She had no idea what she would do if he didn't go.

"All right, Jenny. I'll leave. But I'll be back. You and I -- we aren't finished yet."

* * *

"I could get used to this," Kayla said as Nick handed her a cup of coffee while she was still in bed. It was only eight o'clock in the morning, but he'd already showered. His hair was damp, his cheeks a rosy red. She took a sip of the coffee, pleased to find it just the right strength, the perfect temperature. "Pretty good," she said.

He leaned forward and kissed her on the mouth, then ran his tongue across his own lips. "Hmm, tasty."

"You could get your own cup."

"I like this better." He stole another kiss, lingering this time, reminding her of the passion they'd shared the night before. The sparks were still smoldering. It wouldn't take much for her to go up in flames again. But Nick was already pulling away, reaching for his shirt, sliding it over his head and shoulders.

"Why are you getting dressed so quickly?" she asked. "Do you have somewhere to go?"

"Actually I do. I need to check in at work. I have some days off coming, and I want to make sure they know I'm taking them now. But first, you and I need to talk about the conversation you had with your grandmother."

She sat back against the headboard and sighed. "I was hoping it was all a bad dream."

"Come on, spill it. What did she tell you that rattled you so badly?"

"Where do I begin?" she muttered. "It's a long story."

"Start at the beginning."

"All right. Grandma told me about her relationship with Johnny. Apparently when he went to prison she was pregnant, and yes, he was the father." She saw the jump of awareness in his eyes.

"Are you serious?"

"Yes. Johnny Blandino is my mother's biological father, which makes him my biological grandfather." No matter how many times she said it, it still didn't sound right.

Nick let out a low whistle. "Whoa."

"You can say that again. I'm related to a murderous criminal instead of a respected banker, who was also a wonderful grandfather." She felt her eyes blur with tears, but she blinked them away. She needed to focus on the facts and not on the emotions. She'd deal with those later, much later.

"I'm sorry." He paused. "But it doesn't change who you are, Kayla."

"Doesn't it? I've always thought I knew where I came from, where I got my eyes or my smile or my nose. I was supposed to have inherited my grandfather's knack for stained glass. I got the family gene -- everyone said so -- but that was a lie. I didn't inherit any genes for artistry. I probably inherited a talent for safecracking, only I never knew it." Nick tried not to smile, but she could see it in his eyes. "It's not funny, Nick."

"No, of course it's not. But it doesn't matter who your

grandfather was. The fact that you might not have inherited your talent doesn't make it worth less. It probably makes it worth more, because you did it on your own. You had it in you, and you still do. That hasn't changed."

"Everything else has. Every time I turn around my world starts spinning. I feel like I'm on a merry-go-round and I can't get off. There's something else, something you'll probably find a bit more interesting than my personal family history."

"What's that?"

"I have to get up. I have to show you something. It's in my purse. I think I left it in the living room." She slid out of bed, grabbed her robe off the nail on the back of her door, and went downstairs, with Nick following close behind. She opened her purse and took out the ring box. Lifting the lid, she said, "This key used to be in a small compartment within the case of the watch. Apparently Grandma took it out a while back."

Nick took the key from the box and twirled it between his fingers. "Well, well. I don't suppose she knows what it unlocks?"

"If she does, she isn't saying. She claims she's told me everything, but I'm not sure I believe her. She seems to tell me just what she thinks I need to know at that moment. When I told her my house had been broken into, and I couldn't believe what else they could be looking for, she produced this key."

"And why did she take it out of the watch?"

"I guess I should have asked her that."

Nick considered the implications for a long moment. "I wonder if Evan knows it exists or realizes that it's not in the watch where it's supposed to be."

"If he knew it was gone, he might have come back here to search for it."

"The other watches probably have keys, too," Nick mused. "Which means there's something to be opened. A door? A safe?"

"It's so small. It actually reminds me of the key I used to have to open my diary."

His eyes lit up at her comment. "That's interesting. I wonder if it does open a diary."

"Hard to believe a rough, tough guy like Johnny would have a diary. It's more of a thirteen-year-old-girl kind of thing."

"True. Anything else?"

She nodded. "Grandma said that Johnny and his friends had one thing in common: They trusted their friends more than their families. She thinks that if the watches were passed down, it wasn't through the bloodline. That's why Johnny gave the watch to her and not to one of his sisters or his mother."

Nick nodded. "I'm with you. So did she have an idea who these friends might be?"

"She said Nate dated a woman named Anne Marie Davis. Anne Marie's daughter now runs a flower shop in North Beach called the Flower Boutique. We don't know if Anne Marie is still alive or if the daughter knows anything, but we can go check it out."

"And we will," he said with an approving smile. "Good work."

"You can thank my grandmother, not me. She did the legwork, which is really interesting, since she told me to drop the matter."

"What was her explanation?"

"She's trying to protect me. From what she wouldn't say."

"Why don't you get dressed, Kayla. We'll stop by my office and then go on to the flower shop. Maybe we'll get lucky."

* * *

They got more than a little lucky. Connie Davis was at the flower shop, and while she knew nothing about any watches, she did call her mother, Anne Marie, who was alive and well and living in San Francisco. Anne Marie agreed to see them. Just after noon, they were ushered into her two-story home in Presidio Heights, an upscale part of the city.

A slight wisp of a woman, Anne Marie appeared to be in her late sixties, and had a shy smile and a gracious manner. After exchanging introductions and offering them refreshments, which they refused, she escorted them into her living room. Kayla was impressed by the beautiful, elegant room decorated with expensive antique furniture and amazing art.

"Who's the artist?" Kayla asked. "I notice you have several by the same person."

"That would be me," she replied. "I dabble when I have time." She gave them an expectant look. "Now, I'm not quite sure why you're here. Connie said you have questions about someone in my past. That sounds rather mysterious."

"Do you remember a man named Nate Carmello?" Kayla asked.

A shadow immediately crossed her face. "Nathan Carmello. I haven't heard that name in a very long time. Why would you ask me about him now?"

Kayla hesitated, not sure how to explain. She started with the easiest answer. "My grandmother is Charlotte Cunningham Hirsch. You might have known her as-"

"Sweet Charlie," Anne Marie said. "I remember the name. Nate used to talk about her all the time. She was Johnny's girlfriend."

Kayla exchanged a quick look with Nick. "Was Nate your boyfriend?"

Anne Marie uttered a self-deprecating laugh. "No. He wanted to be, but my father was very strict, and Nate was kind of a bad boy. He was so handsome, though. I really liked him." Her voice faded and she appeared lost in thought.

Nick cleared his throat, drawing Anne Marie's attention back to him. "You said Nate was a bad boy. You are aware that he went to prison for murder."

"That was because of Frankie. Frankie got nervous. He didn't mean to kill anyone."

That was the same story her grandmother had told her, Kayla thought. At least something matched up.

"Did Nate happen to show you a pocket watch that he carried around?" Nick continued. "It was silver, hung on a chain, had an inscription on it."

"Yes, I saw it. Why are you asking?"

"Because my grandmother had a watch like that, too," Kayla said. "She just recently told me that it had belonged to Johnny. The thing is, someone stole it from me before I knew its history. I think that person is trying to find the other watches."

"Why?"

"Because it's possible that those watches in some way lead to the fortune in coins that has been missing from the U.S. Mint since it was robbed by Johnny, Nate, and Frankie back in the fifties."

Anne Marie's eyes widened. "How could the watches lead to

the money?"

"We don't know. Maybe the inscriptions are clues," Kayla replied. "Do you know what happened to Nate's watch when he went to prison?"

Anne Marie tapped her fingers on the arms of her chair. "Nate loved that watch. He said it was a symbol of their brotherhood. They were so close-all of them. They grew up together, you know. I met Nate in church. He went every Sunday. We sang in the choir together. He had a gorgeous baritone."

Kayla wanted to interrupt and ask her to answer the question. Then again, the more Anne Marie talked, the more they could learn. She glanced over at Nick. He gave a slight shrug, as if to say it was her call. She decided to try a different tack. "Did Dominic Ricci make the watches for Nate, Johnny, and Frankie?" she asked.

"Oh, yes. Dominic was a very skilled watchmaker. It was his family business, you know. Nate took me there a couple of times. He always asked me what ring I'd like to wear for my wedding. It was silly. We were never going to get married."

"Dominic went to school with Nate, right?" Nick guessed, bringing her focus back to the conversation at hand.

"Yes, Dominic was a good friend, but Nate wasn't as close to him as the other men. Dominic had a wife and children. He'd married young, right out of high school. He was more stable and settled down than the other boys. It was very sad when he died. He was on a fishing trip and a wave came up and knocked him off the boat. No one could find him. His family was devastated. Lorenzo, Dominic's son, cried like his heart was broken. And I can still see Dominic's sweet little girl, Delores, throwing rose petals onto his coffin. No child should ever have to bury such a young father."

"What about Nate? He must have been pretty upset," Kayla said.

Anne Marie looked away. "Nate wasn't there. None of the men were. They were in hiding at the time. It was just after the robbery."

"So Dominic didn't take part in any of their criminal activities?" Nick asked. "Specifically, that robbery at the mint?"

"No." Anne Marie shook her head. "Dominic didn't participate in any of it. It was just the three of them. I knew something big was in the works. Nate was very secretive, and he kept talking about a big windfall. He said we could run away and we wouldn't need anyone, because he would have enough money to support me the way I was accustomed to. I should have tried to stop him. I sensed he was getting in too deep. I knew he had a good heart. And I knew he loved Johnny and Frankie, but they were greedier than he was. The more bad things they did, the easier it seemed to do something else. I begged Nate to try to break away. He said they were his brothers. He would die for them, and in the end I think that's exactly what he did."

"You don't think there's any chance he escaped?" Kayla asked. "Was it possible he made it back to shore?"

"Oh, no. If he had...well, I think I would have known. I did foolishly hope for that miracle for a while, but time passed." She gave a fatalistic shrug. "Eventually hope dies."

"Maybe he couldn't tell anyone," Nick suggested. "He couldn't afford to get caught."

"I feel sure I would have known," Anne Marie said, more firmly this time.

"You still haven't answered my question," Kayla said. "Do you know what happened to Nate's watch?"

Anne Marie hesitated again. "Is it really important?"

"Yes," Kayla said. "If you have it, whoever is looking for it will probably find you. And he's not a good person either. I don't know to what lengths he'd go to get it or whom he could hurt. He's a con man, a thief, with a very long record. We feel sure he believes that the watches lead to the treasure. And as you said, greed makes men do terrible things."

Anne Marie gave her a long, assessing look. "All right. I will answer your question. Nate gave me the watch before the police caught him. He said he wanted me to have a piece of him that I would carry with me always, that even though we wouldn't be together, we'd be connected."

Kayla felt a rush of excitement. Anne Marie's story sounded similar to the one her grandmother had told her.

"Nate said that one day he'd come back and get it. Of course, that didn't happen. Years later, I gave the watch to my son on his twenty-first birthday. He died last year. He was only forty-eight. It was a tragic car accident. My granddaughters went through all his things. They might have the watch. Or they might have given it away. I don't know. I haven't thought about that watch in years."

"Can we speak to your granddaughters?" Nick asked.

"I suppose I could call them and ask."

"It's important that you do," he said. "As soon as possible."

"I'll call right now. Will you excuse me?" At their nods, she got up and left the living room.

"We found the second watch," Kayla exclaimed. "I can hardly believe it."

"We haven't found it yet."

"But I think we're close, and closer than Evan, because he's probably looking at Nate's family. He might not even know about Anne Marie."

Nick suddenly frowned. He got up and walked over to the window, gazing at the street below. Kayla felt her stomach turn over. "Don't tell me he's out there."

"I don't see anyone. I kept an eye out as we were driving over here. I feel fairly confident that no one was behind us."

"Fairly confident doesn't sound like totally confident," she said.

He shot her an irritated look. "You could have been watching, too."

"I didn't mean to imply I could have done it better. I'm just worried. Evan always seems to know where we're going, almost before we do."

Nick let the curtain flutter back into place. "Yeah, he's a regular Houdini."

"A real bad boy," Kayla said. "He fits right in with the rest of these guys, Johnny, Nate, Frankie. I was just like my grandmother and even Anne Marie, falling for a bastard. I saw what I wanted to see. I was really stupid."

"You're all just too nice, I think," Nick said. "You trust too easily."

"Maybe."

"But in the end your grandmother wound up with a great guy. Looks like Anne Marie did all right for herself, too. The men went to prison and died trying to escape. The women lived good lives."

"Everything worked out," Kayla agreed. "Good triumphed over evil... until Evan got in the middle of it. I wonder if it was Will who brought him in, who told him about the coins and the watches."

"It makes sense. Will talked to the boys in jail. He probably knew as much as anyone who is still alive."

Kayla looked up as Anne Marie reentered the room. "I was able to speak to my granddaughter, Lisa," she said. "She told me that she remembers seeing a pocket watch in her father's things, but she's on her way to work right now, so she can't check until later tonight."

"Can we go and talk to her?" Nick asked.

"I gave her your name, and she said I could give you her phone number. If you call her after ten o'clock tonight, she should be home."

"Where is home?" Kayla asked.

"Oh, I'm sorry. She lives in Reno. She works in one of the big hotels, the Peppermill. She's a blackjack dealer. Her name is Lisa Palmer. My son moved his family there years ago. He always liked the desert." Anne Marie handed Kayla a piece of paper with the phone number. "I told her that I'd appreciate it if she showed you the watch. However, if she wants to keep it, then she should put it in a safe-deposit box at the bank. She's still grieving over her father, and she doesn't want to give away his things. I couldn't tell her the whole history of the watch. I'd rather not get into it with anyone in the family. They don't know about my relationship with Nate. I'd appreciate it if you didn't say anything. I only agreed to help you because I don't want any trouble to come to my girls."

"We understand," Kayla said. She hesitated and then figured she might as well ask. "Did you ever look inside the watch?"

Anne Marie appeared confused by the question. "Of course I opened it to check the time."

"No, I mean there was a compartment within the case. It held a small key."

"I didn't know that."

Kayla gave her a long look, convinced she was telling the truth. "Well, thanks for your time."

"You know, I keep hearing Nate's voice in my head. 'Don't ever tell anyone you have my watch.' I hope I'm doing the right thing."

"You are," Nick said firmly.

Anne Marie didn't look convinced. "I hope so. Nate trusted

me, and now I've broken my promise."

* * *

"You made me a promise," Dana said. "You broke it."

Charlotte stared at her old friend, more than a little surprised to find Dana on her doorstep.

"We need to talk," Dana added, walking into the condo without waiting for an invitation.

"I thought you said we had nothing to talk about," she replied, confused and wary that Dana now wanted a conversation.

"Shut the door."

Charlotte did as she was told. It had always been that way between them: Dana led and she followed. That was their pattern from decades ago. She was too old to be anyone's follower. Still, she was curious.

"You went to see Elizabeth," Dana said.

"How would you know that?"

"She called me. She wanted to know if I had Nate's watch or if he'd given it to that girl he thought was better than me." Dana flung her head back, arrogance etching every line in her face. "Why are you stirring this up?"

"Because someone stole Johnny's watch. I told you that."

"If Nate gave his watch to that stupid girl, I'll kill him."

"He's already dead," Charlotte reminded her. "Isn't he?" There was something in Dana's eyes that she didn't like.

"Yes, of course. It was a turn of phrase. I just hated that girl, that Anne Marie. Nate talked about her like she was some saint, some damn virgin who was better than the rest of us. She wasn't better. She was just luckier. She had parents who had money."

"She was better than us," Charlotte said. "We did some bad things, Dana. I've tried to forget about them, but the past few days have brought back all the memories. I'm afraid my granddaughter is going to find out all of my secrets and hate me for the rest of her life. I couldn't stand that. She's already upset because I had to tell her..."

"About Johnny?" Dana asked.

Charlotte nodded, meeting her knowing gaze. Dana had always known that Johnny was the father of her child.

"You shouldn't have told her."

"I had to. I thought someone else might."

"You mean me." Dana gave her a hard look. "I would have told her if I had to. If it meant protecting my children, my family -- from you."

"I didn't break my promise to you," Charlotte said. "I didn't tell Elizabeth anything. I just asked her if she had Nate's watch. That's it. And she mentioned Anne Marie. Nothing else happened."

"You shouldn't have spoken to Elizabeth at all. Now she's curious about the watches. She's asking questions."

"I didn't have another choice. My granddaughter is being harassed, followed. Her house was broken into."

"Don't say anything more," Dana warned.

"I won't. However, I did find out some interesting news when I spoke to Elizabeth. She said you own three clubs. How on earth did you get so rich, Dana?"

Dana gave her a cynical smile. "Is that your way of asking if I found the coins?"

"It crossed my mind that you had to get your money from somewhere."

"Maybe I'm just a smart investor, or an extremely motivated one. I didn't have the luxury of a rich husband all these years, Charlie. I was a single mother who had to raise three boys alone. Their fathers never stuck around long enough to make a rent payment or make a difference. But I didn't need them. I did it all myself. My sons, Jacob, Albert, and Donald, each run one of my clubs. They're very good at what they do, and each year we make more money."

"I'm happy for you." She still wasn't sure how Dana had gotten the start-up money, but she knew her old friend wouldn't say any more than she already had.

"I don't intend to let anyone mess up my life at this late date," Dana warned. "So stop talking, Charlie. Stop looking up our old pals and stirring up trouble. We had a good fifty-year run of silence. Let's go for a few more."

Chapter Thirteen

Kayla couldn't believe she was on her way to Reno. They'd called the number for Anne Marie's granddaughter a few times, only to get the answering machine, which made sense, since she was supposed to be at work. Nick, impatient as usual, suggested they drive to Reno. That way they'd be close by if Lisa Palmer really did have the watch, and they wouldn't have to wait until tomorrow to see her.

The four-hour trip through the Sierra Mountains had reminded Kayla of her impulsive wedding trip to Tahoe, located just thirty minutes away from Reno. So far, Nevada had not been a particularly good state for her. She hoped this trip would be more successful than the last one.

As they exited the highway at Virginia Street, they drove down the main strip in town, passing the various casinos: Circus Circus, the El Dorado, and the Silver Legacy. Reno had originally sprung to life in the days of the gold rush with the discovery of gold in nearby Virginia City and silver in the Comstock Lode. Visitors to Reno no longer gambled on finding gold in the mountains or the streams; they looked for luck at the casino tables and slot machines. Kayla hoped she'd find her luck with Lisa Palmer.

Walking into the Peppermill Hotel Casino was like stepping into another world, one of pink, blue, and green neon lights, low ceilings, tons of mirrors, thick cigarette smoke, and the nonstop clatter of bells and whistles. Kayla paused to let her eyes adjust to the lights. The slot machines in front of her were packed with tourists. Her gaze caught on the back of a man, a blond man playing a quarter machine. There was something about his posture.

Was it Evan? The thought raced through her mind. Had he somehow followed them here?

"What's wrong?" Nick asked, picking up on her tension.

"That man." She tipped her head toward the line of machines. "Is it-" She stopped abruptly as the man got up from the machine and she saw his face. He walked right by her, gave her a curious smile as if he wondered why she was staring at him, and then with a cheerful little whistle continued on his way. She let out the breath she'd been holding. "I thought it was Evan for a second."

"Well, keep your eyes open. Let's check out the blackjack tables. Maybe we can talk to Lisa now."

They stopped at the first table and asked the dealer if Lisa Palmer was working. She told them Lisa was on a dinner break and would be back in about an hour. Disappointed that they couldn't talk to her right away, they decided to check into the hotel and leave their bags upstairs.

Their room was on the ninth floor at the far end of a long hallway. Kayla didn't bother to unpack. She'd thrown in only a nightgown and a change of clothes. She walked over to the window and glanced out at the view.

She could see for miles. Reno was basically a brown, dusty desert city surrounded by low, rolling bare hills. She could see just about all of it from her window. The only highlights were the casinos, providing an adult playground. She glanced away from the window to the king-size bed and imagined just what adult games she and Nick could play later on.

At some point she really needed to think about what the hell was going on with them, but that point wasn't now.

She glanced across the bed and saw Nick watching her. The tension in the room suddenly went up a notch.

"If we don't get out of here now, we won't be leaving for a long while," he drawled, his gaze taking a leisurely stroll down her body.

"That's a very confident statement," she said with a teasing smile. "You really think it would take that long?"

"Want to try me and see?"

"You're always so quick to rise to a challenge." She dropped her gaze to his crotch. "In more ways than one."

"Are you having fun?" he asked with a dry smile. "Enjoying what you do to me?"

"I could be having more fun if you weren't so far away."

"I can fix that."

"But," she said, putting up a hand, "I am hungry, so maybe we should go downstairs and check out the buffet before we talk to Lisa."

"Now that you've gotten me all revved up, you want me to eat?"

"I think you'll live," she said with a laugh. "Just don't eat any oysters. It might put you over the edge."

He caught her arm as she walked by him. "You've already driven me over the edge, Kayla. You know that, don't you?"

Suddenly all the lighthearted teasing was gone, replaced by something far more serious, far more dangerous. "Nick..." She didn't even know what she wanted to say. She didn't know what they were to each other -- or what she even wanted them to be to each other. They needed time to figure it out, time they didn't have.

"Let's go eat," Nick said abruptly.

As she followed him out of the room, she had the feeling she'd just blown something important.

* * *

An hour later Kayla wasn't thinking about Nick or Evan. She was thinking about how much she'd eaten. "I'm stuffed," she groaned. "These buffets should not be legal. There is way too much tempting food." She sat back in her chair, rubbing her stomach.

"You should know. I think you tried everything they had," Nick said.

She was pleased to hear the light note back in his voice. They had enough to deal with without trying to figure out their relationship in the middle of everything else. "It's not very gentlemanly to point that out," she said, "and you didn't do so bad yourself."

He grinned. "At least we got our money's worth." He glanced down at his watch. "It's almost eight. Hopefully Lisa is back on duty."

"Hopefully," she echoed. She paused as her gaze came to rest on a man sitting across the room. He was dressed in a sport coat, white shirt, and dark trousers. His hair was black and greasy, and he had a rough, weathered face. His eyes were glazed, as if he were tired, or drunk, or maybe on something. She would have put his appearance down to too much gambling, but he was staring at her as if...as if he hated her. The realization took a moment to sink in. How could he hate her? He didn't know her. When he realized she was staring back at him, he quickly looked away.

"What is it?" Nick asked. "Who is that guy?"

"I don't know." She watched as the man threw a few bills on the table, stood up, and left. Something niggled at the back of her brain. "I feel like I've seen him before. He was in the parking lot." Did that mean anything? So what if he was in the parking lot? But the look he'd given her a few minutes ago had made her feel cold. "He stared at me as if he didn't like me much."

"Are you sure he was looking at you?"

Kayla glanced around her. "Who else? There's no one but you and me in this corner of the restaurant."

Nick tipped his head toward the casino floor behind them. "Could be anyone back there."

He was right. She'd probably imagined the whole interaction. "I guess I'm a little paranoid."

"You're not paranoid. I don't want to discount any possibility. But I didn't recognize him at all."

"And it's Evan who is following us," she said.

"We don't know that for sure. He could be working with someone."

"True. Well, the man's gone. So I guess it's a moot point."

"For the moment. But tell me if you see him again."

Nick took out his wallet and put a tip on the table. Then they walked back to the casino. It didn't take long to find Lisa Palmer. She was the only woman dealing blackjack.

"Can we speak to you a moment?" Nick asked.

"If you have something to say while you play, I can listen," she said smoothly.

They sat down at the table and Nick handed her a fifty-dollar bill. She pushed a stack of chips across the table. Nick gave half to Kayla.

"I'm not very good at cards," she murmured.

"Give it a shot."

Lisa dealt out the cards. Kayla came up with a ten and a four. Fourteen. She didn't know what to do. It was such a low number. She decided to take another card. It was a nine-twenty-five. She was out. Nick held at twenty. The dealer drew a seventeen.

"Hey, you won," Kayla said. "Looks like you're the lucky one tonight."

"Let's hope so."

The other two men at the table left, leaving Nick and Kayla alone with Lisa. "We spoke to your grandmother earlier," Nick said as Lisa dealt another hand. "We're the ones looking for the watch."

"Oh," she said in surprise. "I thought you were going to call me later."

"We decided to stop by. Do you know if you have it?"

"It's funny you should ask. I called my sister earlier after I spoke to my grandmother, and she said another man had come by looking for it. He said he was an antiques dealer. It was weird."

Kayla's heart skipped a beat. "Do you know what he looked like? Was he tall, blond, and good-looking?"

"That's what my sister, Beth, said. Why is everyone so interested in an old watch? Is it valuable? Because we could use some extra cash."

"It might be worth something," Nick replied. "Did your sister give him the watch?"

"No, and you're going to have to keep playing, or I'll get in trouble."

They obediently played out the hand. Nick busted. Kayla tried hitting again -- this time on thirteen. She got a nine. Twenty-two -- bust.

"My sister didn't know where the watch was, thank goodness," Lisa continued. "Otherwise, she might have given it to him. She doesn't have a lot of sense. If the watch is worth something, I want to get full price."

"So you do know where the watch is?" Kayla asked.

"Sure, it's in my dresser drawer in my bedroom."

Kayla was relieved to hear it was still tucked away. "That's good. The man your sister spoke to is not an antiques dealer; he's a con artist, and he'd probably steal the watch from you before he'd pay you a dime."

"It must really be worth something if a con man wants it." Lisa dealt another hand of cards. They obediently placed their bets and went through the motions of the game.

"What time do you get off?" Kayla asked. "We're very interested in talking to you some more. You don't happen to know if there's an inscription, do you?"

"Yes. It said...'Until the Day.' I always wondered what that meant. I get off work at ten. If you meet me by the front desk, we can talk more about it."

"What about your sister? Maybe we could talk to her right now," Nick suggested.

"She's at work. Not that I'd want her going through my drawers anyway."

"We'll talk to you at ten then," Kayla said.

They rose from the table and moved away as three other men sat down to play. "She still has the watch," Kayla said as they walked toward the lobby. "That's something."

"I don't think it's a good sign that Evan was here before us," Nick said heavily.

"But it might take him some time to find the watch, if she has it tucked away in a drawer."

"I don't know, Kayla. It doesn't feel right. I wish we didn't have to wait two hours to talk to her," he said in frustration. "That will be too long. I'm going to call J.T. Maybe he can pull some strings, get us an address."

They paused in the lobby by a lounge area so Nick could make the call. "He's not answering," he muttered. "Yeah, J.T., it's Nick. Call me back. I think we found the owner of another one of the watches, and Evan was here before us. Her name is Lisa Palmer. She's a blackjack dealer at the Peppermill Casino in Reno. That's where we are right now. She thinks the watch is at her house. We're going to meet her at ten o'clock. Call me back at this number as soon as you get the message."

"I guess we wait," Kayla said as he hung up.

Before Nick could reply, her cell phone rang. She was surprised. Hardly anyone ever called her on her cell phone. She opened it, not recognizing the number. "Hello?"

"Hey, babe, how are you?"

Her jaw dropped at the sound of a very familiar male voice.

"Don't you know hitting on fourteen is risky?" Evan continued. "Haven't you learned anything from me, Kayla?"

Her heart began to race, and sweat broke out across her brow. "How do you know I did?" She looked around her, sure Evan couldn't be far away. At Nick's quizzical glance, she mouthed, *Evan.*

"I know everything," Evan replied. "Good lead on the watch, by the way. Who told you --Grandma?"

"I don't know what you're talking about. Nick and I just decided to take a little trip."

"The honeymoon you never had, sweetheart?"

Her blood boiled at that comment. "Damn you, Evan. You're a pig."

"That's not what you said before, when we-"

She cut him off, ending the call with a ruthless snap of her cell phone.

"What did he say?" Nick asked.

"He was horrible," she replied. "So cruel. I couldn't talk to him."

"Kayla, what did he say?" Nick repeated.

"He said we gave him a good lead on the watch. He's here, Nick. He's watching us. He knew what cards I played. He's everywhere. I can't find him. I can't get away from him. I can't stand this. And I can't do it anymore." She looked around, feeling a wild desperation to get out of the trap she was in. "I have to take a break."

"Fine, we'll take a break."

"No, by myself. I need some air. I need to be alone." She spun on her heel and headed for the first exit.

The door led out of the casino and into the garden and pool area. The night air was refreshing, and it cooled the furious heat running through her body. She walked to the far edge of the pool, where a fountain ran over a beautiful array of rocks. The sound of the waterfall soothed her nerves. She was grateful for the quiet.

After the noisy chaos of the casino and Evan's disturbing phone call, she needed a moment to regroup.

Maybe Nick could go nonstop without ever taking a breath, but she couldn't. Too much was happening too fast. She felt like a hamster running around on a wheel in a cage, racing as fast as she could but never getting anywhere. And the walls of the cage just kept closing in on her.

She heard a groan, then a thud, and she whirled around. There were only a few soft lights along the path. The bushes and trees in the garden were suddenly filled with dark shadows, and she realized how isolated she was.

"Nick," she called. Had he followed her into the garden but was staying far enough away to give her the space she'd requested? "Nick?"

There was no answer. She started walking back the way she'd come. She kept a wary eye around her as she headed for the door. She was looking up, not down, which was why she almost tripped over Nick's body. She let out a startled gasp. He was sprawled across the grass, facedown, and unconscious.

"Oh, my God!" she said in horror. Before she could kneel down to check on him, an arm came around her neck, hauling her up against a hard male body. She squirmed, trying to see who had a grip on her, but she couldn't move. The man was strong. She kicked out her feet behind her, trying to get away, trying to remember everything she'd learned from her self-defense class.

"Where is it?" he growled against her ear. "Where's the watch?"

It took her a moment to realize what he was asking. "I...I don't have it."

"You're lying." His arm tightened around her neck, threatening to cut off her air supply.

"I don't have it," she said again. "Evan took it from me. The man I married in Tahoe, he took it. He has it. I swear."

"Who has the other watches? Who?" he demanded in a deep, impatient, angry voice. "The girl you were just talking to?"

She put her hands on his arm, trying to pull it loose, but her efforts were futile. "I don't know."

The door to the casino opened and a young couple came out. The man behind her gave her a shove, and she landed on her knees on the ground. She looked around, trying to see who had assaulted her. But he was gone, vanishing as quickly as he'd come. The couple had taken another path, completely unaware of what they'd interrupted. She looked down at Nick. He was starting to stir, thank God.

She crawled over to him, putting her hand on his arm. "Nick, are you all right?"

He groaned and tried to roll over. She helped him sit up. There was blood dripping down his face from a cut on his forehead. He looked dazed, confused, and he put a hand to the back of his head with a decided wince. "What happened?"

"Someone knocked you out."

He stared at her. "Who?"

"I don't know. He grabbed me, but some people came out and he let me go."

"Evan?"

"I don't think so. His body felt different, and his voice was wrong. He asked me who had the other watch." She tried to make sense of what had just happened. "He came up behind me. I couldn't see him. He was strong, though. He had his arm around my neck. I thought he was going to strangle me." She stopped talking, realizing Nick still looked dazed. "We need to get you to the doctor." She dug through her purse, found some Kleenex, and pressed a tissue gently to his head.

"It's okay. I just need some ice," he said, pushing her arm away.

"Nick. You're hurt. You're bleeding."

"Yeah, I noticed. Can you help me up, Kayla?"

She assisted him to his feet, and he hung on to her for one long, unsteady moment. "Whoa."

"Do you want to head for the car? I'll take you to the emergency room."

"No, let's just go to the room. I'm okay."

She could see that he wasn't all right, but that he was going to be extremely stubborn about it. So she let him lean on her as they went back into the hotel and up the elevator to their floor. Fortunately, they didn't see anyone else.

She opened the door and Nick stumbled across the room, sitting down on the bed. "I'm going to get some ice," she said quickly, reaching for the bucket.

"Be careful," he told her.

"I will." As she picked up the ice bucket, she was reminded of when Evan had made the same move on their wedding night, only he never came back. That wasn't going to be the case tonight.

Her pause drew Nick's attention. "Maybe I should go," he said.

"No. You sit." She pushed him gently down on the bed when he tried to stand. "The machine is just by the elevator. I'll be quick. I promise."

As she left the room, she looked down the corridor. There was no one around. She walked to the end of the hall and opened the door to the small room where the ice machine was located. She emptied the ice into the bucket as fast as she could, her heart beating triple-time. At any moment, she expected the man who had grabbed her to come back.

When the bucket was full, she turned to leave. Just then the door opened.

Chapter Fourteen

A man entered the small room. He had bright red hair and wore a yellow Hawaiian shirt that fit tightly over his stomach. He had an ice bucket in one hand. She let out a breath of relief. It was no one, just another guest.

"How you doing, little lady?" he asked in a Texas drawl.

"Okay," she said, trying to move around him, but he was blocking the door.

"Having any luck here in Reno?" he said in a chatty voice.

"Not much."

"You're a pretty thing. You got a boyfriend?"

"Yes," she said quickly, her relief turning to worry. "I have to get back to him. Do you mind?"

He hesitated and then stepped to one side.

As she passed by him, she looked directly into his eyes -- his twinkling blue eyes. Something inside her turned over. She didn't know him. Did she?

"Evan?" she whispered.

"Honey, you can call me anything you want if you let me buy you a drink."

She shook her head. Her brain was playing tricks on her. It wasn't Evan. The man didn't look anything like Evan -- except maybe in the eyes. She pushed open the door and headed back to their room.

Nick was getting to his feet when she walked in.

"What took you so long?" he asked grumpily.

"I ran into someone getting ice. He wanted to chat."

"Who?"

She hesitated. "He had red hair and a paunch and looked nothing like Evan, but there was something about his eyes that bothered me. It couldn't have been Evan. This guy was big and pudgy."

"Ever hear of a fat suit or padding stuffed under your shirt? I'm going down there."

"No, you're not," she said, putting a hand on his chest. "You need ice and rest. If it was Evan, I think he would have said more to me than he did. I'm sure it was just my imagination. I'm seeing Evan everywhere these days."

"You know he wears disguises."

"It wasn't him, okay?"

Nick looked like he was going to ignore her, but as he moved he swayed and had to sit down on the bed. "Maybe I'll check in a minute," he muttered.

"Sure." Kayla went into the bathroom and put some ice in a towel, then took it back out to him.

He placed it on his head with a wince.

"It hurts, huh?" she said sympathetically.

"It's all right."

"Do you want some ice for your forehead, too? I think you landed on your face. Good thing you were on the grass and not on the pavement." She sat down on the bed next to him. "I'm sorry I ran outside like I did. This never would have happened if I hadn't panicked. I just felt like I needed some air."

"I knew I shouldn't have let you go. That's why I came after you. Tell me about the man who grabbed you." Nick swung his legs up on the bed and stretched out, leaning back against the pillows.

"I didn't see him. But he asked me where the watch was -- if I had it."

Nick sent her a puzzled frown. "So he thought you had a watch? I wonder which watch he was talking about."

"He also asked me if the girl we were talking to had one of the other watches. I told him I didn't know. Then some people came out and he took off. Who is he?" she murmured. "What does he have to do with this? It doesn't sound like he's working with

Evan."

"No, it doesn't."

"I wonder if Evan knows about him," she muttered. "This is getting complicated."

"You can say that again," Nick said, closing his eyes.

She stared at his face for a long moment. There was a bump on his forehead that was turning black-and-blue. She had a feeling the bruise would only make him more handsome. He had a beautiful face, she thought idly -- tan skin, thick, dark brows, long black lashes, strong cheekbones, and a wide, generous mouth just perfect for kissing. She had the urge to trace his lips with her fingers, and mentally gave herself a pinch for traveling down that road again. Nick needed to rest.

Unfortunately when she looked away from his face, her gaze moved down his long, lean body, his broad shoulders, and nice chest. She liked the little dark hairs she could see through the open buttons of his polo shirt. She liked running her fingers through them most of all.

Okay, she really needed to put on the brakes. Visualizing Nick naked was not a productive use of her time.

But it was difficult to look away from this man. He was connected to her, in her head, in her heart, under her skin. She could gaze at him all day, touch him, kiss him, make love to him, and once wouldn't be enough. She'd want to do it again and again.

"Kayla?"

She jumped at the sound of his voice.

He opened one eye. "What are you doing?"

"Just sitting here, thinking."

"About what?"

She was definitely not going to tell him. "Everything," she lied. "You should rest, but maybe not sleep. You could have a concussion. I still think I should call the doctor. Don't they have a casino medic or something?"

"I'm fine. I just have a headache. I don't suppose you have any aspirin?"

"Actually, I think I do." She reached into her purse and pulled out a small bottle. "I'll get you some water." She was grateful for the distraction.

Nick took the pills, then patted the bed next to him. "Why

don't you sit down? I just need a few minutes to recuperate."

"I think you're going to need more than a few minutes."

"We have to meet Lisa at ten."

Kayla checked her watch. "We have about an hour, but I don't know if you're going to be in any condition to go anywhere."

"I'll make it. I just need the pounding in my temples to stop."

"Maybe the aspirin will help," she said.

"I hope so."

He closed his eyes, and after a few moments of silence she thought he'd drifted off to sleep. She started to get up, thinking she'd sit in the chair by the window so she wouldn't disturb him, but he reached for her. "Don't go," he said, opening his eyes again. "Just... stay with me."

There was something in his eyes that spoke of a need he couldn't verbally express, and it touched her. Nick was such a strong man. He hated to show any kind of weakness.

"Okay." She stretched out next to him. He put his arm around her shoulder and pulled her up against his side. She rested her head on his chest and let out a sigh as her world tilted back into place. She closed her eyes and tried to relax. It was surprisingly easy. In Nick's arms, her tension evaporated. She felt safe and secure -- and that was the last thought she had until she woke up abruptly, startled by the ringing of a phone.

She glanced at the clock. It was two o'clock in the morning, and Nick's cell phone was ringing. She tried to move, and then realized that she and Nick were completely entangled. His arm was around her waist; one of his legs pinned her down as if he'd worried that she might try to leave while he was sleeping.

Kayla gave him a gentle push. "Nick, wake up," she said.

He blinked sleepily, his face just inches from her own. "Hmm," he murmured, then leaned over and kissed her.

Kayla's mouth opened to say no, but she couldn't get the word out because Nick's tongue was sliding into her mouth, tasting, exploring, driving all thoughts of *no* completely out of her mind. She wrapped her arms around his back, pulling him down on top of her, loving the feel of his chest against her breasts, his leg between her thighs.

She ran her hands under his shirt, tracing the contours of his muscles. He groaned at her touch, and a second later he sat up and pulled his shirt over his head. The sleep slowly faded from his eyes, awareness settling in.

He touched her mouth with his fingers, then let his hand drift down her chin, dropping to her collarbone, skimming her breasts, making her nerves tingle and desire sweep through her. She put a hand around his neck and pulled him down to her. His lips had barely grazed hers when his cell phone rang. She suddenly realized what had woken her up in the first place. "Your phone," she said.

Nick glanced at her, then over at the phone on the bedside table. "It's never good news in the middle of the night."

"You'd better answer it."

He reached out and grabbed his phone. "Hello." A moment later she heard him suck in a deep gulp of air. "What? Are you serious?"

Kayla sat up in bed. Nick's entire body had stiffened, and his lips were drawn in a tight line. "Right. Yes, I've got it."

He closed the phone and tossed it on the table.

"What's happened?" she asked impatiently. "Who was that?"

"J.T." Nick turned to face her. "Lisa Palmer was assaulted when she got home tonight. She's in the hospital.

J.T. said her house was searched. The watch is more than likely gone."

Kayla clapped a hand to her mouth. "Oh, my God! We were supposed to meet her at ten. We fell asleep. We didn't go." It took her a minute to catch up. "What happened to her? Is she going to be all right?"

"J.T. says she's unconscious. It looks like someone pushed her down the stairs."

"Do you think it was the same guy who knocked you out?"

"It's a good bet that it was either him or Evan. We know both of them are here in Reno."

"I can't believe it. Everywhere we go trouble follows."

"J.T. will meet us here in the morning. He said to stay put. Not to go anywhere. Not to talk to anyone. The usual drill."

Kayla drew her legs up beneath her, feeling chilled. "That poor woman. We did this, Nick. We found her. We led the bad guys straight to her. And now she's hurt. God, I feel terrible."

Nick sat down next to her, resting his back against the headboard. "Evan was at Lisa's house before we even got here.

Remember?"

"That's true. He found her first. I wonder how."

"Who knows? The bottom line is that the watch is probably gone. That's two down, one to go."

"Which leaves Frankie and his watch." She slid down in the bed, resting her head on the pillows. "Every time we talk to someone, they get hurt. I don't know how to keep searching without leaving chaos and pain in our wake. I'm frustrated, Nick."

"Me, too." He stretched out next to her, his head propped up by his elbow. "I wish I hadn't answered the phone -- for a lot of reasons."

She felt her cheeks flush at his words and the look in his eyes. "I think that moment has passed, Nick."

"I was afraid you were going to say that. My mind is still a little blurry. What exactly happened? I know we came back to the room, and I closed my eyes for a few minutes."

"And we fell asleep. The next thing I knew you were kissing me," she said.

"Really? I thought maybe you were kissing me," he replied, mischief in his expression, as he shifted closer to her.

She cleared her throat as his hand rested on her stomach, the heat from his fingers burning through her T-shirt.

"I remember thinking how much I like waking up with you. You're so soft, so warm," he murmured, tracing circles on her abdomen.

She caught his wrist. "I think you're ad-libbing now."

He smiled but there was an element of seriousness in his eyes. "I want to make love with you, Kayla. That moment hasn't passed for me."

"You're hurt, Nick. It's not a good idea."

"Haven't you ever heard of kissing the boo-boo?" he asked with a grin.

"I don't think it's your boo-boo you're wanting me to kiss."

"You are a smart woman."

"Am I?" she asked with a sigh. She pushed a strand of hair away from his bruised forehead, reminded that Nick could have been killed earlier, and so could she. "I feel out of my league, in uncharted territory."

"So am I," he said, "and I'm not talking about Evan or

watches or missing coins."

Her heart skipped a beat at the intent in his gaze. "Me?" she asked in surprise.

"Yes, you. You make me want..."

He left his sentence hanging, and it drove her crazy. "I make you want what?"

He shook his head. "I don't think we should be talking right now. I might have a concussion. Who knows if I'm thinking straight? Who knows what I'm saying?"

She frowned. "That's a stall if I ever heard one. You can't just start a sentence like that and leave it hanging."

"Let's leave it at this." His thumb stroked her jaw as he leaned in and kissed her again. "Good night."

"You're just going to sleep?" she asked in surprise as he rolled onto his back. She'd thought one kiss would lead to another.

"You told me to rest," he said, closing his eyes. "If you've changed your mind, just tap me on the shoulder."

She saw the smile play across his lips and realized he was enjoying this a little too much. She had no choice but to turn the tables. She ran her hand down his chest, his abdomen, between his thighs, and along his rapidly arising erection.

"Uh, Kayla, that's not my shoulder," he muttered.

She laughed. "I know. And, Nick -- I have changed my mind."

* * *

If his head wasn't throbbing, he would have felt great, Nick thought as he woke up wrapped around Kayla's soft, luscious, naked body, his face buried in her hair. He'd never felt so much chemistry with a woman, so much satisfaction. When he was with her, everything was right with the world. God, that sounded corny, like some stupid Hallmark card. It was sex. They were just enjoying each other. It was physical.

Maybe it was a little mental. Just a little.

Maybe a few emotions were involved, too. Just a few.

Oh, hell, who did he think he was kidding? Certainly not himself. He liked Kayla. He liked the contradictions she presented, the vulnerability mixed with bravery, the innocence combined with passion, her determination to fight back tempered by her worry that someone else might get hurt. He also liked the way she kissed, the way she moved, the way she generously welcomed him into her body, and he especially liked the way she smiled at him. It quite literally made his heart stop and his body harden, and just like that he was ready to go again.

She stirred in his arms, waking up like a cat with a sensuous stretch against his body that made every nerve tingle.

"Hmm," she said sleepily.

His hand drifted down her stomach, teasing at the juncture of her thighs. He thought he could produce a better response than *hmm* without too much effort.

"Nick," she said, more awake now. She blinked. "Is that the time?"

He gazed over her shoulder at the clock. "I think so."

"We have to get up. We have to meet J.T."

"We have time," he said hopefully.

"I don't think so, Nick. And if we don't meet J.T., I'm sure he'll find his way up here."

"I'll put the Do Not Disturb sign on the door."

"I don't think that will keep out the FBI. I'm getting dressed."

"Really? Now?"

She laughed as she twisted from his arms and jumped out of bed, showing off her gorgeous ass as she walked into the bathroom. She popped her head back out the door. "Of course, if you want to take a shower with me, we could save some time that way."

And now he knew what else he liked about her...she was very efficient.

* * *

They entered the hotel coffee shop an hour later. J.T. sat with his back to the wall, his eyes on the door. He was dressed in jeans and a brown leather jacket. As they drew closer, J.T. gave them a grim nod. He looked tired, as if he'd been up all night. His eyes were bloodshot, and he needed a shave.

"Hey," J.T. said. "At least you two are still in one piece."

"So to speak," Nick replied, realizing he needed to fill J.T. in on some of their other adventures in Reno. "I forgot to mention that someone jumped me last night, and grabbed Kayla, too. It wasn't Evan."

"Why didn't you tell me this before?"

"My head was a little thick when you called in the middle of the night."

"Great, that's great."

Nick pulled out a chair and sat down next to Kayla. "What have you learned?"

"Lisa Palmer recovered enough to say that someone pushed her down the stairs. Unfortunately, she didn't see who it was. I also spoke with her sister, Beth, who confirmed that Evan did, in fact, approach her yesterday about buying the watch."

"Is Lisa going to be all right?" Kayla asked.

"She's lucky. She has a broken wrist and a fractured collarbone. Otherwise, she'll be fine."

"Thank God for that," Kayla said, exchanging a quick look with Nick.

He saw the compassion in her eyes and also the fear. Lisa Palmer could have been killed. They both knew that. "What else?" Nick asked.

"The watch is gone."

"Of course it's gone. Evan got there before us, as usual."

"Because you didn't call me and tell me you were coming here to track down Lisa Palmer. If you had, I might have gotten to her house first," J.T. said pointedly.

"I called you when we got here," Nick retorted, his gut burning at the criticism. Still, he knew J.T. had a point. He could have called him the minute they found out about Lisa's existence, but he hadn't. He wasn't used to asking for help.

"Do you know who else is involved?" Kayla asked, interrupting what had become a tense silence. "The man who grabbed me earlier was shorter than Evan. He seemed bigger, more muscular, and his arm around my neck felt thick, powerful. I wish I could have seen his face."

Nick's stomach rolled at the thought of Kayla being strangled by some stranger while he was knocked out cold. *Dammit.* He'd screwed up there, too. He wouldn't make that mistake again. He'd keep her safe. He'd keep them both safe.

"That's not much to go on," J.T. replied, "but I can run back through some of Evan's earlier cons, figure out if there's anyone out of jail who might be helping him. In general Evan works alone. We did, however, find some prints at Ms. Palmer's house. We'll run them through the system, see if we can ID our third party. In the meantime, has it occurred to either one of you that you're not chasing Evan -- he's using you to get these other watches?"

"Of course that's occurred to us," Nick snapped. "But if you have a better plan, I haven't heard it. You've had years to catch Evan, and you haven't come close."

"That was a cheap shot."

"Just calling it like I see it," Nick said.

"Nick," Kayla warned. "We're on the same side."

J.T.'s gaze didn't waver. He leaned forward. "You're right, Nick. I've made mistakes, and I made them by acting the same way you're acting now -- as if it's personal, as if this is between you and Evan or between Evan and me. It's not. There are other people involved, innocent people who could get hurt, who are getting hurt," he amended. "You and Kayla need to go home and let me do my job."

Nick heard what J.T. was saying, but he couldn't promise to stay out of it. He could only agree to be more careful.

Chapter Fifteen

Nick refused to let Kayla drive back from Reno. Even though his head was still aching, he preferred to be in the driver's seat. At least he could pretend he had some semblance of control over his life. He cast a quick glance at her as he saw her pull out her cell phone. "Who are you calling?"

"My grandmother. I want to make sure she's all right." She waited a moment and then blew out an impatient breath. "She's not answering. I wonder where she is? It's Tuesday morning. I don't think there's anything specific she does on Tuesdays." She shot Nick a worried look. "Do you think she's all right?"

"I'm sure she is. If your grandmother were a target, someone would have gone after her long ago."

"I don't know if that's true, but I appreciate your effort to reassure me. J.T. was pretty annoyed with us."

Nick shrugged. "I don't care."

"Just how close were you two in college? You don't seem all that friendly now."

Nick considered her question, wondering why it seemed so difficult to answer. "We were good friends. We met in the dorms freshman year, then moved into an apartment together our junior year with Evan and another guy named Garrett Thompson."

"Really? Someone else was also there? Is he on Evan's hit list as well?"

"I don't know. Garrett did turn on Evan, but not like J.T. and I did. He was more on the sidelines. After the Evan fiasco, J.T.

moved into a frat house, and I got a studio apartment. We didn't see each other much." He paused. "I probably acted like a jerk back then. I was pissed off at everyone, including J.T. I didn't think anyone did enough to help me nail Evan and get him away from my sister. Evan came between J.T. and myself, and even after he was gone, I guess we just didn't ever get back together as close as we'd been. Neither one of us made the effort."

"What about Jenny? What happened to her after she got hurt?"

"She left school right away. She moved back home. My family lived down in Monterey at the time. She was so angry with me, she told me not to come home. So I stayed away. Eventually, as the years passed, we were able to reconnect. But I suspect she hated me for a long time. She could never look me in the eye. There was a part of herself that she hid from me."

"She must know that whatever you did, you did out of love. You wanted to protect her."

"I think she believed I wanted to ruin her life. She didn't like me playing big brother, or substitute dad, as she used to call it. But I didn't have a choice. When my father left, my mother fell apart. Jenny and my other sister, Dee, needed someone to hold things together, to look after them, so I did. They didn't appreciate it. But I didn't do it for their appreciation. I did it because it was the right thing to do."

"I know," she said.

He gave her a quick glance and saw understanding in her eyes, maybe even a little respect. "Thanks."

He slowed down as they began to weave through the mountains. The two-lane highway twisted and turned as they crossed the summit at Donner's Lake, an area infamous for the Donner party's tragic and cannibalistic journey across the high Sierras. Fortunately, there wasn't much traffic, so they were making good time.

As a curve came up, Nick pressed down on the brake. It was softer than he expected, sluggish. The pedal seemed to be touching the floor, but the car was not slowing down. The road grew steeper. Signs warned of a downgrade ahead, slow trucks, hot brakes.

"Nick, what's wrong?" Kayla asked, her hand gripping the armrest. "You're going awfully fast."

"The brakes aren't working well," he said as calmly as he could.

He could hear her gasp. "What? What do you mean?"

How could he tell her the truth? The brakes were gone. Someone had tampered with them. Someone wanted them dead -- now. It was no longer about what might occur but what was actually happening. He looked at Kayla. She knew it, too.

"God, Nick. We're going to die, aren't we?"

"Not if I can help it."

He hung on to the wheel, steering as best he could as their speed increased. He had to move back and forth between lanes to avoid the slower traffic. He pushed down on the brakes again and again, downshifted as far as he could go. The motor grunted, whirred, but the Honda was still picking up speed. The road was too steep. He prayed for a turnout, but there was nothing, nowhere to go.

If he turned to the left, they would crash into a mountain of rock. If he turned to the right, they'd go over the mountainside, down into the ravines and canyons and rivers hundreds of yards below. He battled as long as he could, but the car was out of control.

The road curved too suddenly. They crashed through a flimsy guardrail, the splintered metal flying past them as they hurtled into space. He couldn't see anything but blue, blue sky. It seemed to take forever to land. Maybe dying wasn't going to hurt that much, he thought, just before they hit the ground with a body-pounding thud.

Instinctively he threw his arm in front of Kayla, but it was futile. He couldn't protect her from what was about to come.

* * *

Evan got back to San Francisco in record time. He'd borrowed a sexy red convertible from the Peppermill parking lot for his trip home. Not for the first time he thought about how perfect Jenny would look in the front seat. She needed to loosen up a little, let her beautiful brown hair blow in the breeze, smile the way she used to, as if she didn't have a care in the world, as if there were nothing but possibilities before her. No limitations. No rules. No big brother trying to make her feel guilty.

Jenny was the only woman he'd ever known who had almost made him believe that life could be good. For those few months, she'd shown him another side of the world, the light side. She'd accepted him as if he were just like any other guy on that college campus. She'd believed in him like no one had ever believed in him. She hadn't thought he was a worthless piece of shit, as his own mother had told him over and over again.

Jenny had looked at him as if he were her hero, a damned white knight in shining armor. Until Nick had gotten into her head, confused her, told her lies, made it all seem worse than it was. So what if he'd made some money off those stupid rich kids. They could well afford to lose every dime, and could always go running back to their daddies and their big, deep pockets of endless cash. But Nick had made it sound like he was some threat to society. That he might even hurt her -0 his sweet Jenny.

No, he would never hurt her. He'd stayed away for a long time. Kept her out of his world. He wouldn't take her back until it was time, until he could show her that he was the best of the best. He would shower her with presents. He would pamper her. He would have the family he deserved.

She might be angry about what he'd done to Nick, but he would talk her around. He would make her see that she didn't need a big brother; she needed him. Together they would conquer the world. She wouldn't have to go to that silly salon, spend all her time on her feet, cutting hair, looking like an old lady by the end of a long Saturday. He'd make sure she had pedicures and manicures and massages. He'd treat her like his queen. He smiled at the thought, imagining them ruling the world.

Jenny had always worked too hard. She and Nick certainly had that work ethic in common. Not that Nick was doing much work now. He was too busy chasing his tail.

Nick and Kayla were playing right into his hands. Kayla must have learned about Lisa Palmer from her grandmother. He'd suspected the old broad knew more than she was saying. His instincts about people were always on the money. He should have played Charlotte for more information, instead of letting himself get sidetracked....

He never should have agreed to work with anyone, especially

not with someone who thought she was calling the shots, who thought she was smarter than he was -- as if that were remotely possible. For the meantime he would let things ride. When it suited him to end their arrangement, he would.

His cell phone rang, and he answered it with one simple word: "What?"

"Did you get it?"

"Of course."

"I can't believe she had it."

"I can't believe I spent two weeks chasing down fruitless leads in Nate's family. I'm done following your suggestions."

"You're not through yet," she reminded him. "And there are others talking now. That old bitch Charlotte is stirring people up."

"She can't stop us."

"What about her granddaughter and her friend?"

"Not a problem."

"I disagree. They've outlived their usefulness, Evan. And they're distracting you. I want them gone."

"I told you to leave Nick and Kayla to me. They won't get in the way again."

* * *

"Forgive me, Father, for I have sinned." Charlotte knelt in the dark confessional, seeing the shadow of the priest through the small window panel. He waited for her to go on. "It has been..." She hesitated before continuing. "It has been a very long time since my last confession."

"And to what sins do you wish to confess?" he asked in a deep baritone that held the wisdom of his faith and probably his years.

She had known that the monsignor was hearing confessions today, which was why she had come. The monsignor wasn't just anyone; he was Johnny's half brother, born to Johnny's mother and another man. Marcus Serrano was younger than Johnny by seventeen years, and he had to be in his late fifties now. He'd been at St. Basil's the past twenty years, and she doubted anyone there knew he was Johnny Blandino's half brother. They didn't share a last name, and they certainly didn't share the same values. She'd never spoken to Marcus, never made any attempt to contact him, to ask any questions, not since Johnny had gone to jail.

She truly had left the past behind -- until now.

"I have lied," she said. "But before I tell you more, I need to ask you a question. I need to know if it's you, Marcus Serrano."

She waited for what seemed like an interminable length of time.

"Why do you need to know?" he asked in a low voice.

"Because it's me, Charlotte Cunningham. I dated your brother, Johnny, a long time ago. We took you to the park with us a few times. We bought you mocha-fudge ice cream. It was your favorite."

The priest cleared his throat. "Go on."

"I have come to ask you a question about Johnny. I couldn't risk speaking to you anywhere in public. I think someone is watching me."

"I'm listening," he said.

"Is Johnny alive? Did he make it to shore? Has he been in hiding all these years?"

"Why would you ask me these questions?" he countered. "He was presumed dead many years ago."

"I understand that, but no body was ever found." She drew in a deep breath. "I need to know if Johnny is behind what's happening now, if he's come back after all these years to reclaim what was his."

"What's happening now?"

"Someone stole his watch, the pocket watch he treasured so much. And the watches belonging to the other men -- someone is looking for them. I believe they are after the missing money and perhaps some of Johnny's other secrets."

"And you know these other secrets?"

Charlotte was almost afraid to answer. But he was a priest. She could trust him, couldn't she? "I know a few things," she said. "But I worry that someone knows more, someone who wants more."

"The treasure," he mumbled.

"Yes," she said. "Johnny loved you so much. I thought he might have told you something, might have wanted to make things easier for you and your mother. I thought if he had come back, you might be the one person he felt he could trust. As a priest, you would keep his confessions."

"I would," he agreed.

"Can you tell me if he's alive?"

"I'm afraid I can't," he said after a moment. "You said it yourself. I'm a priest. What is said to me remains with me."

Her heart sank. "It's just that I really need to know."

"All things are revealed when they should be."

She supposed he meant that statement to be comforting, but it wasn't. She'd had to believe Johnny was dead; it was the only way she'd gotten through the years. But now she wondered.

"Is there anything else I can help you with?" he asked. "Perhaps you can tell me more about the trouble you're in."

Charlotte hesitated, not sure if it was wise to say anything more. She'd kept her own counsel for so long, it was difficult to trust anyone else. "It's all right. But if you do see Johnny or can get a message to him -- if he's alive, that is -- I still don't know..." She tried to gather her thoughts together. "Tell him that if he has anything left to protect, he should do it. Before it's too late. Oh, and tell him that I kept the two things apart as he asked, just in case."

"What two things?"

"He'll know what I mean." She paused. Marcus's answers had set her nerves on edge. If Johnny were dead, wouldn't he have said so? "Can't you just tell me if he's alive?"

"I'm sorry." The window between them closed, and she let out a breath. She said a silent prayer, not sure God would listen to her. She hadn't always acted in his honor in the past, but maybe he'd forgiven her for being young and stupid and in love. Not that any of those traits excused her actions.

She pressed her hands together and murmured, "Dear Lord, please help me to do the right things now. Please help me to make all this right. And watch over Kayla, Lord. She's an innocent girl. Protect her. Keep her safe. That's really the most important thing." She made the sign of the cross and got to her feet.

When she left the confessional, she noticed that the door to the center booth where the priest sat was open, but they were supposed to be holding confession for another hour.

Was it a coincidence? Or had she just made another mistake by opening a door to the past that should have stayed closed?

* * *

Kayla smelled smoke. Was someone cooking? But it wasn't barbecue. It smelled more like gas. She blinked, wondering why she couldn't move. Was she asleep? Was this one of those dreams where you couldn't get out, couldn't scream, couldn't move? She tried to fight the weight holding her down. Her eyes were so heavy. They wouldn't open.

"Kayla."

She heard Nick's voice, but he sounded far away, as if he were in a tunnel or underwater. How could he be underwater? They were... Where were they? Why couldn't she remember?

They were in Reno. Nick got hit over the head. They had made incredible love to each other all night long. Wait, that was yesterday, wasn't it? Why was her head so fuzzy? Why couldn't she think?

"Kayla, wake up. For God's sake, wake up. We have to get out of here."

He sounded so impatient, so determined. But that was Nick. Always in a hurry. He was so strong, so confident. She knew he could do anything he put his mind to. Whenever she thought she couldn't take another step, Nick inspired her to try harder. He'd pulled her out of the hole she'd fallen into when Evan disappeared. Together they were going to beat Evan. They were going to take him down. She would get her life back.

"Kayla, dammit. If you can hear me, open your eyes. Or squeeze my hand. I can feel your pulse. I know you're breathing. But just barely."

She heard the panic in his voice. He sounded scared. Why was he scared?

She felt his hand closing around hers. His warmth seeped into her body, making her realize how cold she felt. She squeezed his hand, wanting to take in more of his heat, wanting to reassure him that she was all right. But was she all right?

Other images flashed through her brain. The mountains, the road, the speed. Everything was going by too fast. She'd begged Nick to stop and then they'd gone over the side....

Her eyes flew open. She stared into Nick's worried face.

"Thank God," he murmured.

"Are we alive?"

He tried to smile, but she saw the fear. "We are alive, but we have to get out of the car as soon as possible." He was speaking calmly, but there was an urgent note in his voice. "First you have to tell me if anything hurts. Do you feel any pain anywhere?"

She tried wiggling her toes. She felt a pain in her ankle. "My ankle hurts."

"Okay. Anything else? What about your back or your neck or your head?"

"I don't think so." She realized then that the air bag was crushing her, and something heavy seemed to be on top of that. "What's on top of me?"

"We crashed into a tree. It smashed in the door. Can you move at all? Don't try if anything hurts."

She tried to push herself up and out of the seat, but she made it only about six inches and then sank back down. "I'm stuck."

"I'm going to go outside and try to get the door off of you," he said. "All right?" He stroked her head with his hand. "We're going to be okay."

"You're scared."

"No, not me. I'm never scared."

She thought he was lying, but she played along. "Okay then, Superman, why don't you see if you can rip that door off?"

"No sweat."

As he got out of the car on the driver's side, the smell of gas grew stronger. And there was some smoke coming from the hood of the car. Kayla realized then where his fear was coming from. If the car caught fire, she'd be trapped. Her pulse began to race as she finally became fully aware of the situation. *Oh, God,* she prayed, *please get me out of here.*

Nick swore as he yanked at the door and nothing happened. He pulled away a large branch from the side of the door. She felt the pressure on her ease slightly. She gave another wiggle and was able to move a bit more out of the seat.

"That helped, Nick. Whatever you did, do it again," she yelled.

"I'm going to stick this branch in through the window," he told her. "Try to get some leverage. Okay?"

She nodded. The window was already shattered, and she realized there was glass all over her sweater. Maybe she was cut. She was starting to feel twinges of pain on her face. Well, it didn't matter. She had to get out of the car; she'd deal with her injuries later.

Nick pushed on the branch. The door groaned. The car slid a few inches forward. She realized they were on the side of the hill. A tree had stopped their forward motion, but if the car shifted a bit more to the left they'd slide farther down the mountain. She tried not to think about it. Nick grunted with his effort, but he still had no luck. The smoke coming out of the hood was getting darker, thicker.

"It's no good," she cried as Nick paused to catch his breath. "The car is on fire, isn't it?"

"No."

She could see the lie in his eyes. "You have to go, Nick. You have to get out of here."

"I'm not leaving you, Kayla."

She didn't want him to leave, but she also didn't want him to die. "I think you have to. I can't get out."

"I'm not leaving you, and you are getting out of that car. Don't argue with me." He leaned through the shattered glass and gave her a quick kiss. "We can do this."

Nick threw all his weight against the branch, trying to use it to crank open the door. The car began to slide. The branch began to crack. And the smoke grew blacker, thicker, hotter.

Finally the door moved -- just a few inches, but it was enough. Kayla grappled with the air bag as she pulled herself out through the open window -- straight into Nick's arms. He caught her in a tight hug. Then he grabbed her hand. "Let's get out of here."

"Wait, my purse. The key is in there," she said.

Nick reached back into the car and grabbed her bag; then they turned toward the hill. "Go up," he said. "We need to get help."

They scrambled up the steep terrain, slipping and sliding. Kayla saw blood dripping onto her hands. She didn't know where it was coming from. She didn't have time to look.

It was a hard climb, but a quick glance back at the car showed bright yellow and orange flames jumping out of the hood. A moment later the car exploded. The force knocked her to the ground. Nick was suddenly on top of her, pressing her into the dirt as rocks and tree branches fell down on their heads. When the fiery rush was over, they bolted farther up the mountain, until they finally got to the top, to the broken guardrail that had done nothing to prevent their crash.

Kayla sank onto the pavement, gasping for air. Nick knelt down next to her, his gaze searching her body, probably noting every cut, every bruise.

"Are you all right?" he asked.

"Thanks to you." Her eyes filled with tears, and her lower lip trembled. "I think I'm going to cry now," she whispered.

He put his arms around her and pressed his lips to her forehead. "I think I am, too."

"You saved my life, Nick. Someone tried to kill us." The realization finally sank all the way in. Someone had tampered with the brakes on their car. Someone had wanted them to die. Evan. It had to be him. *God!* She hadn't just married a con man. She'd married a murderer.

Chapter Sixteen

Kayla and Nick spent the night in a small hotel in Auburn, a city at the base of the Sierras near the hospital where the paramedics had taken them after the accident. Aside from a mild sprained ankle and numerous cuts and bruises suffered by both, they'd escaped unharmed. A hot bath in the hotel tub, a good dinner, and ten hours of sleep had made Kayla feel a whole lot better. She was almost sorry when Nick said it was time to leave. But he was right. They'd eaten breakfast. They'd rented a car, since her Honda was completely totaled. It was time to go home.

They didn't speak much during the trip. Kayla didn't know about Nick, but she was still having a hard time coming to grips with the fact that they'd almost died, that they should have died. The paramedics had taken one look at the crash site and shaken their heads in amazement that they were alive to talk about it.

"You're quiet," she commented as the traffic began to thicken the closer they got to San Francisco.

"There's a lot to think about."

"Like what to do next?"

"Like where to put you so you'll be safe," he replied.

She turned sideways in her seat, hearing the stubbornness in his voice. "We're a team, Nick. Where you go, I go. Don't you know that by now?"

"I didn't think I was going to get you out of that car," he confessed. He glanced over at her, and she could see the pain and fear lingering in his eyes.

"But you did," she reminded him. "You didn't leave me when you probably should have." She was still amazed by the selfless courage he'd shown under fire. She wondered if she would have done the same. It was one thing to be trapped and another to stay in a situation where you could leave. "You didn't quit on me, Nick, and I'm not going to quit on you."

"It's too dangerous, Kayla. I never should have involved you in any of this."

"Involved me? I'm the one Evan started with, Nick. I'm the one who had the watch."

"But I'm the one who encouraged you to go after him."

"It's pointless to argue about it now. We're in too far to stop. And I'm a little pissed off that someone tried to kill me yesterday, so if it's all the same to you, I'm not going to crawl into bed and pull the covers over my head." She saw Nick smile. "Did I say something amusing?"

"I like your spirit. You have a lot of guts, Kayla."

"I think you're inspiring me."

"No, it's all you."

She blinked and turned her gaze out the window, not wanting him to see how his words had touched her. She was feeling emotional after their brush with death, and she was probably reading more into his statement than he'd intended. "So what should we do next?"

"I've been thinking about that. We need to connect even more with the past than we already have. It seems that your grandmother has probably told us most of what she knows." He paused. "You're going to have to tell her what happened to the car. I noticed you didn't mention it last night when you spoke to her on the phone."

"I didn't want to worry her. I just wanted to warn her to keep the doors and windows locked and to keep an eye out for Evan or anyone else. She said she'd be careful, but I could tell she was worried, too. I hope there isn't more that she hasn't told me." She took a breath. "So how else do you propose we connect with the past?"

"Well, we know the men grew up in North Beach and went to Catholic school at St. Basil's. Maybe we should go to the church, see if anyone there remembers them. We still need to figure out what happened to Frankie's watch."

"True," she said. "But I hope we don't bring trouble to the good people of St. Basil's. It seems to follow us wherever we go."

"Let's just hope that whoever tried to kill us yesterday thinks they succeeded."

"That's a lovely thought."

"Do you know where St. Basil's is?"

"Of course. I know where every church in the city is. That's my business. Not that I've spent much time on my business lately."

"I can always drop you off at home. You can catch up on your work."

"We've already discussed this, Nick. I work for myself, so I have a flexible schedule. Just drive and stop trying to get rid of me."

* * *

St. Basil's Church was located in a quiet, residential block in North Beach. It took up most of the block, with the church on the corner and the elementary school right next to it, a large playground running between the two. There were children playing in the yard. It was probably recess or lunchtime, Kayla thought. They all looked so sweet and innocent, dressed in their blue-and-white-checkered uniforms.

"Hard to believe our band of criminals went to school here," Nick said, surveying the scene.

"And they were altar boys," she reminded him.

"Apparently, they didn't learn the Ten Commandments, especially the one about 'Thou shalt not steal.'"

"Sometimes we hear only what we want to hear."

They walked up the steps to the church. Kayla tried the door. It was open. At the far end of the large sanctuary, a group of children and a teacher were practicing a song accompanied by the piano. Another woman was setting up flower arrangements by the altar. It was a beautiful, peaceful church, and Kayla felt a sense of serenity as she walked inside. Sunlight streamed through the gorgeous stained-glass windows.

"These are some of my favorites," Kayla murmured. Her low-pitched voice probably wasn't necessary. No one was paying any attention to them. The children were singing, the pianist was playing, and the teacher was giving instructions in between the beats.

"Nice," Nick said, studying the windows.

"Nice?" she echoed. "They're more than nice; they're spectacular, the way the light comes in through the glass, changing the colors."

He smiled down at her. "Your passion is showing."

"I want you to appreciate what you're seeing. These windows came from Austria, probably in the early nineteen hundreds."

"How do you know that?"

"I've been here before. I've studied every window in every church in the city. They each tell a story." She pointed to the nearest one. "That one is called the Nativity window. See the row of anemones blooming along the bottom lower panel? In German folklore, where every drop of blood fell on the Lord's walk to Calvary an anemone sprouted."

"I never would have noticed that little detail," Nick admitted.

"In the next window, the Annunciation, there are thornless roses blooming at the feet of Gabriel, whose wings shine with the iridescence of a peacock's feather, another symbol of Christ. And some people believe that thornless roses are a lovely way to depict the Immaculate Conception."

"Interesting."

"The best part of stained glass is that different light changes the picture so these very same windows will look different in the morning sun than they will at dusk." She stopped abruptly, seeing the amusement in his eyes. "I'm boring you."

"You're stunning me," he corrected.

"There's just so much to be seen in each window, in the details."

He nodded, a sparkle of awareness coming into his eyes. "That's what we have to do, Kayla: look at the small details and not so much the big picture."

"How do we do that?"

"I don't know yet. How did four altar boys wind up leading lives of crime?"

"They were certainly taught differently."

"I think we should try to find a priest or one of those church secretaries who has been around for a hundred years."

"I'm sure we'll get that lucky," she said dryly.

"You never know."

"Let's go next door to the rectory. That would be the best place to find your secretary."

Unfortunately, the woman who opened the door couldn't have been more than forty years old. She had a round, cheerful face and gave them a welcoming smile. "How can I help you?" she asked.

"We'd like to speak to a priest," Kayla said. "Someone who has been here for a long time, if possible. I just found out that my grandfather used to be an altar boy here," she added. "He's dead now, but I'm trying to get some information about him."

The woman nodded. "Monsignor Serrano has served here for close to thirty-five years. I can see if he's free."

"I'd really appreciate it," Kayla said.

The woman ushered them into a small waiting area.

"That was weird, calling Johnny my grandfather," she said. "I think that's the first time I've said it out loud. It feels disloyal. I haven't had time to decide how I feel about it. I mean, I loved my real grandfather. And Johnny certainly was no prize of a guy. But we are tied by blood. I can't ignore that."

"You don't have to do anything about it, Kayla. They're both dead. You don't have to choose between them."

"You're right. It doesn't matter, does it?"

As she finished speaking, the woman reentered the room. "Father will see you now. He's in his office, down the hall, second door on the right."

"Thank you so much," Kayla murmured.

"Can I bring you coffee or tea?"

"I'm fine."

"No, thanks," Nick said.

They walked down the hall, and after a brief knock Nick opened the door.

A man who appeared to be in his mid-sixties sat behind a large mahogany desk. He wore the traditional black pants and shirt with a priest's collar. A pair of bifocals sat on the end of his beaklike nose. His eyes were a dark brown, his hair completely gray. He had freckled age spots on his face. He extended his hand to each of them as they introduced themselves and sat down in chairs in front of the desk.

"How may I help you?" he asked. "Rosemary tells me you are here to ask about some former parishioners from a long time ago."

"Yes, a very long time ago," Kayla said with a smile. "I understand that my grandfather went to school here and served as an altar boy. His name was Johnny Blandino. I wonder if you might possibly remember him."

His gaze sharpened on her face. "I wasn't aware that Johnny Blandino had any children."

She shifted in her seat, uncomfortable with his scrutiny. "It's a long story, but I have recently learned that I'm his granddaughter. He didn't marry my grandmother. He was sent to prison when she was a few months pregnant."

"I see."

"So did you know him? Can you tell me about him? How he went from being an altar boy to being a criminal?"

"He had a difficult life," Father Serrano said heavily. "His father killed himself when Johnny was eight years old. Johnny was the one who found the body."

It was a similar story to what her grandmother had told her.

"Johnny's mother drank a great deal after that," he continued. "She couldn't hold her life together for a long time. Her children ran wild. For years she struggled to turn things around. Finally she met a man, married him, and had two more children. She was a good mother to those two boys, but the older girls and Johnny didn't benefit from that. They were out of the house by then."

Kayla was surprised to get so much information. She pushed for more. "What about Nate and Frankie? And the other one, Dominic? What was the deal with their families?"

"Nate came from a big family. I think he often felt lost in the numbers, a nameless face at the table. He used to say that his father could never remember his name. I don't know much about Frankie. Dominic was a good man. He was more stable than the others, married young, had children. Didn't follow them down the wrong road like they wanted him to."

"We understand that Dominic disappeared off a boat or something?"

"That was very troubling." Father Serrano played with his fountain pen, twirling it in his fingers.

Silence followed his words. Kayla hoped he'd say more, but

he remained silent. "My grandmother said that Johnny was very religious," she continued. "She told me that he went to Mass every Sunday, and that she found that contradictory part of his personality very attractive. I assume he went to church here."

Father Serrano nodded. "Yes, he did. Johnny never forgot his faith, and I suspect that he came often to ask for forgiveness of his sins. Is that all?"

"Not quite," Kayla said quickly. "I'm trying to find other people who knew Johnny, who could tell me more about his life. I've spoken to people from Nate's family and Dominic's family, but no one seems to know anything about Frankie. Do you know if any of his relatives are still alive?"

Father Serrano set his pen down on the desk. "Frankie's parents died years ago. He was an only child. But he lived just around the corner. He spent a lot of time with one of the neighbor girls, Helen Perrini. She still lives in the neighborhood. She's married now. Her last name is Matthews. They have grandchildren who go to our school. I don't feel that it's appropriate for me to give out her number, but I can have her call you if she'd like to talk to you about Frankie."

"That would be great," Kayla said. She pulled a business card out of her purse. "Here are my numbers. She can call me on either one, and if you could let her know that it's really important, I'd appreciate it."

"I will," he said as he slowly got to his feet.

"There's something I'm curious about, Father," Nick said, speaking for the first time. "It's been more than fifty years since Johnny went to school here, and I suspect you were not a priest at that time. Yet you seem to remember him and the others so well. Why is that?"

The older man smiled. "I don't remember Johnny because he was a parishioner. I remember him because he was my brother."

Kayla sucked in a sharp air of disbelief. "What?"

"My half brother. Johnny's mother married my father. I was one of the two children she had with her second family. Johnny was a great deal older than me, almost seventeen years. But he used to take me out, buy me food, let me spend time with him and his friends."

"I can't believe it," Kayla said. "I guess that you and I are related. I'm related to all of Johnny's family. I didn't even think about that."

"Your grandmother," he said. "Her name is Charlotte?"

"Is that a lucky guess?" Kayla asked, suspecting it wasn't.

"I met her a few times. I could see that Johnny was infatuated with her. I wonder if he knew that he had a child."

"My grandmother says he did know that she was pregnant."

The priest slowly nodded. "I see."

She was glad he did, because she sure didn't. "Is there anything else you can tell me, Father?"

He hesitated. "Be careful."

Her nerves began to tingle. "That's an odd thing to say. Can you tell me why?"

"I'm afraid I can't. I have another appointment. It was very nice to meet you. Please come back another time. We can chat more."

"Thank you, I think I will."

Kayla followed Nick out of the rectory. They stopped on the front steps to regroup. "What do you think of that bombshell?" she asked. "Johnny's half brother is a priest here at the same church?"

Nick shrugged. "I can see why it's interesting to you that Johnny had a half brother, but I'm not sure how it plays out with everything else. He has other siblings, too."

"I just wasn't expecting to run into one here."

"What we really need to do is concentrate on Frankie. One of his friends or relatives has that last watch."

"Maybe this woman that Father Serrano knows will have a lead. But we'd better give J.T. her name so he can make sure nothing happens to her in the meantime."

"Good point."

As they walked down to the car, Kayla asked the most troubling question. "Why do you think Father Serrano told me to be careful?"

Nick met her gaze. "One reason comes to mind. If I escaped from prison and needed someone to protect my secret, I can't think of a better person than a half brother who is a priest, can you?"

A shiver ran down her spine. "Maybe my grandfather is alive. Maybe he's going after the coins. But wouldn't he know where they are? Wouldn't he have been able to get them before now?"

"I've been thinking about the fact that they all had watches and Evan apparently is collecting them. That fact would imply that the watches have to be together in order for something to emerge. We know two of the phrases: 'of Heaven Await' and 'Until the Day.'"

"Which don't seem to tell us anything. We must need the other two phrases. Or maybe we just need the key in each watch. Why would they go to such elaborate lengths? From all accounts the men were best friends, blood brothers, family."

"They were also greedy thieves who might not have trusted one another when it came to their loot."

"They stashed the money somewhere in the time between when they left the mint and were arrested." She thought for a moment. "Maybe that's something else we should investigate, the old robbery. There must be records somewhere."

"Good point. We should follow up on that." Nick paused as he got a call on his phone. "Hello? Jen? What's wrong? I can't understand you." He waited. "How long ago? Damn. You should have called me right away."

Kayla felt a knot develop in her stomach at the anger in Nick's voice. Something had happened. Something bad.

"Shit! Hell, yes, I'm coming over there." He hung up the phone, his face tight with rage.

"What's wrong?"

"Evan stopped by Jenny's shop earlier today. And she just called me now. I can't believe she didn't tell me right away." He hit the side of the car with his fist.

"Nick, you have to calm down. You don't know the whole story yet."

"Evan has some kind of crazy hold over my sister. That's the story. And I don't understand it. After everything she's been through, how can she still have a soft spot for the guy?"

Because Evan was probably still working Jenny, Kayla suspected. And he could certainly be charming when he wanted to be.

"I'm going to get him out of her system if I have to shake him out of her," Nick proclaimed.

"If she's still hung up on him after twelve years, I think you're going to need a better plan than that."

Chapter Seventeen

Jenny was standing at the cash register in her salon when they barged in fifteen minutes later. She was a slender woman about five feet, four inches tall, with dark, wavy brown hair like her brother and hazel eyes. Her pale face turned even whiter when she saw Nick. She finished accepting payment from a customer and put up a hand in warning. She sent one of the other stylists a quick look. "I'll be back in a few minutes. Family business." Taking Nick by the arm, she said, "Across the street. I'm not going to do this here."

She led them to a small park. "What happened to you? You're all banged-up."

"I'll tell you later. First, you talk."

"Okay. I-" She stopped abruptly, her gaze turning to Kayla. "I'm sorry. Who are you?"

"Kayla Sheridan. I can leave you two alone if you want."

"You're not going anywhere," Nick said sharply. "I can't be worrying where you are," he added, softening his tone a bit.

"You're the one who married Evan?" Jenny questioned.

"Yes, that's me," she said.

"You two can bond later," Nick interrupted. "Tell me what Evan said, Jenny. What was he doing here? Were you lying to me when you said you didn't know anything before?"

"Do you want to give me a chance to answer?" Jenny demanded.

"I'm not stopping you," he replied.

"I saw Evan a few months ago. It was a chance meeting, I thought. We ran into each other in the mall. We had a brief conversation. What I was doing, what he was doing."

"What he was doing? As if you could believe a word he said," Nick interjected.

"Please, Nick, if you want me to talk, then listen."

"Fine, go on."

"I admit that I was rattled after seeing him. And then he called me on my cell phone on my birthday. I was shocked that he'd gotten the number. I told him to leave me alone, that we couldn't be friends. I thought that was it until the presents came. I knew they were from Evan even though he didn't sign the cards. But he didn't come by, so I didn't do anything about it. However, after you came to the shop the other day to see me, Evan called again. And later he came to my apartment."

"Are you serious?" Nick asked in shock. "And you never thought to pick up the phone and call me, knowing that he'd robbed me?"

"I know I should have told you," Jenny replied. "I picked up the phone a half dozen times, but Evan said he would tell you something that I didn't want you to know. So I kept quiet. I'm not proud of myself, but I can't take it back."

Nick gave Jenny a long, searching look. "He was blackmailing you? You know you can tell me anything. There's nothing he could say about you that would change how I feel."

Jenny looked down at the ground, shifting her stance from one leg to the other.

Nick glanced over at Kayla, a plea in his eyes, but she didn't know how to help him. This was between the two of them. She almost felt as if she shouldn't be listening, but she knew Nick wanted her here, maybe even needed her here, so she was staying. And Jenny would have to deal with it.

"Just say it, Jen," Nick ordered. "It can't be that bad."

Jenny glanced over at Kayla, then back at her brother. "There was something you never knew about my relationship with Evan. I was pregnant that night I got stabbed. Fortunately, the knife missed the uterus, so it didn't hurt the baby, and it appeared that even though I'd lost some blood and suffered a shock, the baby would survive."

Nick started shaking his head in confusion and bewilderment. "You didn't have a baby. I would have known if you'd had a baby."

"I went back to Monterey when I got out of the hospital, remember? I asked you not to come home. I said I didn't want to see you. I didn't want you to know I was pregnant."

"What about Mom, Dee? They must have known. The neighbors. Our friends? How is it possible that I didn't know?"

"I didn't show for a long time, Nick. I was skinny. I wore baggy clothes. I didn't tell anyone. Mom and Dee figured it out, but I begged them not to tell you. I thought you'd want me to give up the baby or get an abortion, because Evan was the father, and you hated him."

"But I loved you," Nick said.

"You hated Evan more. You thought he betrayed you, took advantage of your friendship. I know you'll never admit that you had a friendship with him, but you did. He took you in. And you liked him. Until you realized-"

"That he was using me and you," Nick finished.

"Maybe. But sometimes I think it was more about what he did to you than what he did to me," Jenny said.

"That's not true."

"Anyway, it didn't matter in the end. I lost the baby when I was seven months pregnant. It stopped moving. They did an emergency C-section and the baby was..." Jenny closed her eyes, biting down on her lip, then finished, "The baby was dead. She had the cord wrapped around her neck."

"God, Jen." Nick put out a hand to her, but she stepped away, folding her arms in front of her chest, as if she needed the barrier between them.

Kayla saw the pain in Nick's expression and wanted to put her arms around him, but she couldn't move. She had to let them finish this out.

"I'm sorry," Nick added. "I'm sorry you went through that. I'm sorry you didn't think you could confide in me. Whatever I did, Jen, I was just trying to protect you."

"It wasn't your job to protect me, Nick. I was an adult, just two years younger than you. I had a right to make my own mistakes and love the people I wanted to love. I still have that right."

"Are you saying you love Evan?"

"No." Jenny immediately shook her head. "I didn't mean that."

"Maybe you did. Maybe it was a slip of the tongue."

"I'm done with Evan, but I will admit that there was something strong between us once, something I can't deny. It doesn't mean I want to go back or try to recreate our relationship. I don't. I am older and wiser. I know Evan is a thief. I understand that he works on the wrong side of the law a lot of the time. So don't look at me like I'm an idiot."

Nick dug his hands in his pockets, rocking back on his heels as he took a moment to think. "Did Evan know about the baby?"

"Yes. I told him," Jenny replied. "I wrote to him when he was in jail. I told him that she died." Her eyes grew misty, and she rubbed them with the back of her hand. "Sometimes when I go to the cemetery there are flowers there, and I think to myself that Evan must have come by. Because no one else, besides Mom and Dee, knows about the baby."

"All these years the three of you kept it a secret from me. Every Christmas, every Thanksgiving, no one said a word. God, what else didn't you tell me?"

Kayla felt her heart breaking at the pain in Nick's voice, and she could see that Jenny was hurting, too. She wished she could push them into each other's arms, so they could take back what they'd lost. But Nick had moved farther away, and Jenny stood alone, unmoving, almost as if she were a statue.

No one spoke for a long minute. Kayla couldn't take the silence. It certainly wasn't getting them anywhere.

"Jenny," she said.

Jenny cast her a surprised look, as if she'd forgotten Kayla was there. "What?"

"Why did you call Nick today? Did something happen?"

"Yes," Jenny admitted. "Evan came by earlier. He scared me. There was a gleam in his eyes that was a little off. He kept talking about impressing me with something. And then he started talking about getting together, being a couple, making a family, the family we should have had. I said we'd never be together again, but he just laughed. And he said I'd see." Jenny sat down on a nearby bench. She let out a breath of relief at finally having finished it all. "I'm sorry, Nick -- sorry I let you down in so many ways. I wish I could take it back, but I can't."

Nick stared at her, his face cold, masking his every emotion. Kayla had never seen him look so... sad. That was it, she realized. It was sadness more than anger, hurt that his family had left him out of something so important. She knew that feeling. She'd spent most of her life feeling exactly that way. There were no words to make it better. Maybe nothing even Jenny could say.

"Did Evan tell you anything else today?" Nick asked a moment later, obviously finished with the personal end of their conversation. "Did he discuss his plans with you -- his plans for Kayla and me, maybe the fact that he tampered with the brakes on Kayla's car and almost got us killed yesterday?"

Jenny's jaw dropped. "What?"

"You heard me. We ran off the road in the mountains. We were coming back from Reno -- where Evan was, by the way."

"He didn't say anything about you or Kayla," Jenny replied. "He just said that you think you know what he's after, but you don't. I'm sure he wanted me to tell you that. He was very deliberate in the way he said it."

Kayla tensed. "What did he mean?" she asked.

"I don't know," Jenny replied. "He smiled as if it were some sort of inside joke. And then he said he'd see me around."

"What the hell is he up to?" Nick muttered.

Kayla sat down next to Jenny. "You know him, right? Better than we do. Why do you think he does what he does? What's your theory?" She put up a hand as Nick started to interrupt. "I know your opinion. I want to hear what Jenny thinks."

Jenny gave her a sad smile. "Evan wants to belong. He wants to have a family, be a part of something. He was abused as a child and left to live on the streets. He didn't grow up with the moral boundaries that we did. You know why he cheated his way into Berkeley? Because he wanted to know what it was like to be a carefree college kid. He wanted to have that experience. He told me that once, and I believed him, because I could see that it was true. Evan has had to lie to survive. I'm not saying it excuses what he does, but you asked me what I thought," she added. "I think Evan tries to fit in by taking over someone else's life. I suspect that's why he lived at your apartment for so long, Nick. He didn't just want to rob you. He wanted to be you."

"That's sick."

"I think he *is* sick," Jenny admitted.

"I think so, too," Kayla muttered.

"Which makes him dangerous," Nick said. "Can we all agree on that?"

Jenny nodded. "Yes. And I promise, no more secrets. You'll know what I know as soon as I know it. But right now I really have to go back to work. I have customers." She got to her feet and gave Nick a hesitant, searching look, as if she weren't sure whether or not she should hug him. In the end she just left.

Kayla stood up. "Are you okay?"

"Me? I'm terrific."

"Okay, that was a little sarcastic."

"My sister lied to me," Nick said angrily. "My mother and my other sister covered it up. They all kept a secret from me. I don't get it."

"They were going to tell you when the baby was born."

"Were they?"

"You would have eventually seen a baby. I know there's nothing I can say that will make this right, so I'm not going to try to talk you out of being mad. But you need to stay focused. If Jenny, Evan's best friend of all time, thinks he's nuts, then he is. And we have to figure out what his next move is before he makes it. Let's go home. We can check in with J.T. and formulate a plan of attack." When Nick didn't move, she took his hand. "It's going to be okay."

He gazed down at her. "You can't make that promise Kayla."

"You're right, but I can make this promise: I'll never lie to you. I'll never keep a secret from you. And whatever it takes, I'm in this with you until the end. Okay?"

"You might be sorry-"

"I won't," she said. "I won't be sorry. Now give me the keys. I'm driving. You need to catch your breath."

Nick didn't know how he could catch his breath when his heart was racing and a thousand hammers of frustration were pounding against his temple. He couldn't believe his own sister had lied to him. He'd done everything he could to make sure Jenny was happy, that she had everything she needed. He'd never asked her to do anything in return, except stay away from Evan, and she couldn't do that one thing, not even now, not even knowing that Evan had robbed him of his life. Jenny had chosen Evan over him again and again and again.

The knowledge burned through his gut, making his stomach churn. It reminded him of how he'd felt when his father had walked out, choosing someone else over him, over his mother, over his sisters. Where the hell was the loyalty? Wasn't blood supposed to mean something? Wasn't family supposed to stick together? Obviously not his family.

He released a breath and rolled down the window, letting the air blow through the car. Kayla turned on the radio, searching for some music. He appreciated her lack of conversation. He needed to think.

A few minutes later, Kayla took an unexpected turn.

"Where are you going?" he asked.

"I'm hungry," she said. "How about a late lunch? I know a great chowder place on Pier Twenty-three. What do you think? Feel like a little break?"

"We have a lot to do." His protest was halfhearted. His conversation with Jenny had left him unsettled. He needed to get his feet back under him before they made another move.

"We'll talk while we eat."

"All right."

The trip across town was fast and easy. They found a parking place right by the pier and even managed to snag one of the coveted outdoor tables on a deck along the bay.

The sun was shining. The water was shimmering, and there was just enough wind to keep the air cool.

Nick immediately began to relax. He'd been feeling trapped ever since he'd come home and discovered that Evan had stolen his life. The view reminded him that the world was much bigger than the one he'd been living in the last week.

The waiter brought them drinks and an array of appetizers, from California rolls to fried zucchini, onion strings and beef ribs. Kayla thought it would be more fun to order a bunch of little dishes and share. And it was clear she was feeling more relaxed. The breeze was blowing through her long brown hair, but she didn't seem to care. She wasn't the kind of woman who had to be styled and perfectly made up every second of the day. She had a natural beauty: rosy cheeks, big eyes, long lashes, a sexy mouth. Even now, with her face scratched and cut, he thought she was the most beautiful woman he'd ever seen.

One look at her and he wanted her again, beneath him, on top of him, surrounding him. Making love to her was fast becoming an addiction he wasn't sure he'd be able to beat. Someday they would have to talk about it. But not today.

Kayla glanced over at him. "Are you feeling better?"

He could see the concern in her eyes and appreciated the simplicity of her question. She hadn't pushed for more discussion on Jenny or Evan, and for that he was grateful. "I'm okay," he said, taking a sip of water. "It's just been a long couple of days."

"You can say that again. And by the way, I don't think I'll be taking any mountain drives in the near future. That crash really spooked me." She shuddered at the memory.

"I can't believe we didn't die."

"It was amazingly lucky."

"It wouldn't have been your fault, you know."

He shrugged. "I was driving. I should have anticipated-"

"How could you have guessed someone would tamper with the brakes?" she cut in.

"Well, someone did knock me over the head and grab you. They didn't get what they wanted. I should have figured they'd try again."

"And they might try again," Kayla said. "I know that, Nick. I've got my eyes wide-open. I'm looking out for myself and for you, and I know you're doing the same. That's the best we can do right now. I just don't want you to feel like you're responsible for everything, for me specifically."

As if he could ever not feel that way. "It's my nature, Kayla. It's who I am."

She met his gaze, and he could see that she understood. "I know, Nick. But try not to be so hard on yourself. We're not dealing with a rational person. Evan is a madman. He's not predictable. He could do anything at any time. He could be anywhere." She looked around as she finished speaking and tipped her head toward a man sitting alone, a newspaper in front of his face. "He could be that guy."

Nick started, wondering if she was right. Then the waiter brought food to the man and he set his paper down, revealing a round face and a bald head.

"Okay, maybe not that guy," Kayla said. "But you know what I mean."

"Yeah, I know what you mean."

"I will admit that I'm glad you're with me," she added. "Evan has me rattled."

"You hide it well."

She sipped her Diet Coke, then said, "I want to stop by my grandmother's house after this, check in with her."

"Good idea." He paused as a small band began to warm up behind the bar area.

"I think we're going to have music," she said.

"Looks like it. I used to play the guitar. Not that well, though."

"Really?" she asked, resting her arms on the table. "I don't picture you as the guitar-picking type. You seem a little too tense for that."

"Are you saying I'm uptight?"

"No, just driven. You're not someone who can easily relax or let go of the little things."

"I'm afraid if I let go, all the balls I'm juggling will come tumbling down."

"Maybe that would be a good thing," she suggested. "Perhaps you try to do too much."

He sat back in his chair. "You might be right. I've been running for so long, I've forgotten how to go slow -- if I ever knew. My jobs are always on deadline, with money riding on every second of delay. There's a lot of pressure all the time. When I work on site, I work sixty-hour weeks. I barely sleep. The time just flies by. I look up and suddenly realize it's been three months, and I thought it was more like three weeks."

"I know what it means to get lost in work. At least it's a happy lost. You love what you're doing. I bet you're good at it. You're a smart man, very intuitive, purposeful."

"And I think you're very intuitive for noticing how great I am," he teased.

"Am I getting too complimentary for you? Making you

uncomfortable?"

Her wide-eyed smile always made him uncomfortable. "No. You can stroke my...ego... anytime."

She laughed. "That was bad."

He grinned back at her, wishing there weren't a table between them. He wanted to kiss her long and hard until she was breathless, until she made those soft little sounds in the back of her throat that drove him crazy. He wanted to touch her, circle her breasts with his hands, and lide into her warmth. He cleared his throat and reached for his water again. A cold shower would have been better, and for a moment he was tempted to dump the water over his head, but he managed to refrain.

"We should get the check," he said.

"You're in a sudden hurry."

"I am," he agreed, giving her a look she couldn't mistake.

She bit down on her bottom lip. "Oh."

"Oh," he echoed, waving to the waiter.

As he paid the bill, Kayla's cell phone rang. She immediately stiffened. "If that's Evan, I really don't want to talk to him right now."

"Do you want me to answer it?"

She let out a sigh. "I'm a big girl. I'll do it." Opening her phone, she said, "Hello? Yes, this is Kayla Sheridan." She paused, listening. "Oh, my God!" She put a hand to her mouth. "Yes, of course I'll come. Right away. Thank you." She hung up the phone and gave him a panicked look. "That was the hospital. My grandmother passed out. It might be a heart attack or a stroke. They don't know yet. They're running tests. I have to go there."

Nick threw enough money down to cover their bill and they headed out of the restaurant. He took the keys from her hand. "I'll drive. Where are we going?"

"Our Lady of Saints. It's only a few blocks from here, near my grandmother's house." She grabbed his arm. "She has to be all right, Nick. I can't lose her."

"Keep the faith, Kayla. Keep the faith."

Chapter Eighteen

Bernice, her grandmother's neighbor, was sitting next to Charlotte's bed in a private room on the third floor of the hospital when Kayla walked in. She immediately stood up, her face lined with worry. "Thank goodness you're here."

"How is she?" Kayla asked.

"She's drifting in and out of consciousness. The doctor says she suffered a mild heart attack. They're going to keep her overnight and monitor her condition."

Kayla latched onto the positive part of Bernice's sentence. "Mild is good, right?" She walked over to the bed. Her grandmother looked small, frail, and very pale. Her eyes were closed. For the first time Charlotte looked old. She was usually so full of energy, with more sparkle than women half her age. But not tonight.

"Your grandmother seems to be dreaming a lot," Bernice said. "She keeps mumbling words and phrases, and sometimes she's agitated. There must be something on her mind."

"What has she been saying?"

"Well, it's not always clear. But a few minutes ago her eyes flew wide-open, and she looked at me as if she were seeing a ghost, as if she didn't even recognize me. Then she said something like, 'Where's Johnny?' Do you know who Johnny is?"

Kayla looked away from Bernice's inquisitive eyes, her stomach beginning to churn. She'd thought her grandmother's age had contributed to her mild heart attack, but maybe there was more behind it. "I'm not sure. Where did you find her?"

"On her porch, her front door wide-open. I don't know if she was coming or going."

"Did she say anything else when she woke up?"

Bernice's brows knit into a severe frown. " 'Johnny's dead. Johnny's supposed to be dead.' I think that's right."

Kayla felt a knot grow in her throat. *God!* Was Johnny alive? Was it possible he'd survived and made it to shore all those years ago? Was he part of this, too?

Kayla tapped her fingers on the aluminum rail by her grandmother's bed, wishing Charlotte would wake up so she could ask her what had happened.

"It's probably just the medication," Bernice said. "I remember waking up from surgery once and having all kinds of crazy dreams."

Maybe she was right. Maybe her grandmother was just dreaming about the past.

Her grandmother stirred and her eyes fluttered open. Kayla moved closer to the bed. "Grandma?" she said. "Are you all right?"

Her eyes slowly focused on Kayla. "Where...where am I?"

"You're in the hospital," she said, offering a reassuring smile. "You had a mild heart attack."

"I did? Am I all right?"

"You're going to be fine," Kayla said, hoping that was true.

"Oh, well, that's good. The way you're looking at me I thought it might be more serious. Who's that behind you?"

"It's me," Bernice said. "You gave me quite a scare, Charlotte. I found you lying on your front porch."

Charlotte's gaze grew big and scared. She reached for Kayla's hand, and as their eyes met, she whispered, "I saw him. He was standing right in front of my house. I went out to the get the newspaper and there he was."

Kayla swallowed hard. "Who, Grandma? Who did you see?"

"Johnny," she murmured. "I saw your grandfather."

Charlotte's mouth started to tremble, and the machine monitoring her heart began to beep. The nurse came into the room. "What's going on in here?" she asked sharply.

"Nothing, we were just talking," Kayla said.

"Well, you both need to leave. Mrs. Hirsch needs to rest. You can talk later. Go," she said, shooing them out of the room.

As they left Bernice offered her a smile. "I'm going home now that you're here. Please keep in touch, won't you? Charlotte is a dear friend of mine. If there's anything I can do, you call me."

"I will. Thanks for taking care of her."

"Anytime."

As Bernice walked away, Kayla couldn't help wondering if her grandmother had imagined seeing Johnny in the shadows. It seemed unlikely that he would have been alive all this time and not contacted her before.

And why would he come back now -- because Evan had stolen his watch? Were the two events connected?

Was everything connected? There was another player in the game, but was it Johnny?

"What happened?" Nick asked. He'd been waiting in the hall, wanting to give her time alone with her grandmother.

"My grandmother had a mild heart attack. She's apparently been drifting in and out of consciousness. When she came to just now she told me that she saw Johnny standing in front of her house. She claims he said her name, and that's the last thing she remembers."

Nick's eyes widened in astonishment, "Johnny is alive?"

"Grandma seems awfully sure."

"I don't know. It doesn't make sense to me."

"Maybe not, but I'm going to sit with her for a while, see if she can tell me any more the next time she wakes up." She glanced down at her watch. "I might be here for a few hours. You should go home. I'll be fine on my own."

"I'll consider leaving you on two conditions: You call me when you're ready to leave, and you don't venture away from this hospital room by yourself."

"I think I'm pretty safe here." She saw his pointed gaze and gave in. "Okay, it's a deal. What are you going to do?"

"J.T. said he'd be here in the Bay Area sometime today. I'm going to try to track him down."

"Keep me posted."

"I will."

As he walked away, Kayla felt suddenly very alone. They'd

spent almost every minute together the last few days. It was hard to watch Nick leave, even harder not to call him back. But she could do this on her own. She could sit in her grandmother's hospital room and wait for her to wake up. Nothing was going to happen to her here.

* * *

Nick met J.T. in a small downtown sports bar later that night. His old friend was standing in front of a jukebox when he walked in. J.T. put a quarter in the machine, and "Born to Run" by Bruce Springsteen blared out of the speakers.

"Interesting choice," Nick said, as he pulled out a chair.

J.T. grinned as he sauntered over to the table. "It reminds me of that time in college when Garrett, you, and me tried to form a band for Lindsay Adams's birthday party."

"I remember. She liked musicians."

"And musicians liked her. She was hot, but I don't think any of us got lucky that night."

"Because we sucked. The dogs were howling," Nick said. He hadn't thought about those days in years. After Evan had messed up their lives, he'd moved off campus and concentrated on getting his degree as fast as possible. It was as if his college life had been divided into two parts: before Evan and after Evan. Now his adult life was fitting into the same pattern. He'd like to start a new chapter with no Evan at all.

J.T. called the waitress over. "I'll have a Corona. What about you?"

"Same," Nick said as the waitress set down two napkins and a bowl of pretzel party mix.

"So, where's your beautiful shadow?" J.T. asked. "I thought the two of you were attached at the hip...or somewhere else," he said with a mischievous gleam in his eye.

"Funny. Kayla is at the hospital. Her grandmother had a heart attack."

"I'm sorry to hear that. Will she be all right?"

"I think so. You'll be interested to know that the heart attack came after a man approached Mrs. Hirsch at her house. She thought it was Johnny Blandino."

J.T. raised an eyebrow. "The dead guy?"

"That's what she thinks." Nick paused as the waitress set down their beers. Then he said, "Do you have any news on your end? Figure out yet who fixed the brakes on Kayla's car?"

J.T. frowned at that. "No, and by the way, I saw the car. You must have nine lives."

"I'm using them up rapidly. Did you track down that Helen Matthews the priest told us about?"

"She says she doesn't know any of Frankie's relatives. She laughed when I asked her if he'd given her a watch. She said Frankie was a cheapskate and a hoarder. He didn't trust anyone with anything, and he hated to share."

"So that was a dead end."

"Yeah. This is different from Evan's usual jobs, you know. It started out the same with the identity theft. He often takes on the lives of others to conduct his scams. But then he veered off into left field. He didn't take Kayla's money. He didn't use his marriage to her to work any other scam. He certainly had the opportunity to clean her out."

"He didn't need her money. He had mine."

"Evan can always use more cash. Since taking the watch, he hasn't worked any of his other scams, as far as I can tell -- no check forging, no telemarketing schemes, no insurance fraud. It makes me wonder what his game is this time around." J.T. took a long draft of his beer. "I think there's a hidden agenda."

J.T.'s words reminded him of what Jenny had told him earlier. "You might be right. Evan went to Jenny's salon today."

J.T. choked on his beer. "Excuse me?"

"You heard me. Apparently it wasn't the first time. He actually made contact with her a couple of months ago. I'm betting that was where he got the information on me, where I lived, what I was doing. It would have been easy for him to learn I was out of the country and move right into my life."

"Shit! And Jenny didn't tell you?"

"No," Nick said shortly, not bothering to go into the other details. "She's upset, though, because when Evan came by today he started talking about how they were going to be together, how he would impress her. She finally seems to think he's flipped out."

J.T. gave him a grim nod. "It sounds like it."

"I want to get some protection for Jenny. Can you recommend anyone?"

"I know some private guys here in the city. I'll make some calls for you." J.T. paused. "What else did Evan tell Jenny?"

Nick thought back to the conversation with his sister. "Something about our not really knowing what he's after. We think we do, but we don't. Whatever that means."

"He could just be playing with you, knowing that Jenny would tell you that. But the idea that he wants to impress Jenny does tell me that his pride is involved. That may be his ultimate downfall. In the past he has never let things get personal. That's one of the reasons he's so good at what he does: He has no compassion or empathy for anyone else's misfortune."

"A sociopath."

"I'd say so. He certainly has no conscience."

Nick was reminded that J.T. had also suffered at Evan's hands. "That's rough, what he did to your father."

"Yeah." J.T. drained the rest of his beer and set the heavy glass down on the table with a forceful thud. "He got me good."

Nick knew that J.T. and his father had had a love/hate relationship most of their lives. Evan had known it, too, and he'd gone after J.T.'s Achilles' heel. "We made a hell of a mistake when we put that notice up on the bulletin board looking for a roommate," he said. "We invited Evan into our lives."

"We thought he was cool," J.T. agreed. "The life of the party. An all-around great guy."

"That's what he wanted us to think. He wanted us to like him."

"And now he wants us to respect him," J.T. finished.

Nick thought about that for a moment. Maybe J.T. was right. Maybe it wasn't just about revenge; it was about respect. Jenny had said that Evan intended to impress her, show her he was the best. What did that mean? "He must think that finding that treasure will bring him a huge windfall of cash. But is it really that easy to sell old coins without anyone tracing their origins to a famous theft?"

"It's not that difficult to find private buyers, coin collectors." J.T. leaned forward, resting his forearms on the table. "I've done some checking on that robbery, our Alcatraz boys, and some of their friends, including Kayla's grandmother. Charlotte ran with a fast crowd. They were questioned extensively after the robbery. Their answers were often evasive, contradictory. For a while the police suspected some of the girls might be harboring the fugitives or hiding their loot."

"Including Kayla's grandmother," Nick said.

"She was a suspect, as well as her good friend Dana, who, by the way, still happens to run that very same club as well as a few other nightclubs in town. And," J.T. added with a smile, "Charlotte paid her a visit a few days ago, which she returned shortly thereafter. Now one might wonder why those two old broads are suddenly having a reunion -- coincidentally just after Johnny's watch gets stolen."

"I don't think I'd call Charlotte an old broad in front of Kayla," Nick said dryly. "That is interesting, though. I've always thought Charlotte knew more than she was telling. She seems torn between protecting the past and protecting Kayla. Maybe I should get back to the hospital, see if she has anything else to say. You know, perhaps it's not such a long shot to think that Johnny is alive. He could be trying to get his money back."

"He'd be in his seventies by now," J.T. reminded him.

"Is there an age limit on greed?" he returned.

"No, but Evan usually works alone. I am going to speak with Delores Ricci again, now that she's recovered, to see if she can give us more information on the watches or her father's death."

"Good idea."

"Tell Kayla I hope her grandmother is okay, and if you hear any more about Johnny Blandino's sudden rise from the dead, let me know."

"Wouldn't that be the ultimate irony? Evan finds the watches, only to discover they lead nowhere and there is no treasure. The Alcatraz boys retrieved it a long time ago. The con man gets conned. He's not so smart after all."

J.T. didn't look convinced. "That's been your problem with Evan all along."

"What?"

"You always underestimate him."

* * *

Everything in her bedroom was white and absurdly feminine, from the sheer canopy over the bed to the lace curtains and soft pillows. Even the thick carpet was a lush white. Did she think she was a virgin? Evan laughed as he sat down on the bed and stretched out his legs, enjoying the fact that his shoes were leaving a dark print on her comforter. It would annoy her, and he didn't care. She'd made him angry. She'd done things she shouldn't. He would have to teach her that he was the boss.

He watched the door open, ready to enjoy her moment of surprise. Her face would change. Fear would enter her eyes. Her mouth might even tremble. She would try to cover her fear with anger, try to take back the control she thought she had. But it wouldn't work. He held all the cards. No one could beat the house, and he was always the house.

She stopped a few feet inside the room, just as he'd expected. No girlish scream for help came from her lips. She just stared at him for a long moment. He gave her credit for showing less of her emotions than he'd expected.

A twinge of uncertainty flashed through his brain, his instincts for survival telling him this was not quite the response he'd anticipated.

"You dare to enter my bedroom without an invitation?" she asked, her voice cold, angry.

Where was the fear, dammit? Didn't she know what he could do to her?

For a moment she reminded him of someone else, another woman who hadn't understood that he was important, that he mattered, that he was a force to be reckoned with. She'd ended up dead.

"You tried to kill my friends," he said. "That wasn't nice."

She shrugged. "They were in my way."

"You failed."

"I've already expressed my displeasure," she said. She walked farther into the room, showing off her long legs, her generous cleavage spilling out of her black cocktail dress. She wore stiletto shoes that were far too high, too sexy, too much for someone her age. Not that he knew exactly what her age was, but he suspected she was far older than she appeared. She could cover up the effects of gravity with plastic surgery, and no doubt she'd done just that. But she couldn't take the years out of her eyes.

"I told you to leave them alone. I have my own plans," he continued. "If you interfere again, I'll take you out myself."

"As if you could," she dared, a smile playing around her raspberry-colored lips.

"I got in here, didn't I?"

"I knew you were here," she returned. "I let it happen. I wanted to speak to you. They've scheduled a date for the auction. It's two weeks from Friday. Everything must be in place by then. If you can't get the necessary materials by the end of the week, I won't need you anymore, Evan. Do you understand what that means?"

"You're threatening me?" he asked in true amazement. "You can't kill me."

"Can't I?" she said with an evil smile. "Try me."

"Then you'll never get what you want," he said with a shrug.

"So do your job and we'll both be happy," she replied. "Now, do you have something to show me?"

He hesitated, then reached into his pocket and pulled out a silver watch. "Yes."

"Very good," she said with satisfaction. "We're almost there. I will get back what's mine, and then I'll get more." She walked over to the bed. "Now, I want you to pay a visit to an old friend of ours."

"Who?"

"Charlotte."

He raised an eyebrow. "Why?"

"You missed something the first time around."

"I got Johnny's watch. She doesn't have anything else."

"I think she does. I think she has Dominic's watch."

For the first time since the game had begun, Evan felt a chill in his bones. Dominic had a watch?

At the look of disbelief on his face, she laughed and laughed and laughed.

* * *

Kayla sat by her grandmother's bedside, wishing she'd wake

up again so they could talk, but Charlotte had fallen into a deep sleep. The doctor who'd stopped by earlier said it was good, that rest would help her heal. She'd asked Kayla if her grandmother had been under a lot of stress lately, which had only made Kayla feel guilty that perhaps she'd created that stress. Her grandmother had been leading a nice, quiet, uneventful life until Kayla had burst in on her with Nick and wild stories of Evan and a con, old watches, missing treasure.

She'd probably brought this on. She should have left things alone.

The door behind her opened, and she started, then relaxed when she saw it was Nick. She got up from her chair and met him by the door, not wanting to disturb her grandmother.

Nick held out his arms, and she walked straight into them. He'd been gone only a few hours and she'd missed him. Missed being in his embrace. Missed the feel of his hands on her skin. Missed his voice, his smile, his strength. She knew they were too involved, or at least she was too involved. They didn't talk about it. But someday they'd have to talk. Someday they'd have to decide where they were going in the future...if they were going anywhere.

For the moment she would let things ride. For the first time in her life she was with a man without expectations, without a plan, without a list of things she wanted. It was freeing. And yet it was also scary. Because she knew deep down that Nick wasn't a man looking to commit to a woman. Their relationship was probably just convenient.

She knew he liked her, enjoyed being with her, but more than that? He was a difficult man to read. He didn't wear his emotions on his sleeve like she did. He didn't use two words if one was enough. She wondered if he'd ever told a woman he loved her; for some reason she doubted it. She knew he could love, and deeply, too. But love had hurt him: Jenny, his mother, his other sister, his father, and even Evan, his onetime friend, had betrayed him, kept secrets, told lies. If she had to pick one thing to give him, it would be honesty. He deserved nothing less.

"How is she?" Nick asked, his hand stroking her hair.

"Okay, I think." She lifted her gaze to his. "The doctor said she's just sleeping. If her heart looks good all night, they'll release her in the morning. They think the attack was more of a warning, telling her to slow down, take it easy, not get too stressed about anything."

"You're feeling guilty."

"And you are starting to know me too well. Please don't tell me it's not my fault, when we both know it's my stubbornness that caused her upset. If I'd left things alone as she asked, she might not be sick."

"Maybe not," Nick said. "But you can't deal in what-ifs. It will drive you crazy."

"You're a likely one to talk. You've been kicking yourself for twelve years over what happened to Jenny."

He nodded. "So maybe I'm an expert on the topic of self-flagellation."

"That's a big word," she said with a smile. "It sounds a little kinky."

"Oh, so you're interested in kinky," he said with a wink. "You should have told me before."

And she never should have started this tease, with her grandmother about six feet away. "Behave," she said.

"You started it."

"And now I'm ending it." She stopped talking as she heard her grandmother mumbling. She walked back to the bed. "Grandma," she whispered. "You're okay. You're just dreaming."

Charlotte opened her eyes and gazed straight at Kayla. "They didn't want to kill him. It was an accident. You understand, don't you?"

Was she talking about one of the guards at the mint? Kayla was confused, but she could see the worry in her grandmother's eyes. "I understand," she assured her. "They didn't mean it."

"He betrayed them. They were brothers. He had to pay. But not with his life. It wasn't supposed to be with his life." Charlotte let out a sigh, her eyes drifting shut, and once again she slept.

"Who on earth was she talking about?" she asked.

Nick stared back at her. "One of the men did something wrong, and he died because of it."

"Frankie? Do you think the other two escaped, but they killed Frankie because he was going to get in the way?"

"Maybe."

She was surprised by the doubt in his voice. "Who else could it be?"

"I can only think of one other person -- Dominic."

"The watchmaker?"

"He did disappear over the side of a boat, as I recall. No one saw what happened. No body was ever found. I wonder who else was on the boat with him that night. It might be interesting to find out. Your grandmother certainly is a fountain of information."

"A slow, trickling fountain. Just when you think there's nothing left to come out, something does." Kayla looked back down at her grandmother, wondering what other secrets this sweet old woman was keeping. "But I don't think we'll get any more information tonight."

"Well, tomorrow is another day."

Chapter Nineteen

"I'm not sure what you hope to accomplish here," Kayla said as they walked down the sidewalk toward the San Francisco branch of the U.S. Mint early Wednesday morning. The mint was located in a historic building on Fifth Street in the heart of downtown. She knew that the U.S. Treasury was still using part of the building, but the rest of the old mint had been converted into a museum. Ordinarily she would have loved exploring a historical landmark, but at the moment she had a lot on her mind, and she wasn't sure this trip to the past would help them figure out how to find the other watches and bring Evan down.

"Haven't you ever heard of returning to the scene of the crime?" Nick asked. "This is where it began. There could be a clue here."

She paused at the bottom of the steps that led up to the massive building famously known as the Granite Lady. It was truly an awesome structure, with its impressive sandstone columns and air of invincibility. It had been built to withstand earthquakes and fires, and it had done exactly that, but time had brought decay to the Granite Lady, and they could see by the signs out front that the building was currently undergoing a massive renovation that would result in a spectacular museum. Public donations were still being encouraged and accepted.

"I guess they don't make money here anymore," Kayla murmured as they headed up the steps.

"I don't think so. I read a bit about the mint on the Internet, and I think it said the last coins were produced here several years ago, the Susan B. Anthony dollar, which no one liked because it looked too much like a quarter."

She smiled. "That sounds like a good trivia question."

"I just wish I'd been able to learn more about the robbery, but it was a long time ago. Hopefully they'll have more of that historical information inside."

"Being here does make it feel more real," she said, gazing at the building. "It's such a formidable structure. I can't believe Johnny and his buddies thought they could just waltz in and rob the place. It's hard to imagine how they even got in."

"I doubt security was as sophisticated in the fifties as it is today. And your grandfather wasn't short on nerve or big ideas, from what I understand."

She frowned at that. "I really don't like it when you call him my grandfather."

"Sorry."

"I mean, I know that's what he is, but my real grandfather, Edward, worked in a bank. He was the president. Isn't it odd that my grandmother fell in love with a robber and then married a bank president? That's bizarre."

"She covered all the bases. Maybe she had a thing for men and money."

"More like a thing for bad boys. I'm still not sure she didn't marry my real grandfather just to give her baby a name and find financial security for herself."

"They stayed together a long time," Nick reminded her. "They had chances to divorce after your mother was grown. Their relationship had to be about more than security."

"I sure would like to believe that. I always wanted to have a marriage like hers. It was the example I held up for myself. I guess that's why learning all this stuff about her is so shocking."

"Just because she's fallen off that pedestal you put her on doesn't mean she's all bad," Nick said. "It just means she's human."

"You and I are alike that way. We expect a lot from the people we love. And we both keep getting disappointed -- you with Jenny, me with my grandmother. The irony is that they're probably just as disappointed in us."

"You're right," Nick said somewhat heavily. "I don't think I'm at the top of Jenny's list, but I suspect I haven't been there for a while. That's why no one saw fit to tell me about her baby. Hell of a secret to keep all these years."

She could hear the tension in his voice and knew he hadn't gotten over that bombshell yet. She, too, wondered why Jenny hadn't told him after time had passed. Kayla doubted that Jenny had ever forgotten about her child. She'd mentioned going to the grave. Kayla thought about what else Jenny had said -- that sometimes there were fresh flowers on the grave, as if Evan visited their child, too. Did he?

It seemed like such a sweet thing to do. But Evan wasn't sweet. He was cold, cruel, and ruthless. He didn't have a heart. She knew that firsthand. Maybe Jenny was wrong. Maybe it wasn't Evan who put out the flowers; perhaps it was someone else, her mother or her sister.

"Ready to go inside?" Nick asked.

"Sure."

They walked through the front door of the building and paused by an information booth to pick up some brochures. A receptionist told them another tour would be starting in a half hour that would take them through the vault areas and down to the basement, where original coin presses were on display. She also pointed out some of the features in the main reception area, including the cast-iron staircases and the gas lamp chandeliers. While they were waiting, she suggested they view a historical video that ran every ten minutes in an adjacent room.

"That sounds like a good place to start," Kayla said. They walked into the small viewing room and sat down. There was an older couple in the front row and two other women in the back, also waiting for the video to start. Kayla checked her watch for the time. She was supposed to pick up her grandmother from the hospital at noon, and she didn't want to be late.

"This shouldn't take long," Nick said.

"I know. I'm just eager to talk more to my grandmother. I'm not sure how hard to push her for information. I don't want her to get upset and have another attack."

"Well, we need to know if she really saw Johnny. That would be huge."

Kayla nodded. "I agree. I also want to know who she was talking about last night when she mentioned someone being killed by mistake."

A few minutes later the lights went out and the screen lit up. The black-and-white film began with the discovery of California gold in 1859 at Sutter's Mill, which triggered one of the most important chapters in history, the California Gold Rush. Pictures from the Gold Rush flashed on the screen.

"Within a few years the mines were producing an abundance of gold, yet there was a shortage of circulating legal coins in the Wild West," the narrator said. "To relieve the problem Congress authorized the establishment of a branch of the U.S. Mint in San Francisco. By 1934, one third of the U.S. gold reserve was being stored in the vaults at the San Francisco Mint. All coins struck there were distinguished by the *S* mint mark. The San Francisco Mint was famous for many rare, legendary issues, including an 1870-S three-dollar piece valued today at well over one million dollars. That particular coin was believed to have been stolen during a robbery in the 1950s by three armed bandits, who not only stole a treasure trove of coins but also killed two guards in the process. It was the worst robbery in the history of the mint, and the coins were never recovered."

Kayla sat up in her chair as the screen showed images of police outside the mint, crime tape, an ambulance arriving. A shiver of excitement ran down her spine as she realized she was seeing the mint minutes after her own grandfather had robbed the place. Someone was brought out on a stretcher and placed in an ambulance in front of a crowd of onlookers, held back by wooden barricades.

Nick nudged her arm. "Those women," he said, "by the ambulance. Isn't one of them your grandmother? The one next to the redhead?"

Kayla's heart skipped a beat. Was that her grandmother?

The image was gone before she could tell, and the narrator continued with the story of the mint after the robbery. A few minutes later the lights went on.

Kayla and Nick sat in the room, unmoving, until they were completely alone.

"I think that was her," she said. "Or am I crazy?"

"Why would it be crazy?" he countered. "She knew Johnny. Maybe she was afraid he was the one being brought out on the stretcher."

She looked into Nick's eyes and saw that he believed what he was saying, and she knew that she believed it, too. "I think it's time to pick up my grandmother from the hospital. But don't say a word to her, not until we get her home, not until I make sure she's strong enough to deal with it."

"It's your call, Kayla. But whether or not she's strong enough to deal with anything, it may be out of our control. If Johnny is alive and he went to see her last night, then something is going down, and probably sooner rather than later."

"I keep coming back to the fact that Johnny wouldn't have stolen his own watch."

"Maybe not. But perhaps he found out someone else did. And he wants it back." Nick paused. "Nate could be alive, too. He could be trying to circumvent Johnny."

"It's been so long. If they made it to shore in the sixties when they escaped from Alcatraz, they would have gone after their treasure sooner."

Nick nodded in agreement. "True, but many a man has found religion in jail. Perhaps one or both decided to change his ways, start over, live a new life, stay hidden."

"Until someone started digging into their secrets," Kayla finished. "Let's skip the tour. I've seen enough."

* * *

Sitting in the wheelchair by the front door of the hospital, Charlotte ran a comb through her hair. The doctor had discharged her a few minutes earlier, and she'd convinced the nurse to bring her down to the lobby to wait for Kayla. She hated being in the hospital. It reminded her of all the weeks she'd spent there while Edward was dying of cancer. She'd watched her once strong and vibrant husband fade away, his body so thin and frail by the end that she barely recognized him.

Edward had always been solid, an anchor in her life, a safe place to rest. She was sure that Kayla wouldn't find that romantic or exciting, and maybe, to be fair, she hadn't felt that way in the beginning either. Those first few years she had yearned for Johnny, wished he could come back and see his daughter and hold her. In the dark of the night she'd had a few dreams of them together as a family. It had felt like a betrayal to Edward, and she'd forced the dreams out of her head as best she could. It had gotten easier with the passing of time.

Watching Edward with Joanna, seeing him treat her daughter as his own, had changed the way she'd looked at him. And she'd gradually begun to realize that the bad boys she'd run with were nowhere near as good or wonderful as Edward. He'd lived according to a high moral compass, and he'd raised her up to his level. She'd become the good woman he wanted her to be.

Or perhaps she'd just grown up. Sometimes she thought that was probably it. Johnny was a part of her reckless youth, a time when she'd played fast and loose with the rules, when she'd lost herself in the excitement of danger, adventure, passion. At twenty-one, she'd wanted to live every moment as if it were her last, so she would have no regrets. Unfortunately, there was always room for regret.

And last night she'd felt the full force of regret when Johnny had emerged from the shadows and looked her straight in the eye. The image of him was so clear in her head now -- his dark, almost black eyes, his square face, prominent jaw, and chiseled bones. His hair had grayed. His skin had drooped, and his eyes were tired but oh so familiar. He'd said her name so clearly: *"Charlie."*

That was all she remembered. The next thing she knew she'd woken up in the hospital.

She cursed herself for fainting at the sight of him. She might have missed her chance to speak to him. But he'd taken her by surprise. All these years she'd thought he was dead.

But he wasn't dead. Was he?

A lingering doubt went through her mind. Was she wrong? Had she mistaken someone else for Johnny? There were lots of senior men living in her condo complex. Had the shadows played tricks on her? Was it just that questions about Johnny were so fresh in her thoughts that she'd created him in her head?

She hoped she wasn't going crazy. She'd always been able to rely on her instincts, if nothing else.

And her instincts were screaming now that Johnny had

survived.

But even as the joy washed over her body, it was tempered by anger. If he had been alive all these years, where had he been? Why hadn't he contacted her? Why hadn't he told her? Why had he let her grieve for him?

She looked up as Kayla walked through the hospital door. She could see by her granddaughter's pinched, tight expression that there were going to be more questions to answer. She supposed she should have been more forthcoming in the beginning, but each time she'd had to tell Kayla anything, she'd felt as if she were putting another nail in the coffin of their relationship. She'd never been as close to her own daughter, Joanna, as she was to Kayla, and she would hate to lose her granddaughter to mistakes made fifty years ago.

"You look better," Kayla said, appearing to force a smile. "Do you feel better?"

"Yes, much. I slept well. The doctor said I'm fine. I just have to watch my cholesterol and get plenty of rest. Drink water, you know, all that." She smiled reassuringly at Kayla, who didn't look convinced.

"Nick has the car in front," Kayla said. "Should I wheel you out?"

"I can walk. This is just for show," she said, getting up from the chair. "Hospital rules or something like that."

It felt good to get up and leave the hospital. The air was brisk. It was a cool day, with scattered clouds in the sky, leaving her with the sense that there was a storm brewing nearby. But for now it was dry.

She got into the backseat and said hello to Nick. He nodded politely. She wasn't sure what he thought about her, and she wouldn't have cared -- if she hadn't seen the look that passed between Nick and Kayla when her granddaughter got into the car. There was an intimacy between them that made her wonder just what was going on. But she didn't dare to open up that conversation now. She suspected there were more pressing matters to deal with.

"Grandma," Kayla said, turning sideways in her seat so she was facing the back, "we need to talk about what happened last night, but I don't want to upset you, so maybe you could just tell me briefly about this man that you saw outside your condo."

"It was Johnny," she replied. "I'm almost one hundred percent certain."

"Almost?" Nick echoed, his gaze meeting hers in the rearview mirror.

"There were shadows," Charlotte explained. "And since I passed out, I'm not completely sure of what I saw, but my instincts tell me it was him. I distinctly heard him say, "Charlie," the way he used to."

"That would mean he's been alive all these years," Kayla said. "Where would he have been?"

"I have no idea."

"Maybe the church," Kayla suggested. "Maybe with his half brother, the priest?"

Charlotte's heart sank. "How did you find out about Marcus?"

"We made a trip to St. Basil's yesterday, thinking someone there might remember the altar boys." Kayla paused. "I was explaining that I was looking for information about my grandfather, Johnny Blandino, when the priest interrupted me to say that he was Johnny's half brother."

"You called him your grandfather?" Charlotte asked, feeling an odd sensation in the pit of her stomach.

"That's beside the point. I've been running all over town trying to figure out the past, and it appears to me now that you're the one who holds all the answers, only you haven't chosen to share them with me."

"That's not true, Kayla. I honestly don't know where Nate's and Frankie's watches are. Did you find that girl in Reno?"

"We found her," Kayla answered. "But she was attacked after we spoke to her, before we could get to her house to retrieve the watch."

"No," Charlotte breathed. "By who? Evan?"

"There was another man there who grabbed me, asked where my watch was," Kayla answered. "And it wasn't Evan, so there are at least two people involved, maybe more."

"Oh, my heavens! Were you hurt? Why didn't you call me right away?" Charlotte said with concern. Kayla did have scratches and bruises on her face, she realized. "You're all banged-up. I didn't even ask you how that happened. It looks like you were in a fight."

Kayla shook her head. "Not a fight, a car crash. We had a problem with our brakes on the way back from Reno. But I'm okay. I'm fine."

"This is terrible," Charlotte said, her heart beginning to race. "I don't like this at all. You could have been badly hurt."

"It's all right, Grandma," Kayla said quickly. "Don't worry about me. We need to focus on the problem at hand."

Charlotte drew in several deep breaths, knowing it was important she stay calm. "What did this other man look like?"

"I couldn't see the guy who came up behind me, but I sensed was that he was stocky, muscular. He smelled, too, as if he'd been sweating a lot." Kayla paused, glancing at Nick. "The guy in the restaurant was sweating."

"What guy?" Charlotte asked.

"Someone I saw in Reno. He had greasy dark hair, not too tall, a little overweight, and he rubbed his face with a napkin to wipe off the perspiration."

Charlotte felt sick to her stomach. Had she inadvertently sent someone after Kayla? Both Dana and Anne Marie had sons, sons who might want those watches. And short, dark men were fairly common in North Beach.

"What are you thinking, Grandma?"

"I don't know. There's so much to take in."

"And so much you haven't told us," Nick interjected. "If you're trying to protect Kayla, you're going about it the wrong way. Information gives her armor. Lack of information leaves her vulnerable."

He had a point. And she realized deep down that she'd been so concerned about protecting her relationship with Kayla that she'd actually put her granddaughter in harm's way. She should have known better. She knew firsthand how dangerous men could be where gold was concerned, especially this particular gold.

"You should have trusted me, Grandma," Kayla said.

"It wasn't about trust," Charlotte answered. "But I'll tell you everything."

"Good."

Charlotte took a breath, then realized they were pulling up in front of her condo. "I guess it can wait until we get inside."

"But only until then," Kayla said firmly. "You said some things last night when you were drifting in and out of sleep that I really want to clarify."

Charlotte pursed her lips, trying to remember. She'd had so many dreams last night. She didn't know if they'd given her medication or what, but the past had seemed so vivid in her head. Nick parked the car, and Kayla jumped out, opening the door for her and offering her a hand.

"I'm all right," Charlotte said, ignoring Kayla's help. "I can walk on my own."

"I never realized exactly how stubborn you are until recently," Kayla said dryly.

"It must run in the family," Charlotte returned. "You certainly ignored my wishes."

"I get my bullheadedness from you then," Kayla said, looking pleased at the thought.

"And your mother. Strong women run in the family."

"You can say that again," Nick muttered.

Charlotte saw the smile in Nick's eyes when he looked at Kayla, and then she realized it wasn't amusement she was seeing, but love, or something very close. Maybe everything did happen for a reason. If Evan hadn't run off, Kayla never would have met this man. And if Johnny hadn't gone to jail, she might never have married Edward. Sometimes the darkest nights turned into the brightest days.

"I guess you don't have your key," Kayla said.

Charlotte suddenly realized she didn't have her purse. It must still be in the condo. "No, I don't."

"It's all right. I have the extra one you gave me." Kayla slipped the key into the lock and opened the door.

As soon as Charlotte crossed the threshold, she realized something was very wrong. Kayla's shocked gasp and Nick's swearing told her that her eyes were not playing tricks on her. Her house had been ransacked, vandalized, searched. The furniture was in shambles, her knickknacks tossed about, her papers, her books, her magazines scattered across the floor.

She put out a hand, reaching for the nearest wall for support. Kayla was immediately at her side. "Grandma, are you okay?"

"I just need to catch my breath."

"What are they looking for?" Nick asked.

"I need to sit down."

"Of course," Kayla said, ushering her into the living room.

Charlotte sat on the edge of her couch, not even sure where to start, how to begin. Who had done this to her home? Johnny? He'd been here last night; she was sure of it. But why would he do this? Because she'd fainted? Because he hadn't had a chance simply to ask her for what he wanted?

"The key," Kayla said. "Maybe they were looking for the key you gave me. They realized it wasn't in the watch, and when they didn't find it at my house, they came here. It makes sense."

Charlotte was tempted to nod, to agree, to let that be that. She might have been able to fool Kayla, who was thinking as much with her emotions as with her head, but Nick appeared fairly sharp-eyed to her. In fact, his gaze was fixed on his face, watching, waiting.

"That's not it, is it?" he asked.

She slowly shook her head. "I don't think so. I have -- or maybe had -- something else."

Kayla sat down on the edge of the coffee table directly in front of her, their knees almost touching. "What did you have?"

"One of the other watches."

"Frankie's?" Kayla asked.

"No. There weren't three watches, Kayla. There were four. I had Dominic's watch."

Chapter Twenty

Kayla had not thought she could be surprised again, but with her grandmother it seemed to be a given. "Why would you have Dominic's watch? Why did he even have a watch? Why?" she asked, waving her hand in frustration and confusion.

"In order for you to understand, I need to tell you the whole story."

"Well, that would be nice for a change," Kayla said, hearing the sarcasm in her voice, but not willing to hide it. She tried to remind herself that her grandmother had just gotten out of the hospital, that she'd suffered yet another shock at finding her condo in a shambles. She had to go easy, or her grandmother would be back in the hospital with another heart attack. "I'm sorry," she said hastily. "Do you want some water? Should you take a rest before you tell us the story?"

"I don't think there's time for any of that." Charlotte glanced down at her hands, playing with her wedding ring; then she looked back at Kayla.

"Dominic was the good one, or at least that's what most people thought. When the boys were childhood friends, it was always the four of them together. But after high school Dominic fell in love. He got married at eighteen to a girl from the neighborhood. They had children right away -- a boy named Lorenzo; then two girls, Delores and Grace, arrived within the next four years. Dominic went to work at the jewelry store run by his father. He had to make a living. He had a family to support.

"Johnny, Nate, and Frankie drifted apart from Dominic. They had bigger plans than working nine-to-five jobs for not very good money. They started out small -- pickpocketing, shoplifting, stealing jewelry from some of the older women in the parish who lived alone. They'd get themselves hired to mow the lawn or trim the trees or do handyman work. Once inside, they'd figure out if they could take anything without anyone noticing. Johnny told me it was surprisingly easy. As they got a taste of success, they grew bolder. They started robbing liquor stores, other small businesses, even banks. They were brash, bold, fearless men. And Frankie, particularly, was big, scary-looking. He was the muscle. Johnny and Nate were the brains." Charlotte paused, taking a breath.

Kayla was fascinated by the story but worried that her grandmother was too pale. "Are you sure you want to do this now?"

"I've already started. Let me finish."

"All right then."

"Dominic grew weary of trying to please his father, who kept him on a tight purse string. He felt like Johnny and the others were having all the fun while he was stuck at home with a wife and kids. He said he wanted back in. They welcomed him back. Dominic did some jobs with them, usually night jobs. No one knew he was part of it. After a while they were so successful that they needed a place to stash their goods. Dana, another dancer at the club, and I knew of this secret room off the basement of the club where we worked. It had been built during Prohibition, when the building was a speakeasy. We'd discovered it one day by accident. We told Johnny he could keep stuff there if he gave us a cut."

Kayla felt her jaw drop. She couldn't hide her shock or dismay. "You helped him?"

"The cut was Dana's idea. She was a very smart girl. I was a lot dumber and poorer. I didn't like to turn down money, and I rationalized that they were going to steal whether or not I helped them hide it."

"Oh, that's great, Grandma. You were an accessory to a crime. You could have gone to jail."

"I told you I made some mistakes," Charlotte said sharply. "Now I'm going to finish this so I don't have to say it again, so I don't have to think about it again."

"Fine. Finish it."

"Johnny and his friends started fighting. Greed has a way of taking apart even the best of friends. They started not trusting one another, worrying that one was getting more than a fair share. So they started putting things in this big old iron box. Dominic made four locks and four different keys that fit in a secret compartment in each watch. They decided to find a better hiding place, too. They didn't say where it was, but the phrases on the watches were some sort of code. They made it so they could open up the box only if they were all there and each had their key. And they kept the keys in the watches. They loved those watches. They were a symbol of their club, their bond, their secrets." She drew in another breath before continuing. "The robbery at the mint was their final job. It was so big. I had no idea they were going after something that huge."

"But you were there," Kayla interrupted. "Nick and I just saw newsreels from the robbery."

"Where would you see those?" Charlotte asked in surprise.

"At the mint. We went there this morning. I couldn't believe my eyes when I saw you and another girl standing by the ambulance."

Charlotte nodded. "I'd heard about the robbery and that two men had been killed. Dana and I went running down there. We thought when they brought those men out that we might see Johnny or Nate. Dana was Nate's girlfriend at the time. But it wasn't them. It was the guards." She sent Kayla a look, pleading for understanding. "They had never, ever hurt anyone before. And now two men were dead. I think that's when I fully realized that it wasn't a game."

"What happened next?" Kayla asked.

"The men went into hiding. I only saw Johnny once before he was arrested. He told me that something bad had happened, that it had been an accident. He wouldn't say more. But he asked me to keep his watch and Dominic's watch. The next day I heard that Dominic had died during a fishing trip. I had a bad feeling about it."

"They killed Dominic?" Kayla asked in disbelief. She wondered what had caused such a drastic break in their friendship.

"I think so."

"Was Dominic part of the robbery at the mint?" Nick asked. "His name was never mentioned."

"He didn't enter the mint. He helped them get away from the building. He knew of some secret way out. No one knew he was involved, except me and possibly Dana."

"And anyone else those boys might have spoken to," Nick said. "It sounds like they talked a little too much if they were telling strippers about their ill-gotten gains. Weren't they worried you'd turn them in?"

"We were in love," Charlotte said. "And Dana and I weren't exactly walking on the good side of the law. We didn't have anything to gain by turning anyone in."

"So why did they kill Dominic?" Kayla asked. "I still don't quite understand."

"I don't know. They had some sort of falling-out."

"You should have told me you had Dominic's watch," Kayla said. "Why didn't you? You knew I was looking for all of them."

"I thought I would wait until you had the other watches. I wasn't sure who Evan was working with and what they might know."

"That is the big question," Nick said. "But obviously someone came here looking for Dominic's watch."

"Or the key," Charlotte said. "But I gave that to you, Kayla."

"I still have it in my purse. Do you know what the inscription was on Dominic's watch?"

"Yes. 'All the Riches.' I figured it had something to do with their loot." She paused. "I kept the watch in my safe in the bedroom closet. The carpet pulls up and you can see a combination lock. The numbers are forty-six, eighteen, twenty-two."

"I'll look," Nick offered.

Kayla was tempted to go with him, but she decided to stay with her grandmother. "That's quite a story."

"And one that doesn't show me in a particularly good light," Charlotte replied. "I tried to clean up my act after I married Edward. He set me on the right path. As the years went by, it was easy to forget I'd ever been wild. It seemed like a dream to me. It was so long ago. I can hardly believe it's all coming up now. I guess you're never truly free of the past. You can't outrun your mistakes no matter how far you go. They always catch up. I don't know if you'll ever forgive me, but I do love you, Kayla, and my biggest regret is that I put you in danger. I never should have given you that watch. I should have held on to it forever."

"I'm glad you did what you did for Johnny out of love," Kayla said. "It doesn't make it right, but it makes it more understandable. I've certainly done some stupid things based on what I thought was love. I have a better idea now of what's real and what isn't."

Charlotte's gaze narrowed on her face. "Is Nick real?"

Kayla started. "Good grief. Why would you ask that?"

"Because I can see the way you two look at each other, as if there's something between you, something deep, intimate."

Kayla felt herself blushing and wished she could stop the spread of warmth across her face, but it was impossible. "We've gotten close," she admitted. "He's a good guy. I don't have the best track record for judging men, though. With Evan I think a part of me always knew it wasn't right. I just didn't want to admit it. I wanted to have the dream he was selling me, so I bought into it. I rushed into marriage so I wouldn't have time to talk myself out of it."

"Is Nick selling you a dream?"

"He isn't selling me anything. We aren't even talking about us. There's too much going on."

"But you want there to be an 'us'?"

"What I want is not to have to answer that question."

Charlotte smiled. "You don't have to tell me, but at some point you have to be honest with yourself."

"I'm afraid," Kayla admitted. "I'm terrified that if I am falling in love with Nick, I'm doing it all alone again. I don't want that to happen. So I don't ask, and he doesn't answer. And you're right: It's not the best way to go, but then I think, why do I have to know right now? For the first time in my life I'm not in a relationship with any expectations."

"Maybe not expectations you've said out loud, but just because you're silent doesn't mean they're not there, and that you won't have to deal with them at some point."

"As long as that point isn't today, I'm happy," Kayla said. She looked up as Nick walked back into the room. His face was grim, his hands empty.

"I found the safe open," he said. "There was no watch.

However, it appears that some other jewelry and papers are still there."

Charlotte's face fell. "How did they open the safe? I guess the lock wasn't good enough, was it? Johnny once showed me how easy it was to crack a safe." She paused. "But I'm an old woman and I didn't have that much to protect. At least, I thought I didn't. It has been so long. I was more careful earlier." She shook her head, her eyes filled with regret.

"It's completely understandable that you grew lax as the years passed. I did the same thing," Nick said. "Evan came for me twelve years after our falling-out. I hadn't given him a second thought in years, and then there he was."

Kayla watched Nick comforting her grandmother with a pleased smile. He could have been yelling in frustration and anger that if Charlotte had just told them all this the first time they asked, things might have turned out differently, but instead he was being nice, putting her grandmother first. She liked him even more, if that was possible.

"Thank you," Charlotte said. "You're very kind to say that. I can see why Kayla likes you."

Kayla shifted in her seat as Nick turned a questioning gaze in her direction.

"Did she tell you she likes me?" he asked with a smile.

Charlotte gave a little laugh. "You should know by now that I can definitely keep a secret."

Nick grinned. "You can say that again."

"Okay, you two, let's focus," Kayla interrupted. "What are we going to do now? There's only one watch left, and it belonged to Frankie. We have no leads."

Nick sat down in a nearby chair, his expression turning somber. "Okay, let's say Evan has the three watches. Either he's waiting for us to lead him to Frankie's watch, he already has it, or he's floundering in the dark like we are."

"But he's not working alone," Kayla said. "We know there's at least one other man involved. Who could he be?"

"Someone related to the Alcatraz guys," Nick said.

Kayla glanced over at her grandmother. "Any ideas?"

"Dana has three sons. Anne Marie had a son and a daughter. Her son had Nate's watch."

"And passed it on to Lisa," Kayla muttered. "So it doesn't seem like anyone else in Anne Marie's family would be involved. That leaves your friend Dana, and her boys. We don't know anything about Frankie. Do you, Grandma?"

"Frankie dated lots of girls. I don't remember anyone special. He had no siblings. There was another girl at the club who used to date both Nate and Frankie. Her name was Elizabeth. She's married to a fine, upstanding man and has left her past behind, but she does have two sons. I spoke to her earlier. She didn't seem to know anything."

"That doesn't mean much," Kayla said somewhat glumly.

"Let's not forget Dominic," Nick interjected. "Someone figured out you had his watch. Someone also attacked Delores, Dominic's daughter."

"They must have been looking for Dominic's watch," Kayla said. "And we thought we triggered it, because we stopped by the store asking her to look up the records. But maybe that wasn't it at all. Or else maybe Evan followed us there and realized Delores might have Dominic's watch." As she finished speaking, Kayla realized they'd done little to narrow down their choices. "Is there anyone else we're missing, someone who might have had an interest in the treasure besides the descendants of the robbers?" She glanced over at Charlotte.

Her grandmother gave a shrug. "I don't think so. Johnny and his friends did brag about their exploits. But it was a long time ago. Most of my generation is gone now."

"Actually, there seem to be quite a few of you left," Nick said dryly. "What do you think about introducing us to your friend Dana?"

Charlotte hesitated. "I guess it's pointless to keep trying to kick that door to the past shut again, isn't it? All right. I'll take you to Dana's place, and you can see the club where I ruined my reputation. Dana owns it now, you know. It's still a strip club. Or maybe more...I'm not sure what goes on in the club nowadays. Dana also owns two other nightclubs. Apparently she bought one for each of her sons to run. She wasn't afraid to be who she was to her family," Charlotte added. "Just to give you a heads-up, she doesn't like me much for turning my back on her. I doubt she'll be warm and welcoming."

"Actually, I'm more interested in checking out that secret room in the basement," Nick said. "I know you said the men didn't put their coins there, but maybe they didn't tell you everything."

"You don't think the money has been there all along?" Kayla asked. "That would be too easy. And Dana could have taken it at any time, it seems."

"Or just used the money as she needed it," Nick suggested. "She certainly turned her life around in a profitable manner, and it would have been easier to sell off single coins to collectors over a period of fifty years than to try to sell a whole stash of coins at one time."

"I don't think so," Charlotte said. "I know Johnny moved the money. He told me so. He wouldn't have had any reason to lie to me." Charlotte stopped abruptly. "Oh, I can see by your faces that you think he could have lied to me."

"It's just that he was a crook, Grandma," Kayla said gently. "If he could rob and kill, I think he could probably lie. And I know better than most that it's pretty easy to believe a lie when a good-looking guy tells you just what you want to hear."

"Johnny didn't lie to me," Charlotte said firmly. "But that's all right. You don't have to believe in him." She stood up. "Let me just change my clothes and get my purse and then we'll go."

"Are you sure it's not too much for you?" Kayla asked. "Nick and I can go on our own."

"You won't get anywhere without me," Charlotte said. "I'll be fine. I'm stronger than I look."

"Should we call your friend first?" Kayla asked.

"Where Dana is concerned, surprise is always a good thing," Charlotte said.

"This is the place," Charlotte said, as they stood in front of Deception, the nightclub located in the heart of the Broadway strip. "I never thought I'd be bringing my granddaughter here."

"If it makes you feel better, I never thought I'd be coming to a strip club with my grandmother," Kayla returned.

Nick opened the door, and Kayla entered first, pausing inside to let her eyes adjust to the dim lighting. It was a Wednesday afternoon, and the club shows wouldn't start until later in the evening. A burly man approached them, looking like some type of bouncer.

"We're not open yet," he said.

"We just want to talk to Dana," Charlotte told him. "Is she in?"

"She's got someone in her office," he replied. "You can wait if you want. What's your name? I'll tell her you're here."

"Charlotte Cunningham."

"Does it look the same as when you used to dance here?" Kayla asked, glancing around at the bar, the tables, the stage area, the shiny gold poles. She couldn't begin to imagine her grandmother dancing around that pole. In fact, she couldn't imagine her grandmother doing any of it.

"It's changed a lot. The stage is bigger. We didn't have the private booths or the poles." She paused. "I can show you some photos. They're down here."

Kayla followed her grandmother into the back hall, which was decorated with black-and-white framed photos tracing the history of the club.

"That's me," Charlotte said, pointing to a photograph.

Kayla leaned forward, seeing her grandmother seated on some guy's lap, a cigarette in her hand, a smile on her face. "Smoking, too, Grandma?"

"We didn't know any better in those days."

"Are Johnny and his buddies in any of these photos?" Nick asked, coming up next to Kayla.

"Let's see," Charlotte said, moving slowly down the wall. "Here they are, all three of them. And that's Dana; she's the redhead sitting next to Nate. The blonde on the other side of her is a girl who danced under the name Lola. Her real name was Elizabeth Hutchinson. She's the one I told you about. She dated both Frankie and Nate."

Kayla didn't want to ask what the term *dated* actually meant. She suspected it had more to do with sex and less to do with dinner at a nice restaurant followed by a movie. These were the bad girls, she realized, the ones who seduced men away from their wives and their "good girl" girlfriends. And her grandmother had been one of them. She looked so young in the photos, so full of life, so happy.

"Where do the stairs go?" Nick asked. "Down to the basement maybe?"

"Yes, but I don't think Dana will appreciate our sneaking

around."

"You're just giving your family a little tour of your old stomping grounds. How bad could that be?" Nick asked.

"I'll let you tell her that," Charlotte said as she led them down the stairs.

The basement appeared to be part wine cellar, part storage area. There was also a large refrigerator and freezer. Charlotte moved to the far end of the room quickly, as if she had no problem remembering exactly where she was going. "We'll have to move these boxes."

"Let me," Nick said, shoving three large boxes to one side. "There's nothing there," he added, running his hands over the wood paneling.

"Third panel from the right-you push it in. There's a release."

Sure enough, one push and the panel separated as a door swung open to reveal a dark space.

"There used to be a light, a string hanging down...." Charlotte stepped forward, reaching inside the blackness. A moment later a light came on.

The room was small, about four by six feet. It was cold and damp and completely empty.

"I knew it wasn't here," Charlotte breathed. "How could it be after fifty years?"

Kayla looked over at Nick, who was examining every inch of the room. He seemed to be looking for something, but she didn't know what. "So this is where Johnny and his friends hid their loot?" she asked.

Charlotte nodded. "They kept the liquor here during Prohibition. That's why the panel is secret. Dana's father worked for the city. He knew a lot about old buildings, and he mentioned to her once that she wouldn't believe what kind of underground network ran through the city. He told us the club used to be a speakeasy and probably had some sort of hidden room in the basement. We thought it was very exciting and dangerous, so we came looking for it, and we found it."

"Telling all our secrets, Charlie?"

Kayla whirled around. A tall woman with bright red hair faced them. Behind her was the man who'd let them into the club earlier. Neither one looked happy to see them.

"It's all right, Stephen," she said to the man behind her. "You can go."

The man looked like he wanted to argue, but after a moment he walked away, leaving them alone together.

"This is Dana," Charlotte said. "My old friend. This is my granddaughter, Kayla, and her friend, Nick."

"What are you doing down here, Charlie?" Dana asked.

"Checking to see if you were still hiding the money," Charlotte said bluntly.

Kayla watched the two women face off against each other and sensed that there was as much hate between them as love. She wondered why.

"I never thought you were that stupid," Dana said. "You really think I had the money all these years?"

"No, but I started to wonder if you knew more than you were saying when you came by my house the other day."

"I came by to tell you to shut up, but obviously that didn't work."

"Someone has three of the four watches," Charlotte said. "The only one missing is the one belonging to Frankie. I feel fairly certain that whoever is tracking down the watches must feel they know where the money is."

"You found Nate's watch? He gave it to Anne Marie?"

Charlotte nodded. "Who gave it to her son, who gave it to his daughter."

"I see. So he trusted her more than me. Shocking."

Kayla couldn't quite read Dana's tone. She seemed to be both furious and hurt.

"I told Kayla and Nick everything, Dana, just so you know," Charlotte added. "I told them that you and I used to hide the money and jewelry here in this room, that we stashed the money from the mint here right after the robbery. We were accessories to the crime. We didn't turn them in even though we knew what they'd done to those guards. We kept quiet."

"You can't prove any of that," Dana said. "It's your word against mine."

"We're not trying to prove it," Nick interrupted. "We just want to find the watches and the money. The person running this game is a con artist and a thief in his own right, and we want to catch him."

"No one is going to find the treasure now," Dana said. "It's been missing for fifty years, and people have looked before."

"No one had the watches before," Charlotte said. "I feel sure someone knows something -- perhaps more than one someone. Maybe you or your sons. They haven't been out of town recently, have they? No trips to Reno?"

"Leave my boys alone."

"As long as they leave my granddaughter alone. Someone tried to kill her."

"It wasn't one of my kids," Dana said quickly. "They're good men. They have wives, children, lives of their own. Don't try to mess with me now, Charlie. You turned your back on this life and this place a long time ago. You have no right to come back here now. I want you to leave, and I want you to keep on walking. Don't come back again. We're done. We've been done forever. Whatever friendship we had ended when you left without a good-bye, without a thank you. I saved you from having to live on the street. But you never acknowledged that. You acted like I was the one who took you down."

"I never said that. I never told anyone that."

"Not even me," Kayla interrupted. "She said you were her friend, and you helped her."

Dana looked surprised by this piece of information. "You told her that?"

"I gave her the truth, all of it. I didn't say it was your idea to help Johnny or Nate, because it wasn't. We were both involved, and I was the one who was madly in love. You always kept your heart out of it."

"Not always," Dana admitted. "Not with Nate. He was special. I just wished he would have left me with a baby, the way Johnny did with you. Then I would have had something of his forever. Well, you'd still best be on your way. There's nothing down here you want. I don't use this room anymore. I keep it empty to remind me to stay on the right side of the road, so to speak. Nate died because of his greed, his recklessness. He never thought anything could happen to him. He was invincible. They thought no one would ever find them, but they were wrong. A week later they were in jail. And five years later they were dead."

"I don't know if they're dead," Charlotte said. "I think I saw Johnny last night. I believe he came by my house, but I passed out from the shock and wound up in the hospital. I don't know if it was a dream, but it sure didn't seem like it." She paused. "Are you sure there's nothing you can tell us, Dana? Nothing more you know about the coins or the watches or who would be looking for any of it?"

Dana took a long moment to answer. "There was that man who wrote that book about Alcatraz and the escape. His name was Joel something. He was here a few months back, doing some research. He used to be a guard at the prison. He said Frankie told him where the money was. I asked him why he wasn't rich then, and he just smiled. He said he was working on it. I thought he was an idiot, but I suppose it's possible he knew something. I think he was just trying to get me to talk, but you never know."

Charlotte glanced at Kayla and Nick. "Is there anything else you want to ask before we go?"

"Just one question," Nick said. He held out his hand, opening up his fingers to reveal a shiny gold cuff link. "Any idea how this got into your secret room?"

Dana stared at the cuff link as if she'd never seen it before. "I have no idea. No one knows about that room."

"Not even your sons?" Charlotte asked.

"Not even them. I've always kept boxes in front of that wall." She paused. "I'll walk you out."

When they got to the car, Kayla asked the question burning in her brain: "What's with the cuff link, Nick? Why do you keep staring at it?"

"Because I think it's mine," he said, meeting her gaze. "The only person who could have taken it is Evan, which means he was in that room. How did he know about it? How did he get in? And why was he there?"

Just once she wished she could answer some of his questions.

* * *

Nick was still thinking about the cuff link later that night. He'd made a quick trip home to check, and sure enough one of the pair was missing, and the one he'd found at the club was a perfect match. Had Evan already found the coins? Or had Dana told them the truth when she said the room had been empty for years? Maybe Evan had just gone to check it out the way they had.

Kayla flopped down on the couch next to Nick. They were sitting in her grandmother's living room, having spent most of the day putting the house back to rights and cooking a good dinner. Now Charlotte was upstairs getting ready for bed.

"I told Grandma I was going to sleep down here," she said. "This couch pulls out into a bed."

"I hope you told her that *we* were going to sleep down here," he corrected. "I'm not leaving the two of you alone in this house."

"I think we'll be fine," she said halfheartedly, but her eyes told another story.

"I'm staying," he said. "Will it bother your grandmother if we sleep together?"

Kayla made a face. "A few weeks ago I would have said yes, but now, knowing what I know..." She shook her head.

"What she did is different from what she wants you to do," Nick said. "You're her granddaughter. She wants what's best for you. That hasn't changed."

"I know, but what's best for me is you, and I'm old enough to make that decision on my own."

He looked into her eyes and saw a truth that scared the hell out of him. They hadn't talked about what was happening between them. He'd been happy to delay that conversation. In fact, he'd like to put it off even longer.

"It's okay," Kayla said softly. "I know it's too soon."

He didn't want to ask, "Too soon for what?" He was afraid of what she would say.

"And there's too much to think about," she added. She smiled again. "The only time you get really nervous, Nick, is when I bring up something personal."

"I'm not nervous," he said.

"You promised not to lie to me."

He looked into her warm brown eyes and knew she was right; he *was* lying. He *was* nervous, because she was getting to him in ways he'd never imagined. He'd always been able to keep his relationships at a distance, even the intimate ones. There were things he didn't share, lines he didn't cross, but Kayla was different. Since he'd met her there had been no lines, no boundaries, and not much distance between them. They'd been living in each other's pockets. They'd faced death together. They'd hit all the emotional high points two people could hit, and he couldn't ignore the fact that he didn't just want her; he was starting to need her. That was what scared him the most. He'd never wanted to be part of a couple, a pair, but now he couldn't seem to tear himself away from her.

Not that he could leave yet, he rationalized. Kayla might be in danger. She wouldn't be safe until Evan was in jail. Until then, he was sticking by her side, even if she begged him to leave. But she wasn't asking him to go. She was looking at him as if she were starving and he were a big T-bone steak. He swallowed hard, trying to think with his brain and not with his body, which was telling him to get her clothes off as fast as possible.

"Nick," she murmured, "you're staring at me. Not that I don't like it, but is there something on your mind?"

"I'm trying to remember that your grandmother is upstairs and these walls are very thin."

"We can be quiet."

"Can we?" he teased.

She blushed. "I can try."

"I don't want you to try. I like it when you let go."

"That seems to happen a lot where you're-" She stopped abruptly, her eyes widening as she stared at something over his shoulder.

"What's wrong?"

"There's someone there," she said, pointing to the window.

He turned his head quickly to see the vague image of a man outside the living room window. Jumping to his feet, he ran to the front door, cursing the time as he undid the new locks he'd put on Charlotte's front door. When he got outside, he saw a dark figure running down the road. He started down the street, but the man jumped into a car, an old sedan, and drove away. It was too dark to see a license plate, and he hadn't gotten a good enough look at the man to recognize him, although he didn't think it was Evan. He'd seemed darker and he'd run with an awkward gait, as if he had a bad knee.

As he turned to go back to the condo, Nick saw something

lying on the ground. It was a wig, he realized as he picked it up, but it was too dark to see it clearly. When he returned to the condo, Kayla met him on the steps. "Did you see who it was?"

"No, did you?"

"He looked dark, Italian," she said. "Older. God, Nick, do you think it was Johnny?"

Nick held up the wig in his hand. "Maybe not."

"What do you mean?"

He motioned her back inside, shutting the door behind him. Then he took a good look at the wig in his hand. The hair was short, black peppered with gray. It was a man's wig.

"Where did you find that?" Kayla asked.

"On the sidewalk." He paused. "I don't think Johnny was here last night. I think it was Evan in disguise."

Kayla met his gaze. "It would certainly make more sense. I'm not sure I want to tell my grandmother, though. She wants to think Johnny is alive."

"Let's leave it alone until we know for sure," Nick said. "I have to admit the guy running down the street tonight didn't move like a young man."

"So what are you thinking?"

"I have no idea," he said in frustration. "Nothing is adding up. We're trying to put pieces together, but they don't fit. The picture coming together is wrong. I feel as if we're missing something important. I just don't know what it is."

Kayla sighed. "I know what you mean. I run into this all the time when I'm trying to restore broken glass. If one piece is off, the whole thing doesn't work. Sometimes it seems hopeless, but then when I least expect it, I find the right piece and everything fits together perfectly."

"How long does that usually take?" Nick asked.

"Sometimes weeks," she admitted.

"We don't have weeks."

She made a face at him. "I know that, but we have at least a night." A sudden gleam came into her eyes. "I have an idea: We lay it out like a puzzle and try to put it together. Instead of trying to figure out what we don't know, let's concentrate on what we have."

Nick followed her into the kitchen, where she pulled out

paper, pens, and scissors. She sat down at the dining room table and proceeded to divide the paper into a dozen squares. Then she cut out each square and gave him an expectant look.

"Hey, this is your game," he said.

"*Our* game," she corrected. "We know there are four watches." She took out four pieces of paper and wrote the numbers one, two, three, and four on separate pieces of paper. Then she proceeded to write down the owner of each watch and the phrase inscribed on that watch.

Nick sat down across from her and laid out the four pieces of paper in front of him. He wasn't sure what order the phrases went in, but so far they had *of Heaven Await, All the Riches,* and *Until the Day.* "I wonder if we put these phrases into the computer what we'd come up with."

"Good question. Unfortunately, my grandmother doesn't have a computer. If you want to run back to your house..."

As much as he was tempted to do just that, he was reminded that only a few moments earlier someone had been watching the house. "We'll do it tomorrow," he said. "What else have we got?"

"All the people involved -- Evan, my grandmother, you, me, Jenny, J.T." She paused, pen in hand.

"Delores Ricci," he continued. "Unknown assailant in Reno, Lisa Palmer, whoever cut our brakes."

"My grandmother's friends-the girls in the dance club."

The tiny squares of paper were soon filled with writing. Nick moved them around and around, but the words just made his head spin. "I don't think this is helping," he said a moment later. "It just makes me realize how much we don't know."

Kayla sat back with a yawn. "Then I guess we'll have to go with plan B -- sleep on it."

"You go ahead," I said. "I'll study this a bit more. Besides, I want to make sure our intruder doesn't come back."

"I can stay up with you," she offered.

He saw the shadows under her eyes and knew the stress of the past few days was taking its toll. She looked wiped out. He felt much the same way, yet there was so much adrenaline in his bloodstream, so much anger and frustration, he didn't think he could relax long enough to sleep. "Go to sleep, Kayla. We'll figure this out in the morning."

"Or you'll figure it out tonight," she said with a confident smile.

"You have too much faith in me."

"I don't think that's true," she said with a seriousness that made his heart catch.

He didn't want to let her down. He didn't want to let himself down. But as he stared at the puzzle pieces, he knew he had no idea how to put them together.

Chapter Twenty-One

Kayla's dreams were filled with images from the past few days. Evan's mocking smile kept popping up. Then she'd feel an arm coming around her neck, threatening to choke off her breath, hear that deep, husky voice demanding to know where the watch was. As soon as she tried to rid that image from her head, another one replaced it. She was driving down the mountain with Nick, and the car was going faster and faster. She could hear herself screaming as they ran off the road.

She tossed and turned, trying not to think about anything. But she couldn't get comfortable on her grandmother's sofa bed, and every time she reached for Nick, he wasn't there.

It was shocking to realize how close they'd gotten. He was the first person she wanted to talk to in the morning and the last person at night, and every time something happened, she had to know what he thought. He was as essential to her as the air she breathed, and it worried her that they'd become so entwined in such a short time.

She didn't want to be a fool for love again. Not that she was in love, she told herself. But the denial sounded weak. Nick might think she was casual about sex, but she knew she wasn't. Her emotions had been involved from the start, from the very first kiss. Oh, sure, maybe she had kissed him in the beginning to get back at Evan, but the second their lips had touched, her motives had changed.

She wasn't as sure about Nick's motives. She knew he was

physically attracted to her, and that was probably all he'd needed to make love to her. Would he be able to leave her bed as quickly and as easily as he'd gotten into it? She was afraid the answer would be yes. She told herself not to think about it. There were other, more pressing matters that should be in her brain, not her personal relationship with Nick.

She just needed to sleep, rest, regroup. Sometime in the night she must have drifted off. When she woke up, the sun was streaming through the downstairs blinds, and Nick was asleep at the dining room table, his head on his arms, the puzzle pieces still spread out around him. She got up, showered, dressed, and made coffee, and still he slept. She hated to wake him, but she had to get her grandmother to a follow-up appointment with her personal physician.

"Nick," she said gently, putting her hand on his shoulder. "Time to wake up."

He awoke with a start, his eyes wild, his muscles tensed as if he were ready to jump into the middle of a fight. Nick was certainly not a man to sit on the sidelines. His gaze slowly focused on her face. "What's wrong?"

"Nothing, it's morning. I have to take my grandmother to the doctor."

"Right." He ran a hand through his tousled hair. "Let me just use the bathroom, splash some water on my face, and I'll be right back."

"You don't have to go with us. I'm sure we'll be fine."

He shot her a look that told her she was wasting her breath and then disappeared into the downstairs bathroom.

"What's all this?" Charlotte asked, entering the room and coming over to the table.

"We were trying to piece together all the information we have."

"Any luck?"

Kayla stared down at the puzzle, in particular the piece of paper that said *Frankie's watch.* It was the only one still missing. It had to be the key. "I don't think so."

"You'll figure it out," Charlotte said.

"That's what I told Nick last night," Kayla replied. "But I'm not sure any of us can figure it out until Evan or someone makes another move. There isn't anything you've forgotten to tell me, is there?"

"No, I swear, you know it all now. No more secrets."

Kayla gave her grandmother a sharp look but saw nothing except clear honesty in her eyes. "Good."

"I'm ready," Nick said as he came back into the room. He smelled like toothpaste, and his hair and face were damp.

Kayla thought he was just about the sexiest man she'd ever met in her life, but she could hardly tell him that with her grandmother standing right next to her.

"I'll get the car, pull it up front," Nick said, walking out the front door.

Kayla glanced over at her grandmother and caught her staring at her with an odd smile on her face. "What?"

"You're in love with Nick."

"No, I'm not," she said automatically.

"Okay," her grandmother said easily.

"I'm not," she repeated, because it was obvious Charlotte didn't believe her.

"Whatever you say, dear."

"Sometimes you can be really annoying, Grandma."

Charlotte simply smiled.

"All right, I like him -- a lot -- but I don't know about the rest of it, and I certainly don't know how he feels. Nick just wants to find Evan, get his money back, and keep his family safe."

"And he wants you," Charlotte said.

"Do you think so?" she couldn't help asking.

"I do, Kayla."

"I've made so many mistakes in the love department."

"So this time you'll get it right."

The sound of the car horn cut off their conversation. Nick was waiting. They had things to do, people to see. Her love life would have to wait.

* * *

After a lengthy visit at the doctor's office, they returned to Charlotte's condo. While her grandmother rested per her doctor's instructions, Kayla made lunch and Nick studied their puzzle. They had just finished eating when Charlotte's neighbor, Bernice, knocked on the door.

"Look who's here, Kayla," Charlotte said, greeting her friend with a hug.

"Hi Bernice," Kayla said.

"Well, it's good to see you up and about, Charlotte, looking like nothing ever happened," Bernice said. "I was so worried."

"Thanks to your quick thinking she got the treatment she needed right away," Kayla said.

"I want to say thank you, too," Charlotte added. "Kayla told me you got me to the hospital."

Bernice dismissed her thanks with a wave of her hand. "It was nothing. But you do owe me a card game." She cleared her throat, darting a quick look in Kayla's direction. "Some of the other girls were thinking of coming over and playing bridge, but only if you're up to it."

"I think I could play a few hands," Charlotte said. "You don't mind, do you, Kayla? You and Nick have been babysitting me long enough. And I'm sure you have other things to do."

"If you're certain you'll be all right, Grandma."

"I'll be fine. Call me later and tell me if you find out anything. Bernice and the girls will be here. Why don't you come in to the kitchen with me?" she said to Bernice. "We can make some tea."

As Kayla returned to the living room, she heard Nick talking on his cell phone. He was pacing, a restless light in his eyes.

"Keep me posted," he said, then hung up the phone.

"Who was that?"

"J.T. I filled him in on everything about your grandmother and Dominic's watch."

"Good. Did he have any news?"

"He spoke to Delores Ricci last night. She told him that the family always believed that their father's death was suspicious, but they never had any proof. She had no idea what happened to her father's watch. I'm sure she would be shocked to know your grandmother had it until now."

"What else?" she asked.

"Will, Evan's old buddy, disappeared the day after we were there. The landlord said he moved out, no forwarding address. I'm sure Evan didn't want him talking to anyone else. And J.T. said that they found fingerprints at Lisa Palmer's house but no match to anyone in the database. Of course, Evan is too smart to leave prints behind."

"Okay. That's all interesting, but you look far more excited than any of those facts should warrant. Why?"

He motioned her over to the dining room table. He pulled out three slips of paper and set them in a line.

"I've been thinking about our pieces, Kayla, and how they fit together. Yesterday when I talked to J.T. he told me about a conversation he had with Helen Matthews." He pointed to the piece of paper where he'd written her name. "She's the woman who knew Frankie way back when. She told J.T. that Frankie was a cheapskate and he liked to hoard things. She couldn't imagine that he'd given that watch to anyone."

Kayla stared at him, trying to follow his train of thought. "So you think Frankie kept the watch. If that's true, we still don't know what happened to it."

"We know what happened to Frankie," Nick said. "He went to..." Nick pointed to the second piece of paper.

"Alcatraz," she finished.

"Exactly, which is where we're going."

For some reason the idea made her uneasy. "Really?"

"Yes," he said. "And our timing is perfect. Remember that former guard...?" He pointed to the third piece of paper, on which he'd written the title of a book, *Tales from the Rock.* "The author is signing copies today," Nick added.

"That's right. I forgot about that."

"I remembered when Dana mentioned yesterday that Joel had come by her place to interview her. If this guard knew about her, what else did he know?"

"But he never spoke to my grandmother," Kayla interjected. "I wonder why not."

"Maybe Johnny didn't talk about Charlotte. But the point is that this Joel knows something about the men and perhaps about the robbery. He might also be able to tell us if Frankie went to Alcatraz with a pocket watch. I think the answers are on that island, Kayla. It would be interesting to find out what happened to any personal possessions the men may have brought with them."

"I agree," she said, beginning to share his excitement. "The pieces are falling into place. My plan worked."

"It did help to lay it all out." Nick glanced at a wall clock. "We should go. I reserved tickets for the three-o'clock ferry. We have just enough time to stop by our houses, change clothes, and get down to the pier. What about your grandmother?"

"Her friend Bernice is here. We can go," Kayla said, feeling suddenly energetic. Nick's positive mood was infectious. Maybe they were about to get the break they desperately needed.

* * *

An hour later, Nick turned into the parking lot across from Fisherman's Wharf. Despite the fact that it was the middle of the week, a large crowd of tourists was strolling along the wharf. Kayla tended to avoid this part of town. The restaurant and shop prices were set for tourists, and it was usually difficult to find parking, but she had to admit that the festive atmosphere made her wish they had time to take a walk. She hadn't eaten clam chowder on the wharf in years.

Nick wasn't paying any attention to the sidewalk entertainers juggling balls, playing guitars, or walking on stilts. He was a man on a mission. Once they'd picked up their tickets, he led her straight to the ferry. After they'd boarded the boat, she pulled her hand out of his with a wince.

He saw her expression and frowned. "Sorry."

"I appreciate the protective sentiment, but you have a really strong grip, and I need these fingers for my work."

"Point taken." His gaze swept the bottom level of the ferry before he nodded toward the stairs. "Let's go up to the top deck. We can get a good view of the wharf and see who else is on the boat."

The top deck was already filling up with tourists. They snagged a spot by the rail and stood quietly together for a few moments, listening to the conversations around them. Nothing seemed out of the ordinary. She hoped that meant nothing *was* out of the ordinary. Taking a band from her purse, Kayla pulled her hair into a loose bun. It was already breezy and would get windier when they were out on the bay. Nick frowned at her action.

"I like it better when you leave your hair down," he said.

"The wind blows it in my face. This is more practical." She had to fight the urge to take her hair down and watch his reaction. She had a feeling it would be worth a little hair in her face.

"I like it better when you're not being practical," he said with a rueful smile.

"I do, too," she heard herself confess. "But I'm trying to focus on the business at hand, so stop trying to distract me."

She turned away from Nick as the ferry began to maneuver out of the harbor. As they passed Pier 39, their departure was greeted by a loud, barking chorus performed by the hundreds of sea lions lounging in the sun on wooden pallets. Sometime in the past couple of years the sea lions had become a tourist attraction, and even now there were dozens of people lined up to take photos of the playful lions.

Once they were out of the harbor, they turned toward the Golden Gate Bridge, lit up by the afternoon sun. A cruise ship sailed under the bridge, probably heading for a port on the east side of the bay. Looking at the turbulent waves, Kayla couldn't help thinking about the past. "I wonder if Johnny and Nate could really have survived a swim across this bay," she said.

"They were young men risking their lives for freedom. I'm sure their will was strong."

"True. Sometimes it's amazing what you can get if you want it bad enough."

"That's what dreams are built on -- desire. Take that beautiful bridge over there. Do you know what it took to build it?"

"I have a feeling you're going to tell me."

"When I was in school I had to do a complete study of that bridge -- the history, the planning, the execution. The builders were fearless, climbing like untethered monkeys some seven hundred and fifty feet above the water. All they had was a safety net, and even that didn't stop eleven people from dying during the construction. But they kept building. And in the end, they created one of the most famous bridges in the world."

She smiled at the passion in his voice. "Tell me more."

He grinned back at her. "I'm boring you."

"Not at all. I'd love to see you in action, climbing like... What was it you said? An untethered monkey?"

"Would it impress you if I said I did that?"

"I think it would. It's very sexy. Not the monkey part, but the daredevil-skywalker part."

"Really?" he murmured against her ear. "Maybe I should tell you more about my adventures in bridge building." He ran his tongue along the edge of her ear.

Her spine tingled, and she couldn't stop the shiver that raised goose bumps along her arms. She cleared her throat. "Nick, behave yourself. We're on a boat."

"Is that why I feel off balance?"

"I wish I could use that as an excuse, but I can't. It's you."

He tucked a stray lock of hair behind her ear. "No, I think it's you, Kayla."

Her nerves tingled at his words, at his expression, which spoke of the same yearning she felt deep within her soul. He got to her, plain and simple -- only there was nothing simple about it. He was complicating her already messy and crazy life, making her feel things she'd never felt before.

The boat suddenly hit something solid, and Kayla stumbled into Nick's arms. "What was that?"

"I think we've landed," he said, stealing a quick kiss.

She suddenly realized the island was right next to them. She'd been so caught up in Nick, she hadn't even noticed that they were docking.

They descended to the lower level with the rest of the passengers. Once they got off the boat, they paused to get their bearings. Alcatraz, often called the Rock because of its rocky formation in the middle of the bay, had originally been a military base, and near the pier were the old barracks from those early days. After pausing for a few minutes to listen to the park ranger's historical presentation, they decided to walk up to the prison, situated at the top of a long, steep hill.

Although she had been born and raised in San Francisco, Kayla had never actually set foot on the Island. She'd been sick the one time her school had taken a field trip to the prison, and neither her mother nor father had ever been interested in taking the tour. When they reached the top of the hill, she and Nick ventured across the large courtyard to stand on the far side, gazing at the amazing scene before them.

"They say it's the best view in the city," Nick murmured.

He was right. The city of San Francisco, with its beautiful shoreline, hilly streets, and tall, sweeping skyscrapers, was spread out before them like a photograph on a perfect postcard.

"The view taunted the prisoners," Nick added. "They could see paradise, but they couldn't get to it."

"That almost seems like cruel and unusual punishment."

"I'm sure it made the idea of escape seem very appealing."

Kayla nodded and turned back to look at the prison. The cell house was a massive stone structure, gray and intimidating. She wasn't sure she wanted to go inside.

"There's our guy," Nick said, drawing her attention to the man signing books near the prison entrance. "Let's get in line so we can talk to him."

"What exactly are we going to say?" she asked as they waited.

"Why don't we start with the fact that you're Johnny's granddaughter? That information ought to get his attention."

She frowned at that thought. "I'm not sure I want to tell him that. I'm not sure I want to tell anyone. You're asking me to rewrite my personal history in a very public way and attach myself to a notorious criminal. Maybe I want to leave Johnny as a skeleton in my closet that no one knows about."

"Okay, I can see where it might be uncomfortable, but he's not going to tell two perfect strangers anything important."

She considered that, suspecting Nick was right. She watched Joel McClain as he signed one of his books for a woman at the front of the line. Even sitting, he appeared to be a tall, lanky man, with long arms and a narrow, skinny face, probably in his mid- to late sixties-which would have made sense if he was a young guard when her grandfather was in prison. She wondered why he'd waited so long to write a book about his experiences. Maybe it was something he'd decided to do after retirement.

"The timing is weird, isn't it?" she muttered. "A new book that features escape attempts by famous prisoners comes out now, just when someone is hunting down the missing money some of those same prisoners stole fifty years ago."

"Do you think there's a connection?"

"I don't know what it could be, but maybe."

They moved forward in line and soon it was their turn.

"Mr. McClain," Kayla said, "we'd love to get your book, but

we'd also like to speak to you if possible. One of my relatives was an inmate here a long time ago."

"Really? Who?" Joel asked. "Perhaps I'll remember him."

"Johnny Blandino," she said, without giving away the relationship.

A gleam came into his eyes. "That's very interesting. He was the mastermind of the last escape attempt, you know."

"That's what I understand. I don't want to hold up your line. Can we speak to you when you're finished?"

He hesitated. "What did you say your relationship was to Johnny?"

"I didn't say, but I will when we meet."

"All right. I'll be here another half hour at least. Perhaps you can come back."

"Great, thanks," Kayla said.

"So you are going to tell him," Nick said as they moved away from the table.

"Maybe. I might lie. Just so you know."

He smiled. "I appreciate the heads-up. I guess we have some time to kill. Shall we take a walk through the prison? Since you've never seen it, I'm sure you'll find it interesting."

"It looks kind of scary."

"It is," Nick said. "You'd better hold my hand."

She grinned back at him "You're always thinking, Nick. Lead on."

The prison wasn't so much interesting as it was disturbing. The cells were small, only about five by nine feet, and there were some six hundred of them in the prison, built one on top of another. Narrow catwalks ran along the upper-level cell blocks. All the doors could be opened and closed automatically.

They paused for several minutes to listen to a park ranger describe an escape attempt-unfortunately not the one that involved her grandfather, but Kayla still found the details fascinating.

"In 1962," the ranger said, "four men attempted an escape from the Rock by digging their way out of the eroding concrete walls, which had been weakened by the leaking pipes of the saltwater toilets. In the end one of the four men chickened out and stayed behind. The other three men were never found."

"Just like my grandfather and Nate," Kayla said to Nick.

"Everyone says no one succeeded in escaping from here, but no one really knows, do they?"

"They just know they haven't turned up alive anywhere else. Let's keep going," Nick suggested.

As they continued through the prison, they passed by the shower room, famous for fights between inmates, who were allowed a hot shower three times a week; the dining room; and the barbershop, infirmary, and library. Last they stopped at D block, isolation, where the most dangerous and violent prisoners were locked up in almost unbearable solitude.

Kayla's skin prickled as they actually stepped into one of the small cells.

She could almost hear the door slamming behind her, trapping her forever. The darkness, the loneliness, would be terrifying. How did anyone survive? No wonder her grandfather had wanted to escape. No wonder desperation had driven him to attempt the unthinkable.

"I have to get out of here," she said, feeling only marginally better once she emerged from the cell. The air was thick with the stench of the past. In her head she could hear the cries of the men who'd lived in the prison, who'd watched the days tick by with agonizing slowness.

She desperately needed fresh air, blue sky, and lots of open water. When they finally exited the prison, they walked across the plaza and paused to breathe -- in and out, slowly, surely.

"That was horrible," she said. "And my grandfather lived here. I'm not surprised he tried to escape."

Nick put his hands on her shoulders and rubbed her tight muscles. "Don't forget that Johnny and those other men deserved to be here, Kayla. You shouldn't feel sorry for them. Two men died during the robbery at the mint, two innocent men with families who loved them. You can't lose sight of those facts."

"I know you're right. I can't forget it. I won't forget it. I'm just trying to understand. I've never been related to a murderer before. God, I can't believe I just said that out loud." Her tension eased slightly under the pressure of his hands, but she still felt cold. She shivered and zipped up her jacket, glad now that she'd brought it along.

Glancing out at the view, she realized that the blue sky was quickly fading. The fog from the Pacific Ocean was coming over the Golden Gate Bridge, covering the towers in thick white puffs. "It's getting late," she murmured.

Nick checked his watch. "There's still a line at Joel's table. We have some time. Let's take a look in that shack over there. It seems to be some sort of exhibit."

They wandered over to a small building not much bigger than the prison cells. On the walls were dozens of photographs of inmates like Al Capone, Machine Gun Kelly, and the Birdman of Alcatraz. In two long glass cases were other memorabilia. Kayla leaned over to read a faded piece of paper that was some sort of journal entry from a former inmate.

"'It's unbearable here,'" she read aloud. " 'I feel as if I will surely lose my mind. I can reach out and touch all the walls of my cell without even moving. At night, I dream those walls are moving in on me, slowly squeezing the life out of my chest. Beyond the prison I sometimes catch a glimpse of the sky, the water, and blessed freedom. My heart yearns for the simple pleasures. If only I could find a way to escape these walls.'" She looked over at Nick. "Wow. You can really hear his pain."

"You're too soft, Kayla. You gotta toughen up. Prisoners, bad guys, remember?"

"I know. I know." She walked down the length of the glass counter, looking at various items, everything from cups to playing cards and prison clothing. And then there was a display of tattered clothes, a hat, and an old-her heart skipped a beat-an old pocket watch, the sign reading, *All That Was Left of Frankie Damon.*

"Nick, look," she whispered. She didn't know why she'd lowered her voice. They were the only people in the room. "It's Frankie's watch. You were right. It was here all along."

They stared in amazement at the silver pocket watch that seemed to be asking, *What took you so long?*

"No one thought to look in the most obvious place of all," Nick muttered.

Kayla bent her head to study the watch. The side that was visible had an inscription. It read, *the Saints Pray*. She thought for a moment, trying to remember the other phrases. "My grandfather's watch said, '*of Heaven Await*.' Dominic's watch said, '*All the Riches*.'"

"And Nate's watch said, '*Until the Day*,'" Nick finished.

She moved the phrases around in her mind, trying to find the rhythm, the pattern. "I've got it. *All the Riches of Heaven Await Until the Day the Saints Pray.*"

Nick stared back at her. She could see the wheels turning in his brain. "I don't--"

"It's the church," she said, snapping her fingers. "St. Basil's. Where the saints pray."

"You could be right," he said, a light dawning in his eyes.

"I know I am. And the engraving on the other side -- I bet it's a picture of the front of St. Basil's," she added, feeling a surge of excitement. "It makes total sense. The boys met there. They were inseparable. They knew all the ins and outs of the old church." It suddenly seemed so clear. "I bet it's there -- the missing money. I bet it's been there all along."

"In the church? Where would it be in the church?"

"I don't know. Maybe that inscription is written somewhere, on a wall, over a door, on a plaque, something that made sense to them. We need that watch."

Nick looked over his shoulder, then back at the glass case.

"What are you thinking?" she asked warily, though she was sure she knew.

"It's a simple lock, probably because nothing in this case is worth much, except for sentimental historical purposes. I think I could get it open. I have a little screwdriver on my key chain."

"Even if you could get it open, we can't break in. Someone will see us."

"We'll wait until the island is closing and everyone is going down the hill. Then we'll grab the watch, catch the last boat, and go to St. Basil's."

"It's stealing, Nick. Someone could catch us. One of the park rangers."

"They'll be busy getting everyone off the island. We just have to wait for the right moment. We grab the watch and go. I doubt anyone will even notice it's gone for a few days."

"Are you sure you can get into the case?" she asked, hardly believing she was actually considering his crazy idea.

"Absolutely. My sisters were always trying to lock me out of their rooms or their diaries," he said with a gleam in his eye. "I can get in, but not now," he said on a hushed note as two other tourists entered the room.

They quickly exited the exhibit, not wanting to be caught standing around, looking suspicious.

"We could get in so much trouble," Kayla said worriedly.

"Or we could finally get our hands on the last watch," Nick said. "We have to take the chance. Don't forget, we have a friend in the FBI. If anything does go wrong and we get arrested, I'm sure J.T. will bail us out."

"Do you have to mention the word *arrested* when we're standing outside one of the scariest prisons in the country? I do not want to end up in a place like this."

"You won't, I promise," he said.

As they walked away from the exhibit, Kayla stopped abruptly. Nick saw the empty table at the same time she did.

"We missed him," she said. "We weren't in the building that long, were we?"

Nick shrugged. "Whatever he knows is probably in his book. We can read that later. I think the place is closing down."

Kayla agreed. Only a few tourists were still straggling out of the prison. The rest were on their way down the hill. The plaza was almost deserted-except... She stiffened as she caught sight of a man at the far end of the courtyard. "Nick, isn't that the guy we saw in Reno?"

As soon as Nick turned his head, the man disappeared, heading down the hill. "That guy who's leaving?"

"Yes."

"I didn't get a good look at him."

"He's gone, so I guess it doesn't matter."

Nick didn't look convinced. "Maybe I should go after him. But if we go down the hill, I don't think we'll be able to return. We'll check the boat for him when we get back on. Let's take a walk so we don't get swept up by any of the rangers herding tourists to the boat. There's a path over there. We'll stay out of sight for a few minutes and then come back here, grab the watch, and jog down the hill."

She followed his lead, and soon they were on a grassy path winding down and around the prison to the other side of the island. It was a quiet and peaceful trail. They hadn't gone far before Kayla began to feel as if someone were watching them, following them. She stopped abruptly and turned. She heard the snap of a branch behind her, but there was no one in sight.

"What's wrong?" Nick asked.

"I think someone's following us," she whispered. "What if that guy turned around and came back after us?"

A flock of birds suddenly squawked and scattered as if someone had disturbed them.

"Let's keep going," Nick said. "The path must wind around."

"Do you think?" she asked, staying close. "Maybe we should go back the way we came."

"We'll run into whoever is following us," he said logically. "You go in front of me. I'll watch your back."

As much as she appreciated the thought, she was disturbed by the fact that the path seemed to be taking them to the far side of the island. A few minutes later she stopped, breathless from picking her way over rocks. "Do you hear anything?" she asked.

"Not for the last few minutes," he said.

"I don't know if this path is going to lead back around."

His expression was grim. "I was wondering the same thing." He looked behind him and swore. "Dammit." He pointed toward the bay, where a boat was heading back to San Francisco.

It took a moment for her to register the fact that it was the same ferry that had brought them to the island. "Oh, my God! Is that our boat?"

"I'm guessing, yes."

"But we're not on it. We have to get on it. Come on." She tried to brush past him, but he stopped her. "Hang on, Kayla."

"What do you mean, hang on? If we get down to the landing, the park ranger or whoever stays on this island overnight will realize we've been left behind. They'll get a boat for us, or maybe there's a small boat they use to ferry the rangers back and forth."

"I don't think anyone stays here at night," he said.

"What do you mean? Of course someone must stay here."

"Think about it. There's nothing to steal. The island is impossible to get to without the ferry, and the guide was talking earlier about budget cuts in the park service. Plus, we still want to try to get that watch."

She swallowed hard, not sure if she was more disturbed

because there might be no one on the island except them or because a park ranger could still find them and arrest them for trespassing or attempting to steal artifacts from a national park.

Her heart skipped a beat at the sound of footsteps and rustling branches. If there were truly no rangers left on the island, then who was following them? "What should we do?" she whispered, suddenly panicked and terrified.

"Hide."

Chapter Twenty-Two

Nick pushed her into some thick brush off the side of the trail. Kayla held her breath as they heard someone coming closer and closer.

Was it a ranger-someone rounding up the last tourists? Or someone who wanted them dead?

Her heart raced a mile a minute. She leaned into Nick, who was in front of her, shielding her with his body.

A few pebbles went flying down the path, as if someone had kicked them. The footsteps paused. Kayla was going crazy from the waiting, the anticipation, and the worry that she wasn't doing the right thing.

Another branch snapped. A bird squawked. A pair of legs came into view. Jeans. Men's shoes. A belt.

The details Kayla could see were not reassuring. Hadn't the man she'd seen in the square been wearing blue jeans? The pants certainly didn't belong to a park ranger. Someone else was on the island with them.

Evan? The thought jumped into her head. She wanted to take a closer look, but she was afraid to breathe. The man began to move again. Kayla let out a breath. Nick flung her a warning look to stay where she was. *Don't say a word,* he mouthed.

That was easy. She was finding it hard to breathe. Speaking wasn't an option.

Nick's instincts were right on the money. A few moments later she heard the person come back up the path. He was walking more quickly now, his feet stirring up loose dirt and gravel as he passed them. He must have decided they weren't there.

They waited for several long, tense minutes. Kayla felt as if her nerves were being stretched so tight they might break at any moment.

Finally Nick murmured, "I think he's gone. I'm going to take a look."

"No," she said. "What if he's still out there, waiting for us to come out?"

He stared into her eyes. "Kayla, if we don't leave now, we may not be able to get off this island tonight."

Even though she had the terrible feeling that was already true, her heart leaped at the possibility that maybe another ferry would be coming back to pick up the last stragglers. "Okay, what should we do?"

"Let's keep going down this path, since he went back the other way." Nick parted the branches for her, and she scrambled out ahead of him. Standing up, she took a look both ways and saw nothing. It was getting darker, and the fog was obliterating any sign of stars or a moon. Nick headed down the path. She stayed close to his back, her hand on his arm, afraid to let him get too far ahead of her.

Nick came to an abrupt halt. The path ended at a wall of rock that went up to the formidable prison behind them. To the right was a steep hillside. To the left were large, rocky boulders wet from the windy spray off the bay. There was nowhere to go but back the way they had come.

"He could be waiting for us," she said, holding on to Nick's arm as if he were a lifeline.

"We'll have to take that chance. We can't stay here. If he comes this way, we're sitting ducks."

It took a few minutes to get back to the stairs leading up to the plaza beside the prison. They climbed the steps slowly, one at a time, pausing at the top to look around. The lighthouse illuminated some of the plaza area, but the shadows had grown longer and deeper. It was impossible to see the far side.

Without words, they walked warily along the edge of the plaza, keeping an eye open for anyone or anything out of the ordinary. It was quiet, almost eerily quiet. They reached the door to the small exhibit shack. It swung open easily, too easily. It hadn't been locked. Or the lock had been broken.

Kayla understood why the door was open when they neared the glass case. The light from Nick's cell phone showed them what she'd suspected: The lock was gone. The case was open. The watch was missing. Whoever had been following them must have taken it.

"We should have grabbed it when we had the chance," Nick said, releasing a frustrated breath. "We blew it. We shouldn't have gone so far away. We should have kept an eye on the building."

"You're right, but what are we going to do now?"

"I don't know," he answered. They stood in the doorway, surveying their surroundings. "I don't think we should stay here, if for no other reason than that we don't want to be accused of breaking into the exhibit."

"Good point."

Nick took her hand as they moved out of the building and into the shadows. She swallowed hard, feeling more than a little scared. "I'd prefer to stay away from the prison. It's too creepy."

He tipped his head toward the area behind them. "Let's go that way."

Kayla could barely make her feet move, she was so tense. She was acutely aware of every tiny sound. Their breathing seemed extraordinarily loud. Their footsteps echoed on the pavement. She was relieved when they hit patches of grass. The remnants of a building beckoned them inside. The walls and floor were bare, the windows long ago blown out, but they were sheltered from the elements, and from their vantage point they could see the empty pier down below. There were no boats, no people in sight. Maybe they really were alone on the island.

Nick stood in the doorway, his eyes focused on the darkness. Kayla leaned against the wall, trying to calm her racing heart. The fog was blowing through the open windows, dampening her face and skin. A foghorn sounded nearby, and as she glanced out the window, she could see the beams from the lighthouse casting a ghostly light over the water.

Despite her best efforts to stay calm, all she could think about was the fact that they were stranded on a spooky island in the middle of the bay. She ran her hands up and down her arms, trying to stop the shivering.

Nick turned and saw her shaking. He moved next to her. "Kayla, are you all right?"

"I don't think so. I'm cold and scared. And this place is terrifying."

"We'll be okay," he assured her.

"You can't know that. We could be all alone on this island. Or there could be a madman looking for us right now, someone who doesn't want us to find the watches or him. We could die here, and no one would know who had done it. We wouldn't even know." Her imagination was running away with her. Her voice rose with each word. "I want to go home. I want to get out of here. I feel trapped."

"You're getting too worked up, Kayla."

"Well, thanks for stating the obvious," she snapped.

He pulled her against him, and she wrapped her arms around his back. One of his hands stroked her hair. "We're together," he said. "We'll be all right."

"I'm losing it."

"You're not. You're a strong woman."

She didn't know what woman he was talking about, because she didn't feel strong. "You obviously don't know me very well."

"But I do." He moved just far enough away so that he could look at her. "I've seen you in action all week. I saw you face Evan with your head held high. I saw you climb out of an elevator shaft even though you were terrified. I heard you order me to leave when you were trapped in a burning car because you were worried about my safety. You are an amazing woman, Kayla Sheridan. Don't let anyone, including yourself, ever tell you differently."

Her eyes blurred with tears. "God, Nick, that's just about the nicest thing anyone ever said to me."

"Hey, I didn't mean to make you cry."

"You're amazing, too, you know. Your determination, persistence, and unwillingness to give up keep me going even when I want to quit-like now."

"It's just one night, Kayla. The hours will pass. In the morning we'll mingle with the tourists and take the first boat back. No one will ever know we were here." He framed her face with his hands. "I won't let anything happen to you. I promise. Trust me."

"I do trust you. I know you'll do whatever it takes to keep me safe. But I don't want you to feel that you got me into this. I came willingly, and whatever happens I don't want you to forget that. I don't want you to spend the next twelve years beating yourself up over anything that might happen to me, the way you did with Jenny."

"Nothing will happen to you or me," he told her firmly.

"Okay." She sat down on the ground and leaned against the wall. Weeds had crept through the cracks in the foundation, and she picked at two long strands of grass with her fingers. Nick stood in the doorway, looking out at the courtyard. She strained her ears to hear signs of someone coming, but there were no footsteps, no sounds of life.

She didn't know how long they waited. It could have been a half hour or maybe an hour, but the minutes seemed to tick by with interminable slowness. Gradually, her heart began to beat more normally. She reassured herself with logic. This was just like camping. She could handle one night in the outdoors. It wasn't that cold. There were no wild animals on the island-at least, she didn't think so. They were reasonably well protected from the elements. And so far it appeared that whoever had been following them had gone or had hunkered down for the night somewhere else.

Nick finally left the doorway and sat down beside her. "I don't see or hear anyone or anything. I think we're alone."

"I think so, too."

He took her hand in his. "You're cold."

"Not too bad."

He put his arm around her and she curled up next to him. She had her head on his chest, and even through his coat she could hear his heart beating. It steadied her. Made her feel she was safe.

"Is this better?" he asked. "Are you warmer now?"

"Yes, in fact I'm getting a little hot." She lifted her head and looked into his eyes.

"Really?" he asked on an incredulous note. "Did I say before you were an amazing woman?"

She smiled at him. "Let's just start with a kiss."

He shook his head. "If I kiss you now, I'm not going to want to stop."

Her heart fluttered at the thought. She was trapped on an

island in the middle of the bay. The menacing prison loomed behind them. The waves pounded the rocks beneath them. It was possible there was a madman looking for them even now. They could die tonight. There had never been a worse time to make love. There had never been a better time either.

She kissed Nick hard on the lips, her need to have him racing through her blood like fire. He kissed her back with the same heated fury, his mouth open, seeking, tasting, taking. She threw one leg over him, straddling him, pressing her breasts against his chest, her hips into his groin. He was hard and she was aching. He rocked back and forth against her, their jeans creating a delicious, delirious sense of need.

"God, Kayla, slow down," he muttered.

"I can't. I want you." She pulled at the snap on his jeans. He arched up and shoved his pants down to his knees while she did the same with her own pants. Then she sank down on him, taking him inside in a white-hot rush of feeling. She leaned forward as he thrust into her again and again. There was so much passion between them. She'd never felt so alive, so wanted, so needed.

His mouth sought hers again and again, as if he were dying of thirst and she was his salvation. She lost track of her surroundings. She was only aware of his touch, his smell, his kiss. It was so dark, so isolated, so primitive and sensual. And she didn't want to stop.

He filled her body in every way, and as they moved together she didn't think she'd ever fit so perfectly with anyone. Each stroke took her to another high. She wanted more and more and more. Her breath came in ragged gasps. Nick's hands clenched on her buttocks as they both hit the final peak and found blessed release. She collapsed against his chest, her arms wrapped around his neck. She had the terrible feeling she could never let him go.

* * *

Nick awoke to the sun streaming through the open windows. Kayla was curled up next to him, her head on his chest, her hand on his abdomen, her long hair hiding her face from his eyes. One of her legs was draped over his, and he felt an instantaneous reaction to the thought of making love to her again. No matter how many times they were together, it was never enough. He wondered if it would ever be enough. But that was a matter for another day. Right now they had to figure out how to get off the island.

"Kayla," he said, stroking her back with his hand.

She lifted her head, her sleepy eyes smiling at him. "Hi," she said.

"Hi." He leaned over and took his time with a leisurely kiss. Then he said, "I think we'd better get a move on."

Kayla blinked and sat up. "Oh, my God, I almost forgot where we were. What time is it?"

He glanced down at his watch. "Seven thirty." He saw wild panic flare in her eyes. "Relax. I know the tours don't start for at least another hour or two."

"Okay, what's your plan?"

He didn't want to tell her he didn't have one, so he improvised. "Stay out of sight for a while. Wait for the first boat and mingle with the tourists."

"And then what?"

"We go back to the city."

"To St. Basil's Church," she said. "I think that's where the answers are, and more than likely where the money is. I just hope whoever stole the watch last night hasn't gotten too big a head start."

After they left the island, Nick called J.T. and told him they were on their way to St. Basil's Church. J.T. said to hang on until he got there. He was across the bay, but he could be there in an hour. Of course, Nick hadn't wanted to wait.

Kayla worried that even if they found Evan they wouldn't be able to take him down on their own, but Nick would hear none of her protests.

"We'll just check it out," he said, as they parked their car near the church and got out.

"Fine, but if we see anything suspicious, we wait for J.T."

"Everything looks ordinary to me," he replied.

She had to agree. It was just after ten o'clock in the morning, and the school must have had some event, because children were pouring out of the church into the adjacent playground. The kids were laughing, playing, skipping. None of the adults looked concerned. If Evan had beaten them here, he hadn't done anything to upset anyone.

Kayla and Nick slipped inside the church amidst the chaos, pausing for a moment in the vestibule while they figured out where to go.

"I doubt it will be anyplace public," Kayla said. "It has to be tucked away somewhere."

"Like where?"

"I'm not sure." Seeing a priest coming down the aisle, Kayla grabbed Nick's hand and pulled him toward a nearby staircase. She didn't want to get caught by anyone before they had a chance to look around. The priest stopped to speak to one of the teachers in the vestibule, so they kept walking down the stairs.

At the first landing they found themselves by an auditorium. The stairs continued downward, and Kayla was curious to see where they led, so she kept going. They ended up in a small hallway facing two closed doors. Actually, one of the doors was ajar. Kayla pushed it open. As she entered into the room, she was shocked to find they were standing in what looked to be a small crypt.

"Nick, what is this?" she asked in hushed tones. There were vaults in the walls, some of them empty, some with open doors, some still closed and locked up tight. The room was dusty, the air thick. It didn't appear as if anyone had been down here in a while. Yet the door had been open. A shiver ran down her spine. She had a feeling they were close to something.

"Looks like a mausoleum," Nick said. "These graves must have been here for a long time."

"The church was built in the eighteen hundreds," Kayla said, moving over to take a look at one of the vaults. "I know burials in San Francisco were outlawed around the time of the 1906 earthquake. A friend of mine is a genealogy buff, and she's done a lot of research on the city."

"Which explains the empty vaults," Nick replied. "They must have moved some of the bodies and reburied them elsewhere."

"Some but not all?" She walked over to one of the vaults and read the name. " 'Mary Ellen Parish, beloved daughter, 1878 to 1898.' She was only twenty years old," she murmured. "I wonder why her grave stayed here."

Nick cleared his throat. "Maybe it didn't. Maybe the vault is just closed." He tugged at the collar of his shirt as if he couldn't breathe.

"You don't like it down here," she said.

"I've never been big on cemeteries," he said tersely. "This is a waste of time. We don't know what we're looking for."

"We're looking for the perfect place to hide something, and I think it's here."

She saw the discomfort in his eyes give way to the realization that she was right.

"Damn," he muttered.

She moved around the room, looking at the vaults, reading the various inscriptions. Finally she found the one she wanted. It was the second one from the bottom, just about waist high. "Nick," she breathed. "Look. 'All the Riches of Heaven Await.' It's the same phrase."

Nick read the name on the vault. "Zacharia Blandino." He glanced at her. "A relative of Johnny's, I'm guessing."

"Maybe my great-great-grandfather," she said with amazement. "I bet they used the phrase to pinpoint the location of the vault."

"What about the other two phrases?"

" 'Until the Day' could have symbolized some specific day they'd meet to split their spoils."

"All Saints' Day," Nick said. " 'Until the Day the Saints Pray.' Only they were captured before they could come back." His gaze met hers. "We have to open that vault."

She couldn't stop the sudden fear his words unleashed. "It's a grave, Nick. Do we have the right?"

"A very old grave that belongs to one of your relatives. No one is tending this place. We don't even know if the vault is empty or if this guy was moved a long time ago. I say we take the chance."

He made sense, but it still felt creepy. "I think we should call J.T. and ask him what we should do."

Nick ran his hands along the front of the vault. "I have a feeling we're not the first ones here."

Kayla looked closer. The side was scratched and bent, as if someone had already tried to pry it open. There was an iron crowbar a few feet away. Coincidence? Had someone been here before them? Maybe they were too late. "Call, J.T.," she said again, watching as Nick pulled out his cell phone.

"Right. I can't get a signal down here," he said. "We'll have to go upstairs."

"I don't think so," a voice said from behind them.

Kayla whirled around, stunned to find herself staring down the barrel of a gun. It took a moment to register that the gun was not in Evan's hands. The man holding the weapon was the same man she'd seen in Reno, stocky, dark hair, dark eyes, and sweating profusely. There was a wild expression on his face. Kayla instinctively moved closer to Nick.

"Don't move," the man warned.

"Who are you?" Nick demanded.

"That's not important."

"What do you want from us?" Kayla asked.

"You have the watches," he replied, a gleam in his eyes. "My father made those watches. They belonged to him. And now they will be mine."

"Father?" Kayla echoed. "You're Dominic's son?"

"That's right, the son of the friend they betrayed."

Kayla shot Nick a quick look, then gazed back at the man holding the gun. "I don't have the watch anymore," she said. "I don't have any of them. They were stolen. You should know that. You've been following us around."

"You're lying. You wouldn't be here if you didn't have the watches. But you will never have the coins. The treasure belongs to me. My father died because of those coins. His best friends killed him. He didn't get what was his, but I will. I knew you would lead me to it. I heard you when you came into the store. I told Delores we would finally have justice. But she didn't believe me. She didn't want to tell me who you were."

"You hurt your own sister?" Kayla asked in shock, putting the pieces together in her head.

"It was an accident," he said, waving the gun at her. "I had to get your name, your address. She was arguing with me. She always argues. I don't like it when people don't do what I say. Now, you," he added, looking at Nick. "Pick up the crowbar and open the crypt. You can finish what I started."

Nick hesitated, obviously weighing the situation.

"Do it!" the man shouted. "Or I'll kill her. Don't think I

won't."

"You'd better do as he says," Kayla said. It was clear that this man was out of his mind. He'd hurt his own sister. He wouldn't think twice about hurting them.

"Okay, all right." Nick said, putting up a calming hand. "I'll do it."

He picked up the crowbar and moved over to the vault. He worked quietly and purposefully for a few minutes. Finally he wedged the bar into the opening and yanked. The door sprang open. Inside was a coffin on a stone slab. Nick slowly pulled it out.

"There could be a body in there," Kayla whispered. "I think this is wrong. We have no right to disturb the dead."

"Open it," the man ordered again. "Do it now."

Nick lifted the lid on the coffin, which was between them. Kayla put a hand to her mouth and then gasped as she saw bones, a skull, a skeleton. Her stomach turned over. She felt nauseous. Who was this man? Her great-great-grandfather? Was this Zacharia Blandino? There were remnants of clothes on the body and a note still pinned to the shirt.

"'You lie -- you die,'" Nick read. "I don't think this body belongs to Zacharia. I think it's-" He stopped abruptly, glancing from Kayla to the man with the gun.

"No!" the man screamed, rushing toward the coffin. He stared down at the bones. "Papa!" he cried. "Papa. They killed you. I knew they killed you. I saw it. I tried to tell the cops. They wouldn't believe me. And they put you here. Damn them to hell."

Kayla was so caught up in the man's raging pain that she was shocked when Nick swung the crowbar at him. The man stumbled but didn't fall. He turned, the gun aiming straight at Nick's heart. Nick lunged forward. The gun went off, the sound muffled between the two men.

Kayla couldn't breathe, stunned by the violence, terrified to see who would go down first. She prayed it would not be Nick. But he started to fall. "No!" she cried, as he sank toward the floor.

The other man began to move. She knew she had no time. She grabbed the crowbar that Nick had dropped to the ground and hit the man in the face. He went over backward this time, his feet slipping out from under him, his head cracking against the stone floor.

She knelt beside Nick. He was bleeding all over the front of his shirt. She couldn't tell where it was coming from, his shoulder, or -- God forbid -- his heart. She cradled his head with her hands. "Nick, Nick," she said urgently. "Please be all right. You have to be all right."

He blinked his eyes open. "What?"

"You were shot. Are you okay?"

"I...I don't know. Hurts," he muttered. "What happened to him?"

"He's unconscious. I've got to get help." She gently slipped her hands out from under his head. Then she took off her jacket and placed it over him. I'm going to go upstairs and call someone. Don't move. And don't... don't die on me, Nick. Promise me."

"I'm okay. It's my shoulder, I think."

She put a hand on his arm as he struggled to sit up. "Just stay put, Nick. I'll be right back."

She got to her feet, only to find her way blocked by another man -- tall, blond, and handsome: the man from her dreams, the man from her nightmares.

Evan. She let out a gasp of disbelief.

He smiled as he picked the gun up off the floor and twirled it around in his fingers. "Hey, babe, how's it going?"

"Get out of my way."

"I don't think so," Evan said, pointing the gun at her chest.

"Get away from her," Nick said weakly, struggling to sit up.

"You don't look so good, buddy," Evan drawled. "Now, now, don't move. You might pass out. I see you took care of Lorenzo for me. That dude is crazy. He knocked that poor blackjack dealer down the stairs for no reason."

"I thought *you* did that," Kayla said.

"I didn't need to. I already had the watch. Thanks for the tip, though. Old Nate had way too many relatives for me to track down." He paused. "Now, Kayla, I think it's time we opened the box."

She'd almost forgotten the reason they were here. She'd been so disgusted by the sight of rotting bones that she'd barely computed the fact that there was an iron strongbox in the coffin.

"Take it out; set it on the floor," Evan commanded.

She debated for a second and then did as he ordered.

Evan pulled out a key ring holding three small keys. "I think we'll need your key, babe. I know you must have it."

"Not a chance," she said.

"Okay, I guess we can let Nick bleed to death. Doesn't bother me," he said with a shrug. "I've got time."

Kayla hesitated, not sure what to do. She didn't want to help Evan, but she didn't want to make this take any longer than necessary. She needed to get Nick to the hospital.

"Or I could just put Nick out of his misery now," Evan offered. "He's already half-dead anyway."

"I'll see you dead first," Nick declared, grimacing with pain and obviously unable to stand in spite of his proud boast.

"I'll do it. Give me the keys," Kayla said impatiently. Evan tossed her the key ring, and she reached inside her purse and took out the key her grandmother had given her. There was a lock at each corner of the box. She knelt down and attacked them one by one. She had to try several times to get the right keys into the right locks. Finally she was finished. She slowly lifted the lid.

Inside were three canvas sacks about twelve inches long, each one tied with a drawstring. Several gold coins were loose in the box. The treasure. They'd found it, the money missing for fifty years. She looked at Evan and saw an expression of pure satisfaction on his face. She itched to wipe that smile off, to find a way to stop him from getting what he wanted.

"Very good, Kayla," Evan said. "Now push the box over here. And don't try anything stupid."

She gave the box a shove, then slowly got to her feet as Evan quickly put the canvas bags inside a backpack he hung over his shoulder. She glanced at Nick. He seemed to be trying to tell her something with his eyes, but she didn't know what. Evan still had the gun on them. What was she supposed to do? Rush him? What if it didn't work? What if the gun went off again and hit Nick, the way it had before?

She turned back to Evan, surprised to see him take an envelope from the bottom of the strongbox and slip it into his pocket. She wondered what was inside.

"You're not going to get away with this," Nick warned him.

"Oh, I think I am. You never appreciated my talents, Nick. You always tried to blackball me, especially with Jenny. You're the one who turned her against me. Told her I wasn't good enough for her. But I'm better than you, Nick. I'm better than anyone. And Jenny will soon realize that."

"She hates you, just as I do."

"No," Evan argued. "You want her to hate me, and it burns you that she doesn't."

As their conversation went back and forth, Kayla realized that they'd completely forgotten about her. She took a step forward, then another and another. Evan wasn't even looking at her. He was looking at Nick. He was taunting him, the gun now dangling from his hand.

This was her chance. She rushed forward, throwing her body toward Evan's arm, hoping to knock the gun out of his hand. Her sudden weight threw him off balance. He went over backward. She landed on top of him and began to pummel him with her fists, hitting and kicking whatever she could reach, the memory of what he'd done to her, what he'd done to all of them, driving her on.

A pair of arms grabbed her from behind. She struggled, not sure who was attacking her now.

"Kayla, it's okay; we've got him," a voice said.

It took a moment to register that it was J.T. talking to her. Then she saw two police officers flanking Evan.

"It's over," J.T. said again, setting her on her feet.

She stopped struggling and let out a breath. "Thank God."

"That was a damn stupid thing to do, Kayla," Nick said, his voice filled with fury. "You could have been killed."

"He's right," J.T. told her.

"I don't care." She looked at the bruises she'd left on Evan's face. "It was worth it. I don't want him to hurt anyone else ever again." She glared at Evan, who was now on his feet being handcuffed. Evan simply smiled at her.

She'd loved that smile once. Now it seemed pure evil.

"Ambulance is on the way," J.T. said, squatting down next to Nick. "One of the ladies upstairs heard the gun go off and called nine-one-one. You hanging in there?"

"I'll live. You took your sweet time getting here."

"Traffic was a bitch. I told you to wait." He glanced at one man on the floor. "Who's our other friend?"

"Dominic Ricci's son, Lorenzo," Kayla replied. "Apparently

he saw his father killed. He seemed quite crazy before I knocked him out. He's not dead, is he? We both hit him pretty hard."

"He's alive," one of the cops told them.

"His father, Dominic, is in the coffin." Kayla tipped her head toward the coffin. "Apparently he didn't fall over the side of some boat. The other three thought he was stealing from them and killed him. They buried him with the money he was trying to take from them."

"Nice." J.T. got up as the paramedics entered the room. "I'll see you at the hospital, Nick. I want to make sure our old friend here goes straight to jail. Looks like you're done, Evan," J.T. said. "Game over."

Evan's arms were handcuffed behind his back, and a cop had a hold of each arm, but even so he shrugged and said, "The game will be over when I say it's over."

"Yeah, yeah, tell that to the judge. We're going to lock you up and throw away the key."

Evan laughed. Kayla could not believe his bravado.

J.T. motioned to one cop to stay with Lorenzo while he and the other cop took Evan out of the room.

Kayla turned to Nick. The paramedics were putting him on a stretcher. His face was white, and beads of sweat dotted his forehead. "It's over," he said. "You did good."

"I'm coming with you to the hospital."

"I'm sorry, ma'am, but we can only take family members in the ambulance," the paramedic said.

"That's fine, because I'm... I'm his wife."

Nick smiled weakly. "Hell of a time to play that card."

"It's true."

"Kayla." He took a deep breath. "I don't want to scare you, but you'd better call Jenny, too, just in case."

Her heart stopped beating at the look in his eyes. She had not come this far to lose him now. "No. There is no 'just in case,'" she said defiantly. "You're going to be okay. You're going to be fine." She prayed to God not to make her a liar.

Chapter Twenty-Three

Waiting for Nick to come out of surgery was agony. Kayla was terrified that he'd lost too much blood, that the bullet had nicked some vital organ, that he would die before she had a chance to tell him that she loved him.

She loved him!

The phrase rang around and around in her head. She'd never said it out loud. She'd never even admitted it to herself. It was too scary. It was too fast. And Nick didn't want her love. Did he?

She knew he liked her. She knew he enjoyed making love to her. He hadn't been shy about expressing those feelings, but something more, something deeper... She didn't know what he wanted from her, what he needed. Her entire life, she'd had a plan to fall in love, marry, have children, but now that plan didn't matter. The only thing that was important to her was that he lived -- even if he lived without her. She just had to know that he was alive, that he was somewhere in the world, that he was happy.

"Oh, God, Kayla, what's happened?"

She turned at the sound of a terrified female voice. It was Jenny. "Nick -- he was shot. He's in surgery."

Jenny's face drained of color, and she started to sway. Kayla threw her arms around her and hugged her tight. When she let go, Jenny was crying. Kayla realized she was crying, too. She wiped the tears from her eyes and tried to smile.

"It's okay. He's going to be okay," she said, trying to believe in that truth.

Jenny sniffed. "Are you sure?"

"He has to be," Kayla said simply.

"Did Evan shoot him?" Jenny asked, fear in her voice, pain in her eyes.

Kayla shook her head. "No, it was another man. Nick fought him, but in the struggle the gun went off, and Nick was hit."

Relief flashed in Jenny's eyes. "Thank, God," she murmured. "I could never forgive myself if Evan hurt Nick in that way."

"He did hurt Nick," Kayla said. "He stole his life from him. Maybe he didn't pull the trigger, but Nick is fighting for his life because of the game Evan started."

Jenny's face crumpled. "I'm so sorry I ever listened to Evan. And I'm so sorry I didn't tell Nick about the baby. I know I hurt him. The other day he looked like he would never forgive me for keeping that secret."

"You did hurt him, but you'll tell him you're sorry -- when he wakes up," Kayla said firmly.

It was after six o'clock that night before either of them had a chance to tell Nick anything. Fortunately, he had made it through the surgery without any complications. The bullet had torn through the muscle in his shoulder and fractured his collarbone, but the long-term prognosis was good. He was going to be fine -- eventually.

Kayla let Jenny go in to see Nick first. She knew Jenny desperately wanted to apologize, but she wasn't just being generous. Inside she was a little scared to see Nick. What would she say? What would he say? Where would they go from here? Would it be "Good-bye, nice to know you, glad everything is solved"? Would Nick return to his old life? Would she return to hers?

She looked up as J.T. entered the waiting room, a tense expression on his face. She hoped something hadn't gone wrong with Evan. "Is everything all right?" she asked, jumping to her feet.

"I was going to ask you the same question. I wasn't able to get away before now. How's Nick?"

"He'll be fine."

"Good, that's good," J.T. said, blowing out a breath of relief. "How are you holding up?"

She shrugged. "I'm still standing. Jenny is with Nick. She had things to say to him. The waiting has been difficult. I kept reliving everything that happened down there, wondering if I could have done something differently."

"It sounds to me like Nick rushed in the way he always does," J.T said. "He has more courage than sense sometimes."

"He was trying to protect me. Lorenzo was clearly out of his mind. I think he would have killed both of us without a second thought."

"Yes, he's very unbalanced. He claims he saw Frankie shoot his father in the heart right there in the crypt. Apparently, they were arguing over the money and the fact that Dominic wasn't being hunted for the crime. He'd driven the escape car. No one knew about him. The other three thought they deserved more of the cut, since their faces were in the news, their lives on the line. Dominic disagreed. He said he'd given them some map to get out of the mint, and that was the only reason they'd been able to escape. They argued and Frankie got mad and hit Dominic in the head with the butt of his gun. Then he shot him through the heart. Lorenzo was hiding in the crypt. He'd followed his father when he wasn't supposed to. No one believed him when he said his father had been murdered, or if they did, they were too scared to say so. Dominic's mother told the police that he'd gone fishing, just the way he'd told her, and since Dominic often went fishing, it made sense. The men must have paid the owner of the fishing boat to lie and say Dominic went overboard."

"So all these years Lorenzo knew his father was dead, killed by his friends. How horrible for him."

"He was only six years old when he saw it happen. It made him crazy, I think. Apparently, he's been in and out of trouble and psychiatric hospitals his entire life. He didn't pop up on my radar screen earlier because Delores told me he lived on the other side of the country. That was a lie. He was in the back room the day you and Nick stopped by."

"I know. And that day when I spoke to Delores, I implied that I still had the watch. So he came after me."

"He's the one who broke into your house."

"And followed us to Reno and knocked Nick over the head, right?" Kayla asked.

"Yes, he was still trying to get his hands on the watch."

"Was he also the one who tampered with the brakes on my car?"

J.T. shook his head. "He's not that smart, Kayla. That had to be Evan."

Evan. She still couldn't quite believe he was in jail. "Has he talked at all?"

"Not about anything important," J.T. replied. "He likes to ask questions, not answer them. He's a tough nut to crack, acts like everything is a joke. I'd like to wipe that superior smile off his face with my fist."

"It felt good to hit him," she admitted. "I can't believe I ever fell for his charm. I must have been insane."

"You're one of many, if that makes you feel better."

She made a little face at him. "Not really."

"At any rate, I don't need Evan to confess. I have plenty of evidence to put him away for a long time."

"So it's over." She could hardly believe it. Evan always seemed to get away. It was hard to believe he was behind bars, that he couldn't hurt them again.

"Thanks to you and Nick," J.T. said, "the money will be returned to the mint. They're very happy to recover the fortune, by the way. And the media is already onto the story. I'm afraid you're going to be famous."

She wasn't sure how she felt about that. "Does that mean that everything is going to come out? About my grandfather and my grandmother?"

"I can't lie to you: It's definitely possible."

She nodded. "I'd better call my mother then and fill her in."

"You have a little time."

"Thanks, J.T., for everything you did."

"I wish I could have done more. I hope Nick's all right. He's a great guy -- a little too impulsive for his own good, but overall he's rock solid."

"Yes, he's a great guy," she agreed, fighting the urge to burst into tears. It had been a long and emotional day.

"Are you going to tell him you're in love with him?"

J.T. asked, a speculative look in his eyes. "Because in my experience, Nick is terrible at figuring out what women think. Of course, I can't blame him -- so am I. We're guys. If you want something specific, you'd better ask for it. Otherwise, who knows what you'll get?" He grinned. "Trust me on this. I know."

"I'll think about it."

"Do," J.T. said with a nod. "The two of you are good together. I'll come back and talk to Nick later. Just let him know that Evan is where he needs to be. Nick can concentrate on getting well."

"I will."

As J.T. left, Jenny came out of Nick's room. Her eyes were puffy and red, but she was smiling. "He wants to see you, Kayla."

"Did everything go all right?"

Jenny nodded. "He said he forgives me. I don't know if he means it, but I hope it's a start. Maybe now that Evan is really out of our lives, we can be more honest with each other. I think I've been holding back for years. I could never quite forgive Nick for ruining everything by forcing me to let go of Evan before I was ready."

"I hope you're ready now, because Evan is going to prison."

"I am. He's not the same man I knew when I was in college. He's harder now. There's a madness in his eyes that wasn't there before, as if he's started to believe his own fantasies." Jenny let out a sigh. "You'd better go see Nick before he tries to get out of that bed and come looking for you. He seems to be very attached to you, Kayla."

"We've been thrown together a lot lately."

"You were the first person he asked for when he woke up. I think he was disappointed when I came into the room. You'd better not keep him waiting any longer. He's not a patient man."

"Don't I know it," Kayla said with smile. "I'll see you later." She drew in a deep breath and pushed open the door to Nick's room.

Nick was sitting up in bed, his arm in a sling, bandages showing under his hospital gown. His cheeks were rough and dark with shadow. His eyes were a little glassy, either from the painkillers or from Jenny's visit-she couldn't be sure. But most important, he was alive. He was going to be well. A weight slipped off her chest. She felt as if she could finally breathe again.

"How are you?" she asked, moving next to the bed.

He took her hand in his. "Better now that you're here. You

had to let Jen come in first, huh?"

"She was desperate to see you. She was afraid you were going to die before she could say she was sorry."

"What about you? You weren't desperate to see me?"

She sat down on the side of his bed and squeezed his hand, wanting to take away the gleam of uncertainty in his eyes. "Do you really have to ask?" She didn't wait for an answer. "When that gun went off, when you went down in the mausoleum and I saw the blood on your chest, I was more scared than I've ever been in my life. When you told me to call Jenny, I thought I was going to lose you. I thought you were dying. All I could think about was that I'd never told you how I really feel."

"Are you going to tell me now?"

She wanted to make him tell her first, but that was the cowardly way to go, and she'd learned a lot about bravery from Nick. "I love you," she said simply.

His eyes darkened with emotion. "I love you, too." His gaze lingered tenderly on her face. "I was scared, too, that I wouldn't get a chance to tell you how much you mean to me." His hand tightened on hers. "I never wanted to hang on to anyone before. But I can't seem to let go of you, Kayla. More important, I don't want to let go of you."

"Really?" she asked. "I don't want to hold you back, slow you down. I know you took on the responsibilities of your family when you were young, that you're not sure you want to be tied to anyone."

He smiled. "You don't hold me back, and what scares me the most is that you don't need me at all."

"That's not true."

"It is. You're strong, Kayla. You took down Evan all by yourself, and unlike me, you didn't get yourself shot in the process."

"That was probably just dumb luck."

"No, it was you." He paused, his gaze serious. "I've never had anyone in my life who shared the burden. You're my partner, someone I can lean on and trust implicitly."

His words made her want to cry. "I feel the same way about you, Nick, but it's too fast. You know it is."

"Yeah, probably."

Her heart sank at his agreement.

"But I don't care," he added. "I know what I feel for you, and it's not going away. We can take as much time as you want to figure everything out. We don't have to get married tomorrow or next month or even next year. But we will get married. Make no mistake about that. I never thought I wanted to spend the rest of my life with one person, but the thought of not seeing you every day for the next fifty years seems completely unacceptable. I know you've been hurt, that it's hard for you trust your feelings or mine, but-"

"I trust you," she interrupted. "With all my heart." She paused, knowing she had to make sure there was nothing left between them. "I know the difference now between what's real and what's not. Evan was just an illusion, a picture of a dream I had in my head. But you're not a dream. You're you -- flaws and all."

"Hey, I don't have any flaws."

"Yes, you do, and so do I. But that's a good thing. It means we're real. And that's all I want, Nick. No more fantasy, no more perfect-family illusion in my head. I'm through with dreams. I just want to live my life, to feel every emotion, to be able to trust someone, to love and to cherish, and to honor and to...well, maybe not obey, but you get the gist."

"I feel the same way, Kayla. And I'll prove to you, no matter how long it takes, that we should spend the rest of our lives together."

She could feel herself getting swept away by the power of his words. This time around she wanted to keep her feet on the ground. "It sounds great, but I think we should have this conversation again when you're not medicated, just in case it's the painkiller talking."

He laughed. "We'll have this conversation as many times as you want. I know how I feel. I've known it since practically the first minute we met."

"You didn't like me at all that first time. You thought I'd robbed you."

"Yeah, you stole my heart."

She grinned back at him. "Now you're laying it on too thick. I think you're delirious."

"For you. What does it take to get a kiss around here?"

"You're awfully demanding. One of your flaws, in case you

didn't know."

"Please?"

"Well, if you're going to be nice about it..." She leaned over and gave him a long, tender, promising kiss.

"Have you ever made love in a hospital bed?" he murmured against her mouth.

She pulled away and gave him a warning look. "No, and I'm not going to start now. You need to rest. No more drama. No more surprises. We finally have the answer to all...well, most of our questions."

"Are you going to fill me in?"

"I'll tell you the whole story later, but the important thing is Evan is in jail. He can't hurt our families or us ever again. The gold coins will be returned to the government. The mystery is solved."

"How's your grandmother?"

"Relieved to know that Evan has been caught and she can finally put the past to rest."

"No more Johnny sightings?" he asked.

"No. I did tell her about the wig. I could see she was disappointed, but to be honest I still think she believes deep down in her heart that she saw Johnny the other night. Maybe when Evan starts talking, we can force him to say whether or not he pretended to be Johnny."

"So he's not talking, huh?"

She shook her head. "Nope, but J.T. assures me that they have enough evidence to convict him of many crimes even without a confession."

"Good. What about the guy who shot me? What happened to him?"

"The police arrested him, too. J.T. said Lorenzo has a history of mental illness, so he'll probably end up in a mental-health institution. Apparently he witnessed his father's murder."

"I remember him saying something like that in the crypt."

"No one believed him, but now I guess they will." She paused. "It's really over, Nick. We can go back to our normal lives."

"I think normalcy is highly overrated," he said.

"Well, I'd like to try it for a while."

"So would I. Will you stay with me, Kayla?" he asked, gazing into her eyes. "I don't think I can sleep anymore without you. In fact, I don't think I can do anything without you, and if you ever tell anyone else I said that...well, I'll have to find a way to punish you."

She loved that he could tell her he needed her when he'd never been able to show that side of himself to anyone else. He'd been carrying his own burdens for far too long, and so had she. "Don't worry; your secret is safe with me."

Epilogue

J.T. stared in disbelief at the open door, the empty cell, the three police officers looking guilty as well. One dazed-looking man wore nothing but boxers and a white T-shirt.

"What the hell happened? Where is he?" he demanded.

"He asked me to bring him a newspaper and a cup of coffee," the man in his boxers replied. "I opened the door for just a second. And the next minute I was on the ground. He put his hand on my throat. He did something weird. I couldn't breathe. I couldn't move. It was like I was paralyzed. He took my clothes, my keys. He walked right out as if he were me."

J.T. couldn't believe what he was hearing. "He's gone. Evan is gone?" He looked to the other officers for confirmation. "Shit! How could you let him trick you like that? Do you know how long I've been trying to catch him?" He paced around the cell, his gaze coming to rest on the newspaper. Something had been ripped from the middle of one page. "Get me another paper," he said. He wanted to know just what story had caught Evan's attention.

"Why?" one of the officers asked.

"Just do it. And seal off the building. Maybe he's still here." J.T. doubted that was true, but he had to make sure. He never should have left Evan alone. He knew better than anyone that the guy was as slippery as a snake.

"He's not here," the other officer said. "We already checked every inch of this building. He's gone. He walked out wearing a uniform. He could be anywhere by now."

Another officer brought him a copy of the newspaper.

J.T. flipped through the pages until he found the one that he wanted. The missing section touted an upcoming exhibition of rare and priceless jewels.

Damn! What the hell was Evan up to now?

* * *

Evan sat back against the plush leather seat of the limo. He took a sip of champagne from the crystal glass and smiled.

"You look far too satisfied for a man who just got out of jail. Although I must admit, I've always liked a man in a uniform," she said with a purr. "How did you do it?"

"That's my secret."

"I was disappointed that you lost the coins," she said, a sharp note entering her voice.

Evan shrugged. "A minor detail. But I got what we really wanted -- the map of underground tunnels in the city. We just have to go to St. Basil's to get it. I left it there before they took me to jail."

Her gaze lit up like a child seeing all the presents under her first Christmas tree. "Very smart."

"Yes, we will soon have all the information we need to pull off the crime of the century."

"I hope we still have enough time to set it up."

"We have plenty of time," he said. "Do you have the things I asked for?"

She opened the bag and handed him a wig, an ID, and a pair of brown contact lenses.

"Perfect," he said.

"You're completely crazy, aren't you?" She sat back in her seat as she gave him a contemplative stare.

"Have you just figured that out?" He took another sip of champagne and glanced out the window. The police officers had been too easy, child's play. J.T. must be blowing steam out of his ears. Evan grinned at the thought.

J.T. had probably thought the game was over. Little did he know it was just beginning.

Book List

The Wish Series
#1 A Secret Wish
#2 Just A Wish Away
#3 When Wishes Collide

Almost Home
All She Ever Wanted
Ask Mariah
Daniel's Gift
Don't Say A Word
Golden Lies
Just The Way You Are
Love Will Find A Way
One True Love
Ryan's Return
Some Kind of Wonderful
Summer Secrets
The Sweetest Thing

The Sanders Brothers Series
#1 Silent Run
#2 Silent Fall

The Deception Series
#1 Taken
#2 Played

Also Available in Print and EBook

The Angel's Bay Series
#1 Suddenly One Summer
#2 On Shadow Beach
#3 In Shelter Cove
#4 At Hidden Falls
#5 Garden of Secrets

About The Author

Barbara Freethy is a #1 New York Times Bestselling Author, who has sold over 2.7 million ebooks since January 2011. Her 31 novels range from contemporary romance to romantic suspense and women's fiction. Twelve titles have appeared on the New York Times and USA Today Bestseller Lists. Her books have won numerous awards. She is a five-time finalist for the RITA for best contemporary romance from Romance Writers of America. She has also received starred reviews from Publishers Weekly and Library Journal.

Known for her emotional and compelling stories of love, family, mystery and romance, Barbara enjoys writing about ordinary people caught up in extraordinary adventures.

Barbara has lived all over the state of California and currently resides in Northern California where she draws much of her inspiration from the beautiful bay area. Barbara loves to hear from readers so please feel free to write her.

For a complete listing of books, as well as excerpts and contests, and to connect with Barbara, visit her website at
www.barbarafreethy.com
You can also visit Barbara on Facebook at
www.facebook.com/barbarafreethybooks and Twitter at
www.twitter.com/barbarafreethy.